LAST TOWER
TO
HEAVEN

ALSO BY JACOB PAUL

A Song of Ilan

Sarah/Sara

LAST TOWER
TO
HEAVEN

a novel

Jacob Paul

C&R Press
Conscious & Responsible

Cover art by Ahmadi, Shiva, 1975 - "Tower"
          Used with permission of Morgan Library & Museum
Exterior design by Sally Underwood
Interior Design by Leland Cheuk

Copyright ©2019 by Jacob Paul

Library of Congress Cataloging-in-Publication Data

ISBN 978-1-949540-02-4
LCCN 2018956129

C&R Press
Conscious & Responsible
crpress.org

For special discounted bulk purchases, please contact:C&R Press
sales@crpress.org
To book events, readings and author signings info@crpress.org

*Birth and death as punctual moments, and the interval that separates
them, are lodged in this universal time of the historian, who is a survivor.*

~~Immanuel Levinas from *Totality and Infinity*

*How can one convey the feelings of a man pressing his wife's hand for
the last time? How can one describe that last, quick look at a beloved
face? Yes, and how can a man live with the merciless memory of how,
during the silence of parting, he blinked for a moment to hide the crude
joy he felt at having managed to save his life? How can he ever bury
the memory of his wife handing him a packet containing her wedding
ring, a rusk and some sugar-lumps? How can he continue to exist,
seeing the glow in the sky faring up with renewed strength? Now the
hands he had kissed must be burning, now the eyes that had admired
him, now the hair whose smell he could recognize in the darkness,
now his children, his wife, his mother. How can he ask for a place in
the barracks nearer the stove? How can he hold out his bowl for a litre
of grey swill? How can he repair the torn sole of his boot? How can
he wield a crowbar? How can he drink? How can he breathe? With
the screams of his mother and children in his ears?*

~~Vassily Grossman from *Life and Fate*

PROLOGUE

SEVEN DAYS BEFORE HIS thirty-third birthday, Jacob Paul discovered, to his dismay, that his life was the dream of a man slowly gassed in the back of a box truck headed from the Chelmno extermination camp to a mass grave in the Polish woods.

This!

Just when Jacob had finally grown into the full range of his faculties, when his professional life was stable, the business he'd founded, profitable and growing, when the same could be said for his relationship with Esther, and for his social sphere, when he actually managed to ride his bike several times a week, and be to bed at a consistent hour, and to drink too much only occasionally and appropriately so that it was ok to drink too much occasionally in the appropriate circumstances, when he'd finally moved past the obsessive, ruminating, second-guessing part of his thinking habits, when he'd at last come to genuinely enjoy his own company.

This!

When the world might end.

When the world was finally survivable.

This.

How long did the gas take, anyway? How long between the onset of dream and the expiration of its dreamer?

Catastrophic to give up this life—catastrophic for the man in the van to succumb—and J searched the walls of his study for an escape from the guilt he felt at meaning 'catastrophic' selfishly rather than on behalf of the dreamer. J hadn't chosen this!

This!

Esther knocked at the door of the study.

"Come in!" he yelled, over-loudly, he thought; and, panicked, he repeated himself in a more moderate tone, "Come in."

The doorknob turned and the brass knob on J's side fell off onto the floor. He startled in his chair. And, while he visualized her annoyance at replacing the knob and its bar on her end, annoyance compounded by the fact that he'd lied that he'd put Loctite on the little screw holding his knob on last time this happened, J tried to will E's breasts a bit bigger, not that he didn't like them fine as they were, but just to see, to test the parameters and impacts and possibilities of this new revelation.

Of course, when E brought into his study the lunch she had fixed him, a pastrami, avocado and sprouts sandwich on pumpernickel bread and a rich dark beer, her breasts were as wonderful as ever they'd been and exactly as they had always been.

He repressed his next thought, which was to ask how he could possibly live.

PART ONE

And God spoke to the fish; and it vomited the Jonah onto dry land.

~~Jonah, Book 2

CHAPTER ONE

TWO YEARS LATER AND everyone else seemed so functional! So synced to a for-granted chronological progression with its desires and expectations and outcomes! They went to work, or failed to work, dated and broke up or married, raised children, mourned death. All around him were people concerned with small things, petty things, minor ambitions. They fretted the purchases of cars of tents of bicycles of cameras of computers of wine of fresh-from-farm cooperative grocery delivery services. J could see no good way to explain to them that they were in a dream, that their time was an illusion.

Two years!

Two empty years since the revelation of the dream and nothing changed: no conjuring, no anxiety, no lucid-dream dreaming having had any material impact but to facilitate a short trajectory, regularly made, an arc down from his apartment and across the street to the despairing vantage of Andy's Bar, where he now surveyed the immutability of his world, the interminability of it.

Andy's patrons had long ago learned the measured doses of their ideal dispatch. And J wasn't any different. Who needs a pleasure palace in which to smoke opium when the whole point of opium is to make pleasure palaces of destitution? Andy's drinks were cheap. Its stools' wooden legs were hand-hacked in a set of efforts to level them, and now leaned at myriad angles and myriad heights like the uneven pistils of wilted tulips. The place chased away young pleasure seekers by laying bare this truth: that all drinks rely on the same chemical formula, that there is no distinction between the hangover begotten by E&J or J&B or Oban or Lagavulin, that the trappings of an elegant nightlife are an expensive excuse for the comforts of inebriation.

J wasn't a drunk, but his tendency to speak in metaphysically whimsical non-sequiturs, as if the visceral questions they masked could be quashed by ornate polysyllabisms, had alienated E. She had moved out. The flat, once something of a salon, always meticulous, first accumulated dishes, then take-out containers, then the boxes of microwavable meals, until one day J simply shut the kitchen door, then E's study's door, and finally the sunroom's. His neighbors whispered of vermin and J could only hear "Judenratz."

No one else paid any mind to the loss of J's origins, of the man who dreamed J and all who were like that man; no one else seemed to mourn, to freak out in the streets. Sure there were remembrance days, and cultural events, and Shoah. But people pursued these by the same logic that they pursued all of their other ambitions, diligently ticking time, as if they were relevant, as if the world was real: I fear, therefore I must be, J countered, unreassuringly.

Everything conformed to physics, to causality based on factors both in and out of one's control. J's progressive dissolution proved this. His personal entropy proved it.

J's boutique marketing firm had slowly folded from inattention. No longer was he the man to go to when a firm demanded the development of sophisticated philosophies around initiatives such that a consumer who agreed to any of a number of premises would find himself or herself completely ensconced in a seemingly flexible worldview that allowed only a single conclusion. J, once the marketer of that deemed unmarketable—the conjoining of pharmaceutical conglomerates presented to ordinary consumers in a way that made them fetishists of childhood vaccinations, connoisseurs of blood pressure medication, fanboys for surfactant-lubed hypodermics—was unable to sell even himself, least of all to himself.

He sat in Andy's because the slowly sipped glass of Ballantine's on rocks made it easier to imagine that nothing existed beyond his periphery, that E, no longer around, ceased altogether, that her new man, her husband, the soon-to-be father of her child, only came into being when J encountered them, which was hardly ever, actually, never.

J sat and sipped the way a monk listens to the pitch of the meditation bowl long after the ringing has ceased.

Sitting at the end of the bar, smarting at the intermittent half-square of afternoon light unleashed when the occasional other patron strolled in or stumbled out, J contemplated his next move, shivering at the cold air the door's opening let in. The attempt to manipulate his existence, he now realized, was selfish, a grab at power. Likewise, his impression of the dreamer's death's imminence was tied to a notion that he would be transported somehow, that he would suddenly rematerialize as the flying Chasidic violinist in a Chagall painting.

"In other words," J mouthed audibly to an audience too far away, and too mesmerized by a telecasted interview of a British chef bent on bringing farm produce to public schools, "I've been seeking some reward, some special recognition, for being the dream of a dying man. It should always, obviously, have been about him."

And something about this recognition, or maybe it was the cause of the recognition, gave J his second ever moment of access to his dreamer, the briefest, briefest of moments, maybe it was just the illusion of connection: a jostle really, a missed synaptic flash, something dizzying, a nonsequitor bridging mitochondria and sunrise, senseless, a wish against held breath, light...Just as quickly, before access had really been granted, connection begun, J was back on his bar stool, the words with which he might clamor too many, too contradictory, to voice.

Instead, he gasped, and—if to be called is to be only partially answered—he was called; called, gasping, he jolted up from his stool that he might answer.

J stood, stood as if for the first time, and the door opened and filled with light and cold air, and then the light and cold air parted to form a tall, stick X made black by the brightness of backlighting, its edges fuzzed and floating in the diffracted glare. A figure with its arms raised. At last, J thought, an answer; and he raised his arms, too, ready.

CHAPTER TWO

THE FIGURE CAME IN through the doorway, and, stripped of its hallowing glare, the figure could clearly be seen to be a woman, prosaic.

She wanted help changing a flat tire.

J, in part to repudiate his selfishness, and in part out of persistence that this sudden calling forth was a recognition of his newest epiphany, followed the woman out onto the tar-pocked sidewalks of a piece of the island so north as to be more Bronx than Manhattan despite its 212-area-code. She was pretty and he was cold, he realized, shoving his hands into his blazer's pockets, shrugging his shoulders for warmth.

A rear tire had gone flat and lowering the spare from beneath the pickup's bed was really a two-person job. That her truck was early eighties vintage would not have made it seem out of place, it was that her truck was both old and meticulous, a metallic off-blue green with softened, chromed corners around the headlights and a thick, cream band running its length, that set it apart from the generally dingy vehicles surrounding it.

J hunched down behind the truck to guide the wheel out of the undercarriage while the woman operated a crank system. As the weight came onto J's hands, he realized that his attempt to stand behind the truck and catch the wheel as it came down meant awkwardly hunching over, his shoulders and face pulling into the tailgate as the wheel descended. He wasn't strong enough to hold the wheel, get it out of its mooring, and get it down to the ground from his angle.

Plus, his back hurt.

He yelled at the woman to stop lowering a second. His pants were clean: brown wool trousers that predated his discovery and decline. His blazer was, well, not yet grease-stained. He was dressed as if for a casual off-site professional meeting. No more meetings, J realized. And barely savings enough for another year in the apartment on a diet of take-out cheese slices and dive bar Ballantine's.

So much for casual professional wear, J thought and lay down in the gutter and slid under the truck, caught the tire, emerged with it.

"You are filthy," the woman said.

"I'm J," J said.

"Stands for what?" the woman asked.

"Jaded, jubilant, jester, junkie, Jew, Jehovah," J said.

"Let's get this tire changed, shall we?"

"Jehovah was a stretch," J said.

The woman gave him a look, and J gave her a looking over. Creased jeans and fringed suede jackets and broken-in cowboy boots weren't usually J's things. Nor, for that matter, were high hard cheekbones and no makeup and the whole grey-eyed blonde-haired shtick, nor turquoise jewelry. The woman looked like she'd just stepped off the stage at a bluegrass festival.

"You got the jack?" he asked.

"You gotta loosen the lugs first," the woman said. "Or you'll bring the truck down on you when you do."

J bit his tongue a second before asking for the tire iron, at a loss of words to describe her modes of attraction. It was as if she'd walked off a commercial set for ranching equipment, not as an actress, but as the character that actress portrayed.

She handed him the iron, and J fixed it on a lug and attempted to turn.

"Haven't you never before?" the woman asked. "You have to jump on that iron to break the lug loose."

J stood up, put one loafer on the end of the iron and bounced. The iron fell off of the lug, and J came unglamorously back to earth.

"Here," the woman said. "I'll hold the iron in place, you bounce."

J bounced; the lug loosened.

For the first time since his thirty-third birthday, J felt the prickling of sweat derived from physical exertion. It felt good to have the blood flowing. Were those who dug their own graves similarly aware of the simple pleasure of their bodies functioning properly? How morbid, he thought, but then, why not? If they dug, they surely weren't sure they were to die, why not enjoy for a moment how well they dug?

Morbid, he thought guiltily.

Besides, there was a difference between refusing to acknowledge one was going to die, and thinking one was to survive. Even then, wouldn't the digging provide a way to suppress fear?

J stopped himself before he could wonder whether those who dug particularly well did so to win favor.

He didn't want to think about these things.

I think, J realized, to not feel. Easier to think about fearful things, awful things, than be surprised by them, by the sense of the immanence of them.

The dreamer could die!

Would die!

Would succumb to the carbon monoxide metering J's elapse, undoing J's life!

The old fear mercurial, fear shimmering, the familiar quicksilver that, just like that, forced itself up from his capillaries into his veins... This seemingly static condition, life, static only conditionally; its foundational certainties—its end and its origin—certain and, yet, unknowable, the end potentially immanent and potentially not immanent, and thus...thus it was, this life; thus it was this lyric leap from intellectual meditation to a literally blinding, physical terror... well, if not fully blinding, a kind of too-bright overlay between his eyes and what they sought to see…how annoying to think this way! To find oneself subsumed by such thoughts, such patterns of thought…well, if not exactly terror, a kind of sentimental over-whelm for which the best, closest, associative phrases, inadequate though they might be, were: sublime dread; great hurt invoked by the recognition of terrible injustice; a portentous despair of the possibility of meaning; mourning that justifies keening; and, wailing inconsolable nostalgia of the sort that would challenge any interlocutor's ability to keep a straight face.

Once upon a time, J and E had used to spend their winter evenings stripped to underpants and panties against their roaring steam radiators' heat, him in the easy chair with a book for pretense, reading the arch of her back and the hang of her chest as she sat cross-legged on the antique Chinese daybed that substituted for a couch, reaching forward to paint on the easel-held canvass before her. Oh, woe was he!

Oh, dumb panic! Oh, how swift its transmutation into simpering tragedy!

J required mere seconds to move from fear to meta-critical self-derision.

What a rare talent! To be expert in the fraught maudlin, an aficionado of one's own neurotic thought, to go agape without warning…

These were the thoughts (and emotional responses to thoughts) from which J's long bouts of therapy and self-work had finally, fully freed him just a few years earlier, back when his business thrived and his relationship was an inspiration for his friends, back before the dreamer's…and there it was again: the emotional heat that drove the quicksilver up his veins from skin to heart…the whole damn sequence…So. Fucking. Tiringly. Fucking. Melodramatic!

"You okay there?" the woman asked.

They'd finished changing the tire and J realized he'd just been standing, holding onto the truck with one hand, apparently staring into space.

"J just stands for Jacob," he conceded.

"Thank you for your help, Jacob," the woman said.

"You're welcome."

The woman began tossing tools into the truck's bed, the clanging of their impact dissonant with the truck's immaculateness. Or maybe not dissonant: It seemed exactly right to the scene. Nonetheless, J didn't see how you could chuck metal on a vehicle and still have the vehicle look so good. The woman turned to look at J, him still standing there, a shrug against a shiver keeping his shoulders high around his ears.

Why stay here? J wondered. There was the apartment with its closed-off rooms. But why really? Because of whatever was the opposite of momentum. His mind provided the antonym: stasis, but that word didn't sound quite right, didn't capture his sense of unease, of frustrated desire. There was a man in a van dying, a man who'd dreamt him, J, into existence, into this world that may or may not be the world that survived the man after his hemoglobin attached to carbon monoxide and ceased to carry oxygen through his body, after his corpse was dumped in a pit filled with other corpses, sprinkled with lye and loosely covered in dirt, only to be dug back up several years later and cremated. *And what do I know of this man?* J asked himself. *And how does this man know of me?*

"Yes?" the woman asked.

He'd been agape again. She hadn't told him her name.

J thought for a moment, didn't answer. If the world was real and he was not, or if the world was the world but J the product of a dream, then was he alone? Were there others like him? Was this woman, who was so much herself, the platonic ideal of herself, the very thingness of the thing that was her, was she the product of a dream, too? Had the flash of light in the doorway created her? Had she existed elsewhere than in this bright afternoon in which they stood? (And if she was created for him, shouldn't he have some special sway over her?)

"Where you headed next?" J asked.

"A gentleman doesn't expect gratuity for aiding a lady in need," she said.

"I don't need money."

"Ok then," the woman said.

"I'm just looking to leave here," J said, and willed the dream mutable with everything he had to will.

"Thought you didn't need money."

"I'm looking for a ride," J mumbled.

"A ride."

"I'm not crazy," J said, making eye contact.

The woman didn't speak.

"I mean of course I'm crazy," J said. "But I'm not psycho or anything. We're all a little crazy right?"

The woman still didn't say anything. J fidgeted.

"Okay, so maybe we're not all crazy."

"If I wait long enough," she finally said, "will you tell me that you are psycho?"

J exhaled and smiled.

"And if I told you where I was headed..." she continued.

J acknowledged that anywhere would likely do.

They waited at each other.

"Shit," she said. "Fine. I've got a last errand somewhere in the Bronx; think you can guide me there?"

She unlocked the passenger door and J climbed up onto a bench seat upholstered with what looked to pass for Navajo blankets. She's a gentleman, he thought, and reached over and pulled up her door's silver lock button. She climbed in, a cowboy hat between them like a chaperone.

"Guess you don't need to grab anything," she said.

"Better if I don't," J said, imagining the doors of his apartment braced against food-stained containers.

"Which way?"

CHAPTER THREE

THROUGH THE TINT ON the windshield's upper margin, the sky looked even brighter than it had from the curb. Yes, J decided, he had been called. He pointed her onto 207th Street headed for the bridge. They crossed onto the trestle, the Harlem River blue and nearly wild below, Fordham Heights sprawling before them, paved in yellow-signed bodegas and thin-strip used car dealerships.

On the far side of the bridge, J realized he'd been holding his breath, as if crossing off the island was the first hurdle in some escape.

Monosyllabically, he guided the woman down between the Bruckner Expressway's high walls and out into the woven overpasses and cobbled byways of the South Bronx's near-defunct terminal markets and up Bronx River Avenue past the sentry box and its armed guard and into ABC Carpet and Home's lot. They parked in an oasis of luxury SUVs tainted by the occasional graffiti tagged delivery van.

She told him she'd need his help, and so he descended from the truck's cab and followed her down a corridor made of greenhouse glass, the mouth of which was guarded by twin Laotian Buddha from some centuries ago.

"Shopping?" J asked.

"It's for my father," she said.

"A gift?"

"Why are you following me around anyway?"

"You asked me to help you?"

She flagged down a salesman and handed him a pink slip of carbon paper. He read it and then called over two helpers, who he directed to a taped-off corner under a balcony. They extracted two wooden straight-back chairs that, like much about the woman, pulled off the curious trick of seeming at once immaculate and dilapidated.

"Looks about right," she said. "Jacob, you mind carrying these out to the truck?"

Blushing happily at his incorporation into the woman's plans, flushed with the fresh air a bridge away from the neighborhood that had confined him, with the sense of being purposeful and of service, burdened awkwardly by a chair held up under each unevenly bent arm, J made it to the asphalt before realizing his task had prevented him from learning the woman's name.

Her name, he thought, and her anonymity reminded him of that of his dreamer, that dark space that continued to ride in a van, continued to die, and whose dreaming continued to lucidly produce staccato wafts of spoiled fish, spoiled fruit, and spoiled exhaust, the olfactory manifestation of a ruined industrial neighborhood, the south Bronx in all its gritty glory. What, J wondered, was he to make of the thirty-three years before the revelation of the man in the van, the gas, the dream? What was he to think of these last two?

Don't think of that, he cautioned himself. Let the carrying of chairs suppress the morbid thoughts, the thoughts themselves an alternative to actual feeling, his feelings being only of loss and of fear of more loss and of keening sorrow at having no one left to hold him while grief and terror wracked him.

They'd be leaving soon, J figured, and the woman's dress, her demeanor, made him suspect Nashville or Ashville or Nacogdoches for a destination: southern cities he'd never bothered to contemplate. That terra incognita seemed about right as a first destination in his newfound quest to somehow reach...well not reach...reach through to…no, not that either…to…something…something…to do something for the man in the van.

He considered setting the chairs in the bed of the truck, but didn't see any good way of securing or protecting them, so he instead left them upright by the tailgate and attempted to brush his pants off until he realized the transfer of road grease and grit from pants to palms was returning grit and grease to his pants, too. He sat down.

He could hear the Bruckner and the Bronx River and the local streets beyond the high-gated parking lot.

What if, J thought, there wasn't a terminal market out there? What if, a few miles down, there wasn't the marshals' mud lot full of impounded cars? What if his company had never been, and E had never been, and his apartment shortly to the west had never been? What if there wasn't this whole business of the van and the Shoah victim?

"What," J asked aloud, "if I'm simply supposed to live?"

He should try to get the woman to stop at the Holocaust Museum in DC, J thought. But what would simply living look like? J could do anything. He'd started his own business once, after all. He'd owned an apartment, lived with a woman, amused himself with intellectual fancies, problems whose successful solving had made him solvent, rich really, for a time. Or maybe his was really a question about God, a question no less trite for being ancient.

"Those aren't for your sitting," the woman said.

J stood.

"Why don't you go ahead and lift those into the truck."

"They're chairs," he complained. "People sit in chairs."

"People don't sit in these chairs," she said.

J lifted the chairs into the bed of the truck under the hands-on-hips watchfulness of the woman, hoping that he projected an appropriate level of woundedness, an attempt that gave the woman time enough to bubble-wrap, tarp, and tie-down the chairs.

She told J to get in; he did.

"Where to?" he asked.

"Isn't that a question more usually asked by the driver?" she said.

"I don't really care where we go."

"There's no 'we,' but I'll take you a few hours and then you're on your own."

J thanked her. He gave her directions back onto the Bruckner, and from the Bruckner she got onto High Bridge and recrossed the Harlem River, risen in the air on stonework better suited to Roman aqueducts. They traversed Washington Heights in a deeply recessed piece of concrete-shrouded road, tunneling beneath residential skyscrapers whose soiled, multi-hued porch walls looked like the faded red and green and yellow plastic of discarded magazine shots from a Cuban tourism brochure.

They drove onto the George Washington Bridge, crossed into New Jersey. But instead of heading south on 95 as J had expected, she turned onto 80, headed west towards Pennsylvania.

"Where are you headed?" he asked.

"Let's keep this impersonal," she said.

"But what if that's where I'm headed to?"

"I'm headed beyond that."

"I'll pay for tolls."

"Yeah? For tolls?"

"Also for gas."

"Gas, too, huh?"

"Where are you going?"

"Pick something on the radio or tell me a story."

J looked at the radio, a long gleaming band of glass bound to the east and west by large polished dials, to the north and south by FM and AM station numbers. He imagined the initial click of turning the volume knob up until the untuned static between stations was audible, and then slowly tuning the red band down those twin rows of numbers, catching clips of broadcasts. He could visualize the smooth dampened feel of big chrome knobs twisted between the pad of his thumb and the edge of his forefinger.

In a car like this, he'd roll the slider down the polished glass to an AM band broadcasting whatever it was that had preceded Willie Nelson and Emmylou Harris, a squawking drawl of banjo-backed ironic rural despair, a recess of the dial left behind for some late night subset of the city's drivers. But he was a marketer, a composer of carefully homogenized identities, and she was an individual, an individual on whom he depended—so he believed. That AM station would suitably soundtrack her, but he couldn't begin to know whether it would please her.

"What kind of story?" he asked.

"Doesn't matter. Something true though, a true story."

"You seem to want to learn an awful lot about me given that you won't tell me your name."

"Chase."

"That short for Chastity or something?"

"Just Chase."

"Okay, then, Chase. I'll tell you a story."

J looked back at the radio dial, regretful. A true story then, a story of what? He didn't want to talk about the time since the discovery, and on reflection, his earlier adult life seemed oddly blank. (To give it form would be to cry in front of Chase.) He absently stroked the high gloss glass of the radio dial, wondering for a moment whether the dream hadn't begun with his realization of its encompassing existence, whether, like the actor in any dream, he'd sprung into being replete with the memory of a past he'd never lived.

"Well?" Chase asked.

"What's so special about those chairs?" J asked.

"Who says they're special?"

"You wouldn't let me sit in them."

"You gonna tell me a story or what?"

"Did they belong to someone famous?" J asked. "Or did someone famous sit in them?"

"What if I told you they were used at Nuremberg or that one of them was kicked out from beneath the feet of a noosed-up Billy the Kid?" Chase asked.

"Were they?"

"Of course not," she said. "Tell me a story."

"At yeshiva, I guess it was our junior year, my junior year, my friend Yehudah and I…"

"What's yeshiva?"

"A yeshiva is a place where you learn Talmud."

"Talmud?"

"Jewish law."

"So are you a rabbi?"

"This was only a high school."

"For learning Jewish law?"

"No. Well, yes. Well, think of it this way: our yeshiva was a boarding school for ultra-orthodox Jewish kids. We had regular high school classes, but also learned Talmud."

"So like a Catholic high school but for Jewish kids?"

"Sure."

"I'm Jewish and I never heard of anything like that."

"You're Jewish?"

"And I never heard of a yeshiva-high school or whatever."

"It's for the ultra-orthodox, you know, the guys in black hats in Brooklyn."

"The guys with the curls hanging out?"

"No, those are Chasidim, though they go to yeshiva, too. Listen: forget it. The important part is that it was a boarding school."

Chase said nothing. J looked at her, waiting, observing the way her double-handed relationship with the steering wheel implied that if she was male, she'd be kicked back, a dangled wrist her only contact with the truck's controls. Finally she turned to him, "Go on then."

J began to talk about the seeds, and then about how they'd planted the seeds in the bottom halves of soda bottles, and how in no time they'd turned his dorm room into a secret greenhouse.

"So what happened?" Chase asked.

"Nothing happened," J said. "We ate the Swiss chard and the radishes and the sweet peas, but the school year ended before the tomatoes ripened, and while the summer squash was only as long as the withered blossoms on their tips."

"That's not a story," Chase said.

"But there's more," J said. "That was the beginning of our freedom. We began to do things."

"What things?"

Right as the first seeds had sent sprouts into the cholent-addled air of the yeshiva, their kitchen cook received, unexpectedly and as part of a shipment of government surplus food, ten gallons of fresh blackberries. The cook, a cantankerous alum from New Orleans, knew the school's forty high school students and twenty seminary students would never consume that many blackberries before they spoiled, even if they had enjoyed eating fresh fruit; the cook had readily surrendered the berries to Yehudah, who had gotten the idea that they might make wine out of the blackberries for Purim.

"Wait, your high school, this yeshiva thing, they let you make wine?"

"Only for Purim."

"Purim?"

"I thought you said you were Jewish."

"My parents are Jews."

"Purim's the holiday that all the kids dress up in costumes for. It's in the spring. Story of Mordechai and Haman, Esther and Achashverus, the Megillah. You eat hamantash?"

"Maybe?"

"Mordechai's the good guy; Haman's the bad guy: after you read the whole Megillah, there's an obligation to get so drunk you can't tell who is who?"

"High school students?"

"That saying, 'the whole Megillah,' because the Megillah is so long?"

"My father might have used a phrase like that when his Hollywood people were old and Jewy."

"The seminary students would go with us to the liquor store to buy us booze. We'd have a giant feast in the afternoon and get drunk with the rabbis."

"Wish I went to yeshiva high school."

"Jewy?"

"Don't worry, you're not Jewy."

J flushed, pleased. He smiled, and then his diaphragm seized with shame: was he a fucking child that a racist compliment was a compliment, still? If he wasn't what a Jew was, then who was, what was? Who was he to claim to be what a Jew was? He who didn't practice, who left yeshiva, who the rabbis called a fool, who didn't have faith? Nothing to be gained in calling out her racism, J told himself. No way to not have felt pleased, viscerally pleased, a base response that preceded language and knowledge. Might as well continue the story, J told himself.

As J shared details with Chase, he could see the old windmill in whose half-basement the wine store was located, a musty, low-ceilinged space run by two old men with matching handlebar mustaches who'd been equally amused with, and fond of, the two young boys sporting knit yarmulkes, tzitzit fringes creeping from the intersections of their almost-dress slacks and nearly-unsoiled button-down shirts, asking about blackberry wine manufacture.

"Where's this all going then?"

"Where's this all going?" This was all headed towards…towards memories that surfaced only now in the telling, memories of the store's collection of antique glass carboys set up on low tables: squat decanter-shaped Venetians alongside thick, green, narrow, British-made jars and common, five-gallon, current-production glass, all filled with shades upon shades of red and purple and yellow and white wines, as if the act of speech were itself generative, creating boys behaving badly, and J was again beset with that feeling which was the opposite of déjà vu, the sense not that what was happening he also remembered, but that what he remembered may never have happened, that he had never sat up late in the basement library, a remnant of when the Yeshiva's building had been a hospital, drinking gut-ugly raisin wine with Abner and Yehudah and Seth and talking about Winnipeg, from whence Abner, the same library in which J found a copy of the Viking Portable Nietzsche, which he read, not understanding, but understanding it as antithesis to the Aramaic, which he also didn't understand, taught him by day.

Still, the memories were true. They belonged to the portion of his brain that recalled rather than invented. He believed it. He told Chase how they had fermented four liters of blackberry juice into potent, must-addled syrup that tasted of prune juice and old socks and mushrooms, smelt the same. He detailed accountings of the chemical processes consequent to yeast's metabolic action.

"You've got some colorful details," Chase cut him off, gesturing one-handed in the space over the wheel, "But you don't have stories. Those aren't stories."

"How are they not stories?"

"Some crap you did isn't a story."

"Formative crap though, shit that creates an identity. My identity."

"So?"

"Identity is always layered, like Talmud, each page an argument from one epoch about an earlier epoch's arguments, and each of these, too, bounded by the arguments about their argument: that's identity; identity is that shit that you reacted to, and to which your future self, remembering your former self, reacts while it simultaneously reacts to the other reactions and their memories, and so forth."

"So what?" Chase asked.

"So what?"

"Even if I could follow that."

"So what is that empathy begins with identity," said J. "For example..."

Here Chase cut J off. 'For example,' she pointed out, already told her that J was going to say something boring. But he insisted that by creating a resume for a corporation, an ethos based in moral problems and philosophic anxieties, he could make that corporation human, more than human, and likable, desirable.

"I make," J said, "of O-rings opera."

"Boring," Chase said.

"But my O-rings have fans!"

"Bored."

"The fans aren't bored!"

"Fine," Chase allowed.

"Great," J said. "So there was this company, I can't tell you the name, but let's call it Acme like we're in an MBA class."

"MBA!"

"What?"

"Snooze!"

"You said–"

"I said, fine."

This company wanted to build a plant just north of Albany. The plant manufactured a medical device that depended upon radioactive isotopes and the local community was anxious that these isotopes would find their way into the Hudson, and, from there, into the drinking water and into the air. Most anyone would have approached the community with a value equation: the company would bring jobs and tax revenue to a depressed area. Safeguards would mitigate the risk of release, a risk already low, and, with proper education, the communities could learn, even were there to be a release, the consequent health risks would be exceptionally low: a low risk of a low risk event was the reasonable cost of bolstering the economy.

Not J.

J exaggerated and then romanticized the risk. He pointed to the long history of human advancement's dependence on boldness and daring. He suggested that residents surrounding the plant had something in common with the Apollo astronauts, that they were like Marie Curie and that it was better to be like her, to risk cancer, die of cancer, than never advance.

J felt a flush along his neck and tightness around his eyes as he told Chase how he construed the residents to sound like the founding fathers declaring an independence for which they'd hang if they lost their rebellion. He explained how he had made it clear that the dangers the plant offered were desirable, necessary, that undertaking the risk of neighboring the plant was deeply part of who the residents were as Americans, as patriots, that failure to house the plant would be a betrayal of their collective and individual honor. J felt an ecstatic scalp tingling no different than he had when Chase told him he wasn't Jewy.

"Compelling marketing, though that may be," Chase said, "I don't care about that town or about whatever that company was doing. I certainly don't care about your great marketing triumphs for their own sake."

"But what about the morality of what I did?" J sputtered.

"It's not really enough of a story to make me care."

"Doesn't the tension between right and wrong, between sacrifice and...between all of the things, doesn't that make it worth... isn't that not boring?"

"You didn't tell me a story of moral conflict."

"Mine! My moral conflict."

"J, I am authentically bored."

CHAPTER FOUR

"There once was a man..."

But that was all J knew, that there was once a man, not his hometown, not his language, not his name, not his loves, aspirations, defeats, triumphs. There once was a man and J desperately wanted Chase to believe that he could tell her a story: "and the Nazis took him to a place called Chelmno."

"Chelmno?"

"A death camp. Look it up. No survivors."

"J...If it weren't that the milieu in which I came up consisted of, competitively consisted of, story."

"One survivor," J corrected.

"You don't need to tell me a story," Chase said, gesturing at the still gleaming dial.

There was a boy with the most amazing singing voice, J continued. When an early trainload of victims arrived, he was picked to work with the Sonderkommandos. 'Sing,' they told the boy, and the boy sang. There was a river, slow, bucolic. The murderers spent their off days rowing boats up and down this river between its tree-hung banks, sometimes in their own company, sometimes with a woman from the town. Mostly, they rode the river with bags of crushed bones leftover from the crematoria, emptying them into the water. On all these floats, they had the boy sit in the bow and sing to them, and so the exhausting monotony of a difficult job far from the front lines was soothed. The boy sang and the war progressed, and the Sonderkommandos were executed time and again, and renewed again from the midst of the about-to-be-killed, but the boy lived, lived because he sang. Eventually, as the front began to retreat, the murderers received orders to close everything down and they took the last Sonderkommandos to a grave in the woods, and the boy with them, and there they shot all of them in the head.

"Wait…what?"

"They did! They shot the boy. And yet…and yet he lived. He crawled as far as a poultry farm and the woman there remembered his singing and that woman bandaged him and she washed him."

"The woman remembered him?"

"It was a teeny town and the trains full of Jews would back up for days and everyone knew what was going on: it wasn't secret. Everyone knew the Nazis who lived there and this Jew, this little boy, she knew too."

"All the Jews she let die and him she saved," Chase said.

"She didn't kill the Jews."

"She was there, she knew…She really didn't just bash his head in with a shovel like you would a…"

"She saved one Jew, him."

"To witness all of that killing and not take it upon yourself to join in! To not kill too! How could she live with herself having sat passively witnessing, not having tried to rescue the others if she was willing to rescue any of them?" Chase asked faster than her too-perfect drawl would imply she could speak.

"That's not the point," J said.

"How could she live with herself unless she believed it morally necessary to kill Jews?"

"Can we go back to my story?" J asked, jiggling his legs and trying not to reach out and touch the truck's radio dial.

"If she believed it moral to kill Jews, shouldn't she have killed this boy, too?"

"Now you care about a moral quandary?"

Chased inhaled through her nose audibly. J waited for her to exhale, waited what seemed an awfully long time, thinking that he didn't need her approval, before she loudly exhaled through her mouth.

"One Jew," she said, "makes a story; many don't."

"Are you suggesting he was saved so as to make for a story?"

"I don't have the words," Chase said.

"Besides, that isn't the story I mean to tell," said J. "That's the story *Shoah* documented."

Chase stared straight ahead, her hands on the turquoise wheel at ten and two, chin slightly up. J watched her jaw visible clenching and unclenching for nearly a mile before continuing:

"There was a man. They kept him in the main house in Chelmno. Then they led him into a van with a lot of other people. They drove the van to the woods."

"The woods where they shot the boy?"

"Yes. The same woods. But the van's exhaust was run into the back, and it killed all the people in the van, including the man."

"That's not a story."

"How is it not a story?" J demanded; and his demand was urgent for though this conversation finally let him feel present, pinchable despite the dream, the interaction's wondrous suppression of fears and doubts also let in the knowledge of those fears and doubts just enough for J to know that talking to Chase was the closest he'd felt to concrete and material in two years. And if she didn't think his was a story...

"Because," Chase explained as they crossed into Pennsylvania, "it's just a..." she sighed and stopped.

"Yes?"

"Look," Chase said, one hand expressively off the wheel, head tilted, as if she were looking at J instead of the interstate. "It's like this: think about your subjects and verbs. Who are they? What do they do? Take your man: he's an object."

"How can you call him an object?"

"Grammatically. Grammatically, he's the direct object of those sentences. He doesn't do anything. They do things. Stories are people doing things, or trying to do things. Unless your story is about the they…"

"But what about with the boy?"

"What about the boy? The boy sang! The boy wanted to survive and he sang and it worked. It worked and he lived."

"Nothing survived. No one survived. There is no redemptive story. The Holocaust cannot have a redemptive story. By your rules, the Holocaust can't have a story," J said.

Chase said nothing; J was now two states away from the amassment of take-out containers he'd once called home. He wanted to express this pleasure of talking to this woman, this relief from the dread, but was afraid to express this pleasure lest the woman stop and discharge him. Why? Why make him aware of the dream? And who was this woman, anyway, that she was such a salve?

They sat silently, Chase looking at the road and J looking at Chase. She was short, J realized, and she bobbed with the truck's motion while she drove.

He understood none of it.

"Your man isn't a story because there was just this thing, an event, the Holocaust, and it…"

"Just an event? You mean The Holocaust, right?"

"Ok, I know, I know," Chase said. "But, his murder was senseless, right?"

"Yes."

"Happened for no real reason, right?"

"Obviously."

"Nothing he could have done to prevent it?"

"How could anyone expect him to prevent it?"

"His is not a story. Horrifying, sure. Awful, sure, but –"

"Tragic."

"No, not tragic. Tragic means tragedy. Tragedy is a kind of story and without story there's no tragedy. Tragedy is a series of events set against each other, dominoes that keep hitting bigger dominoes until they can knock over mountains. And your dude, I'm sorry to tell you, his is not a story. He is, and I know you'll hate this, just the direct object of an awful action perpetrated by an evil actor."

J turned toward the window and pouted at the dense sumac, red-plumed, that divided tall oak from the roadway. Her desire to explain: that had to be out of some kind of caring, didn't it?

"You know how the Jews wandered in the desert for forty years?" J asked.

"J…"

"So that the generation born in slavery could die in the desert?"

"My father knew Charlton Heston."

"Did you know that they only died on the anniversary of the tablets' destruction?"

"I'm not…"

"Yes. On the eve of every anniversary, the entire nation would dig their own graves."

"Jacob…"

"And sleep in them. Those that woke would find fifteen thousand dead, and these dead they would shovel dirt over in the graves they'd died in, and the rest would wander on until the next anniversary. For forty years."

Chase drove, said nothing.

"Some story, right?" J said.

Chase sighed.

"In the fortieth year," J said, "no one died. But the people of Israel didn't believe it was over. Instead they figured they'd miscalculated the date. So for seven nights they slept in their graves, waiting for the fifteen-thousand to perish."

Chase still didn't respond.

"For seven nights, they slept in their graves, their own fucking graves, because they didn't think God was done killing them."

No answer from Chase.

J felt his warmth subside, his forehead pressed as close to the door's window as it could go without putting forehead grease on the glass: Was it any wonder that the people who didn't feel safe enough to leave their graves would commit the serial genocides of the Moabites and Canaanites, the slaughters of *Joshua*? Survivors got to do anything. Chase, a survivor; J...J didn't know if he was a survivor.

Forty years, fifteen thousand times forty, six hundred thousand, an order of magnitude less than the Holocaust; but, then, when the Holocaust happened there were more than two billion people alive. There were less than thirty million people around when the Jews set off out of Egypt to become a nation some supposed four-thousand-years-ago, if the story is to be believed, if, indeed, there's such a thing as a Jew, at least if to be a Jew is for there to be a God to choose a people, and to then choose Jews. Two orders of magnitude less people, meaning, that over forty years, as a portion of world population, an order of magnitude more people died. Numerology. J could do math or he could feel.

J hoped the man in the van could sustain himself against the gas long enough, whatever that meant, and he dreamt of doing the math.

Even the boy in the boat: he sang for murderers, helped them. And the sky darkened further still, a daytime dusk, atmosphere without overcast that denied light nonetheless. Only the killers got stories, J despaired, and in killing the man in the van they were killing J.

I'm just me! J wanted to scream, desperately clinging to the truck's vibrations, the soothing surety of an internal combustion engine's tuned hum transporting them, warm, through the dark, cold rain.

CHAPTER FIVE

J WOULD GIVE HIS dreamer a story. He would make him real. And if he has a story, J decided, and the Holocaust is the absence of stories, then he will escape the Holocaust! J would redeem his dreamer from the Holocaust by giving him a story, and thus J would redeem himself! But this is all a dream, J thought, how will the story matter to the man? How could J matter to anyone, if it was all a dream?

He turned away from the window.

"What are you doing?" J asked.

"Looking for a rest stop."

"Do you have to pee?"

"This might be miles enough for us," she said.

J thought about letting her kick him out, moving on. Perhaps this epiphany of purpose was all he needed from the woman. But the sky was the color of exhaust, of cloying soot. The cab was warm. The woman smelled a bit, just a bit, like a duty-free store at an airport, the hint of cologne tester sheets and once-ago spilled bottles of French brandy: She was destiny, he thought. Tell the truth, he thought.

"I know what I want to do with myself," J said.

"Your career counselor will be ecstatic."

"I want to give that man in the van a story."

"Which?"

"The man I told you about, who gets killed at Chelmno. I want to research him, learn everything there is to know about him, organize it, narrate it."

"Unless you decide to write the tragedy of his heroic flaw that makes, for him, the Holocaust somehow deserved…"

"His story won't be the Holocaust. I don't want to give the Holocaust a story. I want to give him a story, his story without anything to do with the Holocaust."

"My dad's got a ranch in New Mexico. I'm headed there."

"Not Nashville?"

"Come again?" Chase said.

And J thought: the sky is easing out of its threat; and J hoped: maybe the dreamer will hear his story in the dream, and know; and J shivered: wasn't he a survivor also, guilty somehow? Guilty. Because, wanting to do something for the man in the van wasn't the same thing as imagining he could rescue the man from the van.

CHAPTER SIX

J WOKE UP IN the bed of Chase's pickup truck to strains of hotel coffee and melting Styrofoam filtered through damp wool and hunting cabin. He pulled the sleeping bag away from his face to reveal her standing over him, a pixie-sized, steaming cup in one hand and a paper plate stacked with donuts in the other. He immediately realized that he hadn't properly arranged the horse blanket beneath him, and was therefore doomed to spend the rest of the day with the memory of corrugated metal in the interstices of his spine. He wanted to tell Chase that he was too old, but he wasn't nearly comfortable enough yet in their relationship to imply that he belonged inside her room, and he worried that if he paid for his own room, demonstrated that he could pay for his own room, she'd think he shouldn't depend on her for the ride.

On the other hand, J woke up not anxious for the first time in two years. For the first time in two years, his first thought wasn't to try and clutch absent E's arm.

He took the white cup, hardly larger than a dentist's Dixie cup, and yawned, less embarrassed of the sleep-dank that now permeated his everything than of the vestiges of an erection ill-hidden by the sleeping bag's folds and his quickly raised knees. A burgundy leaf fell into his coffee from a slender tree as new as the motel and its fresh white curbs. J idly picked it out, scorching his fingertips, marveling at the grittiness of the dreamscape in which he existed.

J felt an epiphany coming on, and then there it was: anxiety stems from a lack of purpose, not from the challenges posed by a purpose found.

He drank, burning his tongue.

"Thanks," J said.

"Sleep well?"

"You ever wonder if the people in your dreams dream?" J asked.

"Donut?" she asked.

"That's a way in which you remind me of my ex," J said.

"She brought you donuts? Made you sleep in the back of a truck?"

"I made me sleep in the truck," J said. "Can I use your bathroom?"

"That cherry tree too skinny to piss on?" Chase asked.

J pulled off the sleeping bag and stood in the back of the truck, already dressed. He caught Chase squinting at his shoes: maybe he shouldn't have worn with them in her sleeping bag.

"I played on the computer some last night," Chase said.

"Yeah?"

"Look, you've got bird shit in your hair."

"Well let's hope none of it got on your precious chairs," J said, stepping down.

"No joking!"

"What's it about these chairs anyway?"

"I only figured you'd want to know you had shit in your hair."

"Bathroom?" J asked.

"So I found this researcher," Chase said. "Works out of Chicago. It's only a day out of the way."

"Bathroom, please?" J asked, crushing his donut in his urgency.

"This is your life's work, I'd thought, finding your man."

"Can I pee before I address my life's work?"

"It's that which is why you're sleeping in the back of a truck," Chase said, and held out a keycard for which J had no hands.

"Ugh," J said as he tried to hand her the smushed donut back. She smirked slightly, ignored his proffer. He leaned over and took the card with his teeth, too gastrointestinal-bladdery to figure out emptying a hand.

Chase laughed and held onto the keycard an extra moment before releasing it to J's lips, now dangerously close to her fingertips.

"He's a Holocaust historian; focus is on Chelmno!" Chase yelled from behind him as he jogged towards the door.

J actually bent forward in a gesture towards an attempt to use the keycard with it still in his mouth.

"We're going to Chicago!" Chase yelled.

J transferred the coffee to his blazer pocket and his crumbling donut mush to his coffee hand, freeing his left hand to use the card, leant forward to get it in the slot reader and promptly emptied the coffee on his pants' thighs.

"We're gonna give your man a story!" Chase yelled as J finally got through the door, disarrayed, breakfast abandoned to the concrete walk outside the door. They were finally going to give his man a story, he thought, as his eyes adjusted to the motel room's gloom, so glad to relieve his bladder and bowels that he couldn't tell what he felt.

CHAPTER SEVEN

THEY DROVE ACROSS OHIO, where J admired the way Wright's rest stop designs spoke of a crumbling desire to transform plains into sea. They drove across Indiana, both stubbornly refusing to disclose recent personal history. They entered Illinois in a spat because J had told how he'd met E, but wouldn't talk about why she'd left, which according to Chase was to tell only half a story, or maybe even only its prologue, or maybe just to downright lie.

"But how we met is such a great story!" J insisted.

"Ever occur to you that maybe her mother traded seats with you flying back from Spain because they lived across the continent from you?"

"What about our letter writing? Or about how when she agreed to meet me at my talk in Vegas, we'd still never spoken on the phone? How we didn't talk on the phone till we saw each other in the lobby, her in jeans with her giant backpack and me in my most bespoke suit, special for when I presented, and that weird collection of condoms her Aussie friend foisted upon her when she dropped E off at the airport..."

"Why won't you say how it ended?"

"Us meeting was so special, so against the odds."

"Everyone who meets," Chase said, "either meets at random or doesn't."

"It felt like destiny."

"Does it still?"

J didn't exactly pout, but rather willfully didn't expound. He had told the story of his meeting Esther in such detail and even if he wanted to relive her leaving he wasn't free to do so. He couldn't just belt out that he was being dreamt by the man who Chase was helping him research. That would sound crazy, he knew, and more crazy for his inability to explain it, which he also knew. He wanted to talk to Chase about it, about the nature of dreams, but that was, after all, what had driven E away, was precisely why he couldn't tell Chase the other end of the story of E.

That Chase had been willing to let him hitchhike along, he acknowledged, was potentially unwise enough on her part to be not just impulsive and brazen but improbable. Less probable still was Chase's decision on the basis of nothing more than the mention of 'a man' to divert herself and devote herself to J's quest. He tried to convince himself that he could tell her, but Chase had just as good as confessed to not buying into fate or destiny.

"Did you cheat on her?" Chase asked. "Did she? Cheat? Get behind your back with another, maybe one of yours?"

"No!" J said.

"You're still on her," Chase said. And when J sighed, she said, "You are! So are."

"You asked where I was living," he said. "And it was only accidental, habit, telling you how I found home because I'd found E."

"You're hoping to get her back."

"If only there was hope," J said.

"Why? Why? What was so great about her?"

"I don't know," J said. "She was great, that's all. We were great...I thought that was my forever relationship."

"Oh, everything ends," Chase said.

These abstractions, he complained of himself, why not confess that in place of a life, instead of love, friends, job, ambition, joy, he...

"Sorry that was easy and callous," she said.

The relief of her minor concession made him want to fall apart in tears, which left only pugilism:

"Why does anybody love anybody? I mean, I could tell you she was smart, that she's attractive, and interesting, and kind, but so are lots of people. I couldn't tell you why I love her, and even if I could, I don't know that it'd be anything you, or anyone else, would or could believe, anyway."

"You're the worst," Chase said.

"Fine."

"How are we going to figure out if you might still get back together if you won't share at all about why she's gone?"

J stared out the window, jilted.

"Fine," Chase said. "Up to you."

J continued to stare out the window until Chase asked him to reach in the glove compartment and grab out the GPS, unless he knew Chicago as well as he did the Bronx.

Indeed, they had arrived at the forlorn outskirts of a once-industrial city. The layers of graffiti on decrepit factory walls, the strata of innumerable generations visible in the interstices of subsequent scrawlings, blended and reblended such that their colors approximated the solid shimmering of a Rothko. This revelation piqued J's attention. Upright now, fascinated by many-paned windows not only paneless, but stripped of their latticed iron mullions, J imagined these punctuation in the overwhelming homogeneity of cumulative experience.

"Rothko's about excess experience eventually filling in every opportunity for distinction! Every experience jammed up against each other eventually forms a ragged-edged patch of color!" J exclaimed. "It's not that the swath of color is instead of figuration, but that it is the product of infinite overlaid figuration!"

"The GPS!"

"Isn't that kind of modern for this car?"

"Not that it isn't rude to remind the recipient of the gracious-ness of a ..."

"Of course," J said and got out the GPS, marveling.

The GPS wove them over on-ramps and under el tracks until they arrived at a massive office building on the lakeshore, DePaul University's administrative headquarters. J attempted to shake off the realization that the experience of multiple millions of Holo-caust victims must likewise form a compressed solid, a Rothko fash-ioned from genocide, like a brick compacted out of pressed-together sawdust. They circled the block until J offered to pay the fee for a lot.

"Pops is covering my expenses anyways," she said.

"Who are we meeting exactly?"

Chase explained, as they walked to the building, that Pacelli was a Holocaust researcher who specialized in victim transport, and that he'd taken a special interest in Chelmno, for which trans-port records constituted, essentially, the only records.

But wasn't this a Catholic college, J wanted to know.

They rode an elevator to the ninth floor, where they walked past a bank of restrooms to a lobby marked "Special Projects."

"Special projects?" J asked.

"I am trying to help," Chase said.

The woman behind the reception desk, young, pretty, browsing a collection of medieval illustrations culled from illumi-nated texts, rose and asked, "Pacelli?"

"Pacelli," Chase confirmed.

"Pacelli," the woman repeated and grinned. "Pacelli!"

Pacelli strode around the corner of a maze of cubes. Pacelli was a priest, was perhaps ten years older than J. He had very large feet, and though he was otherwise ecumenically dressed, he wore teal, hard leather shoes with rawhide laces.

"Chastity is it?" Pacelli said, bowing, "And this is the friend you spoke of? Jacob?"

"It is Chastity!" J said.

"Chase is fine, Father," Chase said.

"Whatever you prefer," Pacelli said.

"Chastity!" J said.

Pacelli led them to a conference room remarkable for its blandness. He invited them to be seated in chairs that might have done well in AA meetings. They gathered at the end of a Formica-topped table, its surface an odd, flecked off-white that made J cringe.

"Father," Chase said, "We're trying to learn more about a man who was killed at Chelmno."

"What's your relationship to all this anyway?" J asked.

"Excuse me?" Pacelli said.

"Excuse him, Father," Chase said. "I'm not sure why he cares, and I think it's rude to question those proffering a helping hand, but it's upsetting him that..."

"And I thought Jews didn't go in for the whole..." J said.

"It's upsetting him that he doesn't understand your role in all of this," Chase finished.

"The whole 'Father this,' and 'Father that.'"

"It's simply polite," Chase glowered. "Be polite."

Pacelli shifted towards J, his hands clasped penitent before him. J looked at Pacelli. He studied his face: shaven, slightly lined around the mouth, complexion pale on the verge of freckling, skin taught, eyes slightly indented, hair close cropped and greying, but in a way that suggested early-forties, not early-sixties. The face told J nothing, but then, what faces did?

This realization surprised J.

J excelled at conveying messages by using faces and expressions. But he understood, staring at Pacelli, that organizing a series of gestures and facial types into a body of messages for others offered zero insight into what the intellects that owned those faces thought.

"You've come to me," Pacelli said, opening his still entwined hands.

"You were expecting me," J said.

"Naturally," Pacelli said.

"I emailed with him last night," Chase said.

"But he expected me," J said to Chase.

"And?" she asked.

"Why don't we see what we can do for you," Pacelli said.

Chase explained that they hoped—and when she said 'they' she looked meaningfully at J—they hoped that Pacelli might be able to give them some better details about a man who was killed at the Chelmno death camp, because J wanted to tell this man's story but knew nothing about him, not even his name.

"But this is a particular man," Pacelli said, "isn't it? You don't simply wish for a name of a Chelmno victim. You have one in mind."

In a hush, J acknowledged this to be the case.

"Then, what do we know about this man?"

J knew that he died in the van while it drove towards the woods.

"How do you know it's someone in particular," Chase wanted to know, "if that's all you know?"

"Everyone is someone in particular," Pacelli replied.

"Of course they are, but does it matter which man in particular we make our particular man?"

"He has a particular man already. He just doesn't have that man's details yet, which makes it hard to know for which man in particular we're looking," Pacelli said.

"Yes," J said. "It's a specific man."

"How the hell do you know?" Chase asked. "How the hell could you know it's a particular man if you don't which man in particular it is?"

"What kind of a researcher are you, Pacelli?" J asked.

"I identify victims and families and their origins."

"Why?"

"You can't answer me," Chase said, "can you?"

"To pray for them," Pacelli said.

It was the anguish within him, J was certain, that made the Chicago sky turn from autumn to winter in a great gale of grey.

"Pray," J said.

"That would be why you're ignoring me," Chase said, "isn't it?"

"Us priests do that," Pacelli said. "We pray."

"Not the important part, J" Chase said.

"Why do Holocaust victims need prayer?" J asked.

"Why does anyone need prayer?"

"See? Why does anyone?" Chase said, loud and inflected.

"Why do Holocaust victims need the prayers of an American Catholic priest?" J demanded.

Pacelli smiled at him and raised his hands to his lips as if he was about to warm them with his breath, or as if he was indeed preparing to offer up prayer right then and there.

J knew he wasn't any good at this kind of détente, never had been.

"I know that it's a particular man," J said, "because I...because I...maybe all of us are, either way, I am...because I am, because I am in, or am, maybe, this particular man's..."

"Spit it out already!"

"I am in this man's dream," J said. "I am in the dream he is dreaming while he is being gassed to death."

"You are in his dream?"

"Yes. Or maybe I am his dream? Part of his dream? Something like that?"

"Well then," Pacelli said.

"But, yes," J finished. "That's right."

"His dream?" Chase said.

"In that case," Pacelli said, "I suppose we might be able to use our surroundings, ourselves, which if we're in his dream must be the details of his dream, as clues to his identity."

"His dream while he's being gassed to death?" Chase exclaimed. "What?"

"This priest expected me," J said, light-headed.

"He expected you because I made us an appointment with him last night."

Pacelli and J both looked at her.

"If he has a way to decode us into information about the man in the van—it strikes me as a bit of a stretch—maybe it strikes me as a stretch because it would demonstrate that this is all the part of the man's dream, and that the man's dream probably isn't the future of the world, just his imagining of it—but that could be, too. I think I have to give Father Pacelli's idea a shot."

"Dream! What are you even fucking talking about?" Chase asked.

"I guess I thought you knew: you agreed to help give the man a story. I guess I secretly believed you were sent by the man in the van, somehow, to help me."

"To help you? I should have known. What could I have imagined this would be? Raving's are ravings. I should have! Way to break your patterns, Chase! How could I not have known?"

"I thought you were his answer to me," J said meekly. "I thought he was finally telling me what to do, how to help, how to save us both, or even save the whole world, if we're all his dream. I thought that was why I felt so much more real, so much less scared."

"They're all the goddamned same," Chase muttered.

J looked over at Pacelli to see how he was responding to Chase's profanity. The priest seemed unfazed. J wondered what Chase had imagined this would be. He looked back at her. He didn't really understand, but for the first time, or second time, depending on how he wanted to count Chase's arrival, he felt as if the dream was encouraging him, was acceding to being a dream. That it did so should horrify him, but the affirmation of his status and the status of his dreamer, horrifying as those statuses were, gave J something to do and let him at least at last stop questioning the whether of his ontology.

Who else belonged to the 'they' Chase claimed to all be the 'goddamned same,' J wondered.

"Seriously?" Chase said, swinging her head from side to side, "You're just going to stare as if I'm fit to be a five-year-old that's refusing to go to bed?"

Pacelli put a hand on Chase's forearm.

"Isn't it," she said, "hubris to presume to know your creator, heresy even, if that's what we're talking about?"

The windows rattled, gale-blown, the outside sky so dark it seemed to dim the conference room lights.

"To presume to know, yes, to try to understand...that's natural, isn't it?" Pacelli said.

"Listen," J said, "I'm sorry. This is a lot. My deal. I shouldn't have said anything."

"Shouldn't have?" Chase said in her normal voice. "No. You should have—you should have said something sooner is what you should have said."

"I'm sorry," J said.

"And you," she said turning to Pacelli, "I don't even know, or even know if I want to know. Do I? Do I, Father?"

"I'm here to help," Pacelli said.

"I'm out," Chase said.

Pacelli tightened his grip on her forearm and said, "Stay."

"Stay?"

"Jacob believes he needs to learn more about his man. You found in you once the compassion to help him. Why become so upset now?"

Chase slouched, her forearm still firmly in the priest's grip.

"Would you only offer help where there is no need?"

Both were, as far as J could tell, inscrutable, staring at each other as they were. Chase finally, loudly, sighed, a sound consistent with the indigo streaming the windows.

"You can let go of me," she said.

"Of course," Pacelli said, releasing her arm and sitting back in his chair. "Well?"

"Well, yourself," Chase said. "I thought he wanted to do this because he cared about something."

"He does care about something."

"I do care about something," J said.

"Only because he's a crackpot," Chase said. "Delusional."

"So?" the priest asked.

"So," Chase sighed, in a hoarse whisper better meant for microphones and music stadiums.

"All right," the priest said.

"I can't believe I'm giving this the credence of asking," Chase said, "but, isn't Jacob's caring simply self-interest anyway?"

The priest stared at her.

"I mean if J here thinks he's in a dream, is it even in anyway altruistic to care about the man he thinks is doing the dreaming? Isn't it nothing more than survival?"

J thought Pacelli was trying to convey mild-mannered-ness, but if J was to use him in a commercial, it would be to convey...J couldn't quite tell: not caring, not godliness, not even religion. As long as J kept his gaze fixed on the priest and on trying to understand what the priest's aspect meant, he wouldn't have to contend with what Chase was saying, or how she was saying it; J knew that, that that was why he stared at the priest, that that was why he had continued past mild-mannered-ness in his analysis of the priest's facial rhetoric.

The priest's attitude: it would represent something like the unchangeable, or the unassailable. The facial manifestation of pre-fucking-destination: the calm thereof.

"Help him find his damn dreaming man then!" Chase finally broke.

"Of course," Pacelli said. "Let's shall."

"Fine," Chase said.

Pacelli and J sat silently.

"Well?" Chase asked.

"Thank you for your help," Pacelli said.

"I don't get it," Chase said.

"Go get a drink," Pacelli said, "downstairs. Go downstairs and get a drink."

"I'm not a part of this?"

"Of course you're part of it," J said.

"You heard him," Chase said to the priest. "I'm a part of it."

"You should have a drink," J said.

"To hell with you both!" Chase said and stood up fast enough that her chair tipped over backwards. She looked at it for a second, and then half bent, as if she meant to lift it up, but then she stood without touching it and walked out.

"Okay," J said, but the priest put a hand over J's.

Sure enough, Chase stormed back in. Before she could speak, the priest told her to go to the first bar that appealed to her outside the building, he knew which one. They'd find her. Chase made a guttural sound and whipped her hair around, and stormed out, her power, her spell over J, somewhat broken.

CHAPTER EIGHT

"How can we define this dream?" the priest asked. "What features would allow us to understand the one who dreams us?"

Us, J thought, dreams us.

"What," J asked, "if this is actually what the future will look like? What if a version of you and I and the internet and nuclear power plants and a thunderstorm on the day a woman named Chase storms out of a conference room to find whiskey in an afternoon bar will all exist seventy years after the man in the van dies? What if he's dreaming the future as it will actually be?"

"Then He would be the Creator of the Universe."

"But he's just a man in the back of a van being gassed to death."

"Then he dreams the Creator's dream."

"God showing him the future?"

"Yes."

"Seriously?"

"Did God not show as much to Adam?"

"But then am I in the real future too?"

"Isn't this the real future?"

"But I exist in the dream of man who, even now, is succumbing to the gas in the back of a box truck heading from the Chelmno extermination camp to a mass grave in the Polish woods."

J could feel the tears creeping behind his eyes.

"Remember to breathe," the priest said.

"Am I even real?" J asked.

"Aren't you here?"

"I don't even know," J said. "I just need to find this one man."

"To examine the minutiae of our universe is to learn the nature of our Creator, is to come to understand our surroundings."

"Stop."

"Perhaps," Pacelli said, unclasping then clasping his hands back again.

Pacelli began to stand and thunder, rolling, terrific, shivered the conference room glass to the verge of shattering. The priest sat down.

"Help me find a name," J said.

"I have lists of names."

"Please," J said.

Pacelli walked over to a file cabinet in a corner of the room and pulled out a manila folder.

"I've got this here. It's short: 600 names maybe. Children."

"How many names are there total?" J asked.

"Names or victims?"

"Whatever."

"It's you Jews who believe a person's life force stems from his name."

"You Jews," J said.

Pacelli said nothing.

"Is this real?" J asked. "Any of it?"

Still nothing.

"It's bad enough Chase says his death isn't a story. Now you're implying that without a name, he might not even count as a victim."

"For you. You need his name."

"Well he must have had a name once!"

"And don't Jews, at times, change their names to change their fate? Might he have had more than one name? Or do I misunderstand your mythology?"

J almost said, mythology, but then closed his mouth. "Look, I don't need a list of children. I'm looking for a man, an adult."

"Most estimates are that 160-180,000 people were killed at Chelmno and only three people survived, one of whom died at Bergen-Belsen. It's a messy business knowing how many without proper records of names; it's also not easy assigning them names."

J wanted for a sarcastic quip about the names being the messy part of a murder operation so efficient that out of hundreds of thousands of victims only three survived.

"I'll get more lists," Pacelli said, and left the room.

J sat in front of the manila folder waiting for a moment. Either the thunderstorm proved that the world around him was choreographed by the dream, or it didn't. J opened the folder. He read:

> Pinkus Juda Abek, born 1934
>
> Gitla Abramowicz, born 1935
>
> Abram Lajb Abramowicz, born 1933
>
> Mendel Adler, born 1937
>
> Lea Adler, born 1938
>
> Towja Adler, born 1932
>
> Pinkos Juda Albek, born 1934
>
> Wolf Albek, born 1931
>
> Galda Pesa Aleksadrowicz, born 1941
>
> Szmul Altman, born 1936

J tried to stop reading. What did he need with the names of dead children? And his eye caught the hand-typed note stapled to the inside of the folder that said that these were the children of Belchatow, killed August 1942. "Galda Pesa was one year old!" he yelled at the window, before he could stop himself from calculating ages. "A one-year-old! She'd have had to have been carried!"

And the rain, unvaried, on the glass.

He shook his head at water-streaked dark outside—either the dream spoke or it didn't; what J did mattered to the dream, to the dreamer, or it didn't—and then J lowered his gaze towards the page again.

He resumed reading, mouthing the names out loud, softly, only the names, as if they formed the sounds of a prayer in a language he didn't understand:

> Zril Altman
>
> Lajzer Fiszel Altman
>
> Icek Izrael Altman
>
> Ita Basza Altman
>
> Aba Aronowicz
>
> Icek Mendel Arunowicz
>
> Gerzedla Bajgelman
>
> Reszka Bajla
>
> Towia Hanon Baum
>
> Marjem Gulaw Baum
>
> Rywka Mindla Baum
>
> Scheine Zysla Baum

He wanted to cry.

He wanted to call out that these were the names of children whose names would never be called out again.

He wanted to build each of them a story, a life. He wanted to raise a child for every child killed and give these new children the dead children's names. He wanted to exclaim that none of these kids were over eleven years old. And these were only the first twenty names on a list of six hundred from Belchatow. Where the fuck was Belchatow? What the fuck was Belchatow? Did Belchatow exist? Or was it like whatever farming town had once been on the Indiana border south of Chicago that they'd passed on the drive in, turned to outlying industrial space, eventually even that space overgrown, its five-hundred-ninety-three children gone, the place they were gone from razed, erased, replaced.

None of his responses were adequate; none even credible, really. All he was doing was sitting on a chair in a room looking at piece of white paper in a manila file folder under long-tube fluorescent lighting hidden above translucent drop-ceiling panels. Any response was false. These were only names.

He couldn't respond but he could read, and so he read. He read in a muffled singsong, rocking softly back and forth, lulled by the wet of his eyes and the prosody of the list:

> Sura Beczkowska
> Samuel Beckzkowski
> Haim Beckzkowski
> Szmul Alter Beczkowski
> Cywiz Belchatowskz
> Bajla Ruchla Belchatowksa
> Mojsze Belchatowski
> Dawid Hersz Belchatowski
> Szaja Berek Belchatowski
> Dawid Hersz Belchatowski
> Makul Wiger Belchatowski
> Szaja Laby Belchatowski
> Menachem Benjamin

He stumbled over the spellings, the meter of his recitation demanding a spoken speed with which his eyes, his cognition into articulation, could not keep pace. Yet he kept on:

> Itla Berchaja
> Hana Berger
> Michael Izaak Berkowicz
> Symcha Dawid Berkowicz
> Dawid Bienensztok
> Marjem Birencwajg
> Mojsze Birencweig

Tobjasz Bizencwajg

Ajzyk Bjgelman

Names exotic; names overwhelming; names the nightmare of Ellis Island gatekeepers; names and names and names; and he kept on:

Halina Bogdanska

Szymsia Borensztajn

Mordka Bram

Cyrla Perla Bram

Mendel Brandwajn

Szmul Jakow Brandwajn

The hardest thing to do in the world, to recite these names, one at time, stumbled and wrong. Yet he kept on:

Isaak Majer Brener

Bina Bresler

Hema Brilant

Dewora Brum

Miriam Brum

Idesa Bugajska

Margula Bugajska

Mordechaj Bugajski

Jachweta Burman

Sura Bursztyn

Szprynca Burszytyn

Elazer Coldsztajn

Rywen Boruch Checinksi

Szulim Ber Chojnacki

Szaja Chropod

Jacheta Ciechanowska

Izrael Ciechanowski

Wolf Cimberknop
Szaja Ber Cimberknop
Jechudys Cimberknop
Rachel Cimperknopf

And finally he couldn't keep on. Barely to the Cs and he couldn't keep on. Hardly into the list and they were no longer his names to read. J wasn't adequate to the names. Who was he to derive experience, even this unwanted experience, from these dead children? From the murdered? He too was a survivor, the dead unknowable, their names unpronounceable, outside his moral jurisdiction.

He tiptoed across the conference room to the door, turned the knob slowly, and pulled the door open a crack. The corridor of carpeted cube walls was void. He slunk past the reception desk, empty of its undergraduate mistress, and snuck out to the building's stairwell.

The noise of his footsteps, banging down the stairs, echoing in the enclosed well, began to drown out the names. The exertion jostled blood back into his face, which warmed his cheeks and began to heat his tears towards evaporation. Near the ground floor, he began to smell the tanged-humidity of city-rain and soaked clothing and reconstituted fluid, chemical and organic. He ducked out of the building and ran its stretch before ducking into the first commercial doorway he came upon. His face was now soaked, but scrubbed of crying, his clothes wet, but not yet dripping. He was in a bar, and the city-rain smells of the office building were magnified here.

Here, the organic smells smelled of bile and urine, likely were bile and urine. And the rain bonded tobacco smoke to the clothing of those who huddled under the awning for cigarettes. The whole bar reeked of wet wool and wet duck and bad cigarettes and stale beer like spoiled bread. He pressed in to the bar itself and clutched the brass railing that rung its mahogany lip, his hands cold with the metal and the rain.

"Hello," Chase said, next to him, tangled in a stool.

"I can't do it after all," J said.

"That so?" Chase asked.

"Whiskey," J called to the bartender, who demanded clarification. "Ballantine's."

CHAPTER NINE

TWO WHISKEYS IN AND half-way through the third, those fast and this last one slow, J felt a hand alight upon his shoulder like the sword of a queen bestowing knighthood, the hand of a priest giving benediction. He turned and Chase turned too, her shoulder held as well.

"It's hard," Pacelli said.

Chase finished her whiskey with a dramatic toss of her head, banged the glass on the bar, and said, "So a priest walks into a bar…"

The bartender walked over, wiping his hand with a white towel. Chase made a circling motion to indicate all three.

"Not for me," the priest said.

"No?" Chase said. "Insufficient warrant?"

"Ach," he said and made a face. "It's a very bad business."

"When you say dreamer, J," Chase said, "tell me you mean it figuratively."

"It was a list of names of children from Betalow."

"Please?" Chase said.

"Belchatow," the priest corrected.

"Go ahead and tell me that you do not for real believe that you exist in some fellow's dream. I mean you're a smart guy, J."

"Children," J said, trying to finish his drink before another arrived, but another arrived too quickly. "I couldn't even read their names...can't even..."

"Nearly two-hundred-thousand, and only two survivors," the priest said, shaking his head. "Awful, awful, awful."

The priest's pause, choreographed to catch the bartender's attention, caught it, and he ordered a small soda water with lime. J had thought it was more than two survivors: four, maybe even six. But there was no way his dreamer was one of them. J's dreamer belonged to the 'awful, awful, awful,' and so then did J.

"But it's not that this is a dream, not actually, right? It's simply as if this is all a dream, as if it is the dream of a man always dying," Chase said. "And when you say the good Father here expected you, you mean it was as if he expected you, right?"

"Only two," Pacelli said. "Two-hundred-thousand people! Must they not delegate forward someone, anyone, to witness, to preclude absolute erasure?"

"I'm too weak to read a list of names," J confessed. "I'm too timid for print."

"Wait," Chase said. "Wasn't it one survivor only, him that was shot in the head..."

"Simon," the priest said. "Phase two. The boy. Two men also escaped from phase one. One survived the war; one did not."

So now the priest was up to three survivors, J thought. And still, 'awful, awful, awful.'

"Do you also pray for the victims of the inquisition?" J asked. "How about of the crusades? Do you have lists of those names too?"

"See, J? You don't know everything about Chelmno. There's another survivor."

"The escapee who survived the war's name was Mordecai."

"Shit, and what of the Jews killed in the Pogroms?" J asked. "Do you pray for them?"

"Ach," the priest said, and motioned the bartender for a whiskey after all.

"I mean they died Jews," J said. "Aren't they past salvation?"

The bartender brought the priest his whiskey—the priest hadn't needed to specify a brand by name, J noticed—and the priest drank it fast and banged his glass and the bartender standing by filled him another.

"I guess I'd like to hear the story of this Mordecai," Chase said.

"Sometimes," the priest said, his lips tensed, drink savored, the glass never far from his lips. "Forget it."

"Suppose I'm still just chopped liver?" Chase asked.

"Sometimes I," Pacelli started then stopped. "Anyway. Ok. You want to know? Ok: Purgatory. They could be in purgatory, where outside intervention by the living could effect their salvation. That's the concept."

"That's the concept that they've still got the chance, with your help of course, naturally, the chance to get out of being Jews after they've been martyred for being Jews? That's the concept?"

"Ach," Pacelli said.

"Martyrdom," Chase mumbled, "is the endpoint of a narrative arc in the romance genre."

"What?"

"Nothing."

"Ach," Pacelli said again.

"Less the endpoint, maybe, more of an endpoint," Chase resumed nearly inaudible. "In a big Hegelian history, rewritten as romance. A conflict between forces in which individual narrative arcs end in martyrdom so that some larger triumph may be realized even more poignantly, the great telos of eschatology, kingdom fucking come."

J didn't want to think about martyrdom and narrative. The bar was pressed together with rain-wet jackets that arrived in steadily greater numbers as working hours ended. J's side was pressed against the bar to keep space between his shoulder and the priest's. On the stool beside him, Chase's body exhaled warmth in a soft sinus rhythm that raised the small hairs over his ribs and along the curve of his triceps. Her closeness soothed him. It reminded him of tucking into Esther's body when he'd wake up from nightmares, the gentle pull of her nails on his back until he slept again, sleep gained against the desire to stay awake for the pleasure of her nails.

"We are all only as much as we are dreamed to be," the priest said, "performing our part as best we can."

So if the Nazis victims were martyrs then those victims were somehow invested in their own demise? Was that really what Chase meant? That it was romantic, part of the romance genre, part of a quest, an epic and sweeping struggle that they died? What then was their great triumph? What had their martyrdom earned? Surely, J was innocent by any measure. He hadn't chosen the means of his creation anymore than his dreamer had done anything to have SS show up in his shtetl or wherever and load him onto a boxcar, and...it was a stupid line of thought.

"Oh fuck it," J said. "I give up anyway."

"It's a bad business," the priest said, drink finished and another drink already waiting. Another drink already waiting for them all: the bartender at once absent and attentive, his white shirt and black vest a silent shuttlecock behind the bar, gradually pulling everything together into a liquor-fueled opacity.

"Chastity," someone said from behind J in a voice meant for the giant screens and tiny squawk boxes of long-torn-down drive-in movie theaters.

J turned around as did Chase and Pacelli. The woman was built for overalls that suggested bikini-photo-shoots, J thought, the WWII women's factory workers' recruitment poster model recast in corporate wear.

"Delilah!" Chase said. "Hey!"

Something about the way Delilah held Chase at arm's length to look at her struck J as borrowed or staged; he felt the same way about her approving appraisal. In contrast, Chase's goofy grin and flushed cheeks were as unconstructed a response as he'd seen on her yet.

"How the hell is your father?" Delilah asked.

The priest mumbled something about leaving, but the bartender had refilled his glass.

"Got some chairs for him back in the truck," Chase said.

"Chastity," Delilah said.

"What?"

"Chairs?"

"He buys; I fly."

"Really? Chairs?" Delilah asked, her hands still loosely on Chase's shoulders. So staged, J thought, as if Delilah's every movement had been derived from a playbook.

"I was going that way anyway."

Delilah continued to hold Chase's shoulders. J's whiskey-gilded imaginings made him want to invent new marketing campaigns, made him want to express in hues and slogans. He wanted to feel like he was Delilah or Chase, the one touching the other, and this made him long for E.

"I was going somewhere, anyway; going, it didn't matter where, might as well have been there."

"You are something beautiful, aren't you?" Delilah said.

"You know what the old fucker told me?" Chase said.

"Should it matter what Walter tells you, Chastity?"

"He told me, 'Chastity, the thing about young women is that they keep making them.' That's what he told me, sitting on his porch with his one boot on the rail, mud spots on the leather just so, boot toe carefully creased as if he'd hard earned his day's rest before sunrise, as if he'd been out wrangling or some other bullshit."

"What a gorgeous image he makes," Delilah said.

The priest handed her a glass of whiskey.

"What's your father's problem with young women?" J asked, too aware of how close he was to Chase, not wanting to be further away.

Chase made a noise and rolled her eyes, an elbow back behind her on the bar, a shoulder high near an ear, one boot heel hung up on the foot rail. Delilah asked who Chase's friends were, and Chase made a dismissive hand gesture towards J and Pacelli.

J leaned over, took Delilah's hand, and introduced himself and Pacelli. Her scent made him aware of his own common pungency, his odor not just body odor, but the raw chicken thigh smell of dried sweat and raw tobacco ash delivered by the under-awning's cigarette-smoke-in-rain-solution; he asked how they knew each other, Chase and Delilah, and Chase pointed out that the priest was going to tell them the story of Mordecai.

"I began to tell you the story of Mordecai in the car," J said, aware of the way the glow faded from his words someplace between thought and articulation. "Remember, Chase, I told you about Purim in the car? Mordecai was Esther's uncle, or maybe husband. He'd raised her like a daughter and he, it is considered, had to divorce her so that she might marry Ahasuerus so that the Jews could be saved."

"Why are we caring about a Mordecai?" Delilah asked.

"There's always an Esther when the Jews are running up against trouble."

"Our Mordecai," the priest said, "was one of two men to escape the first phase of Chelmno. In this phase, the Jews would be 'relocated' by a van with a windowless box separated from the cab. The exhaust was run into the box while the van drove to the mass common burial area outside town. There, Jewish conscripts were compelled to dig pit graves and to unload the bodies into them. Mordecai was one such conscript. This detail had kept him alive, digging and burying at the edge of the woods. One day, his duties included his wife and child. When he saw their bodies he begged the guards to shoot him. They refused. Later, he and another worker ran away from the graves and escaped into the woods."

"See, J," Chase said. "That is the slim skeleton of a full-fledged story."

"All these stories," J said, "all sound the same. My whole life, they've sounded the same. A man runs from the graves. It's grey. His fellows run with him. Some of them are shot. One escapes, or two. They are all the same story, always."

The priest put his hand on J's shoulder.

"Like they were fighting Nazis their whole lives," J complained. "They weren't. They never fought Nazis. The Nazis just came and took them."

"I can see Mordecai running," Chase said. "He's off, running right before the guards. He wants them to shoot. He's asked them to kill him and they've refused. They raise their guns, but...but... something stops them: the luxury of not finishing their work all at once, perhaps, or the refusal to do what a Jew wants them to do, even when what he wants is his murder.

"'Let him go,' they say. 'We've got a thousand years to catch and kill the Jews!' And Mordecai! Mordecai will long for the bullet in his back."

J felt puny.

"He'll visualize the weapon leveled behind him," Chase continued, "much as I visualize him now, visualize its brass-jacketed projectile nearly overtaken by the sound of the explosion that rifled it through the gun's barrel granting him the microfractional comfort of hearing and knowing before the impact stills the woods' flashing, halts the memory of his family lain amongst all the other bodies. But he'll run, and he'll broach the trees. He'll leap the brush and downed logs, gloom-beset, lungs afire. Run, Mordecai will think, run and they'll shoot.

"He'll mean to run slower, slow enough to be shot. But running is action and action carries its own biological rhythms and imperatives. He'll run like he means it, fast and hard and low and long. When night falls and he stops, the dark will be absent the sound of boots pounding behind. If I can't die, he'll think."

"What bullshit!" J finally exclaimed. "Always the same stories, the same stormy weather. Surely, the Holocaust happened on nice days too! So what? But you have to leave him at least his guilt, leave him the possibility that it feels good to him to run, that he and his friend were calculated and slipped away such that they wouldn't be shot, leave him the dignity of wanting to live...But fuck all this: why this same story over and over? What about my guy, the man in the van, the one dreaming all of this? I mean, is this the only story in the whole fucking world?"

"In the whole fucking world, J," Chase said. "Seriously. What do you think a story's for, anyway?"

"You," Delilah said, "are absolutely Walter's child."

"Mordecai did testify," the priest said, "at the trials after the war."

"All we have are stories," Chase said. "History is stories."

"There is testimony!" J said.

"Which is story," Chase said.

"A question, if," Delilah said, raising a finger and her glass with it, "I may. When you say dreaming, Jacob…"

"I'm not for sure you want to ask that," Chase said.

J mumbled.

"A dream? I couldn't quite hear you."

"The dream of a man being gassed to death at Chelmno," J said louder.

"Excuse me?" Delilah asked.

"Be nice to him," Chase said.

"I exist," J started, out of breath, exhausted, drunk, "or we exist…"

"We do exist," Delilah said. "Certainly."

"Delilah," Chase said.

"…in the dream of man being gassed to death during the Holocaust."

"Yet this man must surely have succumbed by now," Delilah said. "The Holocaust happened before any of us were even born."

"The Talmud teaches that every *neshamah* contains the world entire," J said.

"Neshamah?" Delilah asked.

"Delilah," Chase rolled her eyes.

"Jewish for soul," the priest said.

"It's more than soul," J said. "It's the spiritual entity of the person."

"How's that different than soul?" Chase asked.

"There is no difference. It's his way to pick a fight about why I research Chelmno," Pacelli said.

"I want to pick a fight about patronizing prayer," J said.

"Father's are supposed to patronize, I'm thinking," Chase said. "It's in the title."

They all laughed, even J.

J inhaled. He was drunk, that much he knew. And if the world hadn't survived the Holocaust…He was drunk and he was imagining waking with the memory of a dream in which he was Mordecai at the back of the van and every body he pulled out of it looked like E at first, and so he had to get right up next to their faces. Only then could he see that they were strangers.

The inside of his left upper arm cramped, and he tried to control his breathing to relax his blood pressure. How many times must the Esthers fuck strangers to live? He suspected he'd said that last out loud, but no one had heard him anyway.

"Honey," Delilah said, one hand on Chase's elbow, "are these men planning on staying at my house tonight?"

"No," the priest said.

"Mother," Chase said, "may my friend, Jacob, spend the night?"

J flushed at the warmth of Chase calling him friend, or maybe it was the whiskey. He worried that his body heat would radiate his bad smell.

"What did I tell you about calling me mother," Delilah said.

"That you don't like people knowing you're old," Chase said.

"Chase!" Delilah said.

"Listen," the priest said, holding out a folded piece of paper between his index and middle fingers—more staging, J thought.

"Jacob," Delilah said, "you should know that whatever Chastity's motivation in dragging you alongside her, she is not for you."

"For me?"

"Mother!"

"Chase! It is not polite to entertain a young man's—"

"Mother, stop."

"Stop with calling me mother."

"J's hung up on his ex anyway. Right, J? Esther?"

"Familiar story."

"I'm going home," the priest said. He tucked the paper into J's blazer pocket, and then he took J by the shoulders.

"You," he said.

J thought to respond with something snide, something sarcastic, something anything, to rouse himself into wanting to pursue Chase, to make it so he wasn't hung up on Esther, to refute the uncomfortable soothing of the priest's clutch, of the folded slip of paper in his breast pockets, of the way whiskey worked like brass gilding over lead to let projectiles maintain stable trajectories at ever higher velocities. But the priest held him by the shoulders; the priest did something softer than what J would call holding his gaze; and J settled, calmed by these constraints.

"Ok," J said.

"This is all," the priest said. "Don't forget."

"Won't forget," J said, not knowing what any of it meant.

"You're..." the priest said and, pausing, clapped J on the shoulder, and then, "I'm going home."

CHAPTER TEN

OUT OF THE EVER-DARKENING skyline—a wall of water, wind-driven and raw, skin-penetrating, bone-muddling—they ran from cab to doorman to awning to lobby. And what a lobby! When all was well with J's finances, this sort of thing had been his set's aspiration, if an aspiration never admitted to from the confines of their loudly-announced belief in Brooklyn and Harlem and Washington Heights and Astoria.

An enormous chandelier swayed beneath apprehensively circling cupids painted onto a dome bound by gilt leaves that budded from branches attached to trees within whose trunks boles were filled with minor demons and imps whose platinum and gold pitchforks struck down, dimensional, from the ceiling, their tips orange and red and black spotlights. Where the ceiling met the walls—an uneven progression accounting for alcoves and nooks and room-shapings that defined and defied a catalogue of Euclidian forms—red limestone molding, thickly-veined white, featured carvings of Greek gods acting out mythologies:

Here Zeus birthing Dionysus from his thigh;

Here Hermes flagging Athenian ships to war;

Here Dionysus as Bacchus debauched;

Here Apollo's chariot run wild towards the boiling sea's scalded serpents.

If J had ever smelled frankincense and myrrh, he would have recognized the lobby's smell for that, for burning cedar and frankincense and myrrh, this wafting from several alcoves, each dimly lit and largely occupied by a Chinese wedding bed faced opposite an enormous fireplace in which burned whole trees.

There was a slip of paper in his blazer pocket, J thought, that he ought to be looking at instead of all of this.

As J's brain adjusted to what his eyes readily saw, he realized that he was standing on a kind of parapet that allowed him to survey the actual floor of the room, if one could call it a room. Screens and large potted plants circled by elaborate couches divided the space into a maze of conversation corners. Most of these corners featured the S-shaped couches favored by Louis XIV, but some were simply filled with rugs and skins and pillows like the harem tents of nomadic sultans.

Chase pulled him back from the parapet and along a broad marble walk to a bank of elevators, by comparison disappointingly pedestrian despite their lavish appointment. J expected, at a minimum, a cage for a door and a giant crank for a controller, these ideally operated by a man in shoulder boards and epaulets. Instead, the elevator's car was ornate but ordinary. It ferried them to a hallway with three doors and a third-century marble replica of a several centuries older statue of Poseidon splayed on a cloud, trident gesturing towards a wave below.

"Well done," Chase said, "mom."

"Chastity!" Delilah replied.

"What?" Chase said. "J isn't interested."

Delilah gave Chase a look that made J fear for his virtue.

A handprint reader embedded at the edge of the double-door's join allowed Delilah to simply push open the entrance to her apartment in a muted sweeping gesture. A pair of dogs that looked mostly Pomeranian, white with sculpted fur, ran at them across a white carpet so deep that rather than upon legs, the dogs seemed suspended upon rustlings in white weeds.

It seemed constructed, staged the way Delilah's attitude at the bar had been. J asked if he should take off his shoes and Delilah made a face while assuring him that he need not.

When J considered it, he realized that taking off one's own shoes in a foyer would interrupt the unbroken cinematic shot in which Delilah performed. That act of consideration would imply that Delilah's surroundings operated on a plane in which care was necessary, and in which the absence of care had the power to lead to loss and destruction.

Delilah, J saw, operated in a realm of immutability, inalterability, impenetrability.

CHAPTER ELEVEN

"Do I want you to explain?" Chase asked. "If I do, I guess...I guess. I guess, yes, I probably want you to explain."

Her eyes showed the beginnings of crow's feet. Chase was tired, J realized, and younger than he'd figured. Or not tired so much as weary: weary of what? J wondered.

It still didn't seem possible to him that she hadn't understood about the dreamer, because if she hadn't, then she was nuts for picking up a stranger who spoke in riddles, even crazier for helping him. Still, he thought, she's vulnerable, and the thought surprised him. Maybe it was just that they were all weary, all three of them.

"I'm her stepmother, you know," Delilah said to J, "not a blood relation."

"So you're saying you two are close," J said.

"Saturday afternoon phone calls every week."

"Which calls will cease if you insist on ignoring me," Chase said.

"Petulant much, Chastity?" Delilah asked.

"You know, mother," Chase said, "if it had been you that named me, I might perhaps tolerate your insistence on using all three fucking syllables of it a bit better."

"Don't you mean 'might could?'" Delilah asked.

"Excuse me?"

"You sound more WASP than western when you have your temper up, darling," Delilah said.

"Is it like this on your mother-daughter calls, too?" J asked.

"See, Chastity?" Delilah said. "Now he, as well, has taken to calling me your mother."

"Would you rather you weren't my mother?"

"Chastity!"

J wanted to tease, wanted to be buoyant, but the world was contained in a dying man's last imaginings. He wanted to protect Chase from her stepmother, or at least clearly side with her, but the man-in-the-van's imaginings included the lobby below, and the apartment, and the Pomeranians, which had disappeared, by the way, maybe melded into the carpet as if by slight of hand.

"What you must understand, J, is that we are more like sisters in age. I married Walter when I was only nineteen and Chastity was a little orphan girl of six."

"Girls with fathers aren't orphans."

"Motherless ones might as well be."

"I feel as if there's a syllogism in there by which you're also an orphan, mom, if we take your last two statements for premises."

"At least let's not quarrel like sisters, shan't we?"

They sat in a lavish and entirely white living room. The curtains were drawn but somehow lit to imply bright sunshine, though it was neither sunny nor day outside, which made the room at once welcoming and oppressive, dominant.

"I'll fetch us something."

"No maid to do it?" Chase asked.

"Isn't it stuffy to have staff in the evening?" Delilah replied.

"So it's the stuffiness," Chase said.

"Really, dear."

J remembered spending a full year shopping for a couch with E, because a decent couch was the most expensive thing they could imagine purchasing. They had visited so many stores. The most disappointing thing about shopping for couches was that even expensive couches were rather boring. Then, one afternoon, after a client meeting upstate, he'd gone into a small antique shop specializing in Shaker furniture, and realized that an elaborate bench—well, a very plain, but beautiful, old and heavy, wood bench with gorgeous fanned spindles holding up the back rail—cost no more than their budget. He'd bought it, paid for delivery.

J had felt as if the Amtrak train was too slow getting him back to Penn Station, and the A Train uptown, interminable. It had been the last moment before the ubiquity of cell phones, and all he wanted to do was to tell E about the bench he'd bought them.

J had come home and trilled, I've got news, and then insisted on pouring them glasses of wine before sharing said news. He then set his glass down on the dining table, and in the center of the living room, the lights dimmed, the futon behind him still in the burgundy hemp cover he'd thought fancy at twenty-two; and, he took her upper arms in his hands, and he told her that he'd bought them this bench, that he'd solved their couch troubles.

She had answered that he had broken her heart; J had wanted to know, for all the world, how a bench could break a heart: a bench he had bought because of her! J didn't care about couches or benches: for him, the futon was fine. Couldn't she see he'd bought it for her?

Don't you see? E had said.

"I do want you to explain, J," Chase said.

"I still don't know how I actually broke her heart," J said.

"Don't dare utter another peep," Delilah said, "until I return."

"What?" Chase asked.

"I'm getting tea," Delilah said.

"In the car," J said. "I couldn't tell you why Esther left because I don't really know why. I know what she said, but I don't know why, not really."

Delilah left the room and J asked Chase in a whisper whether there was a towel somewhere that he might put on the couch. The legs of his pants clung to his calves, his blazer wet against his back.

"I meant I wanted you to explain about the man in the van…"

"But I'm soaking wet," J said.

"But now, J," Chase said. "Now, I would simply like to know how it is that men don't understand why women leave, even after women tell them exactly why they've left?"

"I guess," J said, "that the last time anything really made sense to me was the summer after sophomore year of high school, which we spent in DC, or, more precisely in Silver Spring, Maryland. I had this yellow ten-speed Huffy that my parents bought me at a thrift store in Tucson three years earlier after my first bike got stolen out of our backyard."

"Fucking typical," Chase said.

"I know, I should have locked it," J said.

"Seriously?" Chase said, rolling her eyes. "You should have locked it?"

"Right?" J said. "I'd take these long bike rides in the rain. DC would have these torrential summer rains, and I'd ride the parkway towards the capital, winding in the shoulder between afternoon commuters and the Maryland woods. Terrifying, exhilarating. So, fucking, filthy. We didn't wear helmets then. When I'd get home my t-shirt and shorts would be just absolutely saturated with black road spray. My face would be coated in this grit I could feel in my hair, too. I don't know how it didn't run into my eyes."

Chase had her legs crossed and was looking away from him towards the dining table in a way that he found intentionally dismissive. He wanted her, and even more than he wanted her, he wanted her to understand. To understand what though? Was it how much sense he'd made to himself when he'd returned home, triumphant, carrying his bike over a shoulder into the lobby of the posh Silver Spring high rise they'd lived in, and then through the lobby to their apartment with its wall speaker for piping in Muzak? He wanted her to understand his feelings…but his feelings about what? About not having to be beholden to anybody else, perhaps, or maybe the feeling of rejecting shackling claims, his parents' claims…but J was beholden, beholden to the man in the van, maybe to E, too, or at least to the version of E he still argued with in his head…maybe even also to Chase?

J felt tired, tired and judged.

"Fine, Chase," J said.

"What's fine?"

"The last time I saw Esther," J said, "her face had broken out in acne from her pregnancy. She'd only barely moved out a few months before, and all I could think about was this time we'd gotten beets from our local CSA, and I thought I was bleeding to death out of my ass the next morning."

"Every man in my life," Chase said, "no mater how different they are from each other, is exactly the fucking same."

J's soggy clothing chilled him; he was genuinely uncomfortable.

Chase gingerly reached into his blazer pocket and extracted the slip of paper Pacelli had placed there. She looked at it, twisted her eyebrows, and handed it to J. J looked. There was a name, Joe, and GPS coordinates.

"Is that it?" he said to Chase, startled at her quick pivot to the business of their trip.

"How do we not go?" she whispered.

"Do we need to whisper?" he whispered.

"Yes," she whispered.

"Do you have any notion of where those coordinates are?"

"I imagine its someplace we can drive."

"So in the US?"

"Seriously," Chase asked, at her normal volume, "will you please deign to enlighten me about this dream?"

Delilah walked back into the room.

CHAPTER TWELVE

"Perfectly honestly," Delilah said, carrying an ivory tray on which sat a small iron teapot with proportionally tiny china cups and a stack of jam-filled cookies, "whatever Chastity has or has not told you, Jacob, you are truly not her type."

"Her type being?" Chase and J said together.

"Aloof," Delilah said.

"Mother, how best might I impress upon you the full measure of our not togetherness."

"Chastity, please," Delilah said.

"Chastity, please," Chase parroted, mimicking Delilah's affect.

Delilah put the tray down on a kidney-shaped coffee table so identically white to the rest of the room's furnishings that J hadn't registered its presence even when he stepped around it to sit on the couch.

"Tell us about yourself, Jacob," Delilah said.

"Where'd the Pomeranians go?" J asked.

"Little traitors," Delilah said, "unworthy of your deflection."

"I'm sure you and Chase are both more interesting to hear about than me."

Chase rolled her eyes, kicked her boots up onto the coffee table.

Delilah pursed her lips and lidded her eyes and slowly nodded once at Chase, "Chastity always puts her boots where least they belong."

"That sounds like the intro to a story," J said.

"If those dogs betrayed you, Delilah, then with whom?" Chase asked.

"I've said they are not worthy of deflection."

"Betrayal," Chase continued, "I believe it was you who taught me this, mother, betrayal requires a third party."

"They are dogs. Dogs with tiny brains. Leave it."

"Who else is here, mother? Overnight staff? Someone you fuck? Invisible help?"

"Chastity! Language!"

"J has said that he exists in the dream of a man dying in the Holocaust and your passively aggressively sneering at where I put up my feet?"

Delilah didn't speak; but, J noted, hers was a very active and aggressive not speaking.

"Well are you flirting with him?" Chase asked. "Are you?"

"You are too old for me to chastise," Delilah said.

"I'm your family," Chase said. "Side with me."

"Family!" Delilah snapped. "When you are literally living the paragon of virtue and loyalty modeled by your father."

Chase made a noise and held her head away.

"I'm not following," J said.

"When I say Chase is a paragon of virtue and of loyalty, I mean…"

"Family!" Chase interrupted, her face red.

"It is family, your family, that I strive to remind you to mind, Chastity," Delilah said. "Or shall I more bluntly…"

"But in front of J? Really?"

"What in front of J?" J asked.

"Oh, never you mind us sillies," Delilah said.

"I want to hear," J said, looking back and forth between them. "Dish!"

"Dish?" Delilah asked.

"Don't dish," Chase said.

"What does dish mean?"

"Spill," J said.

"Spill?"

"Spill the beans? Tell the story? Dish out the gossip?"

"Oh!" Delilah said. "What queer turns of phrase."

"Well?" J asked.

"Oh, pay me no mind," Delilah said. "What was it you were saying?"

"I was saying?" J asked, and then remembered with nervous excitement. "You wanted to know about the dream. Would you like me to tell you about the dream?"

"Do whatever you think you need to," Chase said.

And why not? Why shouldn't J tell them what he knew about the dream? And a nagging voice suggested that his reluctance to explain, his willingness to take sides against Chase with this bizarre paragon—to use Delilah's word—of vanity, this woman whose affected accent wasn't so much mid-Atlantic as imagined Prusso-parlor, was attributable to his not being able to explain.

The dream was real. J's terror was real.

But J could explain nothing, knew nothing. Even the Prophet Elijah, J thought, had God to tell him what to do.

Chase leaned forward towards her mother, the cusp of her bra contradicting the curve of her cleavage. She was so young, he thought—Twenty-five? Twenty-six?—and so complete in a way that he wasn't. Her anger at her mother countered her weariness, made her seem mature, adult, whereas the weariness had exposed some naïveté.

Buck up, J thought to himself. He needed to tell what he knew because envying the prophet Elijah his mission was untenably ridiculous.

"My life," he began, not waiting for either woman's question, "was as perfect as anyone's life can ever be. I lived with a beautiful woman in a beautiful apartment. For the last two years, I had run my own business out of that apartment, and it was actually a successful venture. I was more than making ends meet and the basic work challenged and intrigued me. We had friends, and interests, and plans. And then…" Then one day while riding the A train back to Inwood, in the middle of Ann Swidler's article, "Culture in Action."

"You wouldn't be the first person what that got claustrophobic on a subway train," Chase said.

"Must you convolute your sentences so, Chastity?" Delilah asked.

It wasn't claustrophobia, J explained. It was all these people, *all these Jews*, crammed together. It was unwashed bodies. It was a cattle car. "And I feel like I should be able to tell you about a too-crying child, or an old man frozen dead, or something like that, but I can't."

"A glimpse," Chase sighed.

"I just knew, for a second, a moment, I knew what he knew, but all he knew was that he was trying to wake up, and that there were two daughters, and that if he didn't wake up he'd be dead by the time the van reached the woods."

They sat silently for a moment, and then Delilah poured herself a cup of tea and drank it.

She muttered under her breath. She sighed.

Chase tensed as if she'd speak but didn't speak.

"Or maybe none of that," J continued. "Maybe I dithered the extra details in over the past few years, imagined them. Maybe all that I discovered was that I exist in the dream of a man slowly gassed to death. That this is true, I know. I exist in his dream. I don't know anything else."

"Amy Swidle?" Delilah asked.

"Ann Swidler," J said. "The sociologist."

"But don't you have to know somehow?" Chase insisted. "What was it that happened on the A train?"

"Or was it the article?" Delilah asked.

"Maybe it didn't happen on the A train," J countered. "I don't know. Maybe I just remember the article because it writes about how one only has the strategies for action that are taught by one's culture and that this is why one person's common sense is an insensible ideology to another, why we try actions we know from past experience won't yield the results we seek: because our culture hasn't provided us with any new strategies. Or maybe I was reading it then. I wish I could tell you for sure. I just know that I discovered this thing that's true. I don't know how; I don't know why; I don't know what it means. I just know."

He paused a moment.

For once, no one interrupted him. Both women sat respectfully listening, waiting.

"How long does it take to know? To really know? To know anything? It takes time to speak, it takes time to read, but knowledge isn't temporal, knowledge happens. It's atemporal. Knowledge is like God that way. You don't have it, and then you do, even if it takes a whole lifetime collecting and assembling its pieces, it's still quantum, its arrival comes in the form of an epiphany. Either you know or you don't. I didn't know and then I knew."

The two women waited.

J found himself with a cup of tea in his hands and the rising urge to speak loudly again, though to say what, he didn't know. It was suspicious that the man had only managed to know what J might already imagine, what anyone might imagine. If there even had been a glimpse in the man's consciousness—that bit about the daughters and the pressed together dying Jews—it was a cliché vision.

"Of course I've considered that I might be crazy," J finally said.

"Perhaps you might tell us about your other endeavors, Jacob," Delilah said.

"I'm boring," J replied. "Tell me more about you, or about Chase."

"But that knowledge," Chase said, "whether or not it is cliché…doesn't it pose some kind of obligation? Have you done anything with it?"

"I can tell you a story about Chase's childhood," Delilah said.

"I'm here with you now, Chase," J said. "That's what I'm doing."

"And if I don't consent, mother?"

"Would you rather the tale to which you truly wouldn't consent?" Delilah asked.

Fine, J thought. If they weren't willing to listen, then he would pour himself another cup of tea.

"Two years later, you are, J, and that's if you count this as doing…" Chase began.

"What would we have done, had we known what Jacob believes he knows?"

"Something," Chase said. "I would have done something, I hope."

"You hope," Delilah said, and extended a hand to Chase's knee. Chase sighed.

"You can trust me, Chastity. You always could."

J looked at Chase. She seemed again a perfect thing, though now he couldn't tell what that thing was.

"Chastity," Delilah said, "was noncompliant as a child."

"Noncompliant?"

"Yes," Chase said. "I was out of spec."

Delilah began a story of a summer; and, though she mimed exasperation, Chase seemed relieved. Chase had been twelve and home from her New Hampshire boarding school, Delilah explained, "a sporting-oriented place. Mind, I had cast my ballot for Swiss finishing school, but nobody listens to me," and would daily strap her fishing pole onto the back of her bicycle and ride up the roads behind their New Mexico ranch to where a cotton-wooded canyon opened into a meadow of savannah-tall grass. She'd fish for trout with worms and spinners, "largely to little avail."

Against this description, J found himself comparing Esther, who, when otherwise free from school and home, respectively finishing school and a creek-side Frank Lloyd Wright bungalow, both in Carmel, had spent her free time modeling for a Japanese cosmetics line.

Chase, as Delilah told it, had persevered in her angling, had spent her evenings over old copies of *Field and Stream*. This all made Walter jealous. By rights, he felt that he ought to be a fly-fisherman himself. But he was busy. He'd had several large movie projects going at once, and the helicopter ferried him near daily from ranch to airport and points beyond. That his daughter refused to use a fly rod bothered him, and that she fished by herself bothered him, and that she fished so much bothered him.

J wasn't sure whether he imagined Chase wiry, slender, and adolescent in red flannel and green rubber, or just felt the images in his jaw muscles and in the part of his scalp behind his ears. He was certain, though, that he didn't want to find himself attracted to Chase because of her childhood, because of how he pictured her twelve-year-old body twisting against the oversized drapery of the red flannel and bellowing waders as she cast. Nor did he want to be attracted to her because of how discordant her childhood had been from E's.

Not that Walter had necessarily wanted Chase cotillion-bound, Delilah continued, but J had tuned out. Of the choices afforded J, the safest was to determine that it was Chase's current blushing, her contorting, on which he could blame his crushing.

For Walter, the daughter as heir ought to comport herself the way the adopted son as consigliore might: sharp, sensible, loyal, and on hand, but also attractive, if never dolled-up. J tried looking away from Chase. His cheeks were tingling. He found himself stealing glances. His fingers moved towards where her hand lay. Walter, Delilah explained, wanted his daughter competent and an ally; presentable, but as a component of his self—for Walter—but J was feeling Chase too lovely, too lovely and too proximate, to hear how Walter was a collector.

J looked at Chase whose eye rolling should have made her seem less like a perfect thing, but the humanity it granted her made him want to kiss her even more. He worried he would; J was terri-fied that he would, that he would lean over out of impulse and put his lips against her lips, before he knew what he was doing, his fingers into her hair...he did! He did want to hear the story, would never have wanted to kiss Chase right there in front of Delilah.

Never.

"Of course, this all is only context," Delilah said, "for the actual story."

"J's the one that needs context," Chase said. "That's what he means by giving the dreamer a story, he means context so that he can understand what the dream is all about."

"So you think he dreamt me to do something," J said, relieved at the return to a decidedly not erotic conversation.

"Or be something," Delilah said.

"I wasn't being serious," J said, remembering that this conversation, too, lay in perilous territory.

"Do you not think that you're in a dream?" Chase asked.

"Chastity," Delilah said, and put her arm around Chase.

His pants and socks were draining into the bottom of his shoes, so that if he were to jiggle his feet they would suction and squeak. He felt rejected, which, given his crush, his flush of a moment ago, made him feel ashamed.

A new tension rose, borne of the stillness of the older woman with an arm around the unmoving shoulders of the younger. Delilah placed her left hand flat beneath Chase's left collarbone.

"I'm still waiting to hear the story about Chase," he said.

Chase found a fishing mentor, an old Ukrainian woman who fished sitting on a bucket that doubled as a live well for her catch. When Delilah explained how this old woman was equally, if not more, excited to catch whitefish on bits of corn as she was to snare trout on worms, J thought to his own grandparents' fondness for old world delicacies: gefilte fish and smoked carp.

J blushed, remembering how awkward he'd felt when he brought girlfriends over for Sunday brunches and his grandparents had proudly laid out spreads purloined from the leftovers of various volunteer board meetings they'd attended over the last week, how glad he'd been that E hadn't known the Yiddish word shnorrer, and so hadn't been able to accuse his grandparents of being shnorrers.

In his shame at having abandoned them, first while they still lived in New York, and then, especially, after his aunt finally got them to move into a facility near her, J barely heard about how the worms the Ukrainian woman used as bait when she did fish for trout were already a sacrilegious departure from deceiving brooks, browns, and rainbows with trinkets wrought of exotic feathers and glinting thread.

So many sources of shame, and yet each only one at a time, J thought, while Delilah described how the woman fed Chase little candies and recipes for breaded fish loaves that reminded Walter not only of his childhood's Jewish cuisine, but of the truth that Jewish cuisine was largely culled from the peasant fare of a dominant, gentile, Eastern-European culture Walter reviled.

There was the shame of his breakup, and the shame of wishing the dreamer away, and the shame of his general terror, when J felt terror, the shame of not feeling terror when he wasn't, the shame of being attracted to Chase, especially, when the attraction came on in response to hearing about her youth, and the shame of his wet clothes on the couch, of being soaked and dependent, and now this shame that predated all of them, the shame of abandoning his grandparents, his ancestors, without whom, and without whose not inconsiderable sacrifices, J wouldn't have been, which, when J considered it, was actually a shame of their origins, their Jewish-ness, and, really, weren't they the same as his dreamer?

Wasn't his shame really at his own Jewishness?

Impossible, he thought.

J dared not query the contradictory ontologies of having both a dreamer and grandparents—and wasn't his shame at telling Chase about the dreamer, not to mention his shame at that shame the same shame?

He was going to throw up.

"I can't," Chase said.

"Ok," Delilah said.

J looked up, puzzled, from his empty tea thimble and his shame catalog, and Chase stood, and Delilah stood and followed her, fingers alight in the arch between Chase's shoulder blades, and only after the two women had disappeared through hallway bends and closed recesses, did a young man in jeans and a plain-front shirt emerge to escort J to a room, Pomeranians at the heels of the man's high-arched bare feet.

CHAPTER THIRTEEN

They left Chicago by the road they'd entered, the coordinates for 'Joe' directing them toward a mostly blank spot southeast of Boulder, Utah. The rain had turned to snow in the night, then stopped without clearing, and the highway's shoulders were splattered with black slush thrown up by the plows and the sky was an oppressively bright gray that made J wince at the ruinously fallow landscape, fields and factories winter-shorn alike.

The man with the Pomeranians had directed J to a guest suite and its marble shower, and when J had finished toweling off, he'd found silk sleep clothes lain out in place of his outfit. He donned these out of consternation that the room's apparent privacy might be less than complete. In his sleep, his contortions elected the nudity at which he'd hesitated, hesitated with good reason: in the morning, he woke to a post-it note on a pillow next to his head telling him to pick anything he wanted out of the room's wardrobe.

Instead, he'd reswaddled himself in foreign silk and, clad thus, padded into the hallway in hopes of finding his own clothes, but Chase had intercepted him and pushed him back into his room— Delilah wouldn't stand for a man not dressed for table at her table. Resigned, J had opened the obligatorily massive wardrobe expecting a selection of clothing.

Inside: seven identical suits, a stack of fourteen identical dress shirts, shelves of socks, sleeveless underwear, thin, blousy boxers, and, on a thin chrome band ringing the wardrobe's interior a foot below the clothes bar, an iridescence of silk ties, uniquely flamboyant, like a string of prayer flags in the walnut alcove of an Oxford library. At breakfast, Delilah had also insisted a set of cuff links upon him, for the shirts all required them. The links were gold circles, convex like shields, and embossed with a crest in which six six-pointed stars circled a rearing, roaring lion.

And now he sat in the truck, clad like a Rothschild or an Oppenheimer in chalk-striped blue wool and a shirt with the slightest tint of lavender and a silver tie with thin red stripes that he would have shed at the far border of Delilah's oversight but for the morning's chill. A brown leather valise behind the bench seat held extra shirts and ties and undergarments. He could stay dressed this way indefinitely, or at least until the suit needed cleaning.

"Are we going to your dad's house first? Or straight to Utah?" J asked.

"Radio," Chase said. "Please."

"I thought we were past this."

"I'd like some music."

The radio knob lived up to J's expectations: damp, smooth. The radio glowed on to static. It emitted a pleasant electric smell, burnt ozone nostalgic of a kerosene heater, that mingled with the musk Delilah had dabbed inside his wrist and the menthol of the aftershave with which he'd salved his bared skin. He slowly turned the tuning dial past hints of sound, decided to find the kind of music he'd originally chosen for Chase's aesthetic. He settled upon an NPR broadcast of twangy mono folk recordings made as part of a depression-era Library of Congress project, sat back to the nasal complaint of a man without work slapping the side of a banjo, though the truck cabin's smells and his clothes suggested Wagnerian opera.

"Really?" Chase asked.

"Wouldn't you say?" J said.

"Would've said Pixies, if you found it," Chase said.

J began tuning further along the dial.

"Leave it," she said. "I'll live."

They'd hardly made their way back south onto I-80 before the music gave out and a talk show came on. J again reached for the knob, but Chase tsk'd. The host introduced himself as a collector of stories about America and Americana, which he claimed, were the same thing; or, rather, Americana was the thing most American about America. J wondered aloud whether NPR had any other kind of shows any longer.

"I guess we are always looking to try to see ourselves a little clearer," Chase said.

"I suppose you could say it's the same way as I'm trying—"

"No."

"Then what am I doing?"

"Would you shush? I'm trying to listen," Chase said.

The show's guest called himself an expert on local museums. He was in the middle of a tour promoting a new book about state park interpretative exhibits and had just come from one such, an exhibit on the Fremont people in central Utah.

"That's about where we're headed," J said.

"Shush."

"Shush, yourself," J muttered; but, Chase ignored him.

What struck the man, it turned out, was not the Fremont exhibit. He'd stopped in Columbia to give a talk at the University of Missouri, and, while there, he'd, by chance, really, swung by the public library. It featured a traveling exhibit, which wasn't usually his thing: his thing was all about how small isolated groups, distant from the commercial world of big-deal curators, presented the world to themselves and themselves to the world. Of course it was, J thought, that's why Chase was interested, because it was Delilah and apparently Walter and probably Chase, too. They were these curators.

Traveling shows were like the worst antithesis, the man said, distributing a one-size-fits-all cultural hegemony to replace and devalue local curatorial mores.

"Sure," J said, still holding against this man Chase's interest in what he had to say. "Fine. But, when he fetishizes these communities, doesn't he objectify them? Need them to stay always pure at what might be their own expense?"

"And, so, what? You: you'd have them travel?"

"He's a chauvinist!"

"I'm trying to listen."

She believed in truth, J realized, that there was such a thing as truth; he didn't. He hadn't anyway. This epiphany, double epiphany, the unnerving part of which was the question—did he believe in truth, now? Was he an essentialist all of a sudden?—nearly caused him to miss the explanation that the exhibit turned out to be a set of detailed accounts of the Lodz ghetto's last days.

"Fuck," Chase said.

"Detour," J said.

The host wanted to know about the show. Just go, his guest said. But surely something must have resonated. All of it resonated. Describe something striking. The man couldn't. But surely, his host insisted, there must've been something.

"There are two problems with my describing any of it," the man said. "First, I might diminish your audience's sense that they need to see this for themselves."

"But what about those who can't go," his host interrupted.

"Second," the guest continued, "I don't feel ethical doing so."

"Ethical?"

"How could I take it upon myself to say anything about the Holocaust? How can I possibly give an account of the Lodz ghetto and its experience? Who am I to do that? To trade in on these people being collected and then murdered? Who says they would want their executions commemorated, shared, talked about, exhibited any more than any other victim would want kill videos of their rapes and murders circulating?"

"Still think he's an asshole?" Chase asked.

"Oh, shut up," J said.

"But surely they don't want to be erased, and isn't the exhibit doing just what you're worried about anyway?" the radio host asked.

"If it's commemorating them, their lives, that you're after, why not make a museum about their lives? Pre-Holocaust?" the man responded. "A museum that shows off how each person lived, and what they cared about, and where they worked, and who they married, and so on and so forth? Why not that?"

"Doesn't it creep you out at all," J asked, turning off the radio and retrieving the GPS, "that we turn on the radio and the first thing it does is tell us where to find information about Lodz?"

"Does it creep you out?" Chase asked.

"It makes me feel, makes this feel…finally like it's real, like the dream is real."

"A real dream."

"Did you see your mother's lobby? Either we're in a dream, or dreams are more plausible than I thought."

"Ha!" Chase said, banging on the steering wheel. "If you took that lobby for a dream, wait till you meet my dad."

"The dad who dispatches you cross-country for plain chairs?"

"It was on my way."

J wanted to ask her whether there was something going on, or about to go on, between them, but for the fear of rejection, and of being kicked out of the truck, and just when she was speaking of introducing him to her father. Instead, he hovered on the edge of speech, antsy in his suit, in his seat, rehearsing conversations; he visualized Chase's hand on his leg, her smile, her words, her pulling over…

When he couldn't take the fantasies any longer, he asked Chase whose clothing he wore: it fit perfectly.

Chase laughed.

"Seriously."

"If the couture suits…"

"Asshole."

"I'm teasing…Do you like the suit?"

"Yes, I like it."

"Ok, then," she said.

J decided that asking questions was perhaps a mistake. And then he couldn't help himself, because it was ask about the suits or ask about whether he could kiss her.

"Are they your father's?"

"God no!" Chase laughed.

"Your mother's lover's?"

"Jesus!"

"Is Delilah magic? Does she have batteries of tailors on call to outfit me in the night? And if she is, why are you driving chairs cross-country for your father?"

"They are divorced," Chase said, plugging Columbia, Missouri into the GPS as a desired waypoint. "And you asked me about the chairs already a moment ago. You need to stop."

"So your mom is magic?"

"Respect that I'm not telling you, J."

CHAPTER FOURTEEN

THEY REACHED ST. LOUIS at four in the afternoon and pushed on without stopping in hopes of catching the exhibit that very day and indeed they did reach Columbia's library by five, outside the door of which a banner hung: 'Last of Lodz.' But, a brass-hooked rope hung between stanchions in front of the exhibition hall, and from it a small sign that simply said, 'Closed.'

They frantically made their way to the library's circulation desk and asked when in the morning the exhibit reopened. It wouldn't, they were told. It was packing up that night. Moving to Jacksonville.

"Jacksonville!" J exclaimed, slapping his hand on the counter.

"But surely," Chase said, "there's a way we can see it, if but for a moment. We've driven from Chicago."

Chase walked away before the young man had finished explaining that far away as Chicago was, they'd been breaking the show down since noon. J apologized and followed her around the stanchion and its braided rope, and into the exhibition hall, in which a few men in beat-up mustard work pants were busy carrying boxes out to a loading dock, cleverly revealed by drawn-back curtains.

"You can't be back here," a worker, hands-on-hips, said to them.

"Your boss," Chase replied. "Now."

The man yelled for a Mary, and a woman, dressed like the workers but not dirty, walked towards them from the trailer's recesses.

"Ma'am," Chase said. "My colleague here, J, is in the midst of in-depth research upon a victim of the Chelmno extermination camp. We were on our way between an appointment with one scholar at DePaul University and another appointment with a most reclusive other scholar in Utah, only first recommended to us by our DePaul contact. I should say, we were on our way, when this, your so very important and relevant show, was described to us on the public radio, and we drove like Gabriel after Lucifer to get here. Is there any way at all that we might chance a glance at your material, even if only at some of it?"

"It's all in boxes," Mary said.

"Anything," Chase said, "would be a blessing."

"Anything at all," J said.

Mary walked over to the man who'd originally stopped them and asked what there was that could be easily opened.

"There's nothing that won't delay us," he said.

"That'll least delay us."

"Fine," the man said. "Whatever, Mary." He flicked open a clasp knife and cut the top of the box next to him.

They walked over to the box, the three of them, costumed like a kind of retold Village People, Philanthropy People: the curator, the donor, and the artist.

The box contained a set of Torah-scroll fragments mounted like butterflies pinned between framing glass and linen backing, the fragments charred at their edges, and a photograph, also glassed and framed. They pulled these out and laid them on the floor side-by-side. The photograph was of a trench, perhaps sixteen feet across, the same deep and three times as long. There were three trees to one side of it, and a group of men in uniforms beside those. In the background's gray horizon, indistinct buildings were faintly outlined, smoke from these blending into the photograph's blown highlights.

The far end of the trench contained bodies, naked, mangled, as if dumped from the tilted bed of a construction truck. The bodies, nude, twined together such that the film's poor resolution coupled with the exhibition-sized enlargement made the shape of the grain more distinct than the contrast between one body and another.

A single woman splayed on the top of the pile, her shorn head draping off into the low-end of the photograph's unrecovered dynamic range, a shadowed range whose detail was sacrificed to an exposure that unrelentingly resolved, made vivid, her pelvis, emaciated so that her white skin barely contained the sharp corners that stretched it to shape, thrust skyward, legs dangling and spread, her pubic mound thick with black hair. J hated that he couldn't help but question what might be his real relationship to this woman's privates.

Gustave Courbet's 'L'Origine du Monde,' seen at the Musee d'Orsay while on European vacation with E, had the same orientation as this woman; they'd giggled at Courbet's lush, enormous, hairy vagina—The Origins of the World!—a giggling begun a week before Paris when E and he had been at the Prado and realized Goya's bird feeding Elijah had a donut in its mouth. Here, in Columbia, that giggling threatened to become a hysteria that might very well get the better of J.

He coughed and blushed and Chase muttered and elbowed him sharply.

The photograph's foreground was the floor of the trench, the puddle-dappled furrows of industrial excavation in bad weather. The three viewers stared at that skyward hip-thrust of that long dead woman, and then at the charred pieces of Torah scroll, and then at that long-dead, long-wasted vagina, and were unable to turn away.

Either this had to do with J's relationship to the dreamer or it didn't. It was the one or it was the other.

Finally, J started to sound out the words on the Torah scroll:

Aleh-zeet turaf bipeeah viyadah Noach kee-kaloo hamaim maiyal ha'aretz.

"What does it mean?" Chase said.

"I don't know," J said. "It's been since high school since I've studied Torah. I think *ha'aretz* means 'the land.'"

"A leaf the size of an olive torn off in her mouth, and Noah knew that water was diminished from on the earth," Mary said.

There was another fragment, and J read: *Vayiven Noach mizbaiach la'Adonai, mi'col habihamah ha'tihorah.*

And Mary translated: And Noah built an altar to the Lord and from all the clean animals…

There that fragment ended, and J read the next fragment: *Viarpachshad vilood viaram…*

Mary cut J off, "Those are just the names of Shem's sons. The rest of that piece of scroll lays out his lineage."

"We should figure out the numerology," J said.

"What's to figure out?" Chase said. "God destroyed the earth, and the earth was repopulated by Noah."

"It skipped the part where God promises Noah he won't destroy everything again," J said.

"From one man, the whole world can be created," Mary said.

"Which means with the murder of any man, the whole world is destroyed," J said.

"Sorry," Chase said to Mary. "He gets this way."

"Imagine if we weren't all the descendants of Cain!"

"Would you two like to join me for a drink?" Mary suggested. "I don't mind this talk."

It was beginning to feel like a pattern, J thought: weird encounter and then the bar.

CHAPTER FIFTEEN

J woke with the curator's knee perilously sharp against his bladder. He slid out from beneath her still-asleep inarticulacies and padded, stocking-footed, thankfully covered by the silk nightclothes slipped into his valise by Delilah's valets, to the bathroom, where he found Chase asleep on the floor.

He shook her shoulder, tried to wake her to lead her to the room's other bed, but she mumbled protests, slapped, and drooled.

"Fuck," J muttered.

He tiptoed back across the motel room. Strong light bent against the corners of the drapes. He peeked out at a back parking lot mostly empty. He stepped into his shoes and walked out, carefully closing the door behind him. He thought to pee beside the truck, but saw a dumpster off behind the building. He slipped between it and a cinder-block wall painted high-gloss, anti-graffiti beige. The bright sunlight was laying groundwork for a wretched hangover. As he peed, he began to hum; and then he found himself mouthing, "Oh one, oh none, oh no one, oh you."

"Oh you," he said. "Ha. Oh one, oh none."

Shaking off, swaying slightly as he checked to make sure he hadn't, and wasn't, splattering his pants, he wondered what he was singing and why. It sounded right, that 'oh one, on none, on no one, oh you,' and when he repeated it, he remembered a ring and the earth. What had he done? He tucked himself away, wondering what mysteries the prior evening had yet to reveal, and caught a glimpse of a head sticking out of the dumpster. His vision blurred with adrenalin surge. He grabbed the side of the dumpster until he could see clearly and stand straight. He looked again. It was a mannequin head with the coarse orange hair of an abandoned doll. Someone had painted eyes onto its neutral surface, but these had chipped, and the edges of the missing paint seemed to catch the harsh light and glint meanly. J kept thinking that the head's mouth gaped, or screamed, but it was closed. He could see that it was closed every time he redirected his attention to it, but as soon as he looked elsewhere, it yawed again.

What had he done last night anyway?

Why wouldn't the dream of a dying man supply such terrors? And why would it either?

He needed to not drink.

J's headache, now blossomed, now still blossoming, frustrated his attempts to make sense of what was at any rate an empty question: it was a mannequin, a beat-up mannequin meant to be thrown away. He walked back around toward the room and the bright sun forced his gaze downward. His pajama pants' fabric had absorbed a drop of urine from his inadequately shaken penis, and a dark wet spread into a splotch.

This was no way to help the man in the van.

The word 'help' sounded so inadequate.

He tried to pull his top down over the pee splotch, but nothing doing. He sighed and continued on, the sockless shoes' leather strange against the skin of his feet. He didn't feel like being in the dream any more, didn't want to pursue the questions it demanded any further. He longed for stasis. He imagined the New Mexico ranch lavish, and wondered how he might dissuade Chase from following the lead in Utah, to just head on through to her dad, take J with her there.

Why had the man in the van dreamt J? J was weak, undisciplined, ineffectual.

But this despair of his mission, this desire to be taken home, taken to a home, any home, tied him further to the suggestion that the world was the world, and the world was also a place into which J might be dreamed. J resigned himself to the notion that while God may well have been the creator of the dumpster and the parking lot and the curator, the dreamer was J's creator: J, his legacy. But legacy depends upon memory, and J bore no memory of his dreamer. How beholden, J wondered, am I? He remembered the damp on his pants. It felt so distant, the man, the van, the man's endless dying. It felt so exhausting.

Last night: he remembered whiskey, and maybe some kind of bar with a disco lit dance floor, but no music.

Mary sat up at the sound when J closed the room door behind him. The cover fell to her waist and J looked at her exposed breasts, which were really quite nice, small and pointed with big purple aureoles that seemed an enlargement of her nipples, raised like mushroom caps.

He wondered what her nudity meant, wondered once again what secrets the prior evening had yet to share, wondered what her nudity meant for him and Chase and the ranch and the lavishness Delilah had promised, and there was always Joe at the end of the GPS coordinates.

He noticed that Mary's stomach was tight, and her skin was brown and almost slightly loose, though not wrinkled, and that she had a scar at her sternum that ran in a long loose coil like an unfurling bullwhip down the side of her ribcage.

"Hey," he said, softly, though it seemed unlikely that Chase would wake out of her stupor, and Mary shook her head sharply, as if a bee had stung her, or as if she was attempting to shift off a daze. She pulled the covers up to her neck. Her fingers, unusually long, clasped the comforter's hem.

"Hey," she said back in a whisper, hoarse, pungent with half-digested whiskey, that made J aware that despite his pants' dampness, his cock was warm. "Where are my clothes?"

He sat down on the edge of the bed beside her, rested a hand on the shape of her legs beneath the blanket. He wanted to reassure her. He wanted to…he didn't want her to feel that his pants were wet.

"No," she said.

"No what?" he asked, running his hand from the leg-shape to the hip shape, running his hand over her hair, which stood to the side like bent straw.

"No, stop," she said.

"Stop, why?"

"I mean it," she said and took his wrist and returned his hand to his lap. "Where are my clothes?"

"I don't have much memory of last night," J said.

"I've got to pee and I don't know where my clothes are."

J, ungainly, began searching the room. He found his suit slung over a chair, but her clothes weren't beneath it. He found his shirt and tie on top of a television, but not her clothes. Mary craned her neck to follow his search, muttering about her bladder. J saw that she had a hickey between her collarbone and her shoulder, and wondered whether he'd given it to her, but all that came to mind was, "There was earth inside them, and they dug."

"What are you saying?" Mary asked.

"Saying what?" Chase said, hanging from the bathroom doorframe.

Full wreckage ravaged her sleep-struck pose: the knot of her ponytail hung over an ear; eyeliner, which J had not realized she wore, spread from her left eye socket onto her nose; her shirt torqued to a side, pants to the other side; the clear impression of her belt buckle indelible upon her forearm.

"I've got words in my head," J said.

"You don't say," Chase said.

Mary clutched the covers closer to her neck.

"Really?" Chase said looking at Mary and then at J.

"I've got another line coming back to me," J said.

"With me in the bathroom?"

"I didn't think you two were…" Mary began.

"But I was right there in the bathroom."

And J worried that Mary's disclaimer was also a disclosure and still most pressingly: "They invented no song. They did not grow wise."

"That's backwards," Mary said. "The poem goes: 'They did not grow wise, they invented no song.'"

"You should know better," Chase said, looking at J. "I thought that you would know better."

J said, "So it's a poem! Did we discuss it last night?"

"Poems are stupid," Chase said.

"Stupid?" J said.

"You're stupid," Chase said. "Seriously, I was right there in the bathroom."

"Ok," J said.

Then Mary cried out, a happy cry, really.

They looked over at her. She had one arm deep beneath the covers, the other still clutching them to her neck.

"I think I found them," she said. "They're under the covers."

"What's the poem?" J asked.

"Found what?"

"You don't remember?" Mary said, reaching further, her eyes focused on the ceiling as if to see into the darkness her hand probed, her tongue between her teeth.

"Remember what?" J said, worried, now, about the prior evening's secrets.

"The poem, you made a song out of it," Mary said, the covers now clutched by her chin against her chest.

"What's she doing?" Chase asked J.

Mary meanwhile had lifted her legs in an attempt to pull on some item of clothing, but misjudged the length of the covers. Chase and J both stared.

"What?" Mary asked.

Chase said, "You're for all the world to see."

Mary blushed and mumbled and set her legs down, them taking, as if token for passage, the blanket from beneath her chin, her chest exposed in her effort to cover her fanny and thighs.

"Great," Chase said. "Fantastic."

Mary began to cry, bent over, her back bare, her spine pronounced, her arms before her like a runner stretching. J apologized to no one in particular, to the room as a whole, to E more than anyone, absent though she was, or to himself, for whatever he'd failed to do, or done unremembered, with the woman on the bed.

Chase threw up her arms, letting them fall loudly at her side. "I'm out," she said; then she pointed first at Mary and then J, "You're not in a dream. This isn't a dream."

Chase opened the door and stood in it, hands on hips. "What you were singing last night, goes like this:

> O one, o none, o no one, o you:
> Where did it go then, making for nowhere?
> O you dig and I dig, and I dig through to you,
> And the ring on our finger awakens.

And then she walked out the door, shoving it further open so that it bounced unevenly off its rubber stop and shuddered in place a moment before succumbing to the return spring's inexorable pull.

"Wait!" J called after her, "What about the line about there being earth inside of them?"

"That is," Mary said, each syllable separated by a loud sniffle, "only the last stanza that she recited."

"We have to go after her," J said.

"I know the rest of the poem," Mary said, sniffle-pausing still.

"We have to go after her," J said. "Her mother gave me my clothes."

"Perfect," Mary said. "I might be pregnant and the father is already chasing after another woman because her mother gives him his clothes."

And J realized he'd made a terrible, terrible mistake.

CHAPTER SIXTEEN

HE LEFT MARY IN a Jacksonville hotel room, empty whiskey bottle and used condom in the miniature trash can beside the bed, those as much a leaving-time offering to their four days cross-country travel to Mary's next installation as was, he imagined, his relieving her of his pugilistic angst, his morose, unpleasant presence. He'd spent the days with his forehead pressed against the passenger pane of Mary's Audi wagon, in part to cool off the heat of his hangovers, in part to not look at the woman taking him further away from Chase, further from Joe, further from whatever passed for destiny or moral obligation, further, really, from just plain old not being a bad person.

He hadn't wanted to sleep with her, hadn't wanted to travel with her, hadn't wanted to talk to her. What he wanted was to call Chase, whose contact information, he realized, he didn't even have.

But, each night, disgusted with himself, he would renege on his commitment to not drink. Then, he would drink, and she would drink, and it was pretty clear she wasn't pregnant, and they'd fuck, and it wasn't particularly good fucking, but it also wasn't like he was sober enough for the fucking to make him feel lonely either. The hangovers were a blessing, too, in that they kept him from thinking, incapacitated him until 4 or 5 in the afternoon. And, then, when he began to feel better, he would begin to remember Esther, who had been his life, and Chase, and the dreamer. He would point out to himself that he'd ruined it, ruined his chance of doing anything.

Why had he?

Because he was an asshole.

Why was he an asshole? It was like he couldn't help himself, or like his night-self secretly hated his day-self. He knew that his disgust with Mary made him an asshole, too, especially as he was fucking her, if only drunkenly and perfunctorily...he was amazed that he'd managed to leave after only four days. Shocked that four days had gotten him all the way to Florida.

If it hadn't been for the Blue Angels' aerial bluster over their hotel, he doubted he would have woken before Mary that morning. He had barely woken before her as it was.

Three hours later and he'd used most of the rest of the last of his money to acquire an F-150 that he wished he wouldn't involuntarily compare to Chase's immaculate truck. It was newer, and it was white, and it reverberated with highway noise. Still, he was pleased with it: who needed four-wheel-drive? he thought, signaling his exit off I-10 onto I-75, one finger tracing the highlighted line he'd drawn on the map, leaving the state. Like the salesman said, "That's how they get you: they sell you features you won't need that complicate the vehicle, guzzle more gas, drive up the price."

Chase would be proud, J thought, of his common sense thinking.

Not to mention, it was a Florida vehicle, basically guaranteed to be rust free.

It felt good to be finally in the driver's seat. He couldn't believe that he'd only left New York a week earlier, if even that. He almost couldn't believe he'd ever lived there. Florida was warm, hot really. In fact, it was hot enough that J had the windows rolled down. A/C was another feature he'd foregone. He did sort of wish the truck had those little pivoting defrost windows, but it wasn't quite old enough for that. Just over a hundred-thousand miles, but, like the man said, that was nothing on a workhorse truck like an F-150. How many miles must Chase's vehicle have, anyway? His was nearly as old as hers, and its wear made him realize just how well restored hers was. Chase owned a classic truck; J had bought a used truck.

It felt so not New York to own a car, to own a pickup truck. A billboard welcomed J into Georgia.

He'd only been in the state once, for a work trip a couple of years before he met E, back before he'd started his little boutique. They'd done a due diligence thing at Stone Mountain Resort outside Atlanta. For two days, all the home office folks from New York had given presentations to the regional office's clients. Then, Saturday morning, they'd played a round of round robin golf. The company folks had all been assigned to teams made up of clients, more meet-and-greet. J hadn't ever played golf before; but, he'd been to the driving range, and he'd done the putt-putt thing. He figured actual golf was just a combination of the two. The three Atlanta guys with whom he was paired had all just gotten back from spring golf camps. J had figured that just meant that the fact that they were playing round robin was a good thing.

The three guys had been curt and polite, not really approachable. The one he shared a cart with was a bit more open. J had wanted to know why it was called Stone Mountain. The man had hemmed.

"Seriously," J had said.

"It's a southern thing."

"Ok."

"It's kind of our Mt. Rushmore," the man had said. "Or I shouldn't say ours. The South's. If I had to say, I would say it's sort of embarrassing."

"Who do you have up there?" J had wanted to know.

Lee, Jackson, and Davis, it turned out. Not that J had gotten to see them. His flight back north left early enough that he'd only made it through about ten holes, which was a good thing it turned out. Because, on the eighth hole—and this was after his stroke had begun to improve, when the men called him Road Rage or New York and did so with a touch of fondness, and when his balls were being chosen at least a fifth of the time if not quite as frequently as were those of the other three—but on the eighth hole: he teed up to drive, carefully swung as smoothly and gracefully as ever he had…the three men, so previously reserved immediately fell onto the green laughing.

It was true, the stroke, which had started off feeling so good, felt strange and light on the follow through. J had looked up, and his ball was arcing towards where he'd aimed it, albeit in a slower, shallower arc than he'd expected. And there behind it, like some graceless clunky cousin, followed the club of his driver.

The men, once recovered, told him that he definitely couldn't borrow any of their clubs, but they did genuinely warm to him. Even so, he'd been glad to get out of there. Driving with an iron on the next two holes had just felt embarrassing.

J thought for a moment about detouring to Stone Mountain, getting a look at those generals. The Nazis of the South, he thought, the Confederacy their Reich. Though, of course, the United States ramped up its genocide of native peoples post Civil War, turning its big, brutalized, leftover army west for what remained of the nineteenth century until the Spanish-American War. That, of course, led to war with the Philippines, which only killed a quarter of a million civilians or so, and all of the other Banana Wars, conflicts so frequent and so enduring, that US involvement in WWI hardly seemed a blip, right up until the second Roosevelt, the one who'd once imposed a constitution on Haiti, finally pulled the US out in 1934.

J sighed. He guessed that he oughtn't waste any time detouring from his course to Chicago where he hoped and believed he could find Delilah's house again where, hope upon hope, he could figure out how to reach Chase.

The US Army, he thought. Though mostly it had been the marines in the Banana Wars, if the distinction mattered. Yet without that army…J wanted to say that without that army, that military, who would lose half a million men in WWII, J wouldn't exist. But, then, they'd certainly not saved his dreamer, and, of course, J didn't exactly know what he meant by the concept 'exist.' So, instead, he laughed to himself and looped around Atlanta, the euphoria of leaving giving way to the beginnings of rush hour traffic and exhaustion and his deferred hangover, which, J supposed, might be withdrawal pangs, or cravings. It was about the time that he and Mary would usually pick up their first six-pack, the one they'd drink in the car before stopping for the night. For, as she'd pointed out, it took them at least an hour to drink their three beers each, they metabolized at least one beer an hour, and it took some time for the alcohol to hit their system, ergo, they were never actually driving with more than about a drink in them, which was fine, exponentially safer than other things, like using a cell phone, say.

There was something monotonous about reaching the Tennessee border, and it was all he could do to not drift off to sleep, drift off the road.

What was he meant to do anyway? J asked of the world, halfway between Chattanooga and Nasheville, startled by how much anger he felt. He was doing it, whatever it was, he soothed himself. He'd been sidetracked, but now he was headed back. But headed back to what? Fuck! To Chase, he told himself which eased the ominousness of the cloud of things J felt he'd already sacrificed for the dreamer, a long list that bored him, a list whose repetition consistently made him feel worse, not for having lost the things, which made him feel bad, but worse for harping on the fact of having lost the things, for caring, for noticing, for complaining that he'd lost the things. What were his losses compared to the Holocaust! He worried again that the dream would end and he with it. Wasn't his life the Holocaust? Enough! But, shit, how was anyone supposed to live if every action and complaint and intention were all compared to the fucking Holocaust? And yet why shouldn't they be?

Seriously, J told himself, enough, and wondered at the possibility of a six-pack, a possibility he resisted when he filled up his gas tank, again, having already racked up a nearly unbelievable $150 gas bill, not quite into Kentucky yet.

Next time, J thought, he'd just walk.

Wasn't he meant for more than simply witnessing the absoluteness of his dreamer's eradication? Surely, J was meant for more than the realization that the Holocaust, like segregation, mullets, gender-based wage inequality, and big box stores had become something a certain set felt it important to identify as evil, such views demonstrated by dutiful occasional checking in, a checking in no more vigilant than the observance of other civic and social duties, like the confines of hygiene and fashion and table manners and commitments to eat more leafy greens and less factory-farmed meat, to get at least twenty minutes of cardiovascular exercise at minimum thrice weekly. Surely J was meant for more than simple witnessing.

The Prophet Elijah must have thought that too, must have thought that right up until he watched his people led into exile and was forced to concede that if he'd done all the good Lord had asked, and the good Lord, being the good Lord, had always known how all that Elijah could do would turn out, then Elijah was always just the good Lord's "you were warned," an "I told you so" hedge should the exiled ever complain that they hadn't known. Smug insurance.

Wasn't J meant to do more than be the audience at a museum? The guy who understands the impact of the smell of a room full of shoes? If what his dreamer wanted was someone to film *Shoah*, well that had already been covered by Claude Landsman, so what did he need J for?

Who was the man?

Where did he live?

What was his name?

Why did he live?

What was his favorite color?

What did he believe?

Whose names did he give his daughters?

How did he meet his wife?

Was he better with his hands or his mind?

Did he wake up happy or groggy or something else?

How did he amuse himself?

From what did he derive a sense of purpose? Of meaning?

Did he work? Did he like his work?

Who were his friends? How did they meet? How did they share time?

Had he ever travelled? Where? Why?

CHAPTER SEVENTEEN

J SHOULD'VE KNOWN THAT Mary wasn't pregnant. He must've known: why then had he followed along with her? Why had she taken him? He didn't want to stop again, but he had to use the john. How his pee schedule had gotten out of sync with his gas refill needs he didn't know, but it was annoying.

Pulled over at a gas station, he considered getting gas too, even though he was only down a third of a tank, but then didn't, thinking to himself that he hadn't stopped at cheap gas; he'd stopped at closest bathroom. He'd just force himself to whiz again when he next got gas. He pulled up besides the restrooms rather than at a tank. The chill outside of the truck's cab surprised J, as did the flatness of the early evening sky over southern Kentucky. Amazing where nine hours driving could take one. To think that it had taken him and Mary four days to get from Missouri to Chicago. Four days bookended by drunkenness and hangover. J resisted the cooler filled with beer en route to the restrooms.

Then back on the road, and he immediately realized the foolishness of trying to adapt his bladder to his truck's fuel consumption, rather than simply resetting the truck's consumption to match his bladder by refilling when he peed.

The sun finished setting as J reached Louisville and the dark offered no protection from nostalgia for how E had given him a ride from a festival to a California airport, how his thank you email strayed into a discussion of what love meant, how her reply talked about the view of the ocean from her bedroom, and of a jogging path at the edge of her backyard at the edge of the bluff above the surf; absent thoughts that coalesced around how E had isolated herself from men, for a time, after a bad breakup, and had gone, finally, to college at 23, where she first checked back in with sex with her French instructor, and then with a man in a drawing class, and then with a bicycle messenger—all of whom J somehow managed to mythologize and envy, though each encounter had told her it wasn't time yet; E had had a clay bathtub and she'd had a cat named Ms. Missy who would invade the surfer boys' house next door.

For some reason, thinking about E reminded J that the Catskills weren't mountains, but were actually eroded plateaus, their tops long and flat, treed with pygmy cypress and dwarf maple. What he wouldn't give to meet up with Esther again at the end of that Las Vegas work trip, to laugh with her from hotel lobby—her in cutoff jean shorts, him in a suit—to his room, to once again rely on the medley of odd condoms E's Australian friend had shoved in her bag before she boarded the plane.

J was into Indiana, the road blurred, when he remembered with an intensity closer to reliving the evening he and E held each other, sitting on an Utah desert overlook thousands of feet high, yards from their rented cabin, drinking wine and watching the sunset, and she'd confessed a teenage night in which a few tabs of ecstasy were worth the exchange of access to her body, and he'd confessed the isolation of not talking to his family for four years and then only barely talking to them after his mother's cancer diagnosis.

Then, just as J really began to struggle to stay awake, right when he'd taken to slapping his own face, and that to no avail, a hailstorm, hood-denting, cab-roof-banging. J couldn't rightly say that it kept him awake as much as that it repeatedly startled him out of sleep, did so at least every other second, so that he was constantly asleep and awake.

He wondered what it was about Chicago that made the weather horrendous whenever he arrived, and he hoped that this minor plague wouldn't actually damage his new used truck much. Regardless, he was grateful.

Finally, fifteen hours after buying the truck, seventeen hours since sneaking out of the motel room, J arrived in Chicago, arrived at Delilah's building, as if by muscle-memory, though Chase had driven to and from the last time. He pulled up abruptly under the awning, paused rather than parked, cab rocking with the force of his stop. He peered in to the lobby to confirm his destination by virtue of its singular opulence, but the atrium lighting over the entryway to the parapet was such that he couldn't make out the interior.

He was ready to find a parking spot based on his limited certainty, when an embroidered grey glove condescended on the truck's silver-button handle.

He stepped out of the held-open door and a second doorman took his keys in another grey glove, and the first doorman escorted him to the elevators, pushed Delilah's floor number. If J had been better rested, if the world in his periphery didn't keep looping forward at the speed of the highway...

J paused before knocking, wondering, were these, his counter-parts, also dreamt-entities each with its own mission? Or were they the equivalents of angels, cognizantly dreamt to guide J? Before he could knock, too paralyzed by his question to ponder it or to knock, Delilah opened the door, said, "Here you are."

"Here?" J asked, misaligned.

"You know."

J stood and nodded and smiled and then just stood.

Delilah insisted him in, told him he needed a sherry and a shower and a nap: then, they'd talk. J protested that he didn't drink, him having made that decision that very morning. Delilah rolled her eyes at him and pinched his bicep through the fabric of his suit sleeve with a long-nailed thumb and forefinger before fetching a tray with a small, crustless, white bread sandwich and a glass of sherry. J ate the sandwich and drank the sherry. He showered, and crawled, naked save his boxers, between the deep covers of the same guestroom bed he'd slept in a week earlier.

When he woke, the sky still hinted at its barely shed cowl, night visible to the west. He slipped back into the shower and then went to the wardrobe. The suit he'd hung up before bed was gone, so he put on one of the six remaining. Now there were five, and he dreaded to what portent, dreaded the seasons and tropes defined by his gradual consumption of apparently predestined couture.

The sun, full above the nearest buildings, haloed Delilah's head in what J imagined must have been a planned pose, her robes reminiscent of late medieval Christ-iconography. Each piece of breakfast was simple, and on its own plate, and shiny: three perfect oranges, reflecting the sun; two scones, reflecting the sun; a serving of scrambled eggs, reflecting the sun; a silver carafe, reflecting the sun. Delilah sipped from a purpled china cup of coffee that turned translucent…in the sun.

Delilah motioned J to sit. He did, wondering whether he could feel any less significant by virtue of being too out of scale. What was the right moment to ask Delilah about Chase?

Delilah presented the table with an open hand by lieu of commanding J to eat. Though he had hoped that Chase would be here, he had also expected that she would have continued on to New Mexico with the chairs. He couldn't believe that he'd almost forgotten about the chairs. J's hand shook as he lifted a scone with a silver tongs that also gleamed in the sun; it shook as he transferred a pat of soft butter, also stage-lit, like deified nectar, like dew-dropped manna, to his plate.

He thought to ask Delilah about the chairs, but the way she lifted her porcelain cup with both hands, or the edges of both hands, thumbs and forefingers, delicately encircling the cup's lip, prevented him from speaking. She sipped and watched him press his butter knife into the edge of his scone, which crumbled and tore. He dabbed at the butter, and then spread it on the uneven crumb inside the scone. What use was he anyway? Of what use and to whom? He wanted to feel sick with his angst and his worry and his fear and his ineptitude, but he'd had a good night's sleep, taken a shower, donned clean clothes. He wasn't hung-over. He felt good, great really, hale and hungry.

Delilah slid an embossed card with a piece of handwriting on it across the table to J. J set his butter knife, loaded but unfired, on the edge of his dish and took the card. GPS coordinates. He didn't have to ask to know that they were in Utah, somewhere east of Boulder, down in the Escalante.

"Chase?" he asked.

"She said to give you these."

"But where can I find Chase?"

"Eat," and a smile, visible even with the sun so bright behind her head.

"I don't even know her last name."

"The card's from Chastity," Delilah said. "This is from me."

She pushed over a purse, literally, a goddamned leather purse that looked like it should be pursed together with drawstrings though it had a brass clasp. J took it, his breakfast untouched right at the moment it was most ready to be touched, this despite Delilah's earlier admonitions to eat—he hadn't had a chance to eat what with her profferings. He half expected the purse to be weighty with gold coin. It didn't have the feel of metal contents though it was certainly filled with something. J started to open it, and Delilah told him, don't, that it was gauche to examine that sort of *thing*. J thought to protest that the kind of gift that shouldn't be opened probably wasn't the kind of gift he could honorably accept.

Before he could do so, Delilah said, "This is for you, but not for you. Chastity wants you to continue your search and your story. I want her to have what she wants."

"Thank you," he said, and lifted his knife.

"Go!" Delilah said.

"Of course," J said. He put his knife down and stood. He took a last longing look at the scone, torn up but unbitten, and buttoned the top button of his suit jacket; at least he remembered that protocol from his years of meetings. So much for breakfast, he thought. And then he thought, what the fuck? Chase wants him to follow some GPS coordinates but won't even tell him her phone number? Won't tell him her last name or how to contact her? For fuck's sakes, J was a person; or something like that. It wasn't as if his nose grew when he lied. He wanted to be treated like a regular human being. A servant saw him to the elevator; when he exited it downstairs, the doorman met him and led him to his truck. Before he started the engine, he checked behind the bench seat. Sure enough, there was a new leather valise. He didn't need to open it to know that it contained fresh undergarments and shirts, just as he hadn't needed to open the purse to know it contained money. They'd filled his gas tank as well.

He started to drive towards Utah. Rather, he started driving with the intention of driving to Utah as soon as he bought a GPS and could figure out how to get there. Then something snapped. J realized that he didn't want to go to Utah.

He didn't want to do any of this.

Sure, he knew what he knew, but nobody treated him sanely for knowing this. It wasn't working out. He wasn't going to do it any more. They had told him the ride wasn't real, the dream impossible, well J would believe them.

J would step off the ride.

Fuck it, he thought.

Fuck Chase, and fuck the dream, and fuck the van the dreamer rode in. (And fuck the fear he thought, and uncertainty, and horror, and loss. Fuck all of them.)

For a whole long minute, he thought about going to NYC. Then he turned west. When he thought about how he was going to need to use Delilah's money to get west, he blushed even though he was alone. It's not like that, he thought. He'd pay her back. She clearly didn't need the money, though he was too sophisticated to buy that line.

He'd get a job, and he'd replace the money in the purse, he assured himself. Then why not bring the money back now? He needed the loan. When, then, and how, would he return the money? He was driving west. He would get a job, a real job, one that was about his hands not his mind. Was he really going to return the money at some random point?

Would he mail it?

They said he wasn't in a dream; he'd act like he lived in the same world as them.

He was driving west, that was it.

End of story.

West. Seriously. J didn't need to be afraid because it wasn't real. The dream was not real. He, J was real, in the real world, with real free will. And he was done.

Truly.

Driving west.

PART TWO

They dug and they dug, so their day
went by for them, their night. And they did not praise God,
who, so they heard, wanted all this,
who, so they heard, knew all this.

They dug and heard nothing more;
they did not grow up wise, invented no song,
thought up for themselves no language.
They dug.

There came a stillness, and there came a storm,
and all the oceans came.
I dig, you dig, and the worm digs too,
and that singing out there says: They dig.

O one, o none, o no one, o you:
Where did the way lead when it led nowhere?
O you dig and I dig, and I dig toward you,
and on our finger the ring awakes.

~~Paul Celan
(translated by Michael Hamburger)

CHAPTER EIGHTEEN

MORE THAN A YEAR after he'd last seen Chase, comfortably into his 38th year, J woke before dawn slightly stronger still, got in his truck, and went to work. Joe's GPS coordinates remained clipped over his driver's side visor; where they belonged, J told himself, though part of him thought that if he didn't need to follow its coordinates, he ought to be able to throw it away. Sure, Chase's nagging insistence that what he had wasn't a story still haunted him towards a discovery of more, but he didn't want more. As best J could tell, nothing good had come to him of his attempts to do something about the dream or the dreamer. Nor, for that matter, had anything good come to anyone else, least of all the dreamer. J categorically rejected the idea that he was meant to do something like read Mishnaiot, which the Orthodox do for the dead that their study might be attributed to the departed and thus increase the departed's share of heaven. Nonetheless, the corollary to his 'ought to be able to throw away this slip with the GPS coordinates' was obvious: if he wasn't able to, then he must be obligated to pursue them. But, much as that sense of obligation to that always-dying man guilted J towards a continued picaresque, J didn't want a mission, didn't want to believe any of it. He wanted a sense of wholesome and had no idea what thing in the world would offer him that feeling.

He was prodigal.

He'd used the first of Delilah's money to buy work clothes as soon as he'd gotten rural of Chicago. He'd driven out of Chicago, west and north to Minneapolis, which immediately failed to meet his image of work that involved dirt and muscle and weather. He had left, heading west on US 12. 12, the nation's first highway, was a two-lane in middling condition advertising 'The Road to Yellowstone' in washed-out primary colors, and it seemed that it would take him where he needed. There had been no question of stopping before the Missouri River. Past the Missouri, he found himself on reservation land. He had filled his tank (again) in McLaughlin, where a young Sioux couple asked him where he was from.

"New York," J had answered.

"That's too far," the young man had said. "No way."

"I am."

"Show us some ID."

J had complied, made friends. He asked about McLaughlin, which they were in, and about where US12 would take him going west. They'd been to Mobridge to the east across Lake Oahe, but they'd never been northwest to the far side of the reservation, seventy miles on. How was that possible, J had wanted to know; they had a car. He'd felt guilty at the blush he saw on the couple's faces when they explained that they didn't really like it there, and he understood them to mean that they weren't welcomed, and J thought, this is what a concentration camp looks like a century after the guard towers and barbed wire are taken down, when the concentrated are expected to keep each other in, and when the gas chambers and shooting fields have done enough work that the people remaining, left to their own devices, will do the rest themselves. How much suffering, J had thought, a people will inflict on another people to maintain the pretense that what they had done to that suffering people wasn't genocide, but natural, though maybe genocide was natural, too, so not natural but necessary, moral even.

Sure, J thought chewing his sandwich in the cab of his car, people have always been willing to do more violence to justify the rightness of the violence they've already done.

J had continued on through the reservation's untrammelled grasslands, thinking about how even the town was named after some Scottish guy, and so too the next town, further in, McIntosh, which wasn't even seemingly open: what of it that was visible from 12 was fenced and chained. He had driven through Lemmon and wondered if it had been worth abandoning the dream for this town's one broad intersection, the billboard celebrating its centennial a coded testament to the clearing of the bison and the arrival of the train. In Bowman, big enough for a coffee shop and small grocery, J had considered turning left and taking 85 south towards Texas. But, he had also liked that Bowman wasn't much, and that of the Laundromat's six machines, two were for 'greasers.' He had begun to feel like this might be the sort of place a man could work. He had tried not to acknowledge that between Bowman and Texas was New Mexico, with all of its forces magnetic and repellent.

Further west and north then it had been, then, because he was done with the idea, then three-years-old already, that he existed in the dream of man gassed in the back of a box truck heading from the Chelmno extermination camp to a mass grave in the Polish woods. He was simply J, he had decided, and he was going west to work.

An hour and a patch of sunset-surrealized badlands later, he had arrived in Marmath, which seemed a ghost town, but for the steakhouse banner strung on a roofless, windowless, brick bank building.

The steakhouse had been closed on account of it being a Monday, but its bar was open, and a man in a western shirt tucked into Levis, no belt, introduced himself as Allen Goldstein of Marmath, North Dakota, and offered to buy J a can of Budweiser with poker winnings which Mr. Goldstein pulled out of a too-ornate, too-old, too-spit-shined cowboy boot. J had idly wondered if this man hadn't once owned an ornate belt and lost it at the table. He'd made an attempt to learn more about Allan Goldstein of Marmath, North Dakota, but the man kept reintroducing himself, Allen Goldstein, and re-offering Budweisers, though J was hardly into his first, and finally the bartender, the only woman in the place, sent Allen home, a destination apparently proximate enough to reach on foot, if, in fact, Allen could walk.

Another man, this one not old, and not dressed for a square-dancing competition, but also wearing his shirt tucked into his beltless jeans, had bought J a second beer, a Coors Light—no one seemed interested in the very good microbrew on tap—and assured J that Allen had not won his money at poker. J understood that he would buy this man a beer back. And so it was night.

In the morning, J had woken up in the bed of his truck so cold that he thought he'd wet himself, nauseous with hunger and hangover. He'd jumped out onto the dirt main street rubbing his arms and shivering, rounded the corner of a the boarded-up two-story brick bank building onto Highway 12, over which banners for Marmath's centennial were affixed to the bank's second-story windows' plywood panes.

He'd walked along 12, here so beaten it seemed more dirt than blacktop, beneath the deep shade of tall old trees, until he'd come to a diner and sort-of grocery store, whose dirt front clearing was all parked up with matching, base-model, white domestic pickups. A young girl had served him eggs while several men at minimum a decade older than himself carried on the slowest conversation he'd ever overheard, the pauses between speech long enough to consume a triangle of toast. By the time one of the men addressed J, he'd reached the realization that a bathroom might mean greater salvation than eggs, bread and coffee, and so he'd truncated his answer to how he was doing to one word in the interrogative: work?

They'd sent him on to Baker, Montana. J drove there wondering whether he'd finally drunk enough to forget about the GPS coordinates clipped to the visor, or to forget the way back to Delilah's, to forget the man, to forget Chase. He'd drunk so much he thought that he'd probably forgotten the list of names from Belchatow and the way E's newborn daughter looked in pictures online.

CHAPTER NINETEEN

J SAT, PULLED-OVER, GAZE wandering a long stretch of uneven rock, purple, ordinarily, but turned alternately black and red by the afternoon's shadow, contemplating:

> When I don't know, don't know,
> without you, without you, without a You,

Where a dirt hill rose high enough to support whimpering grass, BLM land ended at a poor excuse for a homestead turned into mediocre, but private, grazing land. Somewhere inside that confine, J's buddy was sure they'd find a T-Rex.

J had spent the better part of eleven months as a welder's assistant, before working his way up to journeyman welder himself, repairing the pipelines laid all over eastern Montana and western Dakotas. He'd given up drinking because whenever he drank, he told anyone and everyone how shameful it was that he was too chicken to drive to Utah and find Joe and learn about the dream. It wasn't just that this made him feel sad and bad in the morning, it was that he worried that at some point someone would be sober enough to hear him, to actually comprehend what he was saying, and that they'd jump him for being crazy. He also worried that on some night that drunk and morose and ashamed he'd find the pluck to drive to Utah, and then fucking what?

He'd also given up reading because reading did the same thing, except between himself and himself. Reading let him think, thinking led him to contemplate the nature of existence, that led to a consideration of moral obligations, at which point J couldn't hide from the word 'hiding,' and that made him feel chicken and weak and spoiled. Those things, of course, sponsored a restlessness whose only destination was bar and bottle. J was certain this complex, this cycle, would ebb at some point.

He was doing the right thing; he was doing what anyone would do; he was doing what everyone had told him he was supposed to do. It wasn't that he had denied being Jewish so much as that he didn't really bring it up ever. He rationalized that no one would probably care at all, but if he were to start ranting about Holocausts and such, if he started really being Jewish…

J lived in a rented trailer permanently parked on its own lot on the side of Baker inhabited by roughnecks, not to be confused with the side of Baker inhabited by ranchers. For anything better to do, he spent his nights in the bars, drinking club soda with lime, not fully accepted by the men in recovery, who held court in their own corners, until ensued the inevitable fights between their reveling coworkers and the ranchers, which, in acts both penitent and addicted, they would strive to quell.

J became friends with a welder originally from Baker, the man who'd gotten him drunk his first night in Marmath, an actual Baker native, born and schooled, though most everyone was at least local to the region. This man still drank, and in fact gave regular havoc about having drunk J so far under the wagon he was back on it for good, but this man's wife was a bartender in Baker, the bartender for the roughnecks, which oddly forced upon him outsider status, as if he was affiliated with the law. And because his wife was there, he didn't drink as much unless he was in Marmath or Plevna, safe from her watchfulness, but still within range to drive home ripped without real danger of police or behind-the-wheel narcolepsy.

The man was amateur at everything: hunting, paleontology, fishing, cabinet-making, gold-prospecting; J became apprentice to all of that, ended up with a hallway full of picks and shovels, and a freezer full of stringy antelope that he forced himself to make a meal of at least twice a week.

What, after all, J reassured himself, was more real, more visceral, than eating animals he'd killed himself? Had cleaned himself, cutting open their hides, and then their cavities, reaching into the entrails? What proved him more of this land, and not of any dream, let alone one dreamt on the eastern edge of Europe, than swinging a pick to wrest it of its secret bone yards, billions of years old?

There was one hang up to sobriety. When J didn't drink, he dreamt. What he dreamt he couldn't speak of even if he'd been willing to acknowledge the dreams either to himself or anyone else: The dreams were of nothing. The nothing was absolute. It was the primordial void before God created heaven and earth. The nothing of J's dreams seemed like it might well predate even God, have the power to create God out of the awfulness of itself.

The nothing wasn't a place because it had nothing with which to be a place.

The nothing didn't elapse because it wasn't inside of time.

The nothing couldn't be filled because it wasn't a void or a vacuum with an outside from which things might be drawn. It simply was, or rather, wasn't. It would have been horrifying if it could have contained horror.

J refused to believe that this was punishment for not following the GPS coordinates. Nor would he accept that they reinforced the realness of the dream that he had, as he put it to himself, once mistakenly come to believe dreamt him.

What he did do was set several alarms for fear that the nothing, devoid of time, would last infinitely absent outside intervention upon his still temporal body.

Certainly, J refused to worry that he dreamt these blank dreams because the man in the van had lost the energy with which, if not to dream J, to dream J's dreams, and that this emptiness was the first unraveling of J's materiality. Nor would J give credit to the worry that this was the void within which he was meant to create, that this was his prospect, empty, a prospect in which he had created neither heavens nor earth, had not subdivided those into land and water, night and day.

To what end create, J wanted to know. For wasn't it true that if he brought forth dry land by which to divide water from water that then he had committed to one day Noah's generation drowned, and one day the people of Israel damned to elapse their emancipation in the desert, digging for themselves annually graves, and to conquests, and exiles, and pogroms, and inquisitions, and eventually to the rails by which the Jews would be collected from the reaches of the earth to a common evaporation pool, smoke to the firmament, a return to the nothingness that plagued his sleep in the first place? Why fill the irritation of the void to only have it returned unto void?

Whatever it wasn't: absence and lack of absence.

J set the electric clock he'd already owned, a battery powered travel alarm in case of a power outage, a wind-up clock in case the batteries failed, his cell phone too, obviously. He checked each multiple times to insure that it was set before sleeping and yet he woke quaking when they did go off, certain that without their bells and chimes, multiple, he'd never awaken again.

This was just what it would take for now, he told himself.

And during the day!

During the day, his mind flushed by sweat, by labor, by lifting, by negative-twenty winter winds, or now by a strong sun broken only by even stronger afternoon thunderstorms replete with hail, his mind would suddenly produce a line of Celan like a gift from an ex-lover, at once beautiful and inappropriate, tinged through and through with a sense of unwanted commitment.

J rested his chin on his arms folded on his steering wheel. If he still drank, this was when he'd drink a canned beer. If he still drank and was with a friend, he'd set up empties at a distance and shoot at them. Realistically, if he still drank and was with friends, he'd likely not be here at all, but headed for Miles City and bars within which there likely might be women.

"Without you, without you."

And if they found a T-Rex on that private land, they could sell it to Japanese collectors, or so J's friend had told him. They could clear close to a hundred-thousand dollars. That much money meant not having to work for a while. J didn't want to not have to work. Besides, "Without a You." Capitalized pronouns meant God, but the indefinite article refuted God's singularity.

He thought of Chase, and thought that Chase had replaced E in his thoughts, and thought that he was on a year's delay with his woman-wistfulness, and yet there was no one to turn his ruminations to next. He could always drive to Utah. Or could he even?

No, he thought, he didn't have to leave this black-rocked Triassic topography because it was too late. J had missed the chance. If there was something that needed doing, if there really was a dreamer, and that dreamer really could dream a man into being seventy years forward in time, well he'd just have to dream for himself some other Jonah.

J's heart hurt and an RV blew past and blew out a tire, and came to a halt half-a-hundred yards from J's ruptured calm.

J put the truck in gear and drove up to the vehicle. A large tarp obscured the back window down as far as the silkscreened RV-4-Rent slogan. The tarp said, in tall, dancing, font, "Mitzvah Mobile!" and was decorated with Tefillin and Torah scrolls and Shabbat candles. J thought to drive away, and then thought better of it. The common rule of the land was that everyone helped anyone in trouble, and J was committed to the common rule of the land, just as he was committed to his newfound musculature. Plus, he wasn't sure he wanted anyone from Baker discovering what was in a Mitzvah Mobile. He got out of his truck and walked towards the front of the RV. A Chasid, resplendent in black: hat, robe, pants, shoes, beard, payos, velvet yarmulke, glasses frames, a black only broken by the white fringes hanging at the side of each leg, barely visible below the hem of his belted black robe, and by his pink hands and cheeks. He was a small man, and chubby, and he threw up his hands when he saw J approaching.

"A kleyne nes!" the man yelled.

"Kleyne nes?" J said.

CHAPTER TWENTY

"A MIRACLE! IT'S A little miracle!" the man said, his speech apparently confined to exclamations. "I break a wheel and the Lord sends me a strapping Yid to help!"

"It's just your tire, sir."

"And such politeness!"

J wondered at what allowed the man to so easily identify J as Jewish. He was taller than the man; J's hair was tucked under the camo-fronted baseball cap he wore whenever he took off his hard hat. His face was burnt and stubbled and mustached. His dirty black pocket-T was tucked into his dirty, unbelted jeans. He had on steel-toed boots. J was generic! Yet this man knew.

Had everyone always known? Was his shame of being Jewish his alone?

"Your spare's probably under one of those panels on the RV's back corner." J said. "We'll probably have to pull down your banner to get at it."

"Spares! Would you like to *da'aven* a little Minchah with me?"

"Minchah?"

"Afternoon prayers!"

"I know what they are; I don't know why they're little."

"Because we don't have a minyan! Only we have the two of us, and so we can't read the parshah. *Kachah*…little."

"We really ought to get that sign down and get out your spare, sir," J said.

"Spare! It'll keep! I put it out of the back especially in case such a thing should happen. But Hashem won't wait. We da'aven, and then the wheel. Excuse me! Tire! Then the tire!"

Without a You, J thought to himself. Well, he'd have to see for himself about that, and then remembered: I don't know, without you.

"I suppose you've got a spare siddur," J said.

"Not a spare, but for you, a siddur! And a yarmulke!"

"My hat will do," J said.

"Of course, of course your hat will do. But, also, you can wear a yarmulke. Have you put on Tefillin yet today? The sages teach that even though a man is required to wear them with Shachris, if, *mamesht*, by afternoon, he hasn't worn them, nu, he still may wear them up until the last moment to say Minchah."

"I don't think so," J said.

"Don't think so? Then clearly you haven't worn them today. Who could forget wearing Tefillin! Coming right up!"

"No!" J said, louder than he'd meant to, more forcefully than he should have. "I don't *think* I'm going to wear Tefillin today."

"You know," the man said, "when Moishe saw Hashem, what did he see, really? It was the Tefillin knot at the back of his head! That's all! The Holy One, blessed be His name, wears Tefillin, but you, you can't put them on? While you da'aven? Surely this is *mishagas*?"

"Surely this is mishagas," J acceded.

He put on the Tefillin, decades-old memory adequate to wrap the leather straps around his arm such that he spelled out the three letters of God's name: Shin, Daled, Yud. He put on the Tefillin, and because his hat wouldn't fit with the straps and box that went around his head, he put on a thin nylon yarmulke that the wind so obviously threatened that J couldn't think about much other than keeping it on his head; and, standing alongside the man, sun at his back, J faced east into oncoming traffic, in which direction he mumbled the Minchah prayers while the man rocked back and forth declaiming at the top of his lungs, J desperately hoping that the sun, low now, would blind any of his neighbors such that they wouldn't recognize him.

The mumbled prayers had a certain litany, demanded a certain humility, and J felt small, almost as if his body was too big for him. They came to the "Shemah," and the man covered his eyes and shouted for everyone to hear: Shemah! Yisroel! Adonai! Elohenu! Adonai! Echad! Then, to J's great surprise, he shouted the same thing again, eyes still covered, in English: Hear, oh Israel! The Lord our God, the Lord is One! Then, in the booming hush of a stage whisper, the man continued: Blessed is the honored name for eternity and beyond! To J's even greater surprise, the English recitation made him want to hide under the RV lest his neighbors witness him even more than did the Hebrew, even more than did the nylon yarmulke and the Tefillin.

J was ashamed of his ashamedness.

He said the words too, but in his mind he said, "Oh One, Oh None, Oh No One, Oh You!" The dreamer was gassed for being Jewish, practicing or not—J knew not which—and J couldn't even muster the chutzpah to pray before his neighbors, whether or not he believed. Those of his neighbors devout were not shy with their Christian practices; those of them not devout, not critical of those who were.

They recited the thirteen blessings of the "Amidah," their feet together in mimicry of the single leg of the angels, taking three steps backward, bowing in three directions, then walking three steps forward at the prayer's beginning and also at its end, the obeisance of those entering and exiting the presence of the King of Kings, though all that lay before them was wasteland and overgrazed hill, and the strong light at their backs illuminated no presence ahead but the occasionally passing pickup truck at each of which J blushed, though none, thankfully, stopped.

J discovered that his mouth remembered the cobwebbed words, that his body remembered the creaky rocking back and forth, the steps, the bowed head, the prayers he hadn't recited in twenty years. He discovered that his heart rate knew humility and confusion, his cheeks the flush of doing good in the eyes of the Lord. He did not like it, did not want it seen, did not want this Chasid in his black robes and black hat seen. Did not want the flush of the joy of prayer to compete with the flush of shame at being seen praying. For if he was seen, all would see J as well, and this...I'm free! He thought to himself. I'm free and I'm strong! (Free if one left aside the nothingness of the night, left aside the day and its damning verses.)

In the last of the light, the ravines blackened, the ground between them the ruddy orange of still flowing lava, the air cooling but redolent of heated dust and dying grass, J jacked up the truck and changed out the tire, marveling at how much more adept he'd become since he'd done the same for Chase a year ago. The man, who'd introduced himself as Rabbi Rumkowski, stood by and alternately thanked J and thanked Hashem and then thanked J again.

When J had finished, stood and lifted the offending rim and flat tire into the RV while the rabbi waited outside, he brushed his hands off on the sides of his pants. He found himself noticing this gesture, a gesture otherwise second nature since he'd begun out here, and identifying it as a constructed mannerism that reinforced his image as a western laborer, an assistant welder, a roughneck. This identity now felt false, both because he'd become suddenly self-aware of its constructed elements, and because Rumkowski had so easily seen through them. J felt as if there was a smaller version of himself, a little nebbish, hiding out inside of the body he'd built, that his muscles were little more than a clumsy disguise.

It was this nebbish, J didn't want to admit, that kept him from going to Utah and finding Joe.

"So you should know," the rabbi said, "I'm very pleased there's now a fifth Jewish man in the area. We're halfways to a minyan!"

"Are you part of that count?"

"And a fifth invite for dinner tonight! It'll be late before we eat. Nu, so it's late! I can still get to the RV Park and set up."

The RV Park was on the small lake that formed Baker's southern boundary. It had hookups for three vehicles, all of which were essentially visible from anywhere in Baker. J imagined the Mitzvah Mobile parked there. If this Mitzvah Mobile were anything like the ones in Manhattan, Rabbi Rumkowski would probably have a banquet table set up in the morning with Tefillin laid out. At least it wasn't a holiday, like Succos, for which there'd be palm fronds and myrtle woven into lulavs to be shaken at the corners of the world, an esrog clutched against them. Still...

What a nebbish J was, what a chicken-shit.

"Listen, Rabbi," J said. "It's late, the RV Park is expensive. Why not park at my place? You can use my kitchen if you like."

"You keep a kosher kitchen?"

"And the RV Park does?"

"You should, you know."

"Come, park at my place. I'll run you water and electric."

"Only," Rumkowski said, "because it's a mitzvah to bring strangers into your home, something even Lot did, and, *tachah*, who would I be if I were to deny you this mitzvah?"

J wondered if he wasn't indeed Lot hiding his guest from the residents of Gomorrah or Jonah hiding from Hashem. J winced to think he'd used 'Hashem' instead of 'God.' Regardless of which, he thanked his fortunes that he had not daughters to sleep with should the city be destroyed, his wife turned to salt. He also thanked his fortunes that his parking strip was behind his trailer and afforded some privacy by a row of poplar grown as a windbreak.

The rabbi followed him to and through town, and to the parking spot in J's yard. J agreed to come back to the RV in forty-five minutes for dinner—a dinner to which he was to bring nothing, first, because "*Chas v'chalilah* I should invite a person to a meal and then expect that person to bring the meal!" And, second, because anyway the rabbi couldn't eat anything that came from J's treif kitchen.

"But next year," the rabbi said, "when I come back through, if we're not yet in Yerushalaim, you should have a kosher kitchen, *baruch Hashem!*"

CHAPTER TWENTY-ONE

IN THE HALF OF his trailer that passed for a living room, J stripped, tossing his clothes into the pile he'd wear again the next day. He walked into his cramped bathroom and peered into its mirror, a thinly-framed rectangle the size of an 8x10 photograph tacked over the larger, built-in original whose reflective coating had oxidized behind the glass in a dull bloom that probably indicated mold in the walls. Where J's hat had flattened his hair against his forehead, his hair looked thinner than he'd thought it was. The sunburn that began at his cheeks ended in an irritated red line at his collarbone. His chest and shoulders were large, as were, he saw, looking down, his thighs and calves. His muscles didn't have the precise definition of a bodybuilder, but rather the raw mass that comes from lifting and carrying, day in and day out. What did all this strength matter, he thought, so long as he was still the same person, dreamed by the same dying man, and easily recognizable as such? J remembered his father once saying that whenever Jews forgot they were Jews, someone came along and put a yellow star on their chests to remind them.

His doorbell interrupted this reverie.

At the first ring, he looked away from the mirror. At the several subsequent rings, closely spaced and loud, he scrambled to pull on clothing, yelled that he was coming. He raced to the door in time for the third salvo and yanked it open. Allen Goldstein was there, his hair as shiny as his worn boots and bolo tie.

The two men paused, recoiled slightly almost in surprise, evaluated each other. Then, Allen Goldstein asked: "I bought you a Budweiser once?"

"Only once," J said.

"You looked better then. Younger maybe, or slimmer," Allen Goldstein of Marmath, North Dakota said. "That's why it took me a minute, so you should know."

"What can I do for you?"

"Where've you got the rabbi?" Allen Goldstein asked, stepping inside, uninvited.

"What are you talking about?" J asked.

"Come on, come on, he's here. He wouldn't say he was here if he wasn't here. Bring him out."

"How'd you find out that I had a rabbi here?" J asked, feeling more like Lot, the residents of Gomorrah at the door, every moment. If he had daughters to offer them... this brought the little girl in E's pictures to mind, and he found himself suddenly furious.

"*Vus machs da* you should be all tore up for?" Allen Goldstein said. "I've got every right to see my rabbi!"

"And you tell me how you learned he was here," J said, boxing out Allen Goldstein's further advance into the trailer. "Vus machs da? Really?"

But then Rabbi Rumkowski came to the door, arms wide, and shouted, "Mr. Goldstein! I thought, *mamesht*, that is the sound of Mr. Allen Goldstein! This is our new Yid, Mr. Goldstein! Mr. Goldstein! Yaakov! Yaakov! Mr. Allen Goldstein!"

"He was trying to hide you," Allen Goldstein complained.

"*Mishagas*," the rabbi said, wrapping an arm around Allen Goldstein and leading him off towards the yard. The rabbi's free hand bobbed in front of him, fingers bunched as if to blow kisses. J overheard talk of Yaakov Avinu and Dinah and Esau mingled with high notes about cattle prices and broken wheels. He sighed and closed his door, became aware that he had one hand on the knob, the other on the door itself, as if to silence its shutting, felt like he was posing again, and in the absence of a way to put his body that wouldn't be a pose, clutched the doorknob as hard as he could so that he could hope that his finger bones would bruise.

J had one foot in the stall, was wet nearly to his crotch, when the doorbell rang again. He considered ignoring it, pretending he couldn't hear over the shower, and then resigned himself to pulling his clothes back on.

J recognized the man at the door from his first day in town. J had mistaken the visitors' bureau for a visitors' bureau, a reasonable enough mistake. And, therefore, J had also mistaken the man inside, the man now at his door, for someone whose function was to share information. Instead, it had turned out that the man was in charge of promoting Baker, a task that involved raising some grant money for roads and schools and wells, a task not so time-consuming that he couldn't spend a full two hours telling J about how he wouldn't want to find himself in the bars that the oil-workers went to after about five p.m., and that the oil workers weren't like the ranchers that had always been in Baker—not that the town promoter had always been in Baker, though he was an eastern Montanan, through and through, Billings-born, which was technically central Montana, excepting as it was east of the Rockies, or at the eastern foot of the Rockies, which was what made it part and parcel eastern Montana, besides he'd always admired Baker—this all told at a dreadfully slow pace, the pause between each sentence nearly long enough for J to ask about the bathroom, a necessity of his hangover, repetitive since the Marmath greasy spoon counter, but never a pause quite long enough to ask.

Plenty of time too, J remembered, to think about his relationship to a certain set of GPS coordinates. If J's amateur paleontologist pal was part of how he'd ended up working oil and living in a trailer, this man was the rest of it. No way, he had thought, am I letting this kind of obstacle stop me.

"Seen you're a roughneck now," the town promoter said.

J wanted to ask how the man knew—mustaches, sunburns, dirty jeans and dirty T-shirts were hardly trade-specific; ranchers looked like this too—but didn't want to ask the man anything that might prolong their encounter. J opened his mouth to see how he could help the man, but the man had already continued on to say, "Should've figured."

This took J just enough back for him to miss his next opportunity to speak.

"You were a hang of a sight, first time you come into the office," the town promoter said.

J almost got out something defensive but the man breathed loudly to interrupt him, and passed his hat off his head and in front of his face to get it to his side in a way that cut J off again, and then, when J took a deep breath of his own to calm himself, the town promoter beat J to speech again, asking: "Rabbi around?"

"You too?" J asked.

"A Yid is a Yid. Whether or he isn't a roughneck."

J took another deep breath and got ready to say that the rabbi was parked in back, but the man, faster by the thinnest of hairs, said, "Imagine a Jew working oil. A *shikkur* too! A *shikkur* roughneck Yid. Never cease to be amazed, not me."

J was certain that if he hadn't been so thrown off by this fat mustachioed boor's use of the Yiddish slur for a drunk he would have managed to somehow express his outrage at being called a Yid—it was one thing for the Rabbi to do it, another for this guy—but, J was thrown off by the Yiddish slur, and this version of surreality seemed to reinforce J's ontological condition: of being dreamed. But then that distinction implied a space outside the dream from which J might differentiate the dreamlike, so perhaps it was only surprising and skewing and not surreal or dream: J was doing it, thinking to suppress feeling which would lead to other thinking.

Those damn coordinates.

Did it matter whether J was Lot or Jonah? Weren't both eventually found by the Lord? Hadn't the Lord annihilated those around both of them for their troubles?

The town promoter did some more loud nasal breathing before interrupting J's idle wish that the man's windedness indicated a proximity to cardiovascular failure by saying, "Guessing Mr. Goldstein's already there."

J visualized himself screaming in the hopes of some catharsis of screaming, considered actually screaming; with great effort he gained control of himself, or at least grappled with the concept of gaining it.

"Is he?"

J nodded.

"Where?"

J pointed towards the backyard.

"Until dinner then," the town promoter said and walked slowly back down the nailed together scrap-wood stairs pushed up against the trailer door, clutching their two-by-four railing with both hands and bringing both feet to rest heavily on each tread.

J, more worried that he wouldn't get to shower than about discharging his duty to shield the Rabbi from the town, than shielding himself from the town knowing he was hosting a Lubavitcher Chasidic Rabbi and his Mitzvah Mobile, wrote a sign saying, "Mitzvah Mobile parked out back," and taped it to his front door.

He got in the shower that had been running the whole long time of his conversation with the town promoter, determined to enjoy what was left of his diminutive hot water tank, when he heard more knocking.

"Fuck," he drawled, and a full beat later, "you," his eyes shut against the shampoo in his hair. He heard the doorknob rattle and then the door swing open. He opened his eyes and immediately blinked them shut against the soap's sting.

"Hey," J heard his paleo-pal say. "What in the fuck is a mitzvah mobile?"

"Goddamn it!" J yelled. "I got soap in my eyes."

"Does her eyes hurt?" J's friend lilted. And then, "You ready to go out or what?"

J shrieked as the shower water turned cold.

"Or you too busy being buggered?"

"You're an asshole," J said.

"We've got business, my man!"

J came out of the bathroom, fully unsatisfied with his shower, wrapped in a towel.

"Listen," J began, when the doorbell rang again. He shouted to read the fucking sign: the rabbi was out back.

"How should I be out back if I am the rabbi!" the rabbi said from behind the closed door.

"Shit! Sorry!" J spat and opened the door. "Sorry!"

"My!" Rumkowski said. "But you don't have any clothes!"

J's friend snickered.

"And who's your fine friend?" the rabbi continued. "Surely he's not Jewish?"

"Bill, and surely not," J's friend said, walking over and shaking the rabbi's hand.

"A delight!" the rabbi said. And then to J, "Of course you're still coming for dinner?"

"Of course he is," Bill said. "I'm just dropping stuff by, not snatching him off. We'll catch up with you, J."

And Bill was grabbing his bag, and J was embarrassed that he'd cursed at Rabbi Rumkowski and already offended about everyone likely to be at dinner. When Bill opened the door, a couple was standing on the steps.

"Ah!" the rabbi said. "This must be none other than Mr. and Mrs. Frucht! Welcome to Baker!"

"Welcome to Baker to you!" the couple said.

J waved and grimaced and wished he wasn't in a towel. He gently nudged the rabbi out, and all four of them went down the steps, and J closed the door and got dressed in the suit and shirt from

Delilah, this choice of couture at first an unthinking act of deference to dinner at a rabbi's place. Then in his head, sounded slowly out:

> Augenblicke, wessen Winke,
> keine Helle schlaft.
> Unentworden, allerorten,
> sammle dich,
> steh.

"But I don't even speak German!" J cried quietly to himself.

But Mary had, had read to him aloud in the night in the dark in the moments before her insatiability, in the moments before her frigidity. As if the recesses of his subconscious were sufficient to recall something said in those mere days so effectively, as if his subconscious would do so now. He popped his collar and pulled his tie around it. If he were to accept and accede, he would do so in all of the finery wrought for him by the dream.

Suits and chairs, J thought.

He got his wallet and the keys to his truck, glad that he'd parked in front because the Mitzvah Mobile was in back. It wasn't until he was getting off I90 in Gillette, a couple of hundred miles away, halfway to Casper, before he remembered that Rumkoski was the surname of the Jew who headed the Lodz ghetto, who ran a network of factories, sweatshops in which the starved of all ages embroidered insignia on Nazi army uniforms. J shivered and a couple of wild dogs ran out from an empty fence and chased his truck, red from his taillights in the rearview.

Rumkowski. He "deported" dissenters. Deportation meant Chelmno, the van and the gas.

Who was J to judge those who helped the Nazis in hopes that the deaths of a few would forestall, or even preclude, the deaths of all? Look what good Jews we are, J thought with disgust, don't you nice Nazis see that you were misinformed about us? That we can be of service? That you ought to keep a few of us around?

And yet that J was driving south by southwest now meant that he, too, must now acknowledge that he was guilty of shirking the reality of his situation and Rumkowski: Rumkowski and his family eventually ended at Auschwitz. Surely this rabbi was no relation. The last name must be common. J shouldn't have to turn around and confront Rumkowski with his complicity, with his collaboration. Surely he shouldn't. He didn't, but it haunted him. And then it didn't haunt him because after all if this Rumkowski was really Rumkowski, then he was sent back from the dead to teach J not to commit the same sin; if he wasn't that Rumkowski, then it would be stupid and mean and even more running away to go back to yell at him. Running away was always a mistake, J thought. He was beholden to his dreamer. J was his only hope.

But hope for what?

Perhaps this was the curse: The dreamer's desire to imprint himself upon his legacy would doom that legacy. The dreamer would distract J from living, from reproducing, and, thus, from reintroducing the dreamer's creation and continuance into the long lineage of the future world.

CHAPTER TWENTY-TWO

J DROVE THROUGH THE night and through the night, stopping only for gas and gas station food, which meant that by the time he reached Rawlins, on the southern tier of Wyoming, he was too sleep-prone to drive, though it was daylight, and though he pushed on to the Colorado border, where he finally pulled off the side of 789 at the Snake River, just north of Baggs, the adrenaline of fleeing fully flushed, and slept until it was sometime after dark again. He panicked awake, and drove, again in the dark. Because of the dark, and the vagaries produced by his snubbed circadian rhythm, he missed the exit for 24 off of I70. This added time and circuitry, a final dogleg by virtue of which he found himself driving east again, into a dawn no less fantastic than the one he'd left behind a year ago in Chicago. He'd made such bad time: a year to get here from Chicago.

He went into Torrey rather than skirt its edges, found a kitsched-out diner that advertised eggs from local hens. He was less than an hour from Boulder, Utah, and yet this was a detour, another deviation. He parked between a Lexus hybrid SUV and a Ford Excursion whose suspension had been rebuilt to lift the chassis waist-high off the ground. He stepped onto the diner's painted board porch and the air above him filled with the cacophonous tinkling of wind-chimes.

He looked above: a collection of tubes and bells and wooden flappers, all alight in the light breeze.

He looked east: the sun funneled through a series of multi-hued plateaus, as if the day came out of the land; the land, glowing, blended into the sky, a confounding, stirring interpretation of daybreak, a poor imitation of the blended elements so vivid in his last sleeping moment, when last he really slept.

He turned from it, went into the diner. The place was still new with the morning's cleaning, the bar-rag's damp, deposited on blue and green and orange and yellow and red Masonite tabletops, evaporating dew.

A young man in an apron walked over, his yellow dreads up in a teal scrunchee, his glasses taped at the bridge, rag still in his hand, asked J if he wanted breakfast.

J wanted breakfast.

J, legs and vision at sea from driving, swayed in the young man's wake towards a table. The young man asked if he wanted coffee, and J asked himself if he wanted coffee, and for an answer, his brain offered a translation of the Celan that had come to him first in German in his trailer:

> Debris of sleep, wedges
> driven into Nowhere:
> we stay ourselves,
> the steered-
> round star
> avows us.

J said yes to the coffee and slumped into a booth.

Sitting, he saw that he was not alone in the diner. There was a family: a woman, a man, a baby in a car seat turned basinet, a small girl in a booster seat. The girl turned and looked at him and J smiled with what he had to smile. The girl turned away. J's coffee came and he ordered as much food as would fit into a breath. The girl turned back around to look at him again, little hands clutching the back of her booth, little teeth in her grin, chin on her knuckles.

J wrinkled his face over his coffee mug and she ducked her head down. J laughed despite himself. Her head popped back up and he mimed shock with widened eyes, dropped jaw, pursed lips. The little girl shrieked laughter and ducked. Her mother, beside her, scolded her.

"There's a man!" the girl said loud enough for J to hear.

The woman began, "I'm sor..." while turning towards J.

When the woman turned, J had already begun, "It's no..."

E, just as he'd seen her in that first reunion in the hotel lobby, Esther, just as he'd seen her when she sat in a dining room chair that had been their dining room chair, holding by its hose the vacuum cleaner she'd come to pick up, the last of her things left in what had been their apartment, just as he'd seen her, pregnant, on a bench in Central Park beside Rat Rock to whose schist crystals they'd clung at the onset of their rock-climbing, healthy-living phase.

They both sounded out a collection of dissonant consonants that didn't add up to words, stopped, were silent a moment, and then went back to dissonant consonants, stopped again, got half out of their seats, sat back down. Finally, E turned to the man with her, explained, "J. You know: my ex."

"I've heard a lot about you," the man said, his gaze, synced to E's outstretched arm, finding J, aiming at J.

J stood to leave, prepared to make an excuse: that he had forgotten about an appointment or something, when plate after plate of food began arriving.

"Hungry much?" E asked.

"Bathroom," J said, despairing of leaving, fleeing instead to a confusing hallway behind a bead curtain where he found himself forced to decipher which wrought iron Kokopelli signified male.

He splashed water on his face, and then it turned out he did have to use the toilet, and then he splashed more water on his face. He returned from the restroom to E, sitting at his booth, sipping her coffee, and about seven different-sized plates of food. J was starving and had no will to eat.

"How are you?" She began, as soon as he sat. "Are you ok?"

J rocked back and forth in his seat, rubbed his hands up his cheeks and into his hair, rolled up his sleeves.

"What are you doing in Torrey?" she asked.

"What are you doing in Torrey?" he asked.

E described her husband's family vacation home just west of town on the banks of a trout stream backed by sandstone bluffs, and J studied her. She'd grown up. Now she was poised; now she was a more imposing E, identical E, as if she'd been concentrated while accreting more of her own concentrate. Her before-beauty had now become an elegant beauty: The way she'd pulled her morning hair up as well as back, a few bangs spare across her forehead in an allusion to youth, created a kind of shield that prevented J from enumerating the many things he'd thought about her in the past four years. Her posture, erect and easy, her cheekbones, taut but not quite severe, didn't allow him to ask whether he'd been a kind of way-station, a place for her to hang out until she grew up enough to get married and have a baby, things she must've done the instant she left him to judge by the age of the child. He didn't even want her he was so fascinated by each groove and contour and ridge of her; she was utterly untouchable, not just because her husband was there, or because they were in a diner, but because he literally didn't have the strength to reach an arm across the table and make contact with the hands she'd wrapped around her chipped coffee mug, upon which was loudly painted an O'Keeffe of van Gogh, or a van Gogh of O'Keeffe, or maybe just pastel lines tweaked by the twining of her fingers.

"How's the apartment?" she asked.

He didn't want to admit: foreclosed, and lacked the strength to accuse: foreclosed, and so did not say, Has it been that long, said instead, "We stay ourselves, the steered-round star avows us."

"Oh, Jacob," E said, tilting her head, tilting her eyes. "You're really not okay, are you?"

J's pulse raced with the possibility that she might reach out a hand and touch him, that he might actually say something direct, but her hand and his speech lay still. She had children. This, beyond even the husband, or because of how it compounded the husband, put rapprochement out of reach.

"Then where do you stay?"

Where did he stay? He took the card with the GPS coordinates from his shirt pocket and passed it to her. She took another sip of coffee, and he could see that this was her measure of time: when she finished her coffee, she would leave. She was strong-willed. She would consciously ensure that she drank her coffee at her usual pace and would give him no more than what she had allotted.

"Is this where you live?" She asked. "Is it where you're headed?"

J nodded.

"At least you look like you've been keeping in shape," E said.

J turned open his palms to examine his forearms. He had to speak.

"Aren't you going to eat?" she asked.

He lifted his fork and tried to pick up some eggs, but they kept eluding the tines. He took a three-stage shudder-breath. He was tachycardic with unspokeneness. Finally, he managed to gasp out, "The man in the van."

"Oh, Jacob," she said. "Oh, Jacob."

"It's not just him!" J wailed. "It's the children of Belchatow, so young that the small must have carried the smallest. It's the people of Lodz, whose quote unquote mayor fucking deported, and deported also belongs in quotes, fucking deported dissenters to Chelmno. By dissenters I mean those who complained they weren't getting enough food in exchange for embroidering insignia on Nazi uniforms. Those are his grand dissenters he deports to be turned into goddamn soot in the sky. It's the fucking wicker gates at Treblinka through which the naked were beaten from boxcar to gas chamber. It's Mordecai, who, when on burial detail at Chelmno, buried his own wife, his own children, asked the guards to kill him, but him they wouldn't. It's Abe Bomba who cut the hair of Treblinka's victims for wigs, the Germans willing to wear the biology they wished eradicated, Bomba who cut the hair of his own wife and daughters while they sat on benches in the gas chamber and told them not to worry. Abe Bomba, by the way, who if you Google him it's some shit's site that comes up calling him the so-called Barbara of Treblinka and claims that this Barber of Treblinka along with the rest of Shoah is a freaking fabrication by evil Jews attempting to smear honorable Germans. It's Celan and the way his poems could be about bad marriages or could be twisted lullabies if you didn't fucking know better. It's that the charred remnants of the Torah scroll from Lodz tell the story of Noah after the flood. God made a covenant, a rainbow, a fucking pact rendered in split sacrificial animals through which he and Noah walked together to reassure Noah enough that he would be willing to restart the world. What reassurance can there ever be now? How can anyone ever be fucking all right again?"

J felt the wet all over his face and didn't have anything more anyway. And what had he had? Nothing really. The same hack-neyed facts that everyone had. There was nothing new in the Holocaust, nothing unique in the Holocaust, no discovery, no narrative, just manic repetition, and these, his awkward tears. J's vision cleared and he could see E's husband soothing their little girl. J gasped his breath and snuffled his tear-snot, wiping his nose with the back of his wrist, and sighed.

It was either everything or any other thing. The Holocaust. It was either blurry photographs behind glass or it had already killed you.

"Oh, Jacob," she said. "I'm so sorry."

Except for him, for J it was still killing him, or killing whatever had created him. He was still in the Holocaust, unresolved, and that sounded ridiculous, too.

J could see her husband looking at him. They made eye contact briefly, and the husband quickly went back to his children, their children. E's head tilted further, her eyes tilted further, but still, still no hand reached from her coffee mug to touch him. There were no fingers on his forearms, no palm against his cheek.

"It's not me. It's about them," he gasped, "in the van. It's that they're all dying there and I can't seem to do anything."

"Jacob, Jacob, Jacob," E soothed. "It's such a nice surprise to see you."

"I don't want to be this way," he said.

"That's a nice shirt," she said. "A really nice shirt, and those cufflinks. Where did you get all that?"

"From Delilah," J said.

"Delilah?" J could see her almost wink conspiratorially, almost tease, and then the energy left, and she, "That's good that you have her."

"I'm not *seeing* Delilah," J said, his voice betraying him though its betrayal, too, was false. "She's Chase's stepmom."

"And Chase is?"

"I have to go," J said, and snatched the card off the table where E had let it sit in front of her. He fumbled out of the booth and stumbled, bent over, at a rapid clip, to the door. Behind him, he could hear the little girl asking why he was crying, and he turned at the hostess' station and pulled some bills, random bills from his purse, placed them on the stack of menus.

"You always win!" he wanted to shout back at them as he slammed the door open and ran to his truck, but he didn't shout back.

CHAPTER TWENTY-THREE

HE STARTED DRIVING, THE sun fully risen, all hint of new, of green, of late autumn cool, burnt up under its oppressive heat. He promised—who or what he didn't know—but he promised that he'd stop running away, would take no more detours. He made a right onto 12, such a different 12 than the one in Montana, and began driving up the switchbacks towards Boulder. Below Boulder, the GPS directed him down a series of small roads, past at least one sign, perforated with small-caliber bullet holes, that said he'd entered national parkland, the smell of vaporized sage and taxed radiator coolant like the memory of a house fire, and then finally to a pull-off from a dirt road. The several vehicles parked there weren't Chase's truck.

The GPS indicated that he had a few miles of desert to cross from where he was. He was so upset, so upset, he thought. And why? Because E pitied him? He found that assumption repellant: There shouldn't be any shame in insisting still upon caring about the Holocaust at a time when most everyone was ready to consign it to business done. That was unfair, he knew, his was hardly the normal relationship to the Holocaust. E hadn't signed up for who he'd become, or rather, for what he realized himself. He sighed: because of the two girls, the children, the legacy. He'd end like this he thought, here or after forty more years wandering, always in the desert, never allowed to cross into the Promised Land, without even offspring to cross into it on his behalf.

He rummaged around the cab of his pickup for a water bottle, and eventually made do with what was left of a 64-oz Big Gulp of cherry soda, adding to it the melted ice he found in two other combo meal cups, artifacts of time-ago drive-through fast food indulgences.

The GPS traced a dry wash and he walked in its bottom rather than wrestle the brush on its banks. It was difficult progress, the sand bottom soft with mid-summer dryness, as loose as a marooning island. The sun rose out of his eyes to beat down on his head. The drink, at first too noxious to sip, became something he had to ration. He pulled off his shoes for better traction, and the sand burned the bottoms of his soles. He came upon a stand of tamarisk, purple with bloom, and he crawled under their wispy shade, discovered the nettles of near-invisible cactus with his bared toes.

Sighing, he sat, the Big Gulp three-quarters gone, his suit pant legs and shirtsleeves rolled up, his shirt open and hanging, a thin white crust along its sides and back where his sweat had turned to salt before ever wetting him. He remembered reading about people stranded in the desert. They'd survive by digging pits under their cars and waiting out the heat in those shaded caves. He thought about digging a pit, went so far as to idly scoop sand with one exhausted hand. The first scoop left a shallow depression. The second scoop was immediately filled in by sand that cascaded from the depression's walls. The GPS said that he wasn't far.

He let his eyes close a moment. Dreams began almost immediately. In them, Rumkowski and E blended, then Pacelli overlaid their composite, and Chase, too; they split into equal parts, each in a newspaper panel. They spoke. They said: the man in the truck is dying; we sent him to his death.

J shuddered. The sun was higher. His tamarisk stand afforded no more shade. He continued walking. And now the wash became a ravine with low walls of dried mud: teal, red, and purple. The ravine walls rose, and J worried that they would box him in, prevent him from reaching the GPS-appointed destination. He scrambled up the left side, his feet easily puncturing the surface crust and sinking into loose dirt below. It hurt. It taxed. He wanted to put his shoes back on, but felt too unstable on the steep wall to do so. He continued scrambling, managed to exit the ravine.

On the flats above, he again attempted to put on his shoes, but his feet were swollen with walking and the heat. He thought about chucking the shoes. They were awkward to carry. He worried he might need them later. He carried them and the Big Gulp cup, which had been somewhat crushed during his scramble, its wax so hot that it cooled onto his fingers leaving water-permeable shadows of his hands on the paper base. He walked on, barefoot, dizzy under the sun, following winding sand-filled ruts in the overgrown desert to avoid stepping barefoot on nettles and brush. Then his sand path opened onto a sandstone plateau, and J followed his GPS across the rock, searing hot, but smooth and easy to cross, to the lip of a cliff.

He peered over. Directly below him was a trailer, long-ago extended with log additions, the additions roofed with corrugated green vinyl. There was a small corral with a burro. A few cars, dust-beaten, were scattered before the home. There was a road in front of the house, unpaved and uneven, but decidedly passable. Of course there was a road. Of course J wasn't on the path people took to get there.

"Fuck!"

The cliff wasn't particularly high, thirty feet, maybe a shade more. But it wasn't as if he could just jump. He didn't even consider walking back to his car and driving around. He paced the edge, came upon a fissure in the rock, swung down into it, his abraded feet seeping blood like the sand of a late-summer spring. He downclimbed the fissure a body length until it bottomed out at a rock ledge the depth of his feet where it was wide. He walked the ledge obliquely, facing outward, extended arms hugging the rock behind him. The wall above him gradually angled to overhang his catwalk, forcing J off-balance. When he thought he must fall if he scrabbled further, he found another fissure. He tenuously pivoted to face the wall and wedged his feet into the crack and resumed walking down the cliff. The fissure tapered, forcing him out onto the almost vertical rock, his feet still more than ten feet above the ground.

He clung, quaking.

Finally, he let go, sliding down the rock wall on his stomach, his feet raised to not catch and pitch him backwards. He landed— chest scraped, stomach scraped, forearms raw, knees raw, pants legs tattered—and stood. He was a year late, but he was here.

No one answered his knock, a knock confined to the edge of the screen door because the main door was already open. He decided to go in anyway. The trailer's main space was set up as a living room with a kitchenette in the corner. There was green shag carpet on the floor and a few gold easy chairs and a dark wood entertainment center that showed pale composite board through its chips. The carpet stung under his feet, but he forced himself to continue on to the sink, hoping that he wasn't leaving bloody footprints. He found a smoked glass tumbler in the one metal cabinet and turned on the faucet. A blast of air and water and rust from the tap knocked the glass out of his hands with enough force to crack it against the sink's steel basin.

"Fuck!"

He waited for the water to calm down and then cupped his hands to drink. The water was warm and tasted of rust and phlegm. J drank and drank, water running down his chin and his chest, washing blood-tinted wet onto the front of what was left of his pants. He stopped when he felt damp around his feet. He saw that he'd made a terrible mess, but couldn't quite figure out how to fix it. His feet hurt. He was dizzy. He walked over to one of the easy chairs and sat down. His eyes closed and he dreamt, again, of the light and dark that was one with the land and the heavens, the whole thing a single visible entity that he was at once part of and outside of. He dreamt this without pause or change until a guttur-alized, "Don't move a goddamned hair," startled him awake.

"Who," the man said, "are," each word articulated and delin-eated, "you?"

"Debris of sleep," J sputtered. "Nowhere. Wedges. Stay ourselves…"

J's mouth sputtered, continued to sputter, but his brain wouldn't quite turn on, and besides, he couldn't seem to see anything but a slippery surface of sliding pond scum. This, he realized, must be what it was like to see spots.

"Excellent!" the man said. "Well done!"

Then, because the man lowered it, J realized there'd been a gun pointed at him.

J still couldn't really see, or at least not see statically; he became aware of forms as they moved, and now he could see that the man was crossing in front of him. He could tell that the man was tall, had a long-groomed handlebar mustache on the whiter side of grey and hair the same color, straight cut and neck length. He could tell the man wore a soft-brimmed hat. He reminded J of the man who'd run the alternative pre-school in Tucson when he was a child. That man, Gerold, had been a professor of education during the middle of the hippie period, and, in a sudden embrace of the then culture's values, had left theory for praxis, opened a sprawling playland with goats and ducks and geese and children free to make their own risk and discovery. But that had been over thirty years ago; this man couldn't be that man.

What J desperately wanted to know, but couldn't tell with vision that only allowed him to see objects in motion, was whether this man's affect was a self-conscious construction or not. The man stopped moving and, for practical purposes, disappeared. The man whistled, and J caught a glimpse of lip and mustache.

"Joe?" J asked.

"Do you need to ask?" the man said.

"Joe, is there a reason I can't see?"

"Is there a reason you look shipwrecked?"

J saw lips and tongue and a hint of teeth.

"Joe?"

"We established that."

"Joe, I'm J. Father Pacelli gave me your coordinates."

"That must've amused him."

"Sorry?" J said.

"Amused him."

"I heard you. I just wasn't sure."

"OK."

"I can't see," J repeated.

"That Pacelli could've just given you my street address but didn't?"

"No," J said. "I mean that I'm blind. I mean, I'm not usually blind, but I can't see anything right now."

A motion came through the screen door and at its fastest, J saw a still, an image born and lost to blur, to streaks of color, a woman in a white summer dress and flip flops with curly black hair combed out to just wavy. And, he thought, this is how it goes, I exist in a world in which flat tires are harbingers of doom.

"Allie," Joe said. "This man says he's temporarily blinded."

"Maybe he is then, Dad," Allie said.

"I believed him."

"Then why're you asking?"

"Children," Joe said. "Living proof that we all think we're somehow exceptional and our offspring are likely to turn out different than those of every other goddamn human decides on having kids."

"Holy shit, Dad," Allie said. "Did you look at him?"

"I was saying."

"Can you help me?" J asked.

Joe told J to come along and get cleaned up and Allie shushed her father, said that they needed to make sure J could stand. J stood to see if he could, terrified of another basic skill lost, and pitched promptly forward, not out of lack of strength, but lack of balance.

Father and daughter each took a side and wrapped their hands around J's upper arms and lifted him to his feet. Allie asked her father where he'd found this man, and her father said right where she'd found him, on the chair. And J discovered that walking put the world in motion, and he could almost see almost everything around him as they traversed the short corridor, faux-wood-paneled and hardly lit, to the bathroom, the toilet half of which was in the original trailer, but whose handmade clay tub, a clone of E's California bath, was under the addition in the green cast of the addition's plastic roofing.

They stopped at the tub, and his sight worsened, though not nearly so much as before, objects now at least objects, if only objects, green-tinted, fuzzily outlined, indistinct.

"We're sitting you down," Joe said.

J sat onto the edge of the tub, saw the light dim as the object he took to be Allie reached past him to turn on the water. Father and daughter agreed that his clothes had to come off, and argued about whether Allie should stay in the room, an argument that ended when they realized that still-attached strands of his shirt were actually embedded in his skin. Then they argued about whether soaking him, clothes and all, might divide cotton from flesh. They settled on pulling the fabric out of his cuts with tweezers. He winced and sucked his teeth but refused to scream.

Clearly aware of his pain, of his refusal, they asked loud and cheerful questions to distract him:

Where was he from?

What line of work was he in?

How had he met Pacelli?

The pain of the fabric pulling out of his flesh was nothing compared to the pain of hot water on those same wounds, on his abraded and poisoned feet, when they lowered him into the full tub.

While Allie fetched compresses for his eyes, Joe gave him soap and a directive to rub it wherever things hurt. The pain of the hot water was nothing compared to the pain of soap on his peeled skin. J distracted himself from the incrementally rising pain by thinking about the Passover plagues. J wondered whether if God had begun by slaying the firstborn, Pharaoh wouldn't have immediately released the Jews from bondage. Surely doing so would have been kinder to the Egyptians, if less defensible. The same as with Elijah, J thought, nine plagues to justify a tenth, simply so that God couldn't be accused of being unjust.

A thinking being again, J washed, forced himself to wash, penance he thought for Rumkowski, for everything. It was forty-eight hours now since the RV had a blown a tire. Only forty-eight hours, J thought. He couldn't summon a line of Celan or an image of nothingness or a heartbreak over E or Chase, couldn't even muster despair for his dreamer. He was done.

Done, done, done.

CHAPTER TWENTY-FOUR

J SLIPPED INTO A fever. His scrapes, inflamed, oozed puss. His sunburn blistered and peeled. Histamines took their turn inflaming his feet in response to the toxin-tipped nettles and thorns that had savaged them. Several days into his delirium, a delirium wrought with visions of Allie and Joe salving his torn flesh and packing damp towels and ice around his head and body, his dream changed.

Perhaps it is a mistake to say that his dream changed. Rather, something happened, *transpired*, in his dream. A voice spoke, and the voice was a geography in which all was all and one and none. The voice was a location and the location was J and not J, J the voice and not the voice, uncertain, in his less delirious moments, whether he was his vision or only his vision's viewer.

And the voice, infused with dark and light, earth and heavens, land and ocean began, "*Bireisheit barah Elohim et hashamaim vi'et ha'aretz.*"

And the voice was beautiful and the voice was overwhelming and J felt ruptured and raptured and exploded and devastated and complete. But, still, despite the presence of an event, time did not exist in the strange place of J's dreams. It is a mistake to imply that something happened or had happened. The voice was the land and the dry and the light and the dark, all at once and all always, J's rupture and rapture not a process, not an event, but a thing as the voice was a thing, all the words always and never, though those binaries miss the paradox, are the poor limitations of an attempt to comprehend and translate without the benefit of being.

This was J, delirium, visions, great ghastly voice of creation, until Allie shook him awake, and he woke with a start, with sweat soaking him everywhere, his body wet and frigid.

"Your fever's broke," she said.

J gasped and shook. His head was clear. The voice and the place—at least now it was a place!—were gone; and J longed for them, for what he inhabited when he slept. He was on a narrow bed whose springs sunk under his weight in a room that was part of the original trailer. There was a small window at the head of the bed and sunlight through the half-drawn venetians lit Allie in a series of slat-shadows. She wasn't wearing white anymore, and he wondered aloud how long he had been there. In response, she held a coffee mug to his lips and told him to drink. He drank. It took him a moment to identify the salty tang as miso soup. His throat contracted against it; his stomach rebelled long before the liquid reached his esophagus; but his mind swayed dizzyingly with glee at the taste, at taste.

"It's like I've never tasted anything before," he said.

"You've only been able to get down water," Allie said.

"No. This is the first thing I've ever tasted, ever."

She looked at him.

He looked at her:

The skin of her face was lightly brown and smooth and dimpled and freckled. It rose in great contours towards cheeks, dipped, met eyelashes, curved around them, rose again, made the shape of a nose that ran into a brow, into a forehead. Loose hair fell unevenly over this forehead and J could see each hair, the wonder with which they wove together, their thin forms, nearly oval in their cross-section, polished where the window-slats permitted sun to strike.

He felt as if he'd lost his place in a book, followed one narrative too far and along the way dismissed, as digressions, features of fundamental importance. He backtracked, looked again:

He examined the shape of her eyes, the way the viscosity of the fluid on their surface rose to meet the edge of her eyelids in a concave seam. The line that divided iris from eye-white rippled and furred, was not hard or smooth, it rippled again where it met the iris proper, a black smudge that bled into green. And what a green! Speckled with gold and brown, riveleted by blue, hovered above by a giant and pulsating black pupil that moved like an isle of ink pooled on oil. But there was her mouth! He hadn't even looked at her mouth yet!

"What?"

"You're beautiful," J said, his reverie interrupted.

"Thank you," she said. "Drink more soup."

"I love you," J said, and it was so.

"Oh no," Allie said. "No, no, no, no, no."

"I think I love everything," J said, his attentiveness turned to the nightstand beside him, a low table, really, fashioned out of desert juniper, its legs rough, its surface polished. And he saw that it was good.

He looked at the wall, at the wondrous brass sconce that protruded from luminous wood paneling: and he saw that it, too, was good, lovable, loved by him.

"Can I touch your hand?" he asked Allie.

"Can you touch my hand?"

"Please?"

She looked around the room. "All right, then. You can touch it," she said, holding it out and looking away. "Just."

He took her hand between his. It was too much. His head hurt. He felt dizzy. He lay back into the pillows. He whispered that he had to sleep and closed his eyes. J found himself back in the space of his dreams. Though there were more words, they were no longer in Hebrew, nor in any other language, but in what comes before and after language, a space of conception and comprehension, the medium between them erased, and it was all always and at-once as was everything in the dream, a dream comforting if no less impossible than the one of the nothingness.

The voice said, "The breath-wind of the Lord on the surface-face of the waters."

The voice soothed J and J soothed. For the wind of the Lord was the voice of the Lord and the Lord's voice was J's voice and that voice was a gentle breath on his face that brought forth the world and the world was nothing but the breath, J's breath on J's face: a litany, a paradox, an abstraction, a cocoon, and J within.

He woke again in the twilight, the last of the sun projecting the window slats' shadows on the east wall. He rose out of the bed, dank as it was with his days of sleeping and sweating and oozing. His body functioned. He could stand; he could walk. He realized that he was naked. Aside from the rotten bed, the room was clean and put away. J thought to rummage through the dresser's drawers, but that seemed like a violation. He thought to get back under the covers and call for Allie or Joe to bring him some clothing, but instead pulled the top sheet from the bed and wrapped it around his body. Thus clad, he stepped into the short hallway. No one answered his hallo, so he tried the hallway's doors until he found the one that led into the bathroom.

Behind the bathroom's closed door, he allowed the sheet to fall away. He urinated and, turning his head to the side, found himself in a full-length mirror. His skin, he saw, had healed. Scrapes no longer abraded his chest. Sunburn did not infect his face, nor did thorn-stings intoxicate his feet. His muscular bulk in growing lean had gained definition.

"I'm beautiful," he mouthed, hushed.

The moment of discovery of the man in the van came back upon him, crippled him, bent him over into twilight asphyxiation, into a smell, wool not dried but catty still or unburned leaded fuel, cold in the exhaust, and what might almost have been a daughter, or daughters, but the last came as the connection severed, passed like a flash of appendicitis, may well have only been, J would later concede, the nearness of E's young. All of it, J would later concede, may only have been memory.

Shamed, he covered himself in the sheet again, hid his newly beautiful body, and wandered the house in search of Allie and Joe. They were not there. He stepped out of the house onto the dirt parking area. The night settled in now, the heated sage of the air given way to the smell of water wicked by ferny moss, a smell that blurred the boundary between things; de-creation, if creation is division, and J watched the stars appear and appear, and he watched the stars appear.

Beneath his bare feet he could feel each individual gravel, each sand, they as discrete as the stars; and God's two promises of Avraham's fruitfulness—as plentiful as the stars, as numerous as the sands—connected through his feeling body, and in him: the universe, creation, all.

Amazing, he thought, each of these lights differentiated so precisely from the dark around them. And more stars appeared, the moon yet in abeyance. J marveled, awed, These infinite patterns! Amazing! He remembered that in Jewish lore the stars were the *nishamot* of the dead, and he wept for how many stars there were because suddenly he was certain that these were the children of Belchatow, that Pacelli's list was infinitely incomplete, could never be complete. Even were it to finally list every victim of the Holocaust, there were always more victims of the Holocaust.

J went back into the trailer-house to escape them—creation, if still contained within him, imperfect, or at least more than he had mettle for—found his way back to his bed, hid between its covers.

In the morning, J was himself again. Unremarkable, but mostly healed, though not without the traces of abrasion, the drained pool feeling left over after fever.

Allie handed him clothing and he thanked her meekly, embarrassed by her hands, and dressed.

He sat for breakfast in daylight hued green by the vinyl roofing with her and her father.

CHAPTER TWENTY-FIVE

JOE TOOK J ON a walk on the dirt road that ran in front of his house. J, entirely clad in borrowed clothing, borrowed flip flops two sizes too big for his feet, could only move feebly and slowly. Joe didn't rush him, staying a step behind, barely inside J's peripheral vision. When J began to flag, and he began to flag not far at all from the house, despite the road's apparent lack of grade, Joe pointed out the remnants of a petroglyph high above them on a broken section of cliff wall. When it seemed that J had rested long enough, Joe put a hand on his shoulder and pointed him further up the road.

They walked another half mile or so, the drainage narrowing, its walls rising. Then the road ended in a broadening of the canyon, room enough to park several cars, the walls abrupt and tall now. A series of narrow slots broke the yellow and red rock face in front of them, thin, high drainages emptying forty feet up the cliff. Joe led J to a large boulder. They sat together on it, pulling themselves backwards and up so that their feet rested on rock, not sandy wash.

"So," Joe said, "tell me about your dream."

"Where the rock is wet, it's same color red as the anti-graffiti paint they'd use in my old neighborhood," J said, and when it was clear that Joe wasn't going to respond to that, he continued, "I'm not here about my dream."

"Pacelli would only have sent you for help with a dream."

"I figured you were some kind of Holocaust researcher, that you had information about Chelmno."

"Not me."

"Then do you know Chase?"

"It must have something to do with a dream, why Pacelli sent you."

J thought back to the prior night's crippling rediscovery.

"The truth of it is," J said, "is that I'm lost."

"We're all lost," Joe laughed.

"That's too easy," J said.

"And so is that."

"Fine," J said. "This is all the dream of a man being gassed to death in the back of a van at the Chelmno extermination camp in Poland during the Holocaust."

"Ah."

"Ah?"

"Indeed, ah," Joe said. "Sandwich?"

Joe pulled two aluminum-foil-wrapped sandwiches from the green canvas rucksack he'd worn on their walk, those and a thermos, whose lid he unscrewed and filled. J took a sandwich, opened it: dark pumpernickel thick with pastrami and sprouts and avocado. He sipped from the lid of the thermos. It was beer, not tea.

"How?" he asked.

"What?" Joe asked.

"How?"

"How what?"

"How this, these sandwiches in particular?"

"Ok. I'll indulge you: An organic farmer Allie knows about halfway to Hanksville. He orders her all kinds of goodies."

"How did you know that this was what Esther, my girlfriend, she was my girlfriend. It's what she served me the day I discovered that my life was the dream of the man in the van?"

"Not Chase?"

"No, Esther."

"Ah."

"What does it matter whether it was Esther or Chase or fucking Shulamit?"

"Shulamit?"

"Or fucking Margarete?"

"Only that Chase probably told Allie what you liked to eat."

"Chase was here."

"Let's talk about your dream."

"So, Chase was really here, though?"

"Sure," Joe said. "Chase was here."

"It's not my dream; this is the dream, or I'm in the dream in this."

"Do you dream a dream or not?"

"I do dream a dream," J said. He found that he didn't have words for it, for the language that existed before communication and after comprehension. The language infused a world not yet divided into its parts: light and dark joined; land and earth one. And then the land suddenly separated from the other land, called into the light, surrounded by water...J tried to remember what Rashi had written in his commentary on those opening lines of Genesis.

"How long have I been here?" J asked.

"We've been sitting maybe an hour."

"No, here. How long have I been here?"

"Maybe a few months," Joe said. "We're near done with February."

"No," J said. "I'm asking about how long I've been dreamt into this world. Are my memories of my life real? Have I actually been here thirty-seven-something years?"

"Well," Joe began.

"Wait," J said. "It's almost March?"

"Yes."

"Fuck...sorry. I just didn't realize...I was out longer than I... thank you. Thank you for taking care of me."

"I'm not some new-age guru," Joe said. "Nor, for that matter, some salty cowboy full of land-learned wisdom who'll have you do manual labor until the truth becomes apparent. I'm not your dad."

"Then what are you?" J asked.

"I'm the guy feeding you pastrami sandwiches and dark beer."

"I need to give the man in the van his story. I need to figure out who he is, what he's about, why he's dreaming me."

"Chase said you'd say as much."

"I'd ask about Chase," J said, "except that I know you already know I want to know."

"Have you considered just being content that you've been dreamt?"

J didn't answer, and they sat a while, their mouths full of sandwich, dry in the baked desert smell of the place.

"Why not? Why not leave it at grateful that this man in a van you're talking about called you into existence and stop worrying about it? What about that? What about enjoying it, what he's given you, this life?"

"Enjoy? Because I feel like fucking Jonah. Because the head of the Lodz ghetto showed up at my trailer in Baker, Montana posing as a Chasidic rabbi to frighten me back onto the path to you. Because when I tarried in Torrey, my ex, E, Esther, showed up at the diner."

"All one great big conspiracy."

"Exactly."

"To get you to act a certain way."

"Seemingly."

"It's all about you and you don't know why; why you?"

"Yes!"

"And were I to tell you that a cast of individuals all long dead from the Holocaust were offered a one-time chance to project some version of their agency forward, to dream themselves into some other, happier, time, and you're one of those projections, and all of you are working out some intricate and timeless plan bound by destiny...."

"Is that really it?" J asked.

"Were I to proclaim you the center of it," Joe continued. "Were I to proclaim you its messiah."

"Really?"

"Seriously?"

"Right," J said. He bit into his sandwich to hide his blushing, to cover his face with his hands.

"But seriously, fuck if I know."

J took another bite. The sandwich was a marvel, brought him right back to that afternoon in his study, staring out the window at the Dykman farm house's colonial whitewash and stone, anomalous amongst the squat, six-story complexes.

"Aren't you at all curious about what Chase wanted to know?"

"Who are you?" J asked.

"I'm a high school teacher that retired out here with his daughter who likes listening to people's dreams."

"Likes."

"A hobby."

"What are you after?"

"You answer that first."

"I want to be real," J said. "I want all of this to be real. I want to be able to build something. I want to father a child and know that the world in which I raise her won't be obliterated, not in her lifetime, or her kids' lifetimes, or their kids' lifetimes."

"Nothing unreasonable in that," Joe said. "Pinocchio."

"There's no survival," J said, "if this is all temporal, a dream of uncertain duration. Or if only I am that dream, then I at least want to know the man who dreams me. I want to know the purpose for which he dreamed me for."

"Really? Pinocchio? Nothing?"

"Fine. Yes, I got the joke. I get it; I get it; I do. I want to be a real boy. I'm not lying."

"Listen, you think I don't worry the world won't be here for Allie? Stop thinking so much. You're after solace; find solace. Find someone, Chase or whoever. Find someone to think about besides yourself. Find them and be quiet with them."

J contemplated the heat of the ever-higher sun, watched a lizard do pushups in the sand next to a small head of sage: trope or cliché, he wanted to know. He washed the bite of sandwich down with a sip of the beer and felt renewal tingle through his limbs. He decided not to bother asking this man again where he'd find Chase.

Allie, J thought. He'd said he loved her, for fuck's sake.

"You'll be on your feet soon enough, J. Able to go out and do something. Ready for the beyond that's beyond this canyon. But for now, you might as well tell me about it."

"Ok," J began again, and tried, stuttering and halting, to tell of the dream that began in Baker, and how it had grown in Chicago, that it had grown again now.

Joe sat and listened to him and squinted into the sun and chewed with his mouth open, which, it turned out, didn't particularly bother J.

J ate his sandwich, too. The myth of hard labor under the umbrage of his own Mr. Miyagi did still appeal to J, the promise of simple efforts that culminated in epiphany. He could easily entertain visions of spending a year here, working with the dusty animals in the corral, doing whatever it was that Allie and Joe did alongside them. It would be a continuation of his efforts in Baker, except that these could be counted towards his attempts to find answers in a way that welding pipeline simply couldn't.

"You'll tell all of this to Chase."

"Sure," J said. "I can try."

On reflection, the dreams of staying were dreams of rest, of not running, of settling down, settling down with Allie. Even here, even now, while enjoying the way pastrami resisted chewing and avocado didn't, while enjoying a too-hot sun that didn't call forth flies, J found that he had a full fantasy played out of a walk to this very rock in the dark, in the night-cool, beneath this oasis of darkness' infinite stars, Allie as his walking companion, their muscles tingling with the delightful ache of an all-of-daylight's labor, a tingling that kept them in contact with every cell of their being, work gloves folded in their hands.

In the fantasy, they sat on the rock and a word became a brushing of arms which became a touch which became a moment, a moment that evolved into a gentle cupping of her chin in his hand, and then a kiss, and then his hand off her chin and cradling her breast, his other arm around her arching, swooning back...J cut off his fantasy—though surely it wasn't so wrong to want new memories to replace those of riding bikes with Esther across Fordham road and out to City Island for fried fish—and focused on the way Joe only kept one side of his mouth open, the side closest to the sun—a product of his squinting—while he chewed, which ought to have been disgusting but simply wasn't.

"I can find," J said, breath shortened from thinking again of Allie pressed against him, "solace in her arms?"

"She had her existential crises to contend with, too, you know, when she came here."

"But you think I can find peace with her. Quiet?"

"You can't find it with Allie."

"Who said anything about Allie?" J asked.

"Did you hear any of what I was saying?"

"That I should focus on others."

Joe unscrewed the top from the thermos and drank what was left in it. He sat and looked at the cliffs for a while. Joe certainly seemed like the kind of man that might be a new-age guru or a crusty cowboy, not that those were different things, really. Maybe being told to leave was some kind of a test, the way rabbis were supposed to reject would-be converts twice before accepting their desire to become Jewish, and J ought to insist three times before giving into the rejection.

"No time in your dream," Joe said.

"Hasn't been created," J said.

Had he really been asleep since November?

The answer chilled him. It implied that the space of his dreamer's dissolution was without time, and if so, then that the dying man's dream could be boundless, and that the dying man could be the creator, and in the infinity before time, time could be created, itself infinite, though now demarcated, because the space of its creation was not obligated to conform to an ending: "And without time, you can't even wait for time to be created."

"And it isn't an image that you're looking at, a still."

"I am it, not looking at it; and, no, I'm not elapsing in relationship to a static 'thing.' There is no elapse."

"You needed rest before, and you ought to stay here a day or two yet, get back on your feet, but I've got Chase's father's address. He'll know where she is."

Back at the house, Allie gently rocked the porch swing, her bare feet on the railing, little wads of bright white tissue between her fresh painted toes, a yellow cotton dress limp around her flushed body, its lace edges but barely halfway to her knees, her thigh muscles brown and defined when she pushed against the porch rail to swing, her cheeks hollow when she sucked on the straw in her drink from beneath the enormous flax brim of a crushed Sunday picnic hat.

PART THREE

Black milk of morning we drink you at dusktime
we drink you at noontime and dawntime
we drink you at night we drink and drink
we scoop out a grave in the sky where it's roomy to lie
There's a man in this house who cultivates snakes and who writes
who writes when it's nightfall nach Deutschland your golden hair
Margareta
he writes it and walks from the house and the stars all start
flashing he whistles his
          dogs to draw near
whistles his Jews to appear starts us scooping a grave out of sand
he commands us to play for the dance

Black milk of morning we drink you at night
we drink you at dawntime and noontime we drink you at
dusktime
we drink and drink
There's a man in this house who cultivates snakes and who writes
who writes when it's nightfall nach Deutschland your golden hair
Margareta
your ashen hair Shulamite we scoop out a grave in the sky where
it's roomy to lie
He calls jab it deep in the soil you lot there you other men sing
and play
he tugs at the sword in his belt he swings it his eyes are blue
jab your spades deeper you men you other men you others play up
again for the dance

Black milk of morning we drink you at night
we drink you at noontime and dawntime we drink you at
dusktime

we drink and drink
there's a man in this house your golden hair Margareta
your ashen hair Shulamite he cultivates snakes

He calls play that death thing more sweetly Death is a gang-boss
aus Deutschland
he calls scrape that fiddle more darkly then hover like smoke in
the air
then scoop out a grave in the clouds where it's roomy to lie

Black milk of morning we drink you at night
we drink you at noontime Death is a gang-boss aus Deutschland
we drink you at dusktime and dawntime we drink and drink
Death is a gang-boss aus Deutschland his eye is blue
he shoots you with leaden bullets his aim is true
there's a man in this house your golden hair Margareta
he sets his dogs on our trail he gives us a grave in the sky
he cultivates snakes and he dreams Death is a gang-boss
aus Deutschland

your golden hair Margareta
your ashen hair Shulamite

~~Paul Celan
(Translated by Jerome Rothenberg)

CHAPTER TWENTY-SIX

THE RANCH, WHEN J reached it, clung to the last of the late winter sun's warmth. Its gravel drive dissipated into a large dirt patch on which several cars were parked. J couldn't quite tell how close it was appropriate to get to the house. He parked at a distance, at fifty yards, his imagined divide between public and private drives. A few cottonwoods, ancient and accidental, sheltered a long-running, east-facing porch, a boot sole visible on its railing. The sun itself, low over the porch-roof, colluded with the distance to occlude J's view of anything further interior.

J walked up. He had tried to make his hair right and his face clean in a gas-station bathroom that morning, but he lacked confidence in his appearance, and so ran his hands in his hair. A hallo from the porch made J wave and then jam his hands into his pants' pockets, blush at his foulness. He walked closer and saw the man behind the boot sole sitting on one of the two chairs Chase had picked up in the Bronx. The man had the chair tipped on its back two legs, and rocked there, balanced, pushing against the railing with his foot. I'm not allowed to sit on those, J thought, but he can tip them on their back legs.

"You Chase's father?"

"I am," the man said.

J waited and the man continued to look at him. J realized he didn't have a follow-up line. He'd expected Chase's father to ask him a question in return, or to volunteer Chase's location or something. Instead, they were at a standoff: J, dirty, catching whiffs of his own filth, or so he imagined, Chase's father grey-haired and wrinkled and tan, in a tucked-in flannel under a filthy, puffy vest, and brown work pants and boots, a cross between Becket and some movie-version of a fly-fishing guide, tipping back in his inordinately and inexplicably expensive chair. J wondered what Chase's father waited for. After a while, J introduced himself.

"J your name or short for your name?" Chase's father asked.

"Chase tell you about me?"

"Depends on who you are."

"I'm Jacob," J said. "Jacob Paul. I'm looking for your daughter."

"Say it like that, you sound to be the law or some frontier, asshole suitor."

"Why would you tell your daughter that they keep making young women?"

"Which are you, or are you?" Chase's father asked; and then he took his feet off the railing and let the chair loudly drop onto all four legs.

"I helped her pick up that chair you're sitting on," J said.

"And her ex-stepmom dropped by a change of clothes for you. So what."

J stuck his hands back in his pockets, felt the flush of blood all across his face, the hair on his neck straight up. Chase's father laughed and laughed and put his foot back on the railing, pushed, and tipped the chair back to the precarious edge of its hind-legged teeter.

"You're welcome," Chase's father said, "to get cleaned up inside."

"If you could just kindly tell me where to find Chase."

"If you aren't the steered round star. Come in already. Shower."

J capitulated up the porch steps, which creaked satisfyingly, and stepped into the shade, shivered. Chase's father swung the door open for J, giving sight to the living room: The floors were wide-board rough-sawn oak, rubbed with linseed and polished by foot traffic. The space captured a kind of juniper-scented dark cool while still offering mountain views through large windows whose 8x10 panes of age-rippled glass were latticed in painted wood sashes stretched very nearly from floor to ceiling. A couple of canoed logs smoldered in a fireplace, the cobble hearth of which made one think of river bottoms and upstream salmon beneath the felled lumber of a Pacific range. Burnished fir wainscoting bore the overlaid shadows of the window and the fire's grate in shuddering light values, those values complicated by the gradiented honeying of the wainscot's tree-width planks' vertical grain.

Like porn, J thought, not in the sense of sexually explicit material, but in the sense of overwhelming, perfected excess in a particular thing, or rather in an abandonment to a desire manifested in surfaces, in this case, in the creation of the Platonic ideal of the western redoubt, like Delilah's lobby or the view from the Fordham bridge over the Harlem River.

There weren't, fortunately, any stuffed trophies, but the means of killing adorned the wall's plaster upper in three rows of stunningly preserved long guns, the newest of which was a three-shot American-Enfield M1917 that J could identify compliments of his sophomore year of high school spent at a military academy where they'd marched with the WWI-era rifles; theirs, though, had barrels plugged with lead, and, on most, ugly plastic stocks had replaced the original wood. This one had a polished walnut stock with an engraved butt. J could also identify the several lever-action rifles as late nineteenth-century Winchesters. But a stock made out of an exotic wood that seemed to shift between red and yellow in running hues, as if the differentiated tones of the Douglas Fir walls had been conflated, caught J's eye in particular. Intricate manual sights had been carefully brazed on to its exceptionally long, tapering octagonal barrel with generous beads of solder sanded to silver, its bolt double scuppered into a two-finger pull.

"That one," J asked. "What is it?"

"Shower's this way," Chase's father laughed, and gave him a light shove.

J kept barely ahead of the fingers behind his shoulder, which directed him down a hall, and then another hall, and finally into a small teak antechamber. Then the fingers retreated and the door shut behind him.

J stopped and stared.

A single granite boulder floored the hexagonal shower, a stone large enough to preserve a shattered-dory's-worth of Powell's explorers from the Colorado around them, the boulder unblemished but for a groove, cut crude in a side, to drain its slightly concave surface to the void beneath a margin of teak slats between the rock and the glass walls that let the showeree see, to the one way, autumn-bared cottonwoods track a stream's exit from the mountains onto the ranch, the mountains bare of leaves, snow at their upper reaches, and, to the other way, an expanse of scrub desert erode out into a series of red buttes, taller and more massive towards the horizon, so that the reared plane of their unveiled mesas, speckled with what appeared to be either trees or the derelict fabrications of lost dwellers, performed the neat optical trick of escaping the physics of distance and convergence.

Above the rock, overhead, a cast iron tank hung from the peaked ceiling's dark beams, its white enamel glaze mazed by a louched-absinthe-colored oxide that leached from the copper feed pipes resting on its black brim, the tank's base drained by what might have been the spout of a tin watering can repurposed to form an octagonal showerhead flanked by two ceramic hooks, over each of which looped the twine of a sisal satchel. In one, J found soap, shampoo, and sponge. The other held a straight razor and lavender shave cream.

J felt guilty marveling so at a shower, especially at a shower.

He folded his clothes and set them on the teak bench in the shower-room's small antechamber, stepped into the shower-room and closed the door behind him. At the edge of the cottonwoods, a long low animal slunk through lengthening shadows, the sense of her young behind her. J bathed until the sun had set. His skin pink, his mind cleared and clouded again, he turned off the water, the image of the animal echoing in his consciousness, and waited for the basin overhead to slowly drain over him, before retreating into the teak antechamber. Of course, his clothing was gone, replaced by another of the Delilah suits, a pressed shirt beside it.

He emerged shaven and crisp.

Chase's father was sitting on a horsehair sofa in the living room, wearing the work clothes J had retrieved when Joe reunited him with his truck.

"Strong work on the duds," her father said.

J stared.

"My name is Walter, by the way."

"Yeah," J said. "Ok."

Walter gave J scribbled directions to his daughter's house. J wordlessly accepted these and began the hour drive to Albuquerque.

CHAPTER TWENTY-SEVEN

CHASE LIVED IN AN absolutely normal neighborhood, mostly residential but for the occasional tall building and small commercial node. Hers was a modest house with a grass lawn and a brick façade and oak trees in the parking strip. The house was neither new nor old. In fact, if anything could dissuade J of a dramatic reentry into her life, it was this: the sobering plainness of her home, austere in the amber cast by evenly spaced streetlamps.

The weather had turned on his way over: heavy rain that reflected his headlamps and turned the dark invisible. J parked and watched the house absorb the monsoon wet, the late winter storms down off the coast of Alaska, barely tempered by the Sierras and the Wasatch and myriad minor ranges between. He braced himself for the dash to the small portico, an unfolded newspaper at the ready in the absence of an umbrella.

And so, after the elapse of a little more than a year, a year that felt like a decade and no time at all, J found himself knocking on Chase's door, dressed as if for a business meeting, pink and shaven, two clutchfulls of soggy newsprint in his hands, curds of pulp in his hair.

A man in a half-open dress shirt cracked the door and hung out of its frame, the dark hair of his chest, of his cleavage, nose level with J. The man seemed to peer into the street rather than at

J, and J wondered whether he wasn't perhaps less than fully corporeal, fading with his still faceless dreamer, wondered whether Jews forbade the speaking of God's name because that was easier than admitting they didn't know it. Celan: "A man lives in the house he plays with his vipers he writes."

J waited in a deep sense of failure, a sense not limited to his newly (presumably) foiled desire to choose love; yes, that failure, but that failure augmented by his sense that in the end "Death is a master from Deutschland," that Jews, at best, drink the "Black milk of daybreak" until they are reduced to graves in the clouds that are that black milk, drunk at daybreak and by nightfall returned to the sky by those who drank, who followed to their own graves in the sky, failure that he couldn't even find a name for one dead man.

And shame, too: J waited in a sense of shame. He felt ashamed of his failure, of his new failures, of the foolishness of his desire to choose love, as if love was chosen, his to choose; but that he filtered his own minor, not-life-threatening, disappointments through the broad tragedy of the mass destruction of a people, a destruction that by luck of lineage or by magic of dream he'd somehow outlived, shamed him most of all. J wanted to tell himself that he stood neither in the rubble of Jerusalem, watching Babylonians lead his people away, nor in the muck of an earth newly bared after a year of flood, but his capacity to curtail hyperbole could not keep pace with his capacity for it.

The man's focus found J, and the man squared himself and asked how he could help. He was easily six inches taller than J, and a breath of the scent following the man hit J, placed J immediately back in the truck with Chase: if she had smelled of the residue of cologne testers in airport duty-frees, this man was the cologne, and his fragrance, a mix of power and the familiar exotic, flushed over J and forced his gaze down to where the man's trousers broke at his bare ankle to expose well-formed metatarsals and neatly pruned toenails. J explained that he'd come to see Chase, asked whether she lived there, tried to bother to hope that this was a brother or a roommate after all.

The man yelled, "Honey," into the house, his left hand grasping the door.

J saw the thick gold band, the kind of plain wedding ring his parents had worn. J was too ineffectual to put even a name to the man who dreamed him, why should he have expected Chase to wait for him, wait more than a year for him?

(But Delilah's complicity? Walter's? Fate's?)

Chase came to the door, "your goldenes Haar Margeurite." Indeed, casual in sweat pants and a blue oxford clearly her husband's, she looked bred to be next to her too-handsome, too-brownly-manly-Ken-dolly spouse, him either the ashen-haired Shulamith or the man who "shoots you with shot made of lead," which one, J couldn't tell. They stood there next to each other in their half open dress shirts in the cleavage of their doorway, myrrh and lilac and musk, stared at J for a full beat, the Shulamite and her beloved, and J pictured what they must look like from the outside, him in business wear and drenched and not beautiful and them thus: him a Kafka character, them Siegfried and Brumhilde.

"Jacob," Chase said.

"Hey," he said.

"You're shivering," she said, and J swore he could feel the ground beneath him open up and the waters rise from beneath.

He followed them into an absolutely unremarkable home. Where, he wondered, was the great land of the imaginary in which he had found himself until now? Where were the larger-than-life stage sets endemic to Chase's family? He sat on an uphol-stered dining room chair at a perfectly nice, contemporary dining table and relinquished the remains of his newspaper to Chase who gingerly deposited them in a trashcan beneath the sink and went to fetch a towel for his hair.

Chase's husband, Art, gave him a choice of tea or scotch. Against his own wishes, J asked for tea.

Art went into the kitchen and J heard the sound of water against a steel pot, the click of a gas stove's ignition. Art returned to the doorway, carelessly palming a glass of whiskey.

J wondered if he couldn't still change his mind to ask for whiskey. He was distracted, though, by the way Chase's husband seemed to move in stop animation between a series of attractive poses, and now he collapsed into a seat opposite J, Art's last pose simply his scent, which made J a little short of breath and oddly embarrassed.

Art was so obviously complete that J felt he could only be something dreamt.

"So, you're Chase's husband," J said.

"And you're the Jacob I hear so much about from Delilah."

"Delilah talks about me?" J asked.

Art tipped his glass towards J and sipped and winked. The kettle began to whistle.

"Can I have a whiskey after all?" J called as Art stood up.

"You can have both, if you like."

Chase returned with a towel and Art brought in a second whiskey and a steaming mug that trailed a spinning Twinnings tag on a darkening string.

"Well, congratulations," J said, lifting his glass.

"Excuse me?" Chase asked.

"Your marriage."

"Thank you?" Art said.

"Still always nice to be congratulated, right, hon?" Chase said.

"Sure, I guess," Art said. "Been a few years."

"Years?" J asked.

"Honey?" Art said.

"Wasn't exactly a great time," Chase said.

"What does that mean?" Art asked.

"What wasn't a great time?" J asked.

"Here I thought it was Delilah who'd taken to him," Art said.

"How long?" J asked.

"Nothing happened," Chase said. "And even if it had."

"Even if it had what?"

"Don't start," Chase said.

"Don't don't me, Chastity."

J could see. It was pretty clear: J ought to leave. But that Chase had never mentioned Art must have meant...there were the whiskey and the tea and the rain outside. He should go:

> he writes it and steps out of doors and the stars are all sparkling
> he whistles his hounds to come close
> he whistles his Jews into rows has them shovel a grave in the ground

J didn't feel like moving, didn't feel like committing to whatever this thing was that leaving implied and that he couldn't quite name, didn't feel like being bound by the Celan he'd read while with Mary, or by the Celan that had come to him after of its own accord. He should at least offer to go.

This, J thought, is what it must be like to ride a camel over a plain, heat shimmering mirages suddenly breaking into the multi-tiered mosques of Mecca, only to see the long stream of pilgrims before you, only to realize that they're human, that you'll have to dismount and join their ranks, that the owners of the city may exploit you, those pressed too close may trample you, that there will be nobody who notices your piety as different than the piety of all the others.

J tried to convince himself that to not have a story was not to be condemned to the van and the gas.

"J," Chase said, "behold my knight in shining armor, my liege, my very own King Arthur." Here she made a framing gesture with her hands around Art's head. Inside of Chase's frame, Art finished his drink, opening his mouth to let the ice clatter after whiskey.

"So tell us, J," Art asked, "are you a father?"

"I'm not married," J said.

"Have you found the story of your Chelmno victim?" Chase asked.

"Joe wasn't any help," J said.

"Delilah said you'd owned a marketing firm," Art said.

"He who is without sin."

"Oh, I don't mean it like that," Art said.

J confessed that he had, and that afterwards he'd worked oil for a year, but hadn't settled on anything; didn't say: how could he do anything?

"You strike me as a man who could, though, who could do something. You're a capable guy, J! If, you fixed on it, you could do anything; take on a mission. For sure. Do something of meaning."

"Thanks," J mumbled.

"I don't like to use the words 'giving back' because that seems to state a maximum; and, I think the best serve at a value outside of any equational relationship anyway. But that kind of activity, service to others, that's a thing: there's meaning to be found there."

Chase rolled her eyes and stood up. If she had to be married, the least J could do was hear out what was clearly going to be a proposition of some sort from this man who was pretty enough to marry her. J just hoped that whatever Art had in mind was dangerous.

Love frustrated: the joust; love universal: the crucifix; love danced: "A grave in the clouds there you won't lie too cramped."

Art was pretty enough for Chase to marry, and Chase was gone from the room.

Art leaned over and grasped J's folded hands.

Art looked at J in a way that taught him at last the definition of locking a gaze. This was it, J thought, Chase didn't need a home like Walter's or Delilah's, she didn't need their perfect possessions, for she had got for herself a volkshusband; Chase had captured the master aus Deutschland.

Stop, J thought, these aren't a poem.

His exaggerated pulse, the flush of his hands inside Art's hands, his flush: not a poem.

Chase wasn't Margarete. Her husband was neither Shulamith nor Death. Art was her husband, nothing more.

J couldn't have Art, shouldn't want to have Art.

It was all J could do to not kiss Art. If Art hadn't held his hands, J might well have reached over and touched Art's chest, the hair in the opening of his shirt, but J didn't understand, couldn't tell why, or from where, this response. He didn't want Art to hold his hands any longer because he didn't want to involuntarily lean against Art's chest, didn't want to worry that he might do something, didn't want to want to do something, didn't want this same suffocating haze of unwanted impulse Delilah had teased out in J when she described Chase's childhood fishing exploits; this claustrophobia familiar from when J had felt it as an undergraduate in his professors' offices.

J also couldn't bare Art letting go of his hands.

"Can I trust you?" Art asked.

J said yes, because he'd never yet slept with Chase.

"I'm going to put you to work," Art said.

J stood awkward and silent while Chase fetched a sheet and tucked it around the couch's cushions. When she returned with a second sheet and a blanket, he jammed his hands in his pockets rather than speak. She worked efficiently, but took the time to lay out the top sheet and the blanket and make hospital corners and fluff his pillow. He stood, frozen; and into the rain, still falling: Chastity! Chastity! Chastity!

She gave him an eyebrow-raised look that should have led to a pistol-firing duel in an Ozark saloon, her, too, not talking, and then left him for the stairs.

He neatly folded his suit jacket and pants, piled them on the back of the love seat. J wondered at his own sanity, wondered that he didn't often question it. Why ever would he think everything connected? This couple anything more than a couple? Himself in anything other than regular life? Over his clothing, he slung his belt and shirt, the cufflinks carefully buttoned into the sleeves. Ok, so there were a few things that seemed a bit other than regular life...Suit number three, four to go. Unto his grave, then, his hole in the sky. He clicked off the light and the street glowed in the thin space between the drawn curtains. He climbed between the sheets of his monastically narrow rest like the put-to-bed adolescent he'd been on school holidays in his grandparents' New York City apartment.

At the border of a dream in which land and water pulled apart, Chase slipped alongside him. She covered his mouth with her fingers, her satin nightshirt, an odd grey in the streetlight's faint detritus, hanging so that it obscured her breasts. She slipped over him, under the top sheet. Silently, she pulled him inside of her, her knees bent around his sides. They still weren't talking, he thought, as she rocked, her hand over his mouth, her mouth on his shoulder, her teeth sharp. His hands found her. He found her. And afterwards, she whispered that he must go, must leave, must not stay for Art's offer.

In the hushed patter of her feet scurrying away from him he heard:

A man lives in the house your goldenes Haar Margarete
He looses his hounds on us grants us a grave in the air
He plays with his vipers and daydreams

CHAPTER TWENTY-EIGHT

"Let's go out on the veranda," Art said.

J followed him through the house to its modest back patio. They sat in the shade of grapevines beyond whose trellis bloomed purple and yellow, a vista of lavender, Russian sage and yarrow. J sipped the blend of chicory-infused coffee he'd last had at Delilah's. His scalp felt fresh, his skin scoured: Chase on top of him belonged to some oddly distant space, another plane, as did the despair and the Celan. All felt forgiven, different, forgotten in the must Art exuded, in the firmness of his lips, in the intermittent flex of his sculpted brown forearms against the pulled back sleeves of a yellow oxford, the cotton taut then slack then taut then back again, as if the breath of everything bated at Art's movements.

"Listen," Art said. "Why do you think you're here?"

It's Chase he wanted, J urged himself to believe.

"Why are you here?" J managed.

Art did his gaze-locking thing and the diffused sunlight glinted in the flecked gold of his hazel irises. The hazel and gold pressed against the back of J's throat and inflamed his larynx, and he could not speak, and his eyes began to water, his cheeks flush, until, when it was almost too late, Art cupped his mug with both hands and looked away, out at the bright garden. A hummingbird moved between blossoms. Art looked back at J.

"Can I be frank?" Art asked. "Can I confide?"

J allowed that he could.

Art began speaking softly, gradually gaining volume and cadence. Out of that momentum emerged a set of images that were a set of ideas: a people in pain, a God, a Savior, a moral obligation to pursue an end to suffering, a religious understanding of that suffering's inevitability until a second coming. These were Art's two missions: public, democratic service and the glory of a God who bore Christ, a God who might avenge His Son's sacrifice by sword and by fire.

"We were wrong for so long, thinking we were the elect of the Jews, heirs to God, that your role was over, Judaism obsolete. God said you were the chosen people! God's word isn't subject to alteration. He has different purposes for those who follow His Son and for those who were chosen. We are here to serve you to serve God."

Ordinarily J would be immune to such notions, but coming from Art they were the breath of a lover's lips almost against his neck. In desperation, J managed to quip about whether Christians weren't then the new Levites, the Jews all Cohanim now, a dumb joke if it was a joke at all.

When Art said, "You are still the chosen," the garden transformed into Judean hills beset by Roman soldiers, and the sense of a nyloned toe ran along the inside of J's calf, and he found that his chest rose and fell to the meter of Art's speech.

"And you're saying that you don't think Jews should convert," J feebly protested.

"I believe that Christ is personal savior to all who choose Him."

J couldn't bring himself to ask about the whole Jews killing Christ thing, though he wanted to, wanted to in the fashion that a beloved demands of a lover why and how that lover could ever love so, because it can't be real, because it has to be a farce, to feel so, to feel truly. J ordered himself to get ahold of himself, but he was soup, or porridge, or pudding, or gloop.

"Of course I believe Christ is savior," Art continued while J hoped not to cry, hoped not to kiss Art. "Obviously. And if I believe that, how could I not believe that God's decree is His will, and given that decree, that His will is that the Jews are His chosen people? Obviously I believe that."

J had no answer, and J had no answer to why or how it was Art was causing this in him; and Art's wonder-making continued as Art continued to speak: Visions of armored knights galloping down hills towards Muslim armies. Visions of tanned Jewish soldiers fighting out of trenches against overwhelming odds. Visions and visions: seductive, romantic, filled with action. All a series of fragments. Fragments without subjects. Fragments without verbs. Objects on their own. Was this what history looked like when God showed it to Adam? Was this what history looked like when He showed it to Abraham? To David? Ezekiel? Isaiah? Jonah? Did any of them see the Holocaust? Did any of them realize that God's people wouldn't actually survive? Would all die? Was that why Isaiah actually wept, not for Israel led into Babylonian exile, but for the annihilation to come?

I slept with Chase! J wanted to confess. *I slept with your wife!* He wanted to bare his soul to this man, this Art, this specimen of visions, and he didn't want Art to know that he'd slept with Chase, because he wanted to stay in Art's company forever. None of it made sense to J. He also didn't want Art to know, he reminded himself, because that would be a betrayal of Chase; and, he loved Chase, J reminded himself. He wanted both of them, not together, but separately, each of them to the exclusion of the other, J refused to acknowledge; he wanted both of them, nonetheless.

The visions Art projected were strong, implied strength, implied: never again. Shame at even questioning Art's vision, for even questioning, for guilt about clinging to a ravaged past, for clinging to a ravaged past at the expense of an expansive future.

A messenger called from the back gate, and Art excused himself. From where he still sat, J couldn't discern their conversation, but he could see the way the younger man blushed to the roots of his blond hair while Art spoke, and how the younger man's eyes widened and watered. When Art put a hand on the man's shoulder, J could feel the hand on his own shoulder, and J's scalp tingled with the touch of it.

"I don't know why," J mouthed.

Art returned, and the smell of hyacinth and narcissus and honeysuckle and lilac and man and myrrh returned with him.

"Sorry about Karl," Art said. "Where were we?"

But us Jews have been strong, J would have answered. But Art had already again summoned the knights charging down the hill, and Her Majesty and the king were seated in chariots above the battle, directing, benevolent, imminently capable of caterwauling descendency. But for Arthur's crusade's colored costumed regalia, J would've said: we've been Maccabees and we've had King David and we've had Joshua and we've even had Samson and yet still there was a Holocaust so how can there ever really be a never again? Wouldn't there always be an again?

But that was a lie, too: J didn't say these things not because of the visions, but because he could taste Art's heat beside him in the shade's cool, feel Art's blood in his own heartbeat.

"What does all this have to do with me?" J finally asked.

"I need your help," Art said.

"I don't believe what you believe," J said.

"I only believe in God's will."

"I don't see what my role in all of this is."

"Only the role you have already chosen, for which you were chosen."

"I don't know what that means," J said.

"Tomorrow," Art said, standing. "For now, the city calls."

How corny, J thought, the city calls. J stayed seated, staring at the haze, the memory of Art's hand firm upon his shoulder, J's pulse up with jealousy of the young aide, Karl, who'd also felt that hand upon his shoulder, J's breath short with jealousy of the city for whose call Art left him, was willing to leave J. To feel again that hand on his shoulder...to smell Art again...to watch his arm against his sleeve.

Chase did not come in the night.

CHAPTER TWENTY-NINE

IN THE MORNING, ART rose J early enough that only the first rays of sunlight diffracted over the east lip of the backyard wall. They got in Chase's truck. Art winked and let on that his wife would be awful pissed when she woke and only found the Chevy Cavalier in the carport. J laughed, which made him feel giddy and a little guilty. They drove for two hours while the dewy newness of the dawn dissipated into an ever more excoriating heat. They reached the base of a table-topped red stone bluff. J expected that there would be a ladder up to an encamped Pueblo tribe, but Art turned onto a precarious dugway that gurgled up the bluff's backside to reach a mile-wide expanse of car tracks and scrub brush and busted beer bottles. They got out of the car and J fully expected Art to pull out a flask or a bottle.

Art walked J over to the edge. Before them, dry purple rivulets runneled a maroon desert beneath mesa after mesa, mesa walls striated with purple that stretched to black and with yellows banded by all the washed colors of dried corn, the scent of sagebrush arid and ashen in their glands. In the distance, shadows rose in the form of mountains. Over all, whisps of white whirlpooled in the endless blue and into the void between red dirt and a cloud that reflected it as if with pink pigment pregnant plummeted a tremendous eagle, wings hard to its sides.

The eagle struck a lone goose.

The eagle struck with speed and size such that despite its distance out, J flinched, recoiled slightly, Art's arm around his shoulders to hold him steadfast.

Art's arm around his shoulders.

Conjoined, they dropped another hundred hundred-feet, red spray blooming through a contrail of white feathers.

The eagle's wings spread.

It veered upwards, and entaloned providence's offering unto the clouds. Loosed feathers settled gently, white strata against a red gradient in the aspect between red earth and whited-red clouds.

"Ok," Art said. "Let's go."

"What?"

"Tomorrow," Art said.

J tried to stay up in wait for Chase on the couch, but the house, dark, somnambulant, lulled him asleep. He dreamt Adam on the morning's sandstone vantage, before him the animals of the earth cued endless upon the plain. A pair of angels lifted each in turn for Adam's appraisal and these he named: *aryeh, tzvi, lemur, dov, chasidah, kof, nemur.* It continued, the animals named in a Hebrew well beyond J's limited vocabulary, each presented in its glory, sea-flukes and snow leopards, mitochondria and walruses. This dream, though, was not creation. It was simply a dream that happened to be about creation. J was capable of that, too, it seemed, of reflective dreams about generative dreams.

Chase did not come that night either.

CHAPTER THIRTY

IN THE MORNING, ART took him back to the patio.

"Why," J asked, "are you so invested in me?"

"Chase told me everything," Art said.

"She told you everything," J eeked, the memory of Chase's knees gripping his ribs overripe.

"I'm sorry," Art said.

"You're sorry," J said.

"It's ok," Art said. "Whether it's a dream or a metaphor doesn't ultimately matter. Not to me."

J blushed, and then found that he cared less about the flattery than he might have.

"Ok," J said.

"I can help you. I can help you bring back what was taken away. I can help you bring back what was taken away, and if that can happen, then maybe, just maybe, no one will ever seek to annihilate your people again."

"Ever again?" J said. "Really."

"I tremble...I get trembley," Art said slowly, carefully, eyeing J, "around Jews. Now even. There's something...God! I feel all goose bumps! Just...I don't know: you're one of the chosen people! The chosen people!"

"Seriously," J said.

"And to think I'd always thought, always believed, yes, always believed that my legacy and lot would be with the Evangelical Zionists. To have this miracle…"

"Evangelical Zionists?"

J shrugged his back against an ache in his shoulders. His eyes prickled with desert dry. Finally, Art was getting to his pitch, and the pitch J had been so eager to hear now didn't captivate him at all. Had he really been waiting for Chase to come back in the night again? Nothing worked. It all seemed pointless.

"And with your marketing skills! It's almost as if…Almost as if! It is as if, it is: it is that God prepared you uniquely for this calling, made you, J, in a very special image of Himself that you might serve His will."

"Calling?" J twisted his neck, attempting to relieve the ache that had migrated out of his shoulder.

"The work you once did for executive clients, you can now do to give your man, this dreamer you spoke of to Chase, that man, and not only that man…"

"What about the dreamer?"

"Oh, J!" Art said, and this time Art's hand on J's shoulder felt earnest, felt involuntary, and that felt better and worse than it had when all had appeared staged. "J."

"Art."

Art looked into J's eyes, his hand still on J's shoulder, his face close enough for J to hear his breathing, to almost feel the turbulence in the wake of Art's exhalations. What was it about Art's gaze, this time, J wondered, that seemed submissive almost?

"J, you are going to do it for all of them. You are."

"All of who?" J asked. "Do what for all of who?"

Art paused again, said, "J," paused longer.

J's pulse quickened. Art's proximity eroded the peripheries of J's irritation; J wished it wouldn't. He liked resisting, being resistant, finally. A bit of autonomy, J managed to think, was nice.

"J," Art said, his eyes at once moving and still clearly focused on J.

"Yes?"

"I could kiss you," Art murmured.

J swallowed, felt his lids heavy, willed his eyes open, J's weight collapsing through his shoulder and into Art's hand despite himself. Was the proposition to actually be a...

"The murdered chosen people, J," Art said. "That's who you're going to do it for. That's who. You're going to give them all stories. Every last one of them that you can. You're going to give them stories that aren't simply the Holocaust and how they died. You're going to give them the stories of their lives. You're going to give us the story of their lives, J! Can you see it? Their lives restored!"

"I am?" J asked.

J couldn't quite see right. He tried to take deeper breaths. Art could kiss him...Art couldn't mean that he *could* kiss J. Stories for the dead.

"You are," Art said.

J told himself to exhale, to inhale, to stop holding his breath, to not exhale until he'd managed to fully inhale. He hoped his head wouldn't come lose of his neck. Answer the man, J told himself.

"How?" J asked.

"I'd heard about you, you know," Art said. "Before even."

"Before even what?"

Art paused. "I'd heard about you. I had. Thought: that's impossible. And then I thought, what's impossible for God?"

"Before even what?"

"Before you knew," Art sighed, and pursed his lips at J.

"Ridiculous," J said, unconvinced.

"You came up," Art said. "My first run for Mayor. You did. You had your firm then. Out of the box thinking kind of sugges-tion that Louis made, to hire you. Every first-timer is a long shot by definition, me included, and everybody very self-consciously searches for out of the box ideas and we thought about it, thought seriously about hiring you. But you hadn't done a political campaign, and you were in New York, and we certainly had no idea that you were a believer."

"I'm not a believer!"

"Trust me on this, OK?"

"Louis? What? What are you even talking..."

"I'm talking about a museum," Art cut J off. "I'm talking about a place that's like the Holocaust Museum, but the opposite of the Holocaust Museum. A place where visitors go through and they don't see a death. No. Absolutely not. They see a life! Visitors see a life! No more of these homages to what the Nazis committed. You're right about that. No more. Absolutely not. Rather. Instead. Now. You, you, J, you will show them lives. You will show them Jews, Jews as they were before, before there were Nazis."

"Art..."

"I'm talking about a museum, J. I'm talking about what you so bravely and innovatively thought to do for this one man, this one nameless man, who, Chase tells me, you say dreams you from the back of a box truck where he is slowly gassed to death—what a brilliant assessment, Jacob! Of what we are, how we are all just dreams of the Holocaust—yes, yes! What you strove to do for that man; I will give you resources to do for all of those who perished. You'll build a museum, J. That's what you'll do. That's what I'm talking about. I'm talking about you, Jacob Paul, building a museum, showing lives, J, showing Jews."

"Art," J said.

"Would this work better if I resorted to some lofty rhetoric?" Art asked. "Trust me, OK? This is what you've sought; you've sought what has sought after you."

"Arthur, please," J said, exhaling. Lofty rhetoric...so at least they weren't going to kiss, it seemed.

"We all serve humbly as we are called. You as well. As you are called to what you are called to do."

"I guess I'm glad you didn't resort to lofty rhetoric," J said, almost breathing again, slightly too aware of how grounded his feet were.

"Thank you, J. Thank you, and God bless."

That night, too, she did not come to him.

J lay on the couch, his arms crossed over his covers, over his chest, and laughed at the absurdity of Art's language and his earnestness and his talk of callings. For Christ's sakes! J thought. Who the fuck speaks like that? But he was also pleased.

Me! J thought. Art clearly only meant that he could kiss J as a figure of speech. Art had to have.

Called!

Though if J were to be called...

CHAPTER THIRTY-ONE

In the morning, Art and J boarded a plane for Cincinnati.

The city, it seemed, could wait after all. Albuquerque could wait.

J didn't know how, not really, one went about building a museum dedicated to the lives of those who'd died during the Holocaust. He'd figured maybe one way would be to go to the Holocaust museum in DC, or to do research, whatever doing research meant. He was grateful that Chase hadn't brought up Mary as a potential resource; Chase hadn't brought up anything, apparently wasn't talking to him since he'd decided to stay. J figured that he'd need practical things, like an office for example, and a laptop, a phone, paperclips, a stapler and a staple remover: every one of J's office jobs had provisioned him with a staple remover, and he'd never used one to remove even a single staple. He'd also never used tiered trays to sort papers, but they always gave him those things, too.

But Art said there was someone they needed to talk to in Cincinnati first, so off to Cincinnati it was. And, because they flew economy, and at the last minute, they sat in middle seats separated by several rows.

Somehow, on the way to the plane and while boarding, J hadn't noticed that Art traveled completely without luggage. J, on the other hand, was loaded down with what were, in essence, all of his possessions excepting his truck. Granted, his possessions fit into a suit bag and a single black duffel that qualified as a carry-on only after Art's gentle intervention with the gate agent. J couldn't figure out how best to hold his two bags as they walked through the Cincinnati airport, and so kept awkwardly repositioning them as he struggled and sweated to keep up with Art, who ambled along breezily, improbably chomping on an apple, his other hand in the pants pocket of his suit. Art had, of course, offered to take one of J's bags, but J insisted on carrying his own.

Thus they exited security, where a young woman greeted Art, "Mayor."

Art nodded and took a last bite of his apple before tossing it in a providential trash can to free his hand, which he wiped on the back of his pants, to shake hers, still chewing. J moved his bags around again in an attempt to free his right hand, but of course only found himself even more tangled. J wouldn't necessarily go so far as to call himself ordinarily graceful, but there was something about Art's effortless poise, the informalness of it, the way he didn't pair a tie to his suit, for example, that made him obviously the one in charge. That calm wreaked a spasticness on J.

The woman smiled and clasped her hands behind her back, bowed slightly and said her name was Hayley. Her knee-length skirt wasn't pleated so much as plaited, which J found emphasized the energy and power of her hips and thighs. It was true that her black blouse covered everything from wrist to waist to neck, but its silk's luster suggested a casualness, an irreverence for the very modesty it enacted, an ease that stemmed from power. Her suit jacket was short in the sleeves, which bellowed, and collarless. It rounded her shoulders and triceps. She'd taken the elements of a frumpy outfit, something that would've marked her as evangelical, proselytizant, and made of it something that seemed to carry the strength and hope of an Art Deco locomotive's sweeping masculine curves. The sum of her posture echoed Art's; summed with Art's, its effect in J shifted from embarrassed awe to intimidation.

Hayley led them out to the curb, where a man, also young but several years Hayley's senior, stood beside a black Mercedes town car, his biceps and pectorals virtually bursting from his sky-blue polo. The man stowed J's bags in the trunk while Haley situated Art and J in the rear of the car.

"I feel," J said, once they'd begun moving, "as if this is the kind of back seat in which one makes deals or preps for negotiations."

"We could work," Art said. "Or, we could look out the window."

J didn't point out that the window's privacy tinting didn't make for great sightseeing.

"Where are we going?" J asked.

"We'll stay in Kentucky," Art replied.

"We're in Kentucky?"

"Yes," Hayley said, craning around to face them. "The Cincinnati airport is in Kentucky."

"How edifying," Art said.

She muttered a demure apology.

"But I didn't know that," J said.

"You care where the Cincinnati airport is?" Art said.

"Don't we need to prepare?" J asked. "For our meeting?"

Art laughed.

"Dr. Norelius wanted me to let you know that we're all set for any technology you might wish to use," the woman said.

"Doctor!" Art said. "No."

After that, no one spoke.

J woke to discover they'd begun ascending a long gravel drive through dense trees. His confusion and cottonmouth made it hard to determine whether he'd only slept a moment or an hour. Art, by contrast, still looked as peaceful as could be, staring out the window as if it offered a clear view of fascinating scenery.

The drive led out to a broad expanse, a lawn, perhaps, if lawn could be used to describe the mowed bluegrass and clover of a half-a-mile wide hilltop. They parked before a massive stone estate, the peers of which J had only ever seen in BBC films set in manor houses upon the moors. Hayley directed them to follow her along the slate flag walk to the rear of the estate. Before they rounded the corner, J looked back. The driver, who they'd not yet heard speak, was leaning over into the trunk, and where the polo drew tight over the small of his back, just above the brown leather belt that held up his khakis, J could see an oddly square lump, as if the man had tucked away a Walkman there, or an insulin pump.

On the far side of the manor, which had a footprint at least as great as that of J's old apartment building in Inwood, they reached a broad stone terrace that overlooked terraced lawns above a wild-flower meadow that sloped towards the thickly treed embankment of a broad muddy river, beyond which lay a city that J could only imagine was Cincinnati. Three men were seated at an oblong table, covered in a white linen tablecloth, set with six places around a floral centerpiece, the fragrance of which melded with the river air's humid musk on the passing breeze.

The three men stood to greet them and were introduced by Hayley as Drs. Norelius, Graves, and Blanchard.

"Or," Art said, "Harlan, Chuck, and Davis."

"Yes," Blanchard agreed. "No need for honorifics here. Davis will do fine."

"Honorifics!" Art laughed. "Do you all take those honorary honorifics seriously?"

"Arthur," Norelius said, "what's useful is useful! You, of all people, know that."

"Well, I'm Jacob Paul," J said, wondering why Art had brought him across the Midwest to meet with men Art seemingly held in little regard. "I go by J."

"Did you always?" Graves asked.

"When I got to college in Buffalo," J said, "I was fresh out of yeshiva and super innocent and—"

"What's a yeshiva?" Graves asked.

"Why do you go by Chuck, Chuck?" Art asked, sitting. "Can we focus?"

They all sat, J, of course, taking longest to get into his seat, in part because Art moved at the last second to position J centrally between him and Hayley; and then, because J's seat was heavier than he expected, he struggled to straighten it out and pull it in, clumping and scraping the chair on the patio. Finally pulled in, he looked up quickly, aware of the silence, of the sense of eyes upon him. Strangely, the men looked quizzical, benevolent, weren't glaring at all.

"Ok, then," Graves said. "Do you want to tell us who J is and why you've brought him along?"

"He's why we're here, Chuck," Art said.

Hayley had somehow from somewhere produced a leather portfolio, which she now folded open to a yellow legal pad. She took a quick note with a thick fountain pen and then, pen held in air, paused, looking across J at Art, which made J feel like he ought to pull his seat back a bit to better accommodate her gaze.

"And here we were led to believe that we'd assembled because you were at long last ready to move forward," Norclius said.

"This has to happen first," Art said.

"Why are we all here?" J asked, and anxiously looked over at the note Hayley scribbled. But, as J tried to make out her handwriting, he felt Art's hand on his forearm.

"We're here, J," Art said, "to begin building your museum."

"Oh, the suspense," Blanchard said, and rang a bell.

Two servers emerged from the house with soup bowls on trays.

"Isn't it a bit cold to be out here?" Art asked, hunching forward in an adolescent collapse as bowls of crab bisque were placed before them.

Blanchard motioned with his soupspoon that Art should continue, and then began loudly slurping soup off his spoon, as did the other three men. Art straightened a moment, his breath held, and then sighed his way back into his slouch.

"Fine," he said. "I'll explain."

Art ignored his soup, so J did, too, sitting awkwardly proper with his hands in his lap, while Art explained the basic concept of the museum. Hayley continued to take notes. The men slurped their soup, spoon hands held as high as their ears to descend to their curled open lips, as if in wanton mimicry of gluttony's caricature.

By the time Art had finished with the mission statement, and an explanation of J's position, abridged to limit incredulity, the men had finished their soup. Blanchard rang the bell again, and the servers whisked away all of their bowls, only the three honorary doctors' bowls empty; J and Art's were untouched, Hayley's politely diminished.

"Jews as they were before," Blanchard said. "And what is this to us?"

"Something you should enable," Art said.

"Because we enabled the young earth museum?" Norelius asked. "Because of that reproduction of Noah's Ark? Because of our investment in you?"

"You know how," Art said.

"If I may," Hayley interjected.

"This is different," Art cut her off. "It's not some joke thing to stoke outrage and foment distraction."

"It's unseemly," Norelius said, "cutting Hayley off, Art. It's not like you."

"If I may," Hayley said, "the museum you describe, Art,"

"You're quarrelsome," Norelius continued, "preemptively defensive. It has distracted you."

"The museum Art describes," Hayley continued, "would absolutely provoke outrage."

"How could it provoke outrage," Art sad, "to honor all those Jews? To give them stories?"

"How could you not…" Hayley began, and then took a deep breath. "It will provoke outrage because, first of all, you're going to showcase Jews, as they were, whatever that means, which will certainly seem a wee bit weird and fetishistic, and which will likely irk, to put it mildly, actual living Jews. More to the point, people will go apoplectic when you create a Holocaust museum that refuses to discuss the Holocaust."

"The Holocaust Museum fetishizes victimhood!" Art interjected. "This is way better. Necessary."

"Let me finish."

"Fine."

The three honorary doctors began eating the garden salads that
had been placed before them. Art had crossed his arms over his
chest; J decided he better keep his hands in his lap and his mouth
empty, so that he might speak if that became necessary, though the
tang of balsamic in his nostrils filled his mouth with saliva. Hayley
paused another beat. No one spoke.

"My analysis is quantitative," Hayley said. "Qualitatively, I
find your proposal desirable; we can use that outrage. Personally,
which isn't relevant, but nonetheless: sure, I see the merit. I also
like visiting the supposedly accurate Garden of Eden and walking
the four stories of our Ark. My pleasure, however, was not, and
remains not, a factor in the decision to actualize those projects."

J could feel the heat fuming from Art, could see in his periphery—J didn't dare turn to look directly—Art's deep flush. It
seemed, J decided, safe to take a bite of his salad. He lifted his fork
timorously, but Blanchard rang his little bell again, and the servers
scuttled their plates.

"You think we could use it, Hayley," Graves asked.

Hayley made a gesture with her thumbs.

"She's right," Blanchard said. "We could certainly use it. She
always is right."

"You people," Art muttered.

J began to ask what they could use the provocation for, but
Art silenced him by resting his hand back on J's forearm another
moment. J didn't know how he felt about Hayley being right, if
Hayley was right. If she were right, then he would be creating
a museum that provoked outrage, that fetishized Jews, and that
didn't seem right. He looked over at her and she snuck him a
conspiratorial wink. It was possible that she was simply produc-
ing the arguments that would sway these three men, though J

still didn't know who they were, or what all of this was, or how outrage was intended to serve anything. He was hungry, hungry and intimidated.

"One problem," Norelius said. "I don't see how you can run, not for governor, if you immerse yourself in this museum."

Art protested that he absolutely knew this to be true, that's why he wanted to build the museum now, before he ran. He argued that there was still lots of good he could do as mayor, but this was part of his mission and legacy, too, and Art wanted to get it rolling before he had to focus on other things. Blanchard clucked at him with a pate knife en route towards the plate of foie gras and truffles that had been set on the table.

J reached his own pate knife out and lifted a scoop of liver and mushroom.

"The issue," Norelius said, "isn't one of distraction but of affiliation. You can't be associated with a project like this, not now, not later."

"Come on, J," Art said, and grabbed J's arm. The dollop of foie gras fell on the table.

"You mustn't be so hasty, so reactive," Graves said. "You can't be affiliated isn't we can't enable. The impression of impulsivity is less a boon than actual impulsiveness is a bane. Err towards the measured."

Art released J's arm. J scraped the dollop of foie gras off the table with his pate knife. This time, Blanchard looked at him in a manner that was undeniably askance. J blushed and set his pate knife on his plate and put his hands back in his lap.

"Truly, Arthur," Norelius said. "This lack of discipline."

"If Jacob can establish for us a capacity to orchestrate," Blanchard said.

Hayley interjected that even an attempt at orchestrating such a museum's construction would suit their purposes.

"I want the museum actually built," Art said.

"J will orchestrate, Chastity can liaise for you, Art," Hayley continued. "There's distance enough, there; and, it'll explain her absences last year and the year before."

"You'll run," Norelius said.

"I want the museum first," Art sighed.

"You'll run now," Norelius said. "You campaigning while your wife assists in this lets us message both ways."

Art sighed again.

"Be gracious," Norelius said after a pause during which the pate was cleared from the table. "You full well knew what horses you would trade before ever you had boarded the airplane. It is unseemly to pout: you have accomplished what you intended. You are made more than whole."

Art laughed, slouched back in his seat and flicked his butter knife a few inches forward on the table. He acknowledged that he guessed as much was true.

"Come," Hayley said, standing. "I can take you for a tour of the Ark."

"Do," Blanchard said, "but be sure Art's back on a plane to New Mexico tonight."

Hayley asked to what and to where J ought to be sent next.

DC, Norelius told her: there were some offices there, and staff.

"Looks like it's back to the old ABQ, for the both of us then," Art said, slapping J's shoulder. "I'm not sending you to DC without Chase."

J wanted to visit the museum and the ark, but Art brushed that suggestion off, and instead Hayley and the mute driver took the highway back towards the airport.

"You're in luck," Hayley told them craning back from the front passenger seat, smartphone in hand. "You have a new campaign manager, Art, and he has access to a private plane. You'll be able to fly back direct with him without raising any ethics flags."

Art turned from the window to J, who he nudged with his elbow.

"These men," Art said to J in a tone that exuded private confidence, but obviously intentionally loud enough to be heard by Hayley and the driver in the front seats. "The three kings."

Of course, the Mercedes was dead quiet anyway; anything could be heard by those in the front seat. Still, J blushed, embarrassed, and didn't respond.

"Here's an example," Art said at the same volume, in the same manner. "The driver. You saw that bulge under his shirt behind his back? That's a KSN Golan. Only, they care about appearances even more than they do security, so his shirt's tucked in over it."

"Right," J said, not sure what else to say.

"Right?" Art replied. "What does right mean?"

"I'm not sure what I'm supposed to say," J said.

"Right," Art said. "OK. He's got to untuck his goddamn shirt, for Christ's sakes, before he can draw."

"Draw?"

"His gun."

"A KSN Golan is a gun?" J asked.

"Please don't use the Lord's name," Hayley said.

"Oh I'm as holy as any of you," Art said. "I know you, Hayley. And yes, the KSN Golan is an Israeli-licensed version of the Serb Zastava compact, beloved for its stainless steel barrel and ambidextrous usage."

"My request isn't based in holiness," Hayley said. "It's based in discipline. Take care to mind your habits."

"She always introduces herself," Art said, back to his earlier tone and volume. "As if I don't know who she is. I know who she is. I know exactly who she is, that they call her the savant."

"Ok," J said.

In truth, J envied Art's impetuousness, even if it did sadden J to realize that Art had masters, masters Art clearly resented.

CHAPTER THIRTY-TWO

WHEN J ARRIVED IN DC, several weeks after the Cincinnati trip, it was Chase, who refused to accompany him. Her refusal had angered Art, who'd railed about how J needed both a chaperone and an intercessor to not end up neutered before his work ever began. Besides, wasn't J her fucking friend anyway? Didn't she want to look out for him?

J had overheard their low growls from the living room where they'd put him to bed. As a small child, he'd overheard his parents' fights in the same fashion, and this similarity amplified his sense of emasculation.

But, Art had been right. They'd set him up with a perfectly nice office suite in a building primarily tenanted by another of their institutes, one dedicated to something that had to do with young leadership development with some sort of connection to nondenominational Christian values and to Israel. They had a lot of pictures of Israel, pictures with J had grown overly familiar over the last three months, months he'd spent largely in their lobby while he waited with one seemingly basic request or another—a computer, a phone, network access, alarm codes, a spare key to the office, paper supplies, even the compensatory staple remover.

The 'young leaders' all seemed a bit as if they were between a track meet and debate team prep. He wouldn't have picked up on the

Christian part at all—they didn't present as churchy—if it weren't for the conversations he overheard and the hyper-prevalence of crosses. Tasteful crosses, J had to concede, unobtrusive, inornate, demur, but crosses everywhere: on chains, on bracelets, on cufflinks, on stationary, monogrammed on shirt pockets, and patterned into the carpeting. It wasn't that these easy-in-their-skin Christians treated J's requests with disdain; it was simply that he wasn't relevant to them, and they were uniquely focused, being the Young Christian Leaders of Tomorrow's New Zion, on the relevant. J agreed: He wasn't relevant to them. J felt altogether irrelevant.

J was still waiting on the staple remover—he'd broken down and bought his own paper supplies but for that one—but he had finally received network access. And, his first act of research, upon gaining this access, access that magically led to a dial tone on his desk phone, and which was granted him along with a smart phone and a new ID badge, was to google "Holocaust victims' lives." The stupidity, the impotence, of that act was so immediately palpable that he almost didn't bother to look at the results. He looked: the results were about the lives of survivors *after* the Nazis were defeated.

J then set about reactivating his social networking presence. This quickly led down a garden path of clicking on forgot-your-password links, which then sent passwords to other services whose passwords, he discovered, he'd also forgotten.

J took a couple of deep breaths: he didn't to go home to the furnished apartment they'd supplied—he could stay awake. He was fully capable of getting through the account reactivations. And, if he could reconnect…there were any number of research-type people from his past life as a marketer with whom he might reconnect. The yuppies for Christ had begrudgingly authorized J to bring a second on board with the caveat that he subject his final selection to their vetting and potential veto.

And then there it was: an appropriate password reset link!

His scalp tingled. J clicked through and reset his password.

A popup asked if he'd like to update his profile.

He clicked next.

An end user license agreement whose scroll bar indicated an infinitude of legal language popped up. Sure, he thought, vaguely anxious that this, too, was some manner of procrastination. He clicked that he agreed, which brought up a slide, one of eleven, if one believed the navigation arrows in the popup's bottom right hand corner. This first of eleven asked for his occupation and place of work.

Where did he work, he wondered. What was his occupation?

J went to click skip, and then hesitated: who knew better than J the importance of articulate identity? He opened his right-hand desk drawer and took out a legal pad; he opened his left-hand desk drawer and took out a pen. So this was it, three months in and he had all of the tools for work and was about to do work. J set the pen down on the pad, took the elevator down to the lobby, walked the block and a half to the coffee shop, and got in line.

"Fuck," J said to himself. Maybe staple removers really were the talisman prerequisite to doing work.

"Rough day?"

J turned around, and, despite himself, acknowledged to the scrubbed and smiling young man behind him that indeed it was a rough day, but also, in the broad scope of the world, one hardly worth complaining about. To this, the young man offered to see if it was anything J might wish to talk about. J was sure it wasn't worth describing, to which the young man pointed out that it was J's turn to order.

Flustered, J simply ordered what he'd heard the person in front of him order, which, while not something he didn't want was certainly something more complex than the simple drip coffee he'd meant to offer. Procrastination! Committed delay. Submission...

"I'm Jeremiah," the young man said, holding out his hand.

J introduced himself with a haste bordering on franticness and turned back to the counter, but his coffee wasn't ready yet anyway.

"Nice that we're finally past winter," Jeremiah said. "Of course, I'm used to it, being where I'm from."

"Yes, it's very nice," J said, startled that he'd managed to avoid taking Jeremiah's bait. J looked studiously at a shelf full of coffee accouterment on clearance sale, his pose an awkward nonchalance he'd once mastered to avoid idle conversation on elevators and then remembered the new smartphone—J opened the one social networking app he'd uploaded at the office—it took him immediately to a newsfeed featuring the people who'd been his friends when last he'd used the service, years earlier. The second person on the feed was Esther; E had posted a picture of her girls wearing sunflower costumes at what must have been a birthday party in what appeared to be a brownstone kitchen made of natural light and Provençale tile work, the younger of the two girls made up in a chocolate cake and white icing applique. J clicked on the photo to expand it.

The barista called both J and Jeremiah at the same time. Jeremiah touched J on the shoulder. J started, blushed, frantically pushed the buttons on the side of the phone until one blacked the screen. J grabbed his drink from the counter and mumbled a thanks. Jeremiah calmly collected his beverage and said that it had been nice meeting J. They left the coffee shop at the same time and walked down the same block at about the same pace. J didn't care one way or the other about Jeremiah, but he did care about basic manners, and more egotistically, about his own capacity to function gracefully in the world. If J was going to research, fund, and build a museum, he needed to be competent.

To quell this anxiety of competence, J sipped his drink.

Jeremiah, meanwhile, had apparently done the same, because he caught J's attention with a loud request for pardon, and wondered whether they hadn't accidentally picked up each other's drinks. J tried to remember what he'd ordered in order to determine if that was what he'd just sipped. J had wanted a simple coffee, something dark roast. What he had ordered, on the other hand…it wasn't supposed to be this way.

Jeremiah gently took the cup from J's hand and sipped the drink.

"That's mine!" Jeremiah said.

"OK," J said, caught between his surprise at the gesture's implicit boldness and the tenderness of its execution.

Their drinks unswitched, they walked the rest of the way back to the building in which both J and the Christians had their offices. Jeremiah held the lobby door open for J. J held the elevator door for Jeremiah. They parted ways at Jeremiah's floor, which was the reception floor for J's hosts, with smiles and half waves. At least, J figured, he now had some kind of connection to one young Christian leader.

That evening, J picked up a carton of Pat Thai on the way home, and a six pack. Inside, he poured a beer into a stein that had been provided with the apartment, laid out dinner, and delicately opened the laptop. He cancelled out of social network's introductory slides and typed E's name into the search box.

The next morning, two blocks into J's mile walk from his furnished efficiency to the office, Jeremiah hailed him from across the street. J waived back and waited, the sun sharp, while Jeremiah dashed across lanes of traffic to J's side of the avenue.

"Might as well walk together," Jeremiah said.

"What do you do for them?" J asked.

"I'm glad I caught you yesterday," Jeremiah said. "I'm lactose intolerant. That flat white would've capped my day. And sorry about mixing our drinks up."

"Oh," J said. "Sure. Of course."

"Everyone in DC," Jeremiah said, "seems to wake up thinking about next week, really, about next year."

"Oh," J said. "OK."

"Seriously," Jeremiah said, "don't you think? Everyone I meet here isn't simply ambitious; they're dissatisfied with everything but the actuation of their personal monolithic vision of the future."

"I wouldn't know," J said.

"Well," Jeremiah said. "It's true. It informs everything they do. Or who knows, maybe I'm crazy."

"Oh no," J said. "I'm sure you're not crazy."

But, by then they'd reached the building, where a young woman who looked like an immature version of the three kings' savant, Hayley, greeted Jeremiah. The idea of chasing the future puzzled J, who for so long had chased (or fled) from the past. Did J's museum project constitute an ambition to shape the world in his own image? E's daughter's cake face came to mind.

J exhaled the girl's face, though it made him smile to think about, and focused on this question of image: He had never thought about what it meant to make something in one's own image; it was less about replicating oneself in an avatar, he now saw, than it was about enacting one's vision for and of the world. In that case, every aspiration made manifest, every piece of art or of legislation, was a making in its author's image. By the same token, all it meant of man's relationship to God was that God had imagined man.

But then...but then the elevator door opened on J's floor.

A better question might be what it would mean to make something *not* in one's image. He visualized the older of E's daughters turned around in the diner booth in Torrey. He exhaled slowly through his nose and counted while he walked to his suite. The older girl had the indents inside of her eyes alongside of her nose so specific to J's family, to him and his siblings. (And what would it mean if one thought of man as God's avatar, God's player in a virtual game not actually His world? Two versions of image after all then, and which was J to his dreamer: vision or avatar? Vision felt awkward when the word dream was so readily available, and to use the word dream was to collapse into the circularity of tautology.)

He walked into his office and sat down, and then stood up, and then sighed and sat down. Sitting, he sighed again, and opened his laptop. There was Esther's family in front of a wall of red and yellow and orange sandstone spires. He wanted to cry. He closed the laptop. He picked up his phone, set it back in its cradle, tried to cheer himself by remembering the office assistant at his first big boy job whose phone had a Post-it note attached to the handset that read: remember phone etiquette. When J had asked what that referenced, his coworkers had explained that the assistant used to bang the handset against her monitor when she found those on the other end of a call overly imperious. Overly imperious! Like there was an appropriate amount of imperiousness.

J chuckled, sort of, and then sighed, because he should work, and he didn't know what work meant, not in this context.

Was J in his dreamer's image? The world in his dreamer's image? Or was the reverse true? And wasn't the dreamer, who, for dint of details available to J, J had of necessity constructed by act of imagination, actually in J's image?

He tensed his abdomen to not look up E's daughters again: there were so many photos of them online!

Was J's office layout in his image? J sighed. This was all procrastination.

J reopened his laptop and logged back onto his social network, as planned. He'd intended to look up some past colleagues, and J intended to do as he had planned.

The site presented a post from five years earlier and asked if he'd like to share the memory.

Memory! Whose memory? It was the site that had remembered, not J.

E had taken the photo at an Italian restaurant on Crescent Ave. J had clearly come around from E's side of the table to squeeze into a group shot with two of his coworkers from his last corporate gig and their spouses, there were bottles of wine on the table and a large steaming foil bag, in which, J remembered—and he found himself wanting to use scare quotes around every version of the word memory, even in his internal musings, his silent, procrastinatory monologue—J remembered that inside the foil bag there were baby clams steamed in white wine with tiny baby potatoes.

Ward and Dani had come straight uptown from work with their spouses, and thus arrived ahead of him and E. They were seated at a heavy scarred table in the back nook beneath a red brick arch, Bronx Mediterranean villa style. While waiting for J and E, Dani's spouse had apparently asked questions about the wine list in relation to the menu, and the chef had come out and asked for permission to simply feed and wine them. J and E had reached the restaurant from Inwood right in time for the presentation of J's favorite dish, the clams, those preceded by a plate of bread and oils and a small offering of buffalo mozzarella caprese, all already consumed.

What a meal! There had been courses upon courses, never too much of any of them. By the end of the night bonhomie had overflowed into a loud, roundly expressed, desire to work together again; and, those proclamations had, in fact, translated into an important early contract for J. They'd hired him to develop the fictional identities of several types of savers, savers being investors with access only to relatively ordinary income and wealth levels.

J missed Dani and Ward, missed working with them. Chances were they both still had agency jobs, but even if so, Ward might be into side work. Dani had already been too fancy for that even back then. And if Ward wasn't, he almost certainly knew someone research-capable who would be.

A fleeting overcast darkened J's office abruptly, reminding him that this wasn't work, that he had to work. He looked out the window even as the sun came back into full view.

The rat! After their dinner, while walking up Crescent to Fordham, E and J had stumbled across an Italian street fair, threadbare and barely a block long, in honor of some saint's day or other. Humidity had turned the sunset into a pink murk offsetting the streetlights in a way that had romanticized the residential row houses clad in weird 1950's imitation stone and brick. The same pink light cast a dingy mank on the fair's booths and boxes. The fair was dirty. A barker yelled that for a dollar, they could walk up three steps into one of the boxes and see the world's largest rat: over a hundred pounds, according to the rough pink paint on the box's side. J had known better, knew better for E, that she oughtn't go in there; he didn't care to go in, but she oughtn't.

She'd produced two dollars and gone in, J with her.

E had even been to Peru before, knew to call it a capybara, the sad soiled animal they viewed, leaning over the painted-pipe railing over the drop into the animal's tight quarters, a capybara, a kind of guinea pig. She'd said so, as they stood there, the desire to flee the overly bright fluorescent lighting, to flee the stink of piss and hay and shit and fear, to flee the palpable suffering displayed for dollars, the desire to flee so intense it paradoxically paused them, halted their easy egress the few short feet further down the viewing platform. She'd said, "It's not a rat. It's a capybara. I saw them in Peru. I think I'm going to throw up."

And then the barker had yelled to keep it moving or pay another dollar, but wasn't it a sight to behold! And they knew they were not just complicit in that animal's fate by way of the dollars they'd spent, nor only in the gawking they'd done, but in that they shilled for more gawkers and more dollars by simple dint of walking in and through and out again, because they were fresh and dressed and white, those things in combination a potent local signifier of virtue, virtue that authorized, sanitized, the choice of others to go and view, too.

Threadbare, J concluded, fingers still alight upon the laptop's touchpad, a threadbare memory of a threadbare thing.

E had told the barker he ought to be ashamed of himself and the barker had yelled at their backs for her being a hoity-toity downtown bitch and J a vag-man with his oozing cunt showing, and they'd walked together the remaining blocks to Fordham to catch the Bronx 12 Express back to Inwood, though J had wanted to hide his impotence in the ready dark of a gypsy cab's cloister. E wouldn't let him flag any of the many banged up Lincoln Town Cars cruising by.

The poor guy, J thought, now, daydreaming instead of working, to be so desperate as to travel around with a beat up capybara in a box, doing threadbare gigs in whatever was else-where the analog for the most benighted of the outer Burroughs, and to be shamed for it by a fancy lady on her way home from fancy dinner. Or maybe that was condescending, too. Either, way—and at this thought J sighed—he wasn't getting any closer to accomplishing anything with his research, and he wanted to be able to show some progress when Art arrived next month.

J hit up Ward's profile. He began to write a message, and then figured that a preemptive scan of Ward's information was in order. Ward looked the same, but fitter and older, so too his spouse. They'd adopted a child, a two-year-old now four years old.

"Fuck," J muttered for reasons that weren't clear to him.

J had best go ahead and call Ward, whose profile claimed he still worked where J had worked with him. J dialed the number before trying to remember it. Realized that his fingers knew the number even though he couldn't quite recite it.

A receptionist greeted him in a voice that was different but also the same as the one that had greeted him for the better part of a decade.

He asked for Ward and was treated to hold music that defi-nitely dated back to his long-ago tenure there. His chest ached. He wanted to be on the phone and he wanted to write poetry to E. He wanted to replace all of the blood in his veins with new, cleansed blood, and he imagined himself submerged into a saline melt pool in an ice cave, surrounded by ice, freezing. Then, eerily, he heard his own voice, more dulcet, more New York, pitching the agency.

"Shit," J muttered. "I was young."

Ward picked up.

J nearly hung up, but remembered that his phone number would show up on Ward's phone, that Ward would call him back if he fled. Still, what was he to say?

As it turned out, they made easy conversation, caught up a very little bit, J adeptly steering the conversation first to Ward's revela-tion of the adoption, and then conversation about that adoption. When J got around to wanting to hire, having resources to hire,

staff to research installations at a museum, Ward answered enthu-
siastically, emphatically.

Then, Ward asked what the museum was to be.

J took a deep breath held it, exhaled slowly.

Now or never: he delivered the pitch as close as he could
remember to how Art had delivered it to the three kings. There
was a silence. J added more details. Still silence. J began explaining that the museum would be conveniently located a short drive
from the Cincinnati airport. J winced; he knew the location wasn't
persuasive, but there was no elegant way to stop explaining, once
he'd begun.

Thankfully, Ward cut him off before J had a chance to talk
about the neighboring creationist museum.

"J," Ward said. "Do you have someone you're speaking to?"

"I'm speaking to you."

"Of course you are," Ward said. "I'm your friend."

"Ok."

"Fuck," Ward said. "I'm just fucking going to come out and
say it."

"Say what, Ward? That Cincinnati is the wrong place for a
Holocaust museum? Well you'd be surprised to know that there's
really an awfully large historically important Jewish community in
Ohio and Kentucky."

"J," Ward said. "Have you managed to get any help since
you and E split up? We were all worried about you a few years
ago, when you stopped returning phone calls, let alone doing the
contracts folks were calling about. I assumed, when you disappeared altogether that you'd gotten help, but this doesn't sound
like you've..."

J's chest-ache meandered park paths, E's oldest little girl
clutched to his pinkie.

"J," Ward said, "I'd rather you were crazy than think that
you're building a Holocaust museum, the whole fucking point of
which is that it never mentions the Holocaust and that it makes a

fucking Disneyland out of the Jewish ghettos of Eastern Europe. For fuck's sake…"

They'd buy ice cream from one of those vendor carts that lines Central Park's pathways in nice weather, Dove bars, or those Good Humor cones that came wrapped in paper.

"J, I'm married to a Jew, my son is Jewish, I might as well be Jewish, and even if I weren't,"

"You aren't," J interjected. "You aren't Jewish."

"Regardless, it's either willfully fucking offensive or vanilla-ass loony and I can excuse loony a fuck ton easier."

"Fuck off," J said, and hung up.

J sat and stared at the handset in its cradle, stared at the phone's LCD screen and the banks of buttons ringing it. Maybe he needed a phone etiquette Post-it note reminder. Maybe Ward would call back. Maybe what J was doing—which he'd not actually thought to do on his own, after all, it was Art's idea—was, indeed, offensive. J hoped not. He wished for access to the pithy quotables of a self-actualization guru; J could call to mind neither quotes nor guru. He would never have his old life back—Esther would never be with him again, he would never again live in his old apartment with her, he would not marry her, and he would not have those two little girls with her. J would not follow the plot of the life he'd worked for—it was so many years later! Five years—but, wasn't it that he'd never had that life, that he'd simply not then known that his life was always, had always been, beholden to the man in the van—but the illusion! God, he ached today. J clenched and unclenched his hands, which all on their own longed for the mobile welding rig and his torch and his wrenches, longed for grease, for roughnecking. Even that was months and months gone.

J had to go forward with the museum. He did. When they see it, he thought, when they see it… see what, exactly? What would the museum be?

Inhale for a four-count; hold for seven; exhale for eight. Forward.

The pen and blank pad were still on the desk, a memory, such as they were, of how J hadn't articulated for himself an occupation, a mission statement, a role.

J didn't want to think too hard about what Art's influence meant upon him, and he was more than willing to dismiss the savant's assessment out of hand: the men Hayley worked for were conclusively not on the same side as J and Art, and even less so Hayley herself.

Still.

J closed his web browser, and his social network with it. He closed his laptop lid. Coffee, J thought. It was past lunchtime anyway. He returned to the same coffee shop, both hoping for and dreading another encounter with Jeremiah. Of course, Jeremiah wasn't there. However, after he picked his drink up at the counter, he turned around to face the mini-Hayley Jeremiah had been talking to that morning in the lobby.

"Hi," she said. "You were talking to Jeremiah this morning."

She was cute, if clearly, part and parcel, one of the young yuppie Christians. J acknowledged that he had been talking to Jeremiah, that he'd met the man the day before in circumstances almost identical to these, and then ran into him this morning.

"He's absolutely great," the young woman said. "I'm actually getting coffee for him right now, and not even because I lost a bet or anything. I'm in it for the excuse to lean on his door frame and stare at his soul."

"His soul?"

"Which is the most beautiful part of any man, and in the case of Jeremiah is a beauty worth gazing upon."

"Walk back to the office together?" J sighed.

"Well, OK, but I've got to wait on my coffee drink before I can, if that's not too too much of a hold up for you."

"No hold up at all," J said.

"Yay!" she said. "I'm Christian, by the way."

"I know," J said, heat rising to his cheeks, not sure why he was quite so embarrassed.

"How did you know?" she bubbled. "Wait, what have you been up to, you naughty mister?"

"No," J said, "yeah. I mean it's just that you work there, right? At the Christian leader thing with Jeremiah, and aren't you all…"

"Oh!" she shrieked, "no, no, no. I'm not Christian, I mean, I am Christian, like, of course I'm Christian, duh, but also my name is Christian. That's so funny! I never thought of it like that before."

"Oh," J said. "Well, yeah."

He tried to identify what it was he felt as he stood, holding his hot drink, waiting with Christian for her order. His body wanted to lean towards her, but his head wanted to move up and away from her. His feet wanted to get out of there, but his manners kept him rooted. He was embarrassed, he realized, that she had any ability to evoke emotion in him at all. He wasn't drawn to her: he found her annoying and repellent. It was that he had involuntary responses to her, that she could annoy and repel him, that implied that he was drawn to her, and this implication evoked a panicked self-loathing that made her all the more repellant.

Figuring his reaction out, and that his reaction was on him, his fault not hers, was maybe the most self-aware moment of his life J realized, and that made him feel proud and free. Free to stay or free to go?

To leave, J was free to leave. But, as he opened his mouth to own his empowerment, the barista called Christian's name, and it was too late.

They walked together back towards their building. Christian bubbled on and on about all the amazing things that her workplace was about; J kept largely silent in order to not point out that he wasn't Christian. Her shoulders were hunched and her peacoat's collar was popped, but whatever she actually felt about the day's unseasonable raw, J could see it wasn't going to slow her cheer or her chatter.

J was going to have to get comfortable with Christians, with Christianity, he realized. There were Christians everywhere, and they controlled everything.

"But listen to me motor-mouthing," Christian said. "When I haven't even given you a chance to talk even a bit. How is your day going, J?"

"Fine," J said. "My day's going fine."

"You can do better than that," she said. "Come on: tell me."

CHAPTER THIRTY-THREE

J RETURNED TO THE office but the loneliness sang falsetto arias and the apartment's air turned murky with want. J downloaded a photo of E's family and photo-shopped himself in over her husband, just to see how well he'd fit into the composition, and wished and wished that he'd never become conscious of the dreamer, never abandoned his own firm, had married her according to plan. He tried to will his way back to those ecstatic moments in which he had access to the man in the van; he wanted to confront him. Why make me thus? He wanted to ask. Why make me different, make me here? And yet he would not be unmade.

His will failed and he worried that its failure was his failure of will.

J erased the photo-shopped photo because it crept him out. He admonished himself that the dreamer had no choice in his gassing or his dreaming, so who was J to quibble and complain about the impossible time of his existence? J reminded himself that he'd been granted a mission, a purpose, that he'd been granted existential consciousness. This too embittered him: what was he supposed to do with his mission? With this knowledge?

He gave in and went back down to the reception area, still not having written a description of what it was he did, and what it was he would want an associate to do. Even as J announced himself to the receptionist, Jeremiah emerged from the woodwork, popping out through a door in the paneling that J would never have noticed had it not opened.

J started, slightly, though he was glad to see Jeremiah, even if Jeremiah apparently found Christian tolerable. J greeted Jeremiah, asked if Jeremiah might not lend a hand.

"That is exactly what I'm hear for, my man," Jeremiah said, cutting J off before he could specify for what it was he needed a hand, and then stuck out his hand in a way that focused Jeremiah's entire body behind his offer to shake. J gingerly took Jeremiah's hand.

"Great," J said, his hand still firmly in Jeremiah's clasp.

"Shall we get to it?"

"Thanks. Yes, please. I'm here trying to hire someone, so."

"Thought we'd covered that!" Jeremiah said, pumping J's hand. "I'll do it. I'm your man."

"Oh. Thanks! But don't—"

"No questions asked," Jeremiah said, clasping J's upper arm with his left hand. "Everything is arranged. We are good to go!"

"You just came out of the wall," J said, grateful that the aggressive pumping had ended.

"Yes," Jeremiah agreed, releasing J. "Came right out of the sacristy. Bam! Like that. Ready. Prepared. What's first?"

"I guess we should go downstairs," J said.

"Isn't your office upstairs?"

"Sorry," J said. "I meant my office. It just felt for a second… never mind. Upstairs."

"Upstairs!"

Upstairs, J thought, and wondered what he had done. If only Chase had been willing to come to DC, this wouldn't be happening. If only he'd listened to Chase, he wouldn't be in DC at all. She wasn't taking his calls. But, if he'd left, how would he have been any closer to her?

J couldn't answer that last question for himself, but he also felt dishonest claiming that he'd stayed for her. Frankly, at this point, he didn't know what or for whom he'd stayed. All he knew was that he was terrified of his own choices. He held the glass door to his little suite open for Jeremiah and silently addressed the man in the van: "I sure hope this is what you want. I hope this brings us peace."

CHAPTER THIRTY-FOUR

JEREMIAH: JEREMIAH! JEREMIAH WAS a lawyer with a master's degrees in Twentieth-Century European history and divinity. Jeremiah had worked as a legislative aide for several years before moving over to the YCLNZ, which acronym he had a disturbing habit of pronouncing why-clans, which, when Jeremiah spoke fast, as he often did, sounded to J like "Y cleanse." Jeremiah knew when to ask further questions and when to supply answers. Jeremiah decided decisions. Jeremiah knew how to do anything and everything research. Jeremiah kept them on task.

At night back in the furnished efficiency with which the three kings had supplied him, J followed E's children's growth in a stream of on-line photo albums: laughed at their balloon-animaled birthdays, murmured aloud at the colorful Band-Aids masking skinned knees begot of tricycle-borne mishaps. Her oldest child began elementary school, learned letters. None of this assuaged J's hollow want. He loved her children, wept for the notion that the elder of the two would have to carry the younger to the...he dared not name it, but he increasingly believed that his dreams of creation indicated that the end approached. He dreaded that apocalypse more for those two girls than for himself.

How many nights, he wondered, have I gotten back into my own grave, still not certain whether God would not yet smite me in my sleep?

YCLNZ, Y: Young, Yid, Yiddish, Yids.

Somehow Christian had talked her way into being assigned to assist Jeremiah part time, and lolled about their office most of the day, ogling Jeremiah.

Christian was genuinely helpful; J knew it was his own problem that he found her so deeply annoying. It didn't help matters that J also recognized the gendered stereotype in having an efficient assistant who he evaluated, because she was a bubbly young woman unafraid of the title secretary, on a metric of magnetism. This recognition made J feel guilty too, and that guilt led J to find her presence even more repellent.

Progress!

"Choose a city," Jeremiah said.

Because the name of the Vilna Gaon had lingered over J's Torah education during his religious upbringing, and because he knew nothing about either the Gaon or Vilna or even, really, Lithuania, J chose Vilnius. Jeremiah typed that into his search engine, clicked, waited, saw the results, whistled and kicked back in his chair: Lithuania had had the highest extermination rate of any country—about 195,000, roughly 95%, of Lithuania's Jews had been murdered.

J would have preferred to begin with a place from which the man in the van might more reasonably have come. Lithuania's Jews had mostly been shot and buried in pits by Eisatzengruppen A with the active and eager collaboration of Lithuanian paramilitaries shortly after Nazi occupation rather than sent off to death camps. But J couldn't see any good way to raise that contention without confiding that he was the dream of a man being gassed to death. J did not want to confide that particular confidence to Jeremiah.

Within a month, they were sending real data to an advance construction team in Kentucky that Jeremiah had coordinated with the savant, Hayley.

Whereas Jeremiah produced and sorted broad troves of information, J most often found himself at the mercy of small details. Some of these bedazzled, like the fact that Vilna Gaon had actively encouraged emigration to Ottoman Palestine, and that the 500 Lithuanian Jews who heeded him at the tail end of the 18th Century became the Litvaks of Mea Shearim. J marveled at the fact that Mea Shearim had become the great center for what remained of the Hasidic sects of Eastern Europe, despite the Gaon's great opposition to Hasidism, and yet also was the place in the world that most resembled the yeshivish ghettos in which the Gaon had made his home.

Jeremiah, indefatigable, popped his cheerful head into J's office to ask if he'd like a coffee: J turned his laptop around to show a photo of Chagall posing with other Jewish luminaries at a Jewish academy in Vilnius in the 1930s.

"What am I looking at?"

"Chagall," J said.

"Who?"

"I can get coffee!" Christian called from the front office.

"Come in here!" Jeremiah yelled back, outshouting J's acceptance of her offer. "Check out this amazing photograph of Chagall in Vilnius that Jacob found."

"Who's Chagall?" Christian asked?

"He's likely the only in the shot to have survived," J said.

"Why didn't they all just move to Birobidzhan?" Christian asked.

"Birowhat?" J asked. "Jeremiah can explain Chagall to you."

"Wouldn't want to steal your thunder, there, J. You go ahead."

"Birobidzhan," Christian said. "You know, the autonomous Jewish sector in the Soviet Union. All the Jews were like invited to move there and have a totally Jewish state? All the way over on the eastern side of Russia?"

"There was no Jewish region on any side of the USSR," J laughed, "let alone an autonomous one. They were an atheist state! All religion verboten."

"Here," Christian said, handing over a manila folder. "This is what I've found. What I haven't figured out is why they didn't go there."

"Jews belong in Zion," Jeremiah said. "No offense, J."

"None taken," J said, taking the folder.

"If they'd all moved there," Christian said, "the Nazis never would have gotten them. We wouldn't be trying to recreate what Jews were because they would still be Jews."

"Bygones," Jeremiah said, shrugging at J.

"No," J said. "Fuck bygones, fuck the notion that if all the Jews had just moved to some mythical region on the far side of the Soviet Union…I just can't."

"Where they'd have become godless communists," Jeremiah finished. "Sixes really, when you think about it."

"Sixes?" J asked

"It's shorthand," Jeremiah said. "Six of one…"

"I know what it means."

"Living, godless communists," Christian said. "Living."

"Babe," Jeremiah said. "Can you get us coffee?"

"No, no," J said. "I need the air."

He fled the office with the file, eager to breathe anything other than the dank of his own misogyny.

The stream of information flowed steadily to Cincinnati now, dispatched each evening in brown cartons whose daily numbers seemed to increase week-over-week.

E's kids…

"Any word from, Art," J asked.

"He left a message," Christian said. Apparently, Art's campaign was finding its stride—full steam—Art couldn't visit after all. After the general election, Art would fly out to meet up with the Kings, and J could conveniently meet with them at the same time, allowing for a reunion of sorts.

Yet, for all of the bustling activity in the office, J felt ever more adrift in the evenings back in the apartment. Or, more accurately, now that he was only adrift in the apartment, he noticed it more, the comparative formlessness of his time in what passed for a home. He would leave work invigorated, and even reach the apartment building in that state. But, once he got inside a stifling inertia overtook him. He didn't have it in him to do more work, and the thought of going out and socializing exhausted him.

Occasionally, he'd ring Chase. She wouldn't answer. Unless he was a little drunk, he wouldn't bother to leave her messages. Other times, he'd call Art, who would answer, but now conversed only in brief, rah-rah platitudes: All things, full steam ahead! See you in June! Next stop, statehouse and museum!

J turned 38.

Chase sent him a brief email thanking him for his attentions and hoping that J would be understanding if she chose to keep her distance for now. Art called in the morning. Their first two attempts to engage in meaningful conversation were truncated by bad reception in the mountains, or deserts, or someplace else: J could only make out that Art was being chauffeured between campaign stops, presumably had called from the back of some SUV. Art eventually rang back, backstage on his way into the rally, to quickly wish J a happy last year before the big birthday. Before J could ask what that meant, Art intimated a hope that J would enjoy what was in store.

In store was Thai food with Christian and Jeremiah and a few of their YCLNZ friends. After which, Jeremiah announced that they were off to the best whiskey bar in the world. J demurred; but Jeremiah made a great show of his disappointment, and proclaimed that he had a surprise for J.

The whiskey bar's indeed overwhelming selection did little to redeem it from the absolute homogeneity of its patrons, all of whom fit the YCLNZ mold, excepting, for the most part, the ubiquity of crucifix adornments.

The first round came.

"To Zion! New and old," Jeremiah toasted.

They drank. Rather, they competitively shot the expensive Scotch.

A second round appeared.

"To Jacob! To our very own Jew!" Jeremiah toasted.

J awkwardly drank, blushing, grateful that his usual irrelevance was temporarily alleviated. He was their Jew; so be it.

"This isn't much," Christian said, handing him a nattily wrapped box. The YCLNZ had devolved into caste-conforming competitive drinking all around them. But as J began to open the wrapping, they shot their rare sipping whiskeys and then banged their empty glasses on the table in a jarring drumroll, yelling, "Rip! Rip!"

They'd bought him a monogrammed Mont Blanc fountain pen whose logo, J couldn't help but notice, was a six-pointed star, and a stack of heavy linen stationary, also monogrammed, and a bottle of green-blue ink designed to shimmer. He decided not to point out that they'd essentially given him a very upscale version of a cliché bar-mitzvah gift.

He sat for a while, alone amongst them, disembodied drinks manifesting. Drunk, he stood, which got no one's attention. J rapped on the table with an empty glass. Thank them: thank them for what? Apologize then, apologize for not being a Christian leader, for not being young, for being subject to an embarrassingly lame bedtime, for not being Christian. Apologize for their, for their—he was going to apologize for being Jewish. Instead, he tossed down the credit card Haley had issued him.

J bellowed to their server to leave it open for his young friends, and made his exit, only stumbling once, when he tripped over the foot of a young man with yacht club hair, who leaned against a column near the doorway from which pose, even in that pose, yacht club hair heir loomed over his coterie of attendant twined women in mock cocktail dresses.

J meant to take the next day off, but on that next morning couldn't imagine a wardrobe change, and donned his regular suit. He couldn't think of anything better to do than walk to the office.

At the coffee shop, he tried to smell his sweat, prodigious despite it being October; please let it not smell of whiskey. He handed his credit card over, and it occurred to him that he might not have been supposed to use the card the way he had the night before, and that he might have subconsciously known as much. Perhaps, he'd been hoping to get fired.

No one even made any mention of what must have been an unspeakably high bar tab. Not that J had any clear sense of how his compensation worked anyway. He had an account at a bank without any local branches that belonged to some tendril of the three kings' empire, the account set up on his behalf by some third-party HR provider, itself part of yet another tendril, one that handled compensation and benefits for YCLNZ and the museums. His account had the strange feature of staying at a roughly constant balance regardless of whether J spent no money or a lot of money.

He had little occasion to spend a lot of money.

J kept the pen and paper at home, where they sat on the glass dining table that also served as J's desk for what little work he did at home. They sat unused, judging him.

After two weeks of suffering the pen and paper's condemnation, less tempted than ever to go out in the evenings, J sat before them. He took out a piece of paper. He posted the pen's cap. He thought to write to Chase, but her birthday email had apologized for the space she clearly wished him to respect. J sighed. As a younger man, he would have both missed that hint and not respected the request. How long ago would that have been? Before he'd even met E.

J knew not to write to E.

He wrote "Dear Esther," in his most elegant cursive. Those two simple words curved and dipped: needless to say, the stationary wasn't lined.

He sighed, and absentmindedly bit the pen's posted cap. J yelped. It was metal or marble or stone, something really expensive and much harder than his dental enamel. J took a breath and resumed writing.

'I'd driven all night,' he began. 'I was at a breaking point. I'd worked welding pipeline for oil concerns in the far Midwest; clean work *for me*. And then I had to leave that; had to face all I'd been fleeing, all that from which I'd hid. I had driven all night to make an appointment, and then I saw you...'

J stopped. This simply rendered yet another strategic identity, a reconstruction of his old persona to motivate his ex-girlfriend—strange to call a married woman with children an ex-girlfriend; she was a wife, she was a mother, her titles so out of league with 'girlfriend' as to erase that former status altogether especially in its negation through historic relation—motivate her to what anyway? This wasn't work. There was no larger, higher purpose.

He was just writing.

He was just writing for something to do.

It was polite to write. Reasonable.

He tried again: 'I'm sorry if this note feels like it's out of the blue. And, sorry, if I was weird when I last saw you. It was such a surprise seeing you. I'd just pulled an all-nighter and my mind was in that strange state that develops out of an absence of sleep, too many hours on the road. Your daughter, by the way, is adorable.'

But this too felt forced and artificial, too many times saying sorry, for one thing, though it allowed him to realize that he didn't want to write E he so much as her daughter. Not that he wanted to write her daughter: it was the fact of her daughter that unsettled him, led him to wish to reach out. While he'd been chasing ghosts, metaphysical problems and ethical dilemmas, E had produced a child, a living, breathing, smiling consciousness, an adorable little girl who somehow had recognized in him something adequate enough for her to smile and flirt. She'd seen something in him, J thought, some part of herself, some shared thing, there if only by the ethereal trace of his long, if long lost, contact with her mother.

Not consciously, of course: she was a five-year-old, but nonetheless.

He wrote: 'E, so good to see you in the diner. It's been forever: you have a family! Anyway, I'm in DC. I'm doing well. I'm founding,' J paused here in his writing. Anything that had to do with the Holocaust and E would be right back where they were their last year together after he'd told her, or not so much told her as…he wanted her to believe he was doing well. He was doing well. 'Well, founding sounds grandiose. I'm helping develop a really unique museum concept—don't ask, I'm not sure if I could explain it even if I wasn't bound by confidentiality stuff—but I am doing well, and I wish I'd been more with it in Torrey. Do tell me how you are. Keep in touch?'

She wrote back, at length, not on paper with pen, but to one of J's old email addresses that he'd reactivated during his battle with the passwords.

E wrote about her work (she traded in derivatives of overseas companies and commodities that acted as hedges against currency bets); about her children (there were two of them, precocious, lovely, overwhelming); about her husband (a sculptor, just beginning to experience real success, showing in an upstairs gallery on 57th street, balding); about the blessing of her husband staying home most days (the girls had become adept at clay and pigment: they'd had to give up on housekeepers and nice furniture); about her recent family vacations (Torrey, of course, and Denmark for an art show, and Namibia, so many vaccinations for the children); about her surprise at hearing from him; and about how glad she was that he was doing well.

J read her email on his laptop, which sat on a pre-furnished glass-topped dining room table. Only one reading lamp was on and the lights of DC muttered between the pre-furnished polyester drapes. The room held nothing that indicated J except for his suit jacket draped over a chair and a short glass of whiskey (the whiskey was his, not the glass). When he finished reading her email, he read it again because he didn't have any work to do and didn't know what else to do with himself.

He kept rereading her email, progressively less able to contemplate retiring to the bedroom and its landlord-provided bed, whose sheets were changed weekly by the same service that kept the rest of the apartment.

When J was a child, his father would move their family during academic recess to take summer research gigs, and during those stints they stayed in furnished apartments. The furbishing of those accommodations had always seemed so much nicer, so much more exotic, than their own, left back home in whatever city they lived in at the time. The child dreamer, and the adolescent one too, would invent whole new identities for himself, and new parents and siblings too, identities in which he was blond, and strong, and popular, and richly provided with toys and tools to go along with the furnishings. Perhaps, even, those imaginative escapes trained him for his career in marketing. Perhaps they had laid the groundwork for his adult shame.

These current furnishings excluded him as completely as did the YCLNZ, or the Tucson, third-grade, recess girls. Chase excluded him. Art's campaign excluded him.

Obviously, E was no longer interested in him. But, somehow, that child, her oldest child, her description of that oldest child and that oldest child's life. That, that...

...the timing.

When had J last had sex with E?

CHAPTER THIRTY-FIVE

A MONTH AFTER ART won the governorship of New Mexico, he and J landed at the Cincinnati airport in Kentucky on separate planes, though only minutes apart. They met up in the airport's Brooks Brothers outlet because Art needed to buy a belt.

"How did you forget a belt?" J asked, idly thumbing through shirts that were on sale, 3 for the price of 2, and rather predictably preferring the shirts beside the sale shirts that weren't on sale and whose retail prices were nearly twice that from which the sale shirts had been marked down.

"Always forget something each time I fly here."

"Aren't you wearing a belt?"

The woman who ran the store, with whom Art had forged a special relationship over the course of many truculent forgettings, looked away from the belts to glare at J.

"I can't wear this belt to the brunch," Art said.

"I thought you liked showing off how western and casual you are to these guys."

"He is so handsome," the franchise owner clucked. "He looks very good in a suit."

"Wouldn't he look good in a suit wearing his cowboy belt?" J asked.

Art gestured appeasingly. The woman resumed pampering Art. She wasn't flirting so much as kvelling, J realized.

"You know you don't need to shop," Hayley said.

They all three turned towards the store entrance. She straddled the concourse's terrazzo and Brooks Brother's carpeting, as melodically dominant as ever.

"They let you past security?" Art asked, holding up two belts to his suit jacket in the mirror, as if he was comparing ties.

"The left," Hayley said.

In the mirror, J could see Art grimace with wanting to choose the belt in his right hand, though it was clear that the savant was right. Art inhaled, then exhaled his way into a smile. J felt a tenderness towards Art that was so very different than his usual feeling of intoxication, but that by dint of difference also reminded J of that intoxication.

"I'll buy both," the governor-elect said, handing the belts to his mothering friend, who smiled and nodded and complimented and held both belts up, each in their own hand, while she scurried to the cash register.

To J's surprise, he caught a hint of actual mirth around Hayley's mouth and eyes. More surprising still, she didn't seem to mind J noticing. She went so far as to raise an eyebrow and cock her chin at Art's back. J smiled back at her, mimed her gesture, to which she responded with a quick, full smile. Then Hayley gently, deeply inhaled, and as she rhythmically exhaled, she re-centered, sunk into and saturated her center of gravity, her impermeability reacquired.

J walked most of the way to where she stood, her toes barely proud of the concourse terrazzo.

When Art began towards them with his stapled shut bag of newly purchased belts, suit bag slung over a shoulder, J scurried to catch up with Hayley, who'd already begun striding towards the baggage claim. Because Art didn't quite catch up with Hayley, J lingered behind her as well, though not as far back as Art. When J stole a glance back at the man upon whose behest J quested after the perfect museum, Art's side slouch beneath the strap and mantis-like clutch of a sack of tissue wrapped belts came across as awkward. The man was awkward.

Then maybe J's feelings for Chase's knight really were feelings for Chase.

J sighed, and then inhaled. They stepped out of the airport to where the Mercedes waited in December's sliver of a golden hour.

For the first time in a year, for the first time in years, J's diaphragm and lungs and heart did as they might, did freely, unburdened. He breathed deeply again, to test out this newly wondrous relationship to breathing, the bright air crisp within him.

In the caesura after Art got into the car while J still stood beside it, Hayley leaned over the open passenger door, her hands neatly on its window's upper sash, and told J that she would send him her book of breathing exercises. Or at least that's what J decoded her as having said after she smiled again as J entered the cabin, and pushed his door closed with a single thrust of both arms, decoded once her two smiles' echoes subsided to a simple pulse, background crooning dazzle.

J asked Hayley if they could go past the construction site, and this, at least, perked Art up some. He seconded J's request.

"I don't know how satisfying that'll be at this stage," Hayley said.

"You promised this would be real," Art said.

"You are the governor, governor," Hayley said.

"Elect," Art said.

At a billboard for the young earth museum of natural history, the driver turned onto a two-lane road closely hemmed in by thick growth. Hayley explained that this portion of the road could readily be widened once they were set to accommodate visitors. A minute later, they reached a rough mud lot, half-filled with passenger vehicles: parking for the construction workers, Hayley told them.

They drove through the lot and onto a dirt road at its far end. For twenty feet on either side of the dirt road, all the trees had been yanked out, leaving thick ruts in the uneven mud.

"We're in the park experience now," Hayley said, "technically. Visitors will park in a new structure back at the clearing."

"Why then yank all of the trees?" Art asked.

"To replace them," Hayley said.

"Replace them?"

"Scots pine and spruce. Your bidding, governor. The flora of
Lithuania."

"Governor-elect," Art said.

J found something unsettling about the proposed landscaping.
What must the Biro River look like? What flora founded its banks?
What sort of Jews would it have irrigated on its way to the Arun
River, on its way to the top of the Sea of Japan?

"These will be the forests surrounding Vilnius. These are the
specs we get from J's office. Fear not, governor, we'll see Jews as
they used to be yet!"

This comment didn't reduce J's discomfort. But, Hayley had
smiled at him again while she made it. He inhaled, counting; held
his breath—thought about Hayley's book of breathing exercises,
wondered when she'd get it to him and how—realized he was still
holding his breath; exhaled without any sense of calm or rhythm.

A minute later they could hear the machines, and, in another
minute, they reached the site. An area at least a mile across had been
reduced to mud. At its center, giant excavators were digging out
more mud. Construction materials were sorted into heaps mistakable
for reclaimed detritus, and everywhere there were workers in hard
hats doing things. The workers all wore orange mesh safety vests,
and one side of the vests read "Contractor for Christ" and the other
side bore a large Celtic cross. The vests were reversible, and so some
workers had the cross on the front, and others had it on the back.

"What's with the logs?" Art asked, pointing.

They'd stopped now; going any further seemed beyond the
Mercedes' all-terrain capacities. J followed Art's point. Indeed, a
tremendous heap of 4" round logs dominated one corner of the site.

"Building materials!" Hayley yelled over the construction din. "Next time you visit, we should have the right kind of trees in!"

"Eyesore," the driver said. J had expected the driver to have an Eastern European, or maybe even an Israeli, accent. Instead, his one utterance conveyed the totalizing blandness of a TV weather forecast.

"I'm good," Arthur said. "You good, J?"

"Scots pine," J said, "and spruce."

Over the next few days, J and Art were both required to attend a great number of meetings, separate meetings, though often with the same people. Whether it was the three kings, Hayley, or some other aspect of their organization's doing, a real interest in keeping projects separate prevailed; and, Art's political career and J's museum were very different kinds of projects. Art had carved out early morning space for a run each day, and he insisted that J join him on these, their only otherwise unscheduled hour. Of course, J wasn't a very good runner, certainly not good enough to keep up with Art while keeping enough breath to speak, which meant that Art did most of the talking. There was no chance to share anything about Jeremiah and Christian, or DC, or Birobid-zhan, or his growing discomfort, or what J wished most of all to confide, his feelings for E. But then, maybe not being able was a blessing, too—what was he supposed to say? What could Art say? And that J was subject evermore to the little girl's gravitational pull...Instead J learned a lot about the competing pressures Art faced from his New Mexico backers, which included Walter and Walter's friends, and the shadowy national bullshit that trickled down, overlord style, from the three kings.

J panted, heart rate pegged, desperate to allay some imagined suspicion about him and Chase by confiding about E.

Art ambled on about the people he'd met on the campaign trail, and about how relieved he was to have his Evangelical faith without having to display and leverage that faith. Art bragged that he was "the only closeted fundamentalist politician in these United States!" When Art did bring up Chase, it was to dismiss her with a wave of his hand, saying that she was busy being Chase, as per usual. Then, Art would apologize again for Chase not liaising between the two of them, after all.

Ragged breath. Gasp acknowledgement monosyllabically. Ragged breath.

There were no wonders. There was no seduction. An eagle did not snatch a goose out of the air.

These extended sprints would inevitably end with Art resting his hands on his knees in front of the manor. He'd slap J on the back a few times, commenting with each slap on how J had run him straight into the ground. J, struggling to not vomit, wouldn't be able to answer. Art would thank J for motivating him to run, and promise to pick up the pace next time. All of this as if J hadn't heard the same thing the morning before.

Still, J appreciated the joke. He sympathized with Art's distaste for his masters. His distaste made Art more human.

On their fourth day, they reported simultaneously through different doors to the same luncheon to find only Hayley. She stood at the end of a long thick mahogany table—mahogany was the default wood in the manor—an enormous picnic basket in front of her.

"What's this?" Art asked.

"This is a gift, gentlemen," Hayley said, "of time together. Mine to you. Field trip?"

"I'd love a field trip!" J said.

"Careful, Jacob," Art said.

"Oh, Art," Hayley said. "As if you aren't dying to go visit the Garden of Eden."

"Fine," Art said.

"You can drive," Hayley said.

"I said fine," Art said.

They traipsed eccentrically across the hilltop from the manor to the tree line, a zigzagging that, despite Art's nonchalant acceptance of their course, J took as evidence of another ruse until mere yards from the lawn's edge, where the wear of foot traffic from multiple vectors first became perceptible and then eventually merged into a single path trodden into the dirt. The path led to a set of steps, angled to stay out of view until one reached them.

Hayley tossed Art her keys, and he unlocked a rather ordinary mid-sized, mid-model, domestic sedan with a clean but unremarkable cloth interior. They climbed in and, beneath an overtone of Pine Sol and mint, J caught the faintest hint of stale raisins and a scent akin to that of charred plastic. J smirked: Hayley smoked cigarettes. Hayley, the savant, perfect in every way, was a woman who discreetly snuck cigarettes in her car. J leaned across the backseat to see across the center console as Art reversed the car.

When they turned out of the employee lot onto a well lit, well paved, pedestrian road, Art winked at Hayley. Hayley raised an eyebrow and smiled. J expected she'd pull out her cigarettes, and this expectation sparked a longing he'd not experienced since his summer in the Catskills at Camp Mishkon after junior year of Yeshiva when they'd all taken up smoking. He didn't dare ruin the possibility by commenting as much, not even when Hayley handed him back the picnic basket to open the glove compartment. For a second, he even mistook the product of her fumbling for the pack he anticipated. J recognized the prize she held up triumphantly to be a cassette tape, which she promptly inserted into the car's cassette deck.

Three chords of the organ, and J knew it was a hymn. Several bars about Christ's Zion later, Hayley and Art singing together to it, out of key, top of their lungs, and J's only solace was that at least he hadn't suddenly taken up smoking at 38. Art made eye contact with J through the rearview and nodded at J. J shook his head. His friend nodded. J looked away from the mirror. He waited out the ride to the young earth museum as best as he could, him silent, them anything but.

They parked before a concave-fronted building whose glass front was interspersed with sand-colored concrete columns that extended from a grey plaza to the concrete roof, thirty feet above. Art made a snarky comment about a plaster cast of what seemed to be a small stegosaurus in front of the main entrance, while Hayley smoothed the front of her dress with both hands in a gesture that J thought more typical of less licit activities than belting out hymns.

Christian hymns, J thought. Just being in the car felt like a betrayal of the man in the van. Betrayal, and J couldn't stop from running through the list: Esther, Chase, the poor dying man who dreamed him, the girls—the list was fatigued and fatigued J. J opened the car's door, and pulled himself out, upright.

A lilt had infected Art's stride, and his cheeks were flushed. He did a snorting thing, pinching his nostrils with his left thumb and forefinger, his left shoulder swagging. The two of them, J marveled. Could they possibly realize that they seemed as if they'd...Art reached back and clapped J's shoulder by way of bringing J forward to walk alongside them.

"Seems you do have some affection for each other," J said, trying to catch some of their bounce.

Hayley winked and Art took a breath that seemed to sober him. A shame: J liked seeing Art a little loose, happy.

"We have some things in common," Hayley said. "Experiences separated but shared nonetheless. Definitely shared."

"I like Hayley, J," Art said. "I've always liked Hayley."

"Governor," Hayley said. "Please. There's no need."

"Ok. Well. I like you right now," Art said, his grin back.

Hayley beamed and winked; J found himself resenting the hymn.

They walked into the museum's lobby. Art draped around J's shoulders. Hayley waived over the line waiting at the admissions desk, and the clerk there waived eagerly back. Obviously, they were exempt from needing tickets. The guard unhooked a velvet rope from a stanchion, not even requiring that they walk through the small turnstile, and they continued on into a room labeled "The Garden of Eden."

"You've been before?" Hayley asked Art.

"I thought it would be bigger," Art said.

"Then, no, governor," Hayley said. "You haven't."

"Yeah, never really been much of one for museums, per se," Art said.

"Then…never mind."

J looked around. The exhibit was small, certainly, paltry really. But it wasn't the scale of the thing that didn't resonate. Adam was a meek white dude with vaguely long hair and a trim beard. He would have fit in well wearing flannel on a 1970s country album cover, a look that acknowledged a loosening of norms while remembering its Christian country propriety. Eve looked like the Adam's younger sister, but with her face done up and her eyebrows tweezed.

In J's dream, Adam didn't look like anybody, was a presence, a sort of watching wind, and Eve, too, a presence intertwined with Adam's, the two a force, a breath, a consciousness. And whereas in the dream they surveyed the sprawled and endless plain, great hordes of animals in procession, ready to be named, here there were a few whitetail deer and some ibex, the latter seemingly made from the same mold as the deer, but given different horns. There were some fake trees that looked lifted from a suburban backyard, behind which the walls were painted to look like the rolling foothills of the American mountain west. In a nod to less domestic climes, a few tropical flowers were interspersed beneath the trees. And, in a further nod, this one to less contemporary times, there was a large reptilian creature that J at first took for a dinosaur, and then realized was the prelapsarian snake, the snake who still walked upright and spoke in a tongue he shared with God and man, newly made.

Something about it made J want for a sharpie with which to scrawl anarchy symbols all over everything.

"This is all wrong," J said.

"Wrong?"

"Wrong trees, wrong landscape, wrong animals," J said.

"What?" Hayley asked.

"And Adam and Even: they're too corporeal, too human, much too country-club, too rec-room white American," J said, biting his tongue against the qualifier "Christian."

"You should listen to him," Art said.

"It's just an exhibit," Hayley said. "I don't believe in it."

"Well the exhibit is wrong," J said.

Hayley looked at him, her head tilted, her eyes cocked. J felt his face grow warm. She looked over at Art. Art straightened up.

"We expected something bigger; something more…something not as Lilliputian."

"Lilliputian?" Hayley asked, all signs of quizzicality gone from her face. "Really, governor? Lilliputian?"

"Governor-elect, Hayley. Elect."

J took his cue from Art's visible relief at Hayley's redirection. Her mouth twisted, her lids down an f-stop, her nostrils flared. J receded a half step. J watched Hayley discreetly inhale and mimicked her inhalation, his ear receding from his temples as hers did from hers. When she'd finished exhaling, she'd resumed her typically centered, authoritarian disposition and J knew better than to let anyone know of his dream, or of the dream that dreamt him.

"Sandwiches, governor?"

"Starving," J said.

"I hope you knew better than to pack ham," Art said.

"Of us three, only you persist in pretending," Hayley said.

Art's left eye twitched almost shut and his lips tightened. They'd almost gotten along, almost had fun. Of course Art believed. J knew that. And J knew that it must kill Art a little inside to work for those whose faith was a wink and a wink and a nod and a nod. If J had only managed to control himself…and J felt a great surge of gratitude and love for Art.

Who else had ever thrown themselves on their swords for J?

Who ever would?

CHAPTER THIRTY-SIX

AT THE END OF winter, The Foundation for the Preservation of Shared Culture and Heritage—the shell beneath which J operated—summoned J to yet another supposedly important dinner. As he did with some frequency, he arrived late, tardiness the last resistance. When he pulled open the bamboo-framed slide of an upstairs private room at a Japanese restaurant, he saw Hayley at the far corner of the table. He caught himself immediately glancing down at his socks, checking them for embarrassments, blemishes. Hayley acknowledged him with a quick wave and smile, gestures she affected without lapsing in her conversation. J tried not to trip over other diners as he tiptoed his way to the only open spot. J didn't recognize anyone besides Hayley, really didn't know why he'd been told to attend.

J couldn't discern whether the dinner was about Western water rights or whether that was preamble banter.

He ordered a Sapporo from the server, and then someone poured him Sake, and then his phone buzzed. The men beside him encouraged him to go ahead and check it: it was DC, after all. Hayley had texted from beneath the table that he should call her phone. J did so, also from beneath the table, prophylactically covering the phone's speaker that no one might hear the faint ringing, not that anyone could have heard it over the general conversation, which seemed to have to do with fire insurance.

Hayley pulled her phone out of her purse, apologizing, made a big show of flabbergast when she looked at the caller ID, and excused herself to answer the call.

From beyond the room's sliding rice paper walls, she called J.

J gulped the sea urchin in his mouth, unchewed and mucousy, painful in his esophagus, and excused himself. He answered the phone while he laced his shoes in the hallway; she instructed him to come meet her by the bathrooms. She had something to show him.

Celan: "You sublime a prayer / before each."

He certainly could feel excited to meet Hayley and still care about E (and Chase), not E, but E's daughters—

The restaurant was above a club. The club's hostess directed J down another level still to the basement. There, dim bare bulbs encased in safety cages lit a long low-ceilinged corridor and shed patterns like oil-slick rainbows in the concrete floor's uneven polish. A third of the way down the hallway, Hayley leaned against the thick black gloss of one cinder wall across from a row of softly glowing stall doors, her phone yet before her. J, suit jacket still on, left hand in his trouser pocket, heard, acutely, his leather heels on the cement floor, could practically see himself, themselves, shadows in corporate-wear echoing, converging.

Esther had held her thirtieth birthday at a place like this on the lower east side. J had been almost thirty-four, and in the year since his discovery they'd come up with a system to excuse themselves to go fight. That night, they had come down to a set of bathrooms like these, their personal back alley, their outside to which to take it, their after-school schoolyard. E had grabbed his bicep aside a stall.

"Where the fuck are you?" She'd asked.

"Why are you so mad?"

"Did you even care that Aryeh was hitting on me?"

"Should I be mad at him?"

"You should be mad at me!"

"Then why the hell are you mad at me?"

E had thrown up her hands in his face, and the bangles on her arms had flown off. Some had clattered onto the floor, others, impacting on edge, jangled away. J hadn't bothered to explain that he had been distracted trying to will an image of his dreamer onto the Polaroid i-Zone photos the guests kept snapping. Instead, he had leaned back against the wall and, to not reward her behavior, didn't help collect her fallen bracelets. A man at the far end of the hallway had stooped into the oblong light of an exit sign for the furthest one, then continued collecting fallen bracelets as he'd approached so that he and E met midway.

J had stood against the wall; for all the world, anyone in wait.

E had taken the bracelets from that man and started back to the stairs, the man beside her. They had passed J like he could be, for all the world, anyone. J hadn't bothered to follow.

One of the glowing doors to J's left opened and a young woman in a gold skirt exited, revealing a compact toilet and sink. J turned flat to the gloss wall to the let the woman pass.

"What is it?" he asked loudly, still at practically shouting distance.

"Come here," Hayley said, slipping the phone into a bag slung on her shoulder.

He reminded himself that no one was invested in physically hurting him.

J walked toward her until he smelled the citrus of her soap, the hibiscus of her body lotion, her scent like standing outside Art's garden wall in midday, mid-summer Albuquerque.

"Here," she said. "Give me your hand."

He gave her his hand and she took it in both of hers, one of her fists clutching his thumb and forefinger, the other the flesh between his pinky and wrist. The savant held his hand like something large, like an oversize children's book, like a driver's education steering wheel. She pressed his hand under her skirt against her pubic mound, gave a little moan when his fingers went, as if of their own accord between her labia.

"See?" she said. "See?"

He could see that she wasn't Chase or E or even Mary, could see that even if he wasn't devoted to his liege's spouse, Art's wife, Chase, that this was a bad idea. He could see that this would distract him from his ex-girlfriend's children's lives lived on social media— He wondered if could still flee to the Jewish Oblast on the eastern edge of Russia.

Hayley heaved against his hand; thrust his hand into her.

She whispered, all neck and chin, to come on, and pulled him into one of the bathrooms.

She stood one foot on the toilet's tank, braced the other on the far wall. She hung from a hand on an overhead pipe, knotted her other hand in J's hair and pushed his head down, and pulled his head into her crotch. She let go of the pipe to pull her skirt out of the way, her weight braced on his mouth against her, and her skirt draped over his head. Like a nineteenth-century photographer beneath his hood, J performed, his world upside, focused through a dilating aperture.

When her pelvic muscles, when her lower abdomen, when the curve of muscle along the bottom interiors of her thighs, tightened, when they quivered, she pushed his head away, out from under, as it were, and slid down from her perch. She looked at him, eyes a-glint; hers, a broad, closed-mouth smile. J wanted her; he didn't care about anything; he wanted to feel Hayley convulse. She took his head in her hands and kissed him. While they kissed he felt her fingers along his cheeks, felt her fingers in the corners of their lips, felt the introduction of a pill into his mouth.

Is this, J wondered, a giveaway from the dreamer? A bone thrown to compensate J for his romantic failures and the bland outcomes of his professional perseverance? A more earthly compensation? Could the kings gift their savant's body?

J didn't care; he wanted Hayley; J yearned to live inside her; he swallowed.

She grabbed his hand.

Giggling, Hayley dragged him back out of the stall and led him running down the hallway, their hard-heeled shoes loud and echoing. The stall door slammed and re-slammed behind them. They pursued the winter city, venal and vernal in their touch of ecstasy, the bathrooms of nightclubs the hopscotch squares of their buoyant seductions. The pills subsided, bite-marks like leopard prints across their bodies, their desire more for touch and kiss, for scotch than cigarettes, they wandered into the almost dawn, stumbled into a taxi, and then to the room at the St. Regis that Art kept for the unexpected, now that he was installed as governor.

They woke to the day half-finished, fucked for the hangover, champagne for the hangover, room service burgers and fries, and hid from the sunlight until at five-thirty Hayley slipped her dress over her bra and panties. J leaned forward to stand, but she pushed him back onto the chair beside the glass-topped desk from which he'd been picking cold French fries, dipping them in relish. She knelt in front of him and slipped her hand into his boxers. The angle seemed as if it would be awkward for her wrist, but she left his underwear in place, slowly tugging on his cock until he grew hard, as if he possessed some dignity his flaccidity might impugn and she wished to save him from dishonor.

Then she pulled down his underwear and put her mouth around his cock. When J thought he was far enough from orgasm, but also too close, he tried to lift her up, pull her towards him, but she withdrew barely enough, her tongue still against him, to say, "No. Sit."

He came. She stood up and tousled his hair. She was going to leave now, and when she left, that would be it. They would return to their roles: museum-maker and savant, nothing more or less. Then Hayley slipped on her shoes and left, put together, fresh even, for all that, self-possessed.

J waited a moment, then dressed and left the room too, set off in search of a cab, as if in ordinary return commute.

CHAPTER THIRTY-SEVEN

A FEW BLOCKS SHY of his building, J asked his driver to take him to the Holocaust Museum instead. (The other Holocaust Museum, he thought.) The car turned south. The scent of Hayley, her and fancy hotel room soap, enticingly putrid on his fingers, why the museum, why now? His thoughts shellacked in sooty grease.

He waited in a line of tourists to pass through the metal detector. His skin an uneasy interface between his internal temperature swings, the legacy of the cab's brisk AC, and the late afternoon's muggy sun. His few cultural encounters in this city had all been under the guise of galas. J wondered if he should check in with Jeremiah. He walked past a guard on the hard stone floors ubiquitous in museums, and into a black room that housed the first section of the permanent exhibition.

It featured glass-cased photos of American-liberated concentration camps. He stopped and looked at one. Skeletal men in striped pajamas with matching railroad conductor hats stood clustered against a wire fence, the towers to either side of them empty of guards. Presumably the men had gathered to stare at the approaching American army. They didn't smile, but clearly wouldn't have gathered if they feared the soldiers. This was the last moment of their captivity, J thought, though he knew this was an idealized myth, that their liberation wouldn't offer them any return, or, for a period of years, anywhere to even go. The gates would open, the guards carted off, but these men would stay.

They would stay in the camps, quarantined for dysentery, which disease received no notice of the end of hostilities, and so cheerily murdered for months beyond when there last were Nazis to do the killing. They would stay in the camps because no one would know where to put them. No one would want to take them. There would be no place to go. Some would sneak out in the night, escape to Israel, hunted by the British along the shore, conscripted to fight the Arabs intermingled in the British mandate's countryside.

None of this was news, not to J, not to anyone.

Still, J thought, an army approaches; the murderers flee their elaborate crime scene. The murderers intended victims, those still able to stand, obviously, horribly decimated, approach; and the photographer calls a halt. The photographer tells the army to not advance, to not grant aid and the army defers. First the photographer must make pictures of what they find. The photographer, the vanguard of history, halts its human impulse to give aid (and retards its rearward impulse to flee in revulsion).

In high school, J had an American history teacher who had liberated Dachau, had literally been at the front of his troops when they stumbled into that first concentration camp. The teacher, Major Stuart, had told this to J and his parents as they toured the school's campus, a nineteenth-century collection of white-trimmed brick buildings surrounded by long lawns divided from the wooded Pennsylvania hills by long low stone walls. Major Stuart had told this, his hands clasped behind his back, as they walked around the stereotypically lovely summertime grounds. J didn't know whether the Major told it because he had nothing else in common with the Jewish family, or because he wanted to point out to them the unique importance of military aptitude for Jews, or because a stunning summer day spent wandering bucolic fields were reminiscent of Dachau for him.

Perhaps it was J that triggered Stuart's memory.

J wondered whether Major Stuart had participated in the summary execution of the Dachau guards. J hoped that he had, wished that he could do so as well. He really did, J realized; he longed to line up SS guards against a wall and then fire into them, the reverberations of a heavy-caliber automatic weapon buffeting his arms until his muscles seemed as if they might separate from his bones, until he screamed. Final catharsis. Revenge. He wanted revenge on those men for forever sealing the story of the man in the van who dreamt him. J wanted revenge against those murderers who denied him access to his own creation.

Shooting was tame, humane even. He knew that some of the American soldiers had simply shot the guards in the legs and then handed blunt instruments over to the camp inhabitants still strong enough to wield them. J knew all about the prisoner who beheaded a guard with an American-lent bayonet. Those people belonged to history, could, as Chase might point out, be the subjects of stories.

He thought of Chase and he wanted to kill Nazis. He wanted to kill Nazis and he thought of Hayley, of her smell with his tongue pulling up against her clit and the stubble above her engorged labia rough against the shadow on his lip, his nose pressed against the top of her pelvic bone as if to long for what lay behind her skin.

J thought: the man whose life has nothing to do with the day he obeys an official notice and uncomfortably boards a train with his fellows to several days later disembark into the flash of Treblinka's tunnel, beaten naked into the gas, dead twenty minutes after arrival, that man's death has as little to do with his life as the death of the man who succumbs in his sleep.

In one of his Tucson childhood synagogues, a congregant who inevitably dressed in a turquoise bolo tie, matching boots and belt, had been enslaved at Auschwitz. Twice a year, during the *shalashudos* meal between afternoon and evening prayers on Shabbat, on the *yartzeit* of two relatives whose relation to the ex-slave J could not remember, the man would stand up, and in place of the usual *drosha* about the week's Torah *parsha*, so the young shouldn't forget, he would begin, "The soldiers came to our village…"

He would end with mumbling; sometimes tears would end his account. At other times, he would end in rage. A congregant would take his arm and ask him to sit, "Nu, the children." Those same children the man so wished to give his real memory, to give his experience at Auschwitz.

How could the young forget? All their grandparents had been soldiers in the war. J's own grandfather had shot Germans in Holland until leaving the battlefield with a bullet in his thigh. There was Major Stuart, of course, but then also all the people who'd lost cousins in the camps, or who knew someone who had. J had seen Elie Wiesel speak! As far as J knew, back then, at any given moment Israeli Nazi hunters were operating in Argentina. It seemed impossible that these people would disappear. Yet die they all had. Inevitably, inexorably.

There was no one left to act out violence against, except that the man was in the van anyway, slowly succumbing.

He's outdreamt his relevance, J thought: will he outdream the memory of what was done to him? Dream a world in which the Holocaust has been forgotten? In which things like this museum have been repurposed to document newer and hipper genocides? Is that the dying man's fantasy? Will our museum in Kentucky somehow better preserve him? Or will his dream extend all the way until the next murderous impulse towards the Jews takes hold, and we are once again herded down the streets towards boxcars and camps and death chambers? Will he finally dream another man who, like him, ends in the back of a van with a pipe from exhaust to box chamber, surrounded by dying children?

The dreamer had dreamt J just far enough away that J's life shouldn't be all about the Holocaust, but just close enough that he could still access its legacy.

J was bereft of his serotonin, had the smell of hotel soap on his skin, of the savant on his clothes.

J left the museum, flagged another cab home. He had work to do, obviously, always. He sat on his couch and looked out at the still bright street. It was certainly too early for bed. His apartment felt small, as if he'd abandoned it for much more than a night, had come home to it expansive beyond its provincial margins, its enactment of a self that J had molted during his absence.

J thought about not wanting to work on the museum: what would the museum even be? He would turn thirty-nine in less than a year and had never been on a real adventure, never been further away from his home culture than a ferry ride to Tangiers from Spain. *Catharsis,* J thought, *violence.*

How does one express the desire to feel one's work? The desire to feel? How does one ask for wonders and signs? How does one ask for the arm around their shoulders that holds them steadfast and also the chance to be that arm? How does one remain patient before the outcome of that patience is revealed? How does one feel? Find feeling?

And in the end, we pursue what we do not want for lack of what we do want. For some reason, he remembered his mother's funeral, and how the yeshiva boys taking turns throwing dirt into the grave had been eager to perform their religious duty, and how J's father had chided them: *not so fast, not so much in a hurry, slow down.*

The last of the Jews would have perished had the US not first financed the Soviet efforts, and then entered the war with its great wealth and power and twisted mythology; all predicated on land and opportunity seized through genocide and developed by the enslaved labor of real humans, Africans seized and exported. The rationales that justified those actions evolved into proper ideologies in the 19th Century, and those ideologies, the ideology of racism, was weaponized by the Nazis and used to murder the Jews, just as the exploited wealth and power from that ideology built the country that saved the Jews. They were all guilty, J knew that, and still he wished there was more that he could do, personally, with his hands, to bring about justice, even if that meant finding some ancient perpetrator and compelling them to justice.

J was only a dream, and yet even a dream has some agency, and if it has agency, it can follow a set of ethics. Ethics and agency alike require parsing. J was exhausted.

Of course he was tired: he'd been up all night with Hayley, high and fucking.

PART FOUR

*In every stone, there is an appeal of the
stone.*

*In every spring, there is an appeal of the
water.*

*In every Jew, there is an appeal to the
day.*

*For the stone can longer stand to be
stone.*

*The spring dreams forever of being held
back.*

The Jew expects each day to live.

~~Edmond Jabes
The Book of Questions: Volume 1
(Translated by Rosemarie Waldrop)

CHAPTER THIRTY-EIGHT

ON AN OCTOBER DAY whose warm weather suggested early September, Chase picked J up at the Albuquerque airport. J had only seen her on TV since he'd left New Mexico, except for once across a DC ballroom she'd traversed on Art's arm. He shifted his roller bag from his right hand to his left, and his scalp tingled when the bag rocked as if it might tip. He caught his breath despite himself, smiled and blushed.

Chase smiled back as she strode towards him. She'd mastered the trick of interweaving layers of clothing such that it seemed as though she moved nakedly beneath a billowing mass of rich fabrics that hovered around her, a kind of crushed velvet posh iteration of a Renaissance painter's conception of angels shielding an innocent Eve, Eve modeled on Diana, that and a touch of the flamboyance of Bedouin banners. She was tan and bright and coiffed.

J extended an awkward right hand and Chase spread her arms, palms open, thumbs turned out, threw her head back, her mouth squashed in mock confusion, kept on toward him. Chase embraced him. J hugged her back gingerly, holding his body away from hers in deference, but she was strong. He relaxed into her hold even as he tightened his grip, clung to her, her pulling him further against her, against her breasts, crushed, soft and bra-less, her hips matched against his hips, her breath on his neck, and everywhere around him that airport duty-free smell, though now it had acquired another strain, too, a musk that wasn't quite sage and wasn't quiet feline but somehow Arabian.

"I love you," J whispered. She gently rubbed his back with one open hand, the other still firmly securing his waist. He hadn't meant to speak, hadn't meant to tell her he loved her; but she hadn't let go. He held on to her with all of his strength. He felt real. He tried not to cry. He felt all of his skin tingling. Behind them, his suitcase fell over with a thud, and he pulled back a few inches.

They looked at each other and laughed.

"Come on," Chase said. "There's a birthday celebration waiting for you."

"I can't believe you've done all this for my birthday," J said, though beyond broaching their caesura, bridging it for now, he didn't know what she'd really done for his birthday, or really what anyone had done for that matter.

"You only become a demi-octogenarian once," Chase said, moving forward, twisting her head to speak to J, who raised his roller bag handle and hastily reassembled his briefcase upon it and scurried after her.

"Excuse me?" he asked.

"Forty. You only turn forty once."

"Wait," J said.

"We're late," Chase said.

"I'm not turning forty," J said, stopping.

"What?" Chase asked.

"I'll be thirty-nine Sunday."

"Are you sure?"

"Am I sure?"

"Get the fuck out! Really?" Chase said, and laughed. "Holy shit!"

"You guys are throwing me a fortieth birthday party," J said. "Seriously. How the fuck did that happen?"

"We just thought," Chase said, and then bent over, clutching her side laughing. "You can't tell them! You cannot. Please!"

"How?"

"They'll be heartbroken."

"Can't tell them?" J exclaimed, mock querulous, mock outraged, but he was laughing now, too. "But I'll have to lie forever!"

"You've always seemed young for your age? You've always seemed mature beyond your years?"

"Stop!"

They stumbled out of the terminal, trying to catch their breaths between bouts of hysteria, and crossed the street to where Chase had parked her truck in the shelter of a bank of solar panels. They stepped into the shade; blind a moment before their pupils dilated, freed from the stark afternoon light.

"So, seriously?" J asked, resting a hand on Chase's shoulder.

"I don't really care," she said.

"It'll be fun being forty a year early."

"Who ever said that in history?"

They smiled at each other, and then they were kissing. J clutched her, and her lips mashed into his so hard that he thought their teeth would bang against each other and he felt as if a molten core was climbing his spine and screaming its way out of his scalp.

"Holy shit," he said. "I've missed you."

Chase gave him a peck of a kiss and stood back. They looked at each other. Then she wrapped her arms around his neck and kissed him again. J closed his eyes and swooned. She took his face in his hands and pushed herself away. He opened his eyes.

"I've missed you, too," she said, her eyes scanning his, her voice that old opry stage hoarse and coarse that so smote him.

They got into the truck. J ran a finger along the gleaming radio dial, nostalgic for that first drive out of New York. She looked over at him and smiled, turned the key in the ignition, grabbed the shift wand, underhand, and pulled the truck into gear, her head tilted, her lower lip between her teeth.

They barely spoke on the drive to Walter's ranch, too busy smiling and blushing and reveling in hormones that shifted blood pressure and neurology in unpredictable patterns across their bodies, the city opening up into desert, and then into buttes and mountains. Home, J thought, his lips tingling where her lips had bruised his against his teeth. He savored the pain, thought: home.

J wished that he wouldn't have to hide this connection with Chase and, paradoxically, he looked very much forward to seeing everyone, to seeing Art. His brain bubbled lenticular puffs that couldn't think through anything in words, anyway. He laughed quietly.

"Yes?" Chase asked, eyes wet, smiling, all melody.

"Forty," J said. "You. I can't even make words."

She smiled at him again, left the road to take care of itself. He reached over and took her right thigh in his hand, rubbed it through her folds of fabric.

"I'm glad," she said, gaze fixed forward on the carless road through the yellowed landscape.

"Me too," J said. "Me too."

At the ranch, Walter walked down off the porch to greet them, wearing what J was pretty sure were the clothes J had shed on his first arrival, a year earlier. Chase grabbed J's bag out of the back of the truck while Walter pumped his hand and clapped his shoulder. She brought the bag over to J, touched his arm while handing it off to him to tiptoe to kiss her father's cheek.

"Dad," Chase said.

Walter laughed, clearly pleased, and wrapped an arm around J's shoulders to steer him. J looked back at Chase, and she smiled and touched his arm again.

"I see you two have made up," Art called from the porch, walking into the sunlit swath at the edge of the steps.

J blushed.

"Made up from what?" Chase asked, walking behind J and Walter.

"Whatever works," Art said. "I love everybody."

Walter laughed again, and directed J to a spare bedroom while Chase collapsed onto the couch. The bedroom, J was dismayed to see, featured an iron cot with a true-to-period, thin, straw mattress.

He was too tired to demand a transfer from the ranch hand special to more brothel-fabulous quarters. He hung his suit jacket and lay down, tingling with the sense of Chase, straw ticking tickling his back, Chase off elsewhere in the house, and fell asleep.

As if it had always waited here for his return, the voice of creation imbued his sleep world.

> *Viyihee erev viyihee boker:*
> *It was evening and it was morning.*
> *Viyihee erev:*
> *It was evening*
> *Viyihee boker:*
> *And it was morning.*
> *Viyihee erev viyihee boker*
> *Viyihee erev viyihee boker*
> *It was evening and it was morning.*

Each time the voice said, *erev*, the world turned dark and the moon and the stars shone. When it said, *boker*, all turned to light, sun high in the sky. Each repetition began without pause at the conclusion of the last, as if God, drifting off in imagination of new worlds, had absentmindedly leaned against the switch that flicked between day and night.

Day and night.

Night and day.

Day and night.

Night and day.

J woke to a hand on his shoulder.

"You'll want to shower before the rest get here."

But J could not tell what this was, or what 'the rest' were, or what a 'shower' might be.

"It was night and it was day, *Yom Shishi.*"

"Wake up, buddy," Walter said.

Yom Shishi: one day; Day Six. The completion of the sentence returned J, the first day's completion, the equation in which "it was night; it was morning" equaled one day, equaled day one, the sixth day. Who and where he was came into focus sufficient for J to not tell Walter that in his dream the night and day must not have been different nights and different days, but the same one, skipping, repeating, unable to conclude without a name for what it was.

"Genesis," Walter said.

"The day."

"Would have made magnificent cinema. I've always believed that."

"I was just dreaming," J said. "And it was only the first day, but it was also the sixth."

He was a man about to celebrate his fortieth birthday a year early, who existed in the dream of another man, who was being gassed in the back of a van during the Holocaust, and he was at the house of the father-in-law of his employer, his employer who was also his friend, his only real friend, a friend he'd met because he, the governor of New Mexico, was married to the woman with whom J was very much in love. He was J. He was Jacob, and he was in an elaborate and eccentric ranch house in New Mexico, in which he was about to celebrate his fortieth birthday a year early. And, J was fully awake.

"Creation! What imagery! Out of the void: Earth! Water! Light! Dark! Trees! Animals! And then a man with only an invisible, unknowable deity for company, Adam, a man very literally God's son, who longs and because he longs is forever split into parts, one part leading the other into violation, into sin. Obey God or love a woman! If that isn't the beating heart of cinema...to choose love and thus be cast from paradise!"

"Whatever," J said.

"Milton got it. Especially when he wrote about their doing it."

"Walter…"

"Beautiful, dutiful sex in the garden, then sin, then the real sex. Needy, rough, intoxicating, passionate sex! Flowers crushed, bramble bower thrashed! Beautiful!"

"Ok," J said.

Walter paused a moment, then exclaimed: "Philistine!"

"Whatever you say, Walter."

"Fine. Go clean up."

J was not, this time, to stand on the granite boulder and survey the ranch's disposition while water from an overhead porcelain tub drained over him. Instead, his shower, his bath, consisted of a large tin washtub filled by an elbowed faucet that swung out from the wall at waist height. Beside it were a stiff brush and crude soap flakes. A concession, J thought, that he didn't have to boil water over an open fire to fill the thing. There was something gross about squatting in his own wastewater, also something cold.

Scoured, de-scented, he dressed.

He overheard the mutterings of arrival, greetings and counter greetings, the sound of ice poured into glasses. J went to open his room's door—this by means of a cut glass knob inlaid with brass ribbon that formed a swan with a woman's torso rising up out of swirls and traces. Of course that was the doorknob—and then hesitated.

Two dreams: one of creating something, a museum, a story, a Nazi-hunting agency, whatever, and another of creation skipping. Esther. Chase. Neither dream was plausible; J understood that.

He'd had no success pursuing his dreamer. He dreaded what the museum might turn out to be.

Cut the rope, he thought. You're here now. And J remembered that he did indeed love Chase, and that Chase loved him, impossible for it to turn out though it might be.

J sighed, breathed, resigned himself to opening the door. If he wasn't always looking into the Promised Land from a mountain beyond its borders, not worthy of the sanctum of the Holy Grail...

"A drink for this man!" Art greeted him, stretching an arm out to clasp J's shoulder, Art's thumb's pressure in J's collarbone relieving the tension at the base of J's spine, spreading warmth down into his hips.

"A drink for me!"

And with what a hand Art clasped J's shoulder! Manicured to the rough edge of reasonable, the forearm above it bared beneath the pushed-up sleeve of a crisply starched pink dress shirt J knew to be custom-sewn, the bared forearm leanly muscled, its lightly sun-browned skin and sun-bleached hair neatly groomed. From Art's far side, Chase raised her glass and winked at J.

From beside Chase, Hayley raised a glass and winked as well.

The wink, the winks, shamed J. The winks exposed J. So did his desire for Art's hand on his shoulder. Art's hand braced him. The hand of Chase's perfect human on his shoulder and Hayley's shoulder whispering against Chase's.

Walter's objects froze time; Chase's perfect human enacted it; maybe Walter was right to point out that the thing about the young was that they kept making them, that the thing about humans is that they're susceptible to desiring those that desire them, and everyone wants their own Arthur, wants that Arthur to publicize his desire for them.

J wanted to ask Chase whether she'd slept with him so he'd leave, or if she'd asked him to leave because she'd slept with him, and whether, whichever, she would have followed had he left. It angered him that he had these questions loudly, now, when finally Chase had warmed to him, when the questions' persistence threatened his ability to navigate towards Chase. If Chase hadn't abandoned him for the last year, he wouldn't have followed Hayley into that basement bathroom after she put his hand under her skirt; if J had left, he never would have met Hayley. And still, still J had done nothing of substance for the man in the van, who continued to die. What, then, of J's petty discomforts? So, he was uncomfortable. So what.

So what?

Hayley was here. So what. Fuck.

What did J expect of the farce of a fortieth birthday on his thirty-ninth birthday? It was too perfect an allegory to bother to examine.

Walter brought J a drink. Judging by the odd shape of the ice chunk inside of it, someone had put pick and hammer to work on a hand-sawn block of solid lake. J raised his glass, and the rest of the room did as well, ten guests in all. Aside from Walter, Chase, Hayley and Art, J recognized three more. Margaret was a donor to Art's enterprises. Her husband, Louis, ran an investment firm with offices in DC. Karl was Art's aide in New Mexico, the man J had seen at the gate his first morning on the patio with Art. Karl: the man by whom the city once had called. Beyond these, Art introduced a mother and her daughter, Rachel and Chrissy, and a young woman named Erin. J assumed that either Chrissy or Erin was Karl's date, whether Karl knew it or not, but J couldn't tell which woman was whose date.

Walter suggested the porch and pre-dinner cigars.

That Chase obeyed the gender divide, and stayed in the house with the other women, surprised J. He was equally surprised the men hadn't simply instructed Hayley to join them; J imagined the pull of tobacco must sting for her. Regardless, J followed the four men onto the porch. It was the only fortieth birthday party he was likely to get, damn it. J could have a cigar.

The men assembled in a rumbling of porch boards. Walter, of course, bit the end off his cigar, tipped back in one of the Bronx chairs, and spat the plug between the men perched on the railing and into the yard. Louis sat in the other Bronx chair, and, with thumb and middle finger in a monogrammed silver cutterp's loops, clipped his cigar then passed the cutter on to the others. They lit up in a ritual of massive matches. It occurred to J that all the people at his fortieth birthday party were someone else's friends, and for that matter, were something closer to allies to each other than friends.

His phone buzzed in his pocket. J checked it out of habit, fumbling his cigar. Hayley had texted, "Happy birthday, old man!"

Walter asked whether it was his girlfriend texting, and the other men tittered.

J blushed and said that he didn't have a girlfriend, though he felt as exposed as he had when Chase had winked at him.

"Mistress then, lover, partner, whatever the hell they're calling it now," Walter said.

"Nor by any other name," J said.

"Sure," Art snickered. "But you're a terrible liar. For the record."

J could date; he didn't need to be so damn coy about it; he could sleep around. He wasn't though. Whatever. Or was he? His scalp revealed his anxiety by tingling and prickling, and when it stopped tingling and prickling, J missed its energy.

"The thing about the indulgences of power," Walter said, "Is that none of them are new."

"Meaning?" J asked.

"Brothels," Louis grunted, grinned.

"Brothels?"

"Means that the ultimate indulgence of powerful men is the compulsion of servitude," Louis said. "Such indulgence culminates the night with the servitude of indentured loving."

"Or in a DC hotel room," Karl said.

"Or indeed."

"Excuse me?" J asked.

"Now, now," Art said, "It's J's birthday."

"And?" Walter asked.

"I'm sure J could use a break from Washingtonian antics," Art replied.

J sucked deeply on his cigar, retracted the last trace of his exhalation deep into his lungs, set his head buzzing. Chase was married, for fuck's sake: why was J beholden to not sleeping around? Couldn't Art see that shaming J for Hayley would...J didn't know that Art even knew. Who knew what they were on about? If they kept teasing they'd fuck everything up.

If Art really didn't know anything, and it led to some kind of blow up from Hayley, and then...J didn't feel like considering it.

J sucked on his cigar and winked at the men. The cigar would make his mouth taste like he'd eaten a burnt rabbit, fur and all, in the morning, J knew that, but for now it felt indulgent and powerful, which was a way of saying that because they all smoked cigars, too, he was, while he smoked, one of them. He almost told the story of his night with Hayley. Why not? But he didn't. Why not own it if they already knew? He allowed himself to believe that Karl really was referring to the general mythology of DC hotel rooms as loci of illicit debauchery. Even if they did know, so what? He was single and the savant was of age and single, though the drugs weren't smart, and Hayley worked for the three kings, was the three kings. But why would they care about the drugs?

It had been months ago!

Hayley was right inside. Inside, Chase sat next to Hayley. Hayley: J's lips tingled where Chase had bruised them earlier.

The museum curator; Hayley; Chase.

"I should know of better brothels," Walter said, upset, as if the scrim hiding a gaping hole had been lit. "The ideal brothel."

Louis laughed, told Walter he'd be happy to help field test; he even had some ideas for where they'd maybe start. Art chuckled and nodded, but even from the side, J could see Art's eyes darting. Surely, J thought, Art's evangelism is not some secret he protects by pretending he's ok with the idea of prostitutes. Surely, Art didn't use prostitutes.

"Shit, Art," Walter said. "You don't have to come. In fact, you are married to my daughter."

"I don't have to go either," J said.

"Now it's not even a party." Walter said.

"Art bailed on the hookers first."

"Hookers!" Walter exclaimed. "New York and your penchant for street-walkers and crack-aficionados! We're talking about going to a proper brothel, gentlemen! Ladies in corsets playing piano!"

"Aficionados," Karl said, "of crack. Nice."

"Crack cocaine, Karl, crack cocaine," Walter said. "The indulgence in which makes for the worst kind of whore."

"Never mind," Karl said.

"I guess, Walter," Louis said, "I could always picture you with some hussy, bust booming over her corset, hair tied high. Sure enough, I can picture her scrubbing your back with a bristle brush while you sit in one of them wooden barrel tubs dreaming of your gold panning's prophets of profitry. Miser!"

"Walter has one of those tubs," J said. "I just bathed in it."

"Louis," Walter said. "Fetch you a drink?"

"I'll drink your whiskey," Louis said.

"You guys are just joking, right?" J said. "This is joking, yes?"

Walter popped his feet off the railing and let his chair drop to the porch boards with a bang. He took up Louis' glass and went inside. They all could hear Chase yell at her father to take the cigar outside and the answering slap of his hand on her ass, his guttural laugh distorted by the tobacco chomped in his mouth. The slap jostled J out of his contemplation of whether he might not want to perhaps go to a brothel after all.

"This what you figured on for your birthday?" Louis asked.

"Aren't fortieth birthdays about acknowledging that nothing you've figured on is likely to turn out?" J asked back.

"Fuck," Louis said. "I at least had a kid and a wife and a company of my own when I was forty. Now all I've got are erratic phone calls from the other end of the country asking for more and goddamn more: more things, more money, thanks, Daddy, I love you, Daddy, as long as I give. I've got a succubus of a grown child and a woman who's cranky with new power, desperate for extra time out of the house, and a conniving board what that wants me to appoint a successor. Forty was good. Forty was god damned fucking fantastic."

"You're a cliché, Louis," Art said.

"An entertaining one, I hope."

"That's also a cliché," Art said.

"Don't I damn well know it."

Forty, J thought. The seven years since his last birthday party were enormous. Wrong he corrected himself: thirty-nine. The six years since his last birthday party. He and E had celebrated his thirty-third with a sodden dinner in their Inwood apartment. Not one of the many guests had been anything other than a hand-selected friend. Not with even one of those former friends was J in contact anymore, the abortive phone call to Ward not withstanding. Back then those friends' only questions about his future had been whether he and E would stay in the city after they had kids. A third had favored raising children in the city; a third championed the respective commuter enclaves to which they'd recently retreated; and a third demanded that they forestall procreating at all, but none of them were here and J had no progeny.

J already adrift then, just a week after the revelation, had willed them all silent. They had been all silent. He hadn't even realized yet that he wasn't keeping it all together: the relationship, the apartment, the business. J thought of the dreamer's two girls, and wondered whether already, and whether when, they would ride the box truck to the woods, and who would hold their hands and who would comfort them.

E had chosen, chosen to raise children in the city, was living out that dream if not several more dreams as well. I live in a dream, J thought, thinking literally of the ranch, which was infinitely more impressive a destination than New York. The ranch shone like a pinprick in the fabric dividing power's resting place from the rest of the world, shone like a chink in the wall that separated the Holy of Holies from the rest of the Temple, through which an enterprising explorer might witness a refraction of the Shechinah, see God's presence manifested on earth.

He wanted to dream the man grabbing his daughters and kicking out the back door of the van and jumping, and fleeing—but J knew that didn't happen because the man was dreaming J, was dying and unconscious and, thus, dreaming J.

J took cigar smoke into his mouth, sipped whiskey through it, exhaled the mingled fumes through his nose. Smoke and vapors, he thought. All the very different meanings of living a dream.

Fuck having a calling, J thought, for the umpteenth time, bored of himself.

They stubbed out the cigars on their boot soles and chucked them into the dirt drive, into the stubbled autumn grass, still brown in advance of early winter's coastal storms. They mocked the dangers of wildfire, wildfire's vowels in Louis' mouth a contagion of incendiary color.

Maybe it was better to comfort the two little girls rather than scare them in trying to save them.

CHAPTER THIRTY-NINE

BACK INSIDE, THEY PULLED chairs around a long table that ought to have been rough but for centuries' worth of accidental polishing by ranch-hand suppers somewhere, certainly not here, not recently. When J had half sat into his chair, was mid-lowering himself, still reliant on a hand upon the seat, Walter yelled, "Catch!" and tossed over a badly wrapped object that could only be a gun. J managed to get his hands up to grab at it, but fell back into the chair. "Happy birthday!"

"Do I open this now?" J asked.

"Wrapping isn't going to get any prettier," Walter replied.

J pulled open the gift to chants of, tear it, tear it, which made him worry that pre-dinner drinks had already gone too far. It was the hand-made rifle from over the mantle he'd first asked about. He heard Chase whisper, "Father," in a tone that implied the utterance was despite herself. J looked up to see Art's lips pursed and eyes narrowed, though he smiled when J made eye contact.

"Holy shit, Walter," J said.

"What kind of a gun is that?" Erin asked.

"Big," Karl said. "It's the big kind."

"Can I see it?" Erin asked.

J pulled the bolt open, checked the chamber; then, left hand holding the stock, right on the ball of the bolt, handed it to her.

Across the table Hayley raised an eyebrow. Hayley rested her drink on her lower lip, touched her tongue against her upper lip. J gulped.

"The young man knows how to present arms," Louis said.

"It wasn't going to be loaded," Karl said. "Birthday boy didn't need to clear the fucking chamber."

"Hell," Louis said. "I'm just admiring that he knew that the lever thingy opened the bullet holder thingy."

"Please," Karl said.

"I know the words for bolt and chamber," J said, looking surreptitiously over at Hayley, which ensnared his gaze in Chase's, Chase, whose cheekbones had grown magically more pronounced, her mouth so tight it was nearly imperceptible.

"I've gone to military school," J continued, much less emphatically. "I have a varsity letter in rifle team. I've hunted. Well... junior varsity letter."

"Who said I know the words?" Louis countered, as Walter announced that if J had an appreciation for hunting and game, he'd be delighted that they were eating antelope.

"What kind of gun is this?" Erin asked J.

"What kind of a gun is this?" Hayley mimicked, barely audible, but no one other than Chase had acknowledged Hayley all evening. Chase quietly clinked glasses with Hayley and everyone ignored her, too, as if contact with Hayley made one invisible.

Fuck, J thought.

"What kind of a rifle," Karl corrected.

"There's such a thing as junior varsity letters?"

"I'd like to know what kind of gun it is, too, Walter," J said.

"That's the weapon given to my grandfather by the Bedouins he rode with against Rommel, father," Chase said.

"Hell," Walter said. "Giving it on to Jacob is keeping it in the family, isn't it?"

"Father," Chase said.

"Figuratively a letter. I was on junior varsity."

"It was the first thing the guy ever asked about when he first came here. Figured it for his fortieth."

Erin handed the rifle back to J, commenting again on its beauty, said, "I love to shoot."

"Thank you," J said.

"Thank you," Chase mimicked, in a low groan that everyone managed to not notice except Hayley, who reciprocated Chase's earlier quiet clink.

"There's evidence that J knows how to work in the prone position," Karl said.

Chase rolled her eyes at Karl and then said to her father that she wasn't suggesting he not give the gun to J.

J's phone buzzed. He snuck a peak at a text from Hayley saying she hadn't flown all this way to not handle his gun. He blushed and looked up at her. She winked, which Chase couldn't see, but Art's smirk demonstrated that Art clearly could see both the look and the blush.

"Whatever his proclivities, prone or otherwise," Art said, sort of laughing again, and then not, "I'm not sure, Walter, why you think J needs something as concrete and as active as a gun, let alone that gun."

"Proclivities?" J asked.

"All that mythology and legend, the seduction of it. Bedouins," Art said. "I don't know…for J?"

"The man's sitting right here," Walter said, holding a hand in J's direction.

"We're past the era of shooting Nazis," Art said.

"Who said anything about shooting Nazis?" Chase asked.

"I'm sure J's a gentleman," Erin said, blushing, "and a delightful shooting partner. If you'll let me join you, J."

"Certainly," J said. "Come by, Erin, and we'll pop some cans."

"Pop some cans!" Walter exclaimed. "Chastity's grandfather logged forty-three kills with that damn thing. It is not for the popping of cans!"

"Delilah's father was a sniper?"

"Chastity's birth mother's father."

"Right," Chase said. "My birth mother's father. Not my father nor his father."

Hayley gave a half nod towards Chase while making eye contact with J and mouthed, "What the fuck?"

J widened his eyes in what he hoped communicated that, first of all, he didn't know what Hayley was 'what the fucking' about; and, second of all, that he couldn't exactly respond while everyone gawked at him and the rifle.

"My father-in-law gave it to me," Walter said. "To my sights, it is up to me to pass it on to J."

A rib roast on a slab of tree appeared, succulent and tender from afar in a way that made Walter's claim that it was antelope seem specious, but then so did forty-three Nazi kills in Africa. Red wine also appeared, and glasses. Walter stuck to whiskey, but J leaned the gun against a post behind him and filled his glass. It was his birthday. He could mix whiskey and wine. They chanted, "Toast!" and he stood up with his glass.

"To new friends! To killing Krauts!"

There was a silence. J blushed. Fuck it. It was his birthday. The Nazis weren't something other than Germans. If he had earned the right to kill them, then he'd certainly earned the right to slur them, surely he had. There was generally subdued sipping from the toasted drinks. Had he earned the right to kill them, though? Didn't the man in the van earn him that right; not only a right, but, for J, a mandate? But how did that help the man in the van? Fuck it. It was J's birthday. His birthday.

"How does forty feel?" Chase asked.

"I wouldn't know," J said.

"You wouldn't know?"

"Not yet."

"Sunday, isn't it?" Hayley asked.

"So they claim," Chase replied.

"It's his gifts that have delivered early," Karl said.

All the men snickered. J caught Art and Karl stealing glances at Hayley. Louis had shifted from ignoring Hayley to outright ogling her, which, given the lack of response that got, must have been standard for Louis, or for Hayley, or both. J couldn't tell whether he actually overheard Karl sniggering something snide or imagined it.

"So tell me about yourself, J," Erin said.

"I'm not interesting," J said. "You tell me about you."

Art winked at J.

Erin blushed and tittered.

Chase rolled her eyes. J took a bite of antelope, drank wine, nodded at Erin, who almost immediately into explaining her job exclaimed that J had duped her; her life wasn't interesting at all, she'd much rather hear about J. Everyone would much rather hear about J.

"Everyone would definitely much rather hear about J," Hayley said. "That much I know is true."

"There's nothing to hear about me," J said.

"Nothing to hear?" Hayley said. "Except that you're the best kept secret of DC's nightlife."

"I hear otherwise," Art snapped.

J blushed, panicked at how visible his blush was, looked over at Chase, who cocked an eyebrow.

"What you need to know about J," Karl said—and J just barely caught Art giving Karl a tight shake of the head, a short slash of the hand—"is that he's all passion."

J saw Art squint at Karl.

"All dedication," Karl said. "He's passionately dedicated."

Clearly, J realized, they knew about something. Was there anything to know about other than Hayley (and Chase)? But if Hayley, surely they wouldn't have invited her. Or had they invited her? J was entitled to do what he chose to do. He wasn't even pursuing Hayley! (She'd told him he couldn't.) J was pursuing Chase, or something like that. If they did know (if they knew about Chase it would all really be over), if they knew and that night was the subject of their innuendo, if they knew and that was what their weird behavior was about, then Erin and Rachel must be potential replacements. If replacements, what they hell were they thinking with Hayley here?

"Passion!" Erin said. "Passion is the best."

Or, maybe, they were goading him into acknowledging Hayley, wanted him to pursue Hayley, and couldn't directly tell him that because Hayley was here.

"Passion is the best," Hayley said, which made Chase laugh into her wine glass.

No, that wasn't it.

"He's dedicated to passion, too," Karl said. "Passionately dedicated and dedicated to passion. That's our J."

"Thanks, Karl," J said. "I'm glad the news of my museum project has reached you in such passionate and dedicated and dedicated to passion terms."

"Your museum project," Art said. "I didn't realize it was yours, per se."

"Ours?"

Hayley texted that she knew where J was sleeping.

"Those people the Nazis killed don't belong to us, J. They don't belong to anyone."

J tossed his wine back and poured himself another glass.

"Fine," J said. "Fair. Well played."

"It's amazing what you're doing," Karl said. "Seriously."

Could be Karl that wanted to make J squirm a bit.

J texted Hayley back, one hand on his wine glass, the other punching in letters beneath the table.

"Tell me about passion, J," Erin said, just as J remembered that Karl was German. "Tell me about this museum. Tell me about the Holocaust."

J drank half of his new glass of wine. He got a text back from Hayley that read, 'panx?'

She texted again: 'I'll panx you later, just you wait.'

Art looked at Karl. Karl flushed.

Fuck.

"J's passion," Karl said, "motivates an army of young bright things to abandon everything in pursuit of his dreams."

"His vision," Art said.

It could even be that Karl's competitiveness was itself a ruse, a move to get J to pursue Erin. This would have been much easier if J had just stuck with whiskey.

"Vision," Karl said.

"Ooo," Erin said. "How does he do that?"

"Well," Karl said, following a bite of antelope with wine, "there are hands on ways and less hands on ways."

Did Karl expect to be provided with women also? Art tilted his beautiful head and tilted his luscious eyebrows, and narrowed just one eye, all of which constituted an actor's dictionary's definition of glower. Or had Art simply figured two women, two men, however it pans out, and as should have been expected, it panned out that both of them favored the same woman. Naturally, Erin wanted to hear about the less discrete ways.

"Correct me if I'm wrong, J," Karl continued, "but your trick is that you quietly paint an image, a golden image if you will, of the vision, and of the relationship to that vision the person you'd like to motivate might have. Am I right J?"

"You've got it, Karl," Art said.

"Ok then," Karl said. "And if that fails, there's always incrementally exposing small glints of a less than savory other image, held in reserve, until the subject determines they'd prefer the vision after all. It's always J's way in the end."

"If I even ever could do that, it was way before, back in New York," J said. "And I'm not saying I ever could."

"I don't get it," Erin said.

"Sure you can, J," Karl said. "Sure you do. Why do you think everyone is here? Why do you think everyone is there in DC?"

"I'm confused," Erin said, practically out of her chair—J could imagine her raising her hands frantically. He looked over at Art, who shrugged with half of his face and smiled with the rest; and the rest, all mesmerized by Art's focus, shrugged smiles at J as well. This woman, J thought, this Erin.

"We're human," J began. "We're…" He struggled to figure out how to begin. Why the fuck was he trying? Wasn't Chase enough? Hayley? He'd lost both: J would lose both. He couldn't face either. This was easier. He didn't know.

"J," Chase interrupted, "invokes something in a person that makes J seem trustworthy to them."

"Really," J said. "DC, the museum, that's all Jeremiah."

"I don't get it," Erin said.

"Honey," Chase said to Erin. "What's to get?"

"Jeremiah's there because of you," Art said. "You're there because you were called."

"I'm not a bad person," J said.

"This isn't about individuals," Art said. "It's about a people."

It's about a people, J repeated to himself, and wondered what he'd ever done for his people, wondered whether these were his people. J had a gun now.

"Now," Karl said, "if we could put J's talents to use in our pursuit of policy, if we could lift him out of this museum nonsense and put him to work lobbying on behalf of the great state of New Mexico, and if we could pair Chase's capacity for narrative and genre with his ability to make people believe that how he sees them is who they are or ought to be…"

Chase, J thought. His throat choked up again on his Adam's apple the way it had in the car when he'd had his hand on her leg, when she'd covered his hand with hers. Chase slouched.

Karl paused and smirked at J, then he shook his head and said, "If you're J you've got the unique ability to make lots of kinds of choices seem bad. If we could just steal J away from the past, then, as I've been loudly advocating for, we could deploy him to lobby congress, put J's talents to some immediate use, have him get congress to imbue a legislative vote about allocations for road development with the heady aroma of anonymous afternoon sex in an airport bathroom.

"That's it, J, isn't it? You know how to make a sex scandal into a chaste romance. Right? That's your talent."

"Sex scandal!" Erin said, an octave too high and a few watts too powerful.

"See," said Karl, "That's why J's the genius and I'm not. All you heard when I said it was sex scandal. If J had been the one talking, you'd never think to ask about drug-fueled sexual escapades at the St. Regis Hotel on the company dime, about the abuse of position and power and the misuse of resources and morality and bodies. You'd instead feel that excitement you feel now, that blush of new, impossible love, of transcendence that negates any necessity of any kind of adult scruple."

"That's so crazy!" Erin said.

"And you know," Karl said. "If on the one hand, J can make that debauch romantic, on the other hand, we can threaten to take J's visioning away, return it to what it was. There's nothing that feels as tawdry, nothing so clammy and cold on the soul, as the recognition that one is not in the coddling swaddle of romance's embrace, but simply debauched."

J shouldn't feel guilty.

He could tell Karl was going to reveal the night with Hayley in the hotel room (and in the city's clubs and bars and bathrooms). He had sex, yes, whatever, consensual sex with an unmarried woman who was age appropriate and not in his employ.

Whatever.

Why did J care? And how did they know? Why hadn't Hayley known that they'd know? Why did Karl or any of them care?

"I suppose you're the one whose job is that he puts the tawdry back in romance, Karl," J snapped.

Chase sat up in her chair some.

Seriously: whatever.

"Tawdriness and debauchery!" Erin said. "Love and romance!"

"Sure," Karl said. "I'm the reveal. Of course I am."

J did everything he could to keep from blushing. It was hard not to look at Chase.

"The reveal," Chase said.

"The reveal. The one to reveal to Art that a Holocaust museum that never mentions the Holocaust is not only dumb, it's very fucking offensive," Karl said.

"I told the governor that," Hayley said, "clear as day."

"You are the tawdry debauch, Hayley," Karl said, looking between J and Hayley: so the fight was with Hayley, this was about Hayley and Karl. "You goad with your claims of offensiveness, and then you revel in the offense you've goaded straight into being."

"Hayley is the tawdry debauch," Chase lilted. "Huh."

"I thought you were on my side, Chastity," Hayley said.

J watched Chase breathe, which she did through both her nose and her mouth. He blushed again, looking at both women, watching both women see his blush, read his blush, as for them and not for them.

He watched the back wall appear between Chase and Hayley's previously conspiratorial shoulders, their shoulders not visibly moving at all, yet parting, and he felt fade the flush of the whiskey and wine, of his birthday, of his embarrassment, of his flirtation with Erin. J felt it fade. He resented the fade, resented the guilt that caused the fade. How was J to have known that Chase would warm to him again? How was he to have known that Hayley was actually interested in something ongoing after she hadn't allowed him to dare broach the topic for months? Really, how was he to have known?

"I'm sorry," Karl said.

And where was his own sense of agency and choice, he chided himself.

"Really?" Chase said after a while. "The St. Regis?"

J pretended it wasn't a question for him, or about him.

"It's just my role to play," Karl said.

"Missouri?" Chase asked, only loud enough to draw the others' attention back. "My grandfather's rifle?"

"I didn't have the rifle yet," J said, wanting to say that he'd thought she wasn't interested at all back in Missouri, had thought Chase was gone for good when Hayley summoned him to the basement bathroom; Chase hadn't even told him she was married in Missouri! But then, that was probably the clue that she was interested, except how was J to have known that clue given that he didn't know she was married?

What else wasn't he picking up on?

"Happy fucking birthday," Chase said.

She shoved her chair back loudly and walked out the front door.

"Why," Art asked, "does my wife care?"

"I just want to do real work," J said, "something with my hands."

"But you're building a museum!" Erin said.

Karl flushed in the general silence.

"You're good at a thing," Art said quietly. "Be good at that thing."

"I want to act," J said. "I want to feel things, concrete things."

"You already act too much," Art said, still without raising his voice.

"What do you know, Art?" J said. "Really? Tell me already. What do you know about me?"

"I am your friend," Art said.

"Chase took a huge chance recommending you to Art, J," Karl said. "Didn't she, Art? When she thinks about your reckless-ness...How can Chase not be angry with you when you jeopardize her family's mission? That's why, Art, if you ask me. That's why she's pissed at him."

J took a moment to consider whether Karl was finishing him off or rescuing him from Art's deductions.

"Her family's mission?" Art snapped, snapping back into focus. "I thought it was my mission."

"You're our mission, Art," Walter said.

"OK," Art said.

"Part of it anyway."

"What the hell does that mean?"

Fine, J thought, "Fine. Let's have it straight: me and Hayley. Who knew, who knows, who cares?"

"Fuck you, Jacob," Hayley said.

"I'm sorry. I know it's your birthday dinner," Art said. "But Karl's right."

"Seriously," J said. "Enough with the fucking innuendo."

"And fuck you, too, Art," Hayley said.

"Come on, Hayley," Art said.

"I'm a human fucking being, you asshole."

"Hayley," Art said.

"No," Hayley said, beginning to cry. "No."

"Hayley," J said.

"I just…" she stood up.

J rose, too, said her name again. She pushed her chair back and walked through the arch into the living room. J started to follow her and she paused and shook her head and held out her palm to halt him. J stopped, crooked between the table and his seat, holding onto the back of his chair. Everyone else was silent.

"See, J?" Art said.

"Holy fuck, Art," Hayley said, turning back. "Do you ever wonder why you're only ever surrounded by men?"

"Consider it under advisement," Art said.

Hayley made a disgusted noise and stormed out of the house. J blushed for the umpteenth time, this time out of worry that what he found attractive in Art was, perhaps, something that turned ugly for women.

When the noise of the two departures had finished settling, Art said in a low monotone without making eye contact with anyone, "Anyone but that one, J. If it's women you want, I can help with that, we can help with that, but not that one. Not her."

"Don't count me in that number," Rachel said.

"Seriously," Chrissy said.

J had forgotten about the mother and daughter.

Erin blushed and looked down at her hands.

"She's the fucking savant," Art said. "How can you not fucking see that? How can you not see what…what getting with her means, what that means for your integrity, for your moral compass? Where are your boundaries?"

"You don't know my compass," J said, "or my boundaries."

"You are my brother," Art said, "and I love you."

"Then send me to kill Nazis, not build museums."

There was silence, and then Walter laughed that at some point a man just wanted to see an enemy at the end of his rifle sights, didn't he.

To this, Louis quipped, "Sometimes a man wants to do something more with his saber than rattle it!"

And the eye rolling, the moans, the overly vocalized bereaving at Louis' sexism, broke the tension.

"She's a good woman," J said. "Hayley really is a good woman. I'm the asshole."

The room was quiet for a second, and then Walter yelled, "Birthday shots!"

"Shots!" Louis yelled.

"Shots!" Walter yelled.

"Shots!" Erin yelled, but not for J.

They all drank again, and J considered that he would indeed have liked to have lain beside and behind Erin while she aimed the rifle down a long stretch of dirt at a can or a bottle or an overripe pumpkin, his arms outlining her arms, his breathing training her breathing, his finger telling her finger when, and how, and how hard. They drank and drank and when it was late and there were stars to watch, there were cigars to smoke again.

And after most everyone had already left, it was just Walter and Art with J on the porch. Walter sat tipped back in his chair and J stood and Art was on the railing.

"It's a thing," Walter said. "Forty."

Art looked silently at J, and J stood and looked back at Art with eyes strangely open and his drunkenness seemingly a distance out beyond the umbrage of the house's lights.

"Fifty is too, I suppose," Walter said. "And sixty! Sixty certainly. But forty is a thing."

"Can I trust you?" Art asked.

J heard the question, he did, and he wanted to ask it back because the only person who even knew J's age, J had somehow betrayed; and, that woman was married to Art. But J also could hear in Art's plaintive tone that Art wasn't asking, Art was pleading. J could feel Art's vulnerability and J knew that he loved Arthur.

Walter lowered his chair quietly, chucked his lit cigar into the yard and went in.

Besides, J couldn't imagine he would ever again sleep with Chase; he told Art that he could trust him.

"Ok," Art said.

"I'll do it, this work," J said.

"Jacob," Art said.

"I'll build the museum."

"Shut up," Art said.

"Thank you," J said.

They sucked on their cigars and J started coughing.

"Was there something you wanted to trust me with?" J asked.

Art started to speak, stopped, then said: "Just if I can."

"Yeah," J said. "Absolutely."

"Why are we smoking these fucking things?" Art asked, coughing, holding his cigar out in front of him, laughing.

"Seriously!" J said. "They'll make us feel like shit tomorrow."

"Such shit."

They laughed but didn't put their cigars out.

"Why did Walter give you that gun?"

"Haven't the goddamnedest," J said.

"It's important, the museum," Art said.

"Fucking hell, Arthur," J said. "Obviously I know that."

"Find someone, Jacob," Art said. "Find someone who'll love you. Who you'll love. Not like Hayley, not like me."

"Arthur," J said.

"We need love," Art said. "All of us. You, too, especially you. I can almost get by with Christ and the work and the people, almost. You're different."

"I have my work, too. And I have you. And besides, you have so much love."

"Come on."

"Chase," J said.

"Do you need me to help you find someone?"

"Shut up," J said.

"Thanks," Art said and laughed and coughed and laughed again.

CHAPTER FORTY

J SPENT A FEW days at Walter's house, mostly hungover, days in which he saw Chase not at all. Nor did he see Hayley, nor any of the other dinner guests. He shot through a box of the heavy caliber cartridges the big gun took. Because Walter was too particular to allow that gun to be fired at plinking targets on the ranch's pastures, J invariably shot up in the canyons. He trudged to alpine meadows dormant in anticipation of snow, his arms cross-hatched by scrub oak. He consoled himself that this was where Chase had established her independence, pulling carp and whitefish out of trout streams.

There had been the girl who worked at the restaurant across the street from his first job when he was barely twenty-one. He'd met up with her for drinks a few months after whatever it was was over. They'd fallen under the purview of an older man at the small dive bar on 39th Street who bought them drinks and did coke with the girl in the bathroom and over the small wedge of marbled plastic vanity told the girl to ditch J, which she should have, or perhaps shouldn't have. They'd bought condoms in the corner market beneath her apartment where once he'd picked up flowers for her. She told him she'd thought he was the one, she told him he was a dog, and during sex she asked if he was clean and he didn't know how the hell to answer that, so the condom stayed on.

And he thought that his chance to have children was quickly passing.

He remembered the woman whose Halloween party he'd gone to dressed as Uncle Sam shortly after the love of his middle twenties left him and he thought about the love of his middle twenties who'd ended things in a room borrowed from a friend in Seattle after giving him head before leaving for a play, all while the friend showered. The hostess of the Halloween party had followed him into the street, called him back, and he'd boasted that she'd better be up for sex more than once, boasted because he was afraid he'd climax quickly when they had sex first. They'd fucked, and he'd said he had to go home, and she'd said wasn't that kind of weird, and he'd insisted that he had to be at a brunch party in his apartment building two boroughs away, and she asked wasn't that weird, that he was leaving in the middle of the night after sex.

He had known her for two years and he had admired her, and she'd followed him out into the street to call him back and he had left in the middle of the night.

He wondered whether he'd ever be anyone's one, and he despaired of it.

He remembered the night the love of his middle twenties had called, a year after swearing she'd never speak to him again, ten months after she'd moved back in with her mother in California, ten months after the Halloween party and J's hook-up there, and asked if he'd meet her for dinner, and they stayed at the restaurant, *their restaurant*, until it closed, and the cab driver had told them no sex in the car, and on J's couch, the same couch that he would later abandon to take-out containers months before fleeing NYC with Chase, they'd agreed, clothes mostly off, to elope in the morning, and in the morning, he'd thought better of it, and within the month, over the phone, her back in California, he had told her that their trust was too battered to continue.

And J yearned for the life they might have had had he not told her their trust was too undermined, had she not ended it in Seattle; he yearned to have ever married, to have ever had children, yearned for the dream she'd confessed to him of coming home to find him behind the French doors of their study, working, their toddler at ease in a mess of papers.

He thought too about the woman he'd met at a Comfort Inn bar in Pennsylvania while traveling on business. He thought about all the women he'd desired but abandoned when they didn't respond quickly enough, and wondered whether it was his lack of patience that was at fault. He thought about the sister of a coworker he'd made out with at a work party. He thought about Hayley.

He thought about Esther.

His pain swaddled him, his indulgence in wallowing.

It was awfully suspicious, how quickly E had had her daughter after leaving him.

What did any of it matter? The man in the van had had children who either survived or didn't survive. The man in the van had either loved and been loved or not loved and not been loved or loved and not been loved or not loved and been loved. Whichever and whatever had been the moments of his existence, all now were relegated to a simple fact, an ending that did not flow narratively, logically, justly, or emotively from his life, an end unbound by karma or poetry: he was being gassed to death along with people who he either knew or did not know, and though the temporality of his dream was seemingly infinite, or at least adequate for J to continue, the dream's chronology had long eclipsed the man, the man had long ago died, become unidentifiable, become a success of his murderers, been erased.

J lay in ravines in mountain air that turned colder daily, aspen leaves yellowing and falling, his fortieth year eroding, trying to drown his thoughts in the concussive discharge of slug after slug from the gun. The umbrage of Art's governance, palpable to J, though absent of any actual manifestation.

These were the forty years wandering in the desert, knowing that one night, sleeping in a grave of one's own digging, the end of the world would come.

But a child!

I am the man's child, J thought.

But then who would be his child? His legacy? His progeny?

Absent any other means of delaying his return to Washington DC, J determined to fly from Albuquerque to Cincinnati to visit the museum in progress. He told Walter this. Walter had neither endorsed J's additional days holed up at the ranch nor complained about them. Mostly, he'd moved wraithlike about, an old man possessed of the strength of his routines, few of which involved direct engagement with other people. Whether it was because this quiet offered J the peace he strove for, or because he simply lacked the temerity to ask, J hadn't moved out of the room in which Walter had first placed him. So, he was surprised when Walter asked if it was the straw ticking that was forcing him to leave, and suggested that if he wanted to stay longer he was welcome to move into any of the other bedrooms.

J did want to stay longer, but he also wasn't yet ready to become a co-wraith, wandering the ranch's quiet, waiting as winter gradually shut down the cottonwoods and the scrub oak, the sun lost to the shadow of the mountains.

CHAPTER FORTY-ONE

IN A KIND OF preemptive nostalgia, J stopped by the Brooks Brothers outlet after he landed at the Cincinnati airport. He'd thought to call Hayley, and then thought better of it, reserved a rental car instead. But now, as he fingered the shirts stacked near the store's entrance, the shopkeeper's glare palpable, J found that he missed Hayley. When he broke the spell of the store and of his own longing, headed off in search of the rental car place, the shopkeeper scurried out after him.

She handed him a small, stapled shut bag. "For your friend," she said. "You give it to him, to Mr. Arthur."

"Of course," J said, and put the bag in his briefcase.

"Make sure," she said.

J promised he would. But the sense of the bag in his bag broke J's heart before he even made it to the rental car line, which made it unbearable to wait behind a group of boisterous vacationers a generation his senior, decked in bolos and ten-gallon hats, a vertiginous echo of New Mexico, as if he'd arrived back in Albuquerque. That Art's friend at the Brooks Brothers had remembered not only Art but J, J as a symptom of Art, and who would remember J? Who remembered airport retail clientele? Who would remember J?

What was J going to do, though, get rid of the gift? No, he'd schlep it in his bag until the next time he saw Art.

The vacationers took what seemed an infinite amount of time, and then J had to ask for directions, and for a map. By the time he was situated in the car, the marked-up sheet of paper the rental car place passed off as a map beside him, J couldn't help himself, he texted Hayley that he was on his way to the museum site.

The drive went quickly, and to his surprise, there were already giant billboards advertising the museum. These featured images of things like Hasids in streimels and robes holding Torah scrolls, which, leaving aside historical distinctions between Lithuania's Litvak and Hasidic communities, seemed reasonable enough, J supposed. That some of the billboards also advertised children's ice cream cones and hot dogs at discounted prices disconcerted him more, but, still, it was America.

An even larger sign, this one an enormous LCD display, marked the turnoff to the parking lot. J tried to ignore that it referred to the project as "Yid World & Pre-Shoah Musuem!" There were only a few cars, a couple of church vans, and several RVs in the lot, which, given the museum's newness—J hadn't expected it to even actually be open yet; it certainly wasn't completed—and that it was a random weekday at the end of October, also seemed in in keeping with expectations. He parked and walked to the newly made, narrow path.

As Hayley had told them it would be, the path was lined with newly planted Scots Pine forest, and from the lot, the line between evergreens and leafless deciduous trees was bizarre. Still, once he stepped onto the crushed cinder path, the new forest blocked the old forest from view, and did give an exotic feel to the walk that J was ready enough to associate with pre-war Lithuania. As he walked, he began to notice that some of the trees had died, and others leaned at crazed angles. Growing pains, J thought. He wondered where they'd even managed to get so many full-grown trees.

The walk down the path was longer than he remembered it, and he encountered several museum guests headed back to the lot. To a person, they were eyes alight, and this gave J some greater confidence, even if they were all wearing the thin nylon yarmulkes

distributed at bar and bat mitzvahs, and at weddings, and by synagogues whose congregants were less than uniformly practicing
Orthodox. He nodded at a couple in matching convertible, nylon
expedition pants and shirts, both of whom wore white yarmulkes
imprinted with the Yid World logo stamped in gold ink.

"Murse Hatchem," the man said solemnly.

"Yas-ser ko-ach-ah," the woman added.

J covered his flinch with a nod and a thank you, determining
that to correct them was to pretend that *Mertz HaShem* and *Yahser
Koach* were somehow greetings appropriate to this couple.

And then J reached the edge of the forest.

The logs had been used to construct what J imagined an
American frontier fort might look like, a sort of walled village
constructed out of round logs that Art had pointed out on their
visit to the construction site. J stopped and gawked at the main
entrance: spread open wooden gates over which arched lettering
spelled, "Welcome to Our Shtetl!"

A man bounded out towards J at high speed in an outlandish
side-to-side dance, his black pants tucked into his white socks, his
tzitzit swinging from beneath his halat, which J could see wasn't
even real silk, the gartel around his waist wasn't tied, but used some
sort of clip system. He wore an enormous streimel, from beneath
which what appeared to be stick-on payos swayed to nearly the
bottom of his enormous, potentially fake, beard.

"Mazel, mazel, mazel!" he greeted J. "Shall we dance a little
horah?"

"What?" J asked.

"Welcome to Yid World!" the man shouted, before dropping
into a bit of a crouch and cocking his head to the side. He put a hand
up to his ear, "What's that I hear? Wait, wait...yes! Baruch Hashem!
I hear that this fine mensch before me shall be a Yid for today!"

With that, the man pulled one of the white nylon yarmulkes
out from behind his ear, birthday-party-magician style.

"Won't you join me in Yiddishkeit, kind sir?" he asked. "It's a magical world in which Yids can be Yids!"

"No thank you," J managed.

"Don't be shy! Come inside! It's always Shabbos in Yid World and there's always cholent on the table!"

And then J did something he hadn't ever done in his adult life. He positioned his hips the way his tennis camp counselor had instructed him for hitting a forehand, and swung as hard as he could, hitting the man in the nose.

The effect was immediate.

The man howled and reeled backwards, holding his hands up to his face.

"What the fuck, man!" he yelled, his Yiddishe accent abandoned. "Security! Fucking security!"

J stood, stunned by his own action, as a number of guards rushed out from the woods. The man was bleeding from his nose. J's hand hurt. The guards grabbed him. The man kept yelling that J had hit him.

"Are you an anti-Semite, sir?" one of the guards demanded, leading him away by a painful clutch on his upper arm. Another guard had an equally over-strong grip on his other arm. "Sir, are you an anti-Semite? Are you affiliated with an anti-Semitic organization? Are there more of you?"

"Are you Jewish?" J asked quietly, trying to keep pace with the guards to not be dragged by them.

"Are you an anti-Semite, sir? Is this a hate crime?"

"Are any of you Jewish?"

They took him into a well-lit windowless concrete holding room that could have been anywhere, and might easily have passed for a corporate conference room were it not for the heavy metal door, which had only a small, security-glassed, window, and that the floors were also concrete. They sat him down forcefully and told him that if he didn't tell them everything they wanted to know, they'd hand him over to the police and press assault and hate crime charges. If he dished, they'd limit it to trespassing.

"I hit him," J said aloud. The world rests on the prayers of righteous men.

Within moments, Hayley stormed in. The security guards snapped to attention.

"What the living fuck?" she asked.

"How'd you know it was me?" J asked.

"Well you texted me," she said. "And I rushed over to meet you, because I had, note the past tense, wanted to see you, and I got here just in time to watch you hauled off."

"I'm glad you're here," J said.

"You broke that man's nose."

"I did?" J marveled.

"I've got it," Hayley said to the guards. "You can go."

"He's violent, ma'am," one of them said.

"This is his park," Hayley said. "Sort of."

"Ma'am."

"He's not part of an anti-Semitic conspiracy," Hayley said. "I'll be fine."

"Yes, ma'am," the guard said; and they left.

"Park?" J asked after the guards had left and Hayley had sat heavily in an office chair opposite him. "This was supposed to be a museum."

"Park, museum: what's the difference?" she asked.

"I'm sorry I broke that man's nose," J said. "Will he be OK?"

"Who hits people?" She asked. "I didn't think you were a hitter."

"I'm not a hitter," J said.

Hayley gave him a look and crossed her arms over her chest.

"There's a difference between a park and a museum," J said.

Hayley shook her head.

"It's fucking offensive," J said.

Hayley shrugged at him, arms still crossed.

"It is."

"I liked you," she said.

J sprawled his arms across the table towards her, hand out, stretched out towards her to look up at her, supplicant. "Can you forgive me?" he asked.

"You and Art asked for this," she said. "You and Art can have it."

She stood up and walked to the door.

"Hayley!"

The guard opened the door, and she told the guard to let J go, but only after a few minutes.

"Hayley, wait!" J called after her, but the door had shut.

And after a few minutes, the guard opened the door and told him he was free to go. J stood and straightened his suit jacket. He walked out through the lobby of the administrative offices, where a paramedic was treating the man J had punched. The man gave J the finger; J muttered that he was sorry under his breath.

CHAPTER FORTY-TWO

J WALKED OUT OF the park offices. He walked the Scots Pine flanked path to the parking lot. He stepped from crushed cinder to asphalt and his quads quaked; he hurried the last yards to the car for fear of falling over before reaching it. He leaned heavily on the rental's roof. Then the exhaustion left his thighs and moved for the briefest of moments to the self-indulgent wallowing of the last few days, to the predictable heartache of the litany of misplaced loves, but that didn't deliver, skipped straight to the immanence of the world's end.

That ever-accessible sense of demise only hid another eschatology, one in which native woods were torn up to make way for imported woods, one in which the world might die not for ideology made military but for the blithe haste of a species built to build. Only at the pale of this vision of civilization and J found it too painful to proceed; he forced himself to focus on the car roof, on the parking and suddenly the most exhausting thing he could imagine was getting back into the vehicle and driving to the airport. He could not imagine getting into the rental car. He could not imagine flying to DC, to the furnished efficiency apartment, to the ministrations of Jeremiah and Christian.

Come on: unlock the car.

He stood back up, sucked in his breath, straightened his lapels.

He had punched a man. He, Jacob Paul, several days past his thirty-ninth birthday (fortieth as celebrated), had decided that he was entitled to avenge his own frustrations on another human being. Who the fuck did he think he was?

Who the fuck was he?

All of this should have carried some pathos: nothing. J didn't feel it at all. He walked across the parking lot to the main drive. He began up the main drive. The bright October sun made him squint into a smile. Within a few steps, he realized his shallow fast breaths and trilling heartbeat. He inhaled deeply, nasally, let the pine fill his nostrils, the chill sharper in his sinuses, in his throat, his lungs, the longer he drew. Exhaling as slowly as he could, he smiled again, the sun warm. The end of the slow exhale forced another deep inhale and his cheeks tensed with pleasure at the intake, his eyes opened, lifted, shrillness shed.

J walked.

He came to the end of the drive and stood on the fallow shoulder of Route 20, sheltered by the giant billboard advertising the turn-in for Yid World. J unknotted his tie and pulled it out of his collar, folded it four times and tucked it into his jacket's inner pocket. He made to move, then paused again to shed his jacket and unbutton his collar and cuffs. Nothing extended within him from fingertip to toes to nose. It felt great. His arm, already elled to bear his jacket, could turn him hitchhiker with a simple extension outward, a lift of his thumb, but an echo of gravity, a mote of E's girls pulled to the east: J turned right.

He'd walk a while. (He could always turn back to the car.)

The road was flat and between fields stubbled with shattered stalks were fields rolled up into great big wheels of hay, some of which were shrink-wrapped in white or black plastic. A man mowing the still green lawn of one of the every-so-often houses called out to J if he it wasn't time to stop for a cold drink.

J tipped two fingers off his brow back at the man and nodded and smiled, but kept walking.

After an indeterminate spell the road bent right, and the sun, behind, but also to the right, now danced at the back corner of his eye and J found that he enjoyed this minor discomfort. New woods replaced fields, and low brick walls at the entries to new roads named subdivisions in fanciful pairings of earthly and ethereal topographies, that J repeated to himself, nearly involuntarily, caught in a contest of merits between 'Heavenly Hills' and 'Eternal Springs.'

"What about Hades Caverns?" he said aloud to himself, and laughed at himself, pleased. He shifted his suit jacket from one arm to the other, as he had so many times already that afternoon.

The road bent again and the subdivisions lost their cloaking woods, bare beyond supermarket parking lots and fast food gas stations and ordinary fast food. He crossed an enormous road, dodging a crush of oversized family cars fetching schoolchildren. The houses got squat. Overhead engine roar overwhelmed the traffic's tinnitus at regular intervals. J looked up: a line of jets extended up and to the north. Trees to his north and a runway up ahead.

The road turned to parallel the runway, and every ninety seconds J flinched at another landing's roar. In the intervals, J consoled himself, caught his breath, promised himself he wouldn't flinch at the next. Then tires and dust and full bore reverse thrust and he ducked and cowered and breathed wrong and checked himself for engine grime and broken body parts. The road turned right again at end of the runway, and J had to close his eyes and slow his breathing to go beneath an underpass, the intermittent havoc of overhead vehicles between the landings. A hundred feet clear of the overpass, concrete flared around the road beneath the runway's grassy overrun.

J stopped. He could do it, he thought, he could.

In the tunnel, he crept along the eighteen-inch-wide high concrete curb, hemmed against the tunnel's grimed tiles by dense traffic, exhaust rough in his throat, every iridescent seep stain down ceiling and wall proof that at the next subsonic shake the concrete would fracture, the roof collapse. His shoulders were up to his ears, and his knees buckled at every horn at every blast and boom. Fuck, he thought, fuck, fuck. He tried to force a smile the way the climbing books he'd read in his twenties had recommended: if you're clutched, smile, and your legs and hands will follow. Instead, J ran the last third, a lopsided lope to daylight, and as he cleared the far flare, someone yelled from a slowed car wanting to know was he ok. J gave the same two-fingered salute he'd give the guy on the riding mower, stumbling to a walk.

J wondered at his acquisition of this new gesture, mock salute, mock hat tip.

He walked alongside the airport traffic, the terminal buildings visible, planes launching and landing everywhere. Gradually his breathing slowed. He tried on a smile again, and this time the smile didn't feel like the verge of tears. He felt almost confident when he came to the bridge over the freeway, but the further out along its span, the higher up he went, the more it shook with each car and truck, and when the traffic geared to a near halt the whole thing trembled with engine vibrations. Harmonics, J bleakly remembered his father telling him, had collapsed early attempts at suspension bridges. No way off but over, J muttered to himself, a mantra by which he inched along yet another curb also only half the width of a sidewalk square, one arm raised over the guard rail that curved in towards him. He felt far too on par with the landing planes.

His mouth was dry and his shirtsleeves were greased and when he made it back to ground he felt that he'd been through something meaningful, though he knew no language by which he could meaningfully share the trials and triumph of walking a mile of road. There were trees again, and then, to his left, a Baptist Church, which J gave the finger for reasons he couldn't articulate, and then immediately felt like crying, and then worse, worried about what the cars' drivers would think; but, J had become invisible to them again.

The woods offered some sense of peace for a mile or so, until he came to a series of long term parking lots and the angry drivers who seemed to want to run him over as he tried to cross the lot entrances. Past these, J reached an intersection at which a sign welcomed those who followed the road to his right to Cincinnati/ Northern Kentucky International Airport.

This was it then: walk straight or walk to a plane.

Home.

(How could he return to the airport and not return the rental car? How was it better to not return to the airport and not return the rental car?)

Home?

Anywhere: DC, Albuquerque, Bowman, New York...New York! Ha.

(But wasn't he headed to New York anyway? Headed to that city that was for him six-story Deco apartment buildings, a version of city E had abandoned for the conforming contours of a lower Manhattan lifestyle? Wasn't he?)

J crossed the street and kept on Route 20. He went a few feet further and stopped. Took a deep breath. He could still turn around. Turn around to what? For what? And if he didn't look at his shame would it not exist? J shrugged on his suit jacket, and continued, decided, relieved.

He walked on.

He reached a road that ran through the woods along the wide muddy Ohio, and he turned away from the lowering sun, followed the road through the trees as it curved along the river. The river, and his mouth was still dry but he forgot that, walked, walked until he reached an emulation of a city, the quaint riverfront, revitalized zone of a sleeper community, pressed up against the great moat securing it from the uncontrollably urban.

J stopped at a card store and bought a bottle of water.

He walked.

Then, at what he took for peak satellite city downtown density, a square with commercial high-rises and a strange building with a neon-lit, topsail fin, he crossed onto a suspension bridge.

J walked into Cincinnati, he walked through its downtown, he walked past its churches and shops and office buildings; he walked and resisted the urge to have urges, settling instead for the easy emptiness of his legs' repetitions.

He passed rows of bulletproof apartment buildings, dormant despite the hint of warmth in the late fall evening air. Some metabolic wave made him sweat and he sweated through his undershirt, felt the back of his dress shirt, damp and clinging. Walked. Walked through the dark, piecing his way eastward, piecing his way northward. He negotiated a tangle of overpasses and expected to find himself on the far side of city, but remained on main roads bounded by neighborhoods upon neighborhoods, neighborhoods interrupted by shopping centers distinguished from their humdrum analogues elsewhere only by a greater propensity for travertine and glass facades. Walked. Aimless, not interested in thought or food or sleep, the notion that tonight he might witness (again, Genesis Chapter Two, now) the creation (redux, second telling) of animals a source of fatigue worse than the numb ache in his shins from extended travel in dress shoes. He came to a series of high-rises, their red brick austerity unmitigated by their bordering flowerbeds and flowering shrubs and flowery vestibules. Walked. He followed a road whose sidewalk disappeared as it became a winding rolling highway bisecting a large inner-suburb park whose dense sumac and maple and oak blackened the night but for passing car headlights, the hummus alloyed with exhaust.

Hills made xylophones of J's shins, their splints hammered upon by cacophonous toddlers. Walked. He emerged from the park, his pants' legs splattered with road-spray, his mind melodiously blank, to post-war homes with lawns that extended to rounded curbs that mirrored the contours of their curving side streets. He stuck to the thoroughfare, here a broad commuter road whose accidental sidewalks were randomly absent for blocks at a stretch.

Walked. By meridian moon, he'd reached an actual country road that went through actual woods, though the woods were fragmented by developments and the road as traveled as any down-town's arterial streets. J kept walking.

Late in the night he chanced upon a diner as fortuitous as the rock with which Moses transgressed. He wasn't hungry so much as weak, wasn't tired either, or at least didn't want to sleep. He went in and began to shed his suit jacket, but the clammy cold of his wet shirt, which he remembered was grease grimed from his circumvention of the airport, led him to pull the jacket back tight, button its top button.

The waitress paused some steps away from him, but he smiled at her the way he'd learned to smile at clients and subjects, and she seated him in a booth with a view of the parking lot's enormous flag, its weight more than the wind could bear, as if the empire it represented had grown too overgrown to fly. Once food arrived, he discovered that he wanted to eat, though none of it, not the chicken fried steak, not the mashed potatoes, not the coffee, not the pie that followed, none of it tasted to him at all. Because the waitress kept giving him increasingly skeptical looks as the hours waxed—he had ordered dishes one at a time to stretch out his tenure in his booth—he handed her his credit card while a last slice of pie and a full cup of coffee still sat in front of him.

His card was visibly fancy, black, metal, and the waitress, hesi-tatingly, asked if she might see some ID. He showed her his license and she rang up the bill. When she returned, by way of apology, she made light of asking to see ID.

"I guess I look a bit haggard."

"I didn't see you drive up."

"I walked," J said.

"From where?"

"Never ask where a man's headed," J said. "Ask him only where he's going."

"Are you all right?" she asked, sitting down across from him on the very edge of the booth.

J turned and looked out the window at the parking lot and the giant, drooping flag. He willed himself to not acknowledge what he was doing. He was walking east-northeast. There was a waitress sitting across from him, a woman who couldn't but barely be out of college, if she'd gone to college. Or she was in college, or not, he thought.

"Sure I am," he said, collecting himself. "Where's the closest motel?"

"About two miles down the road towards Madisonville."

"Madisonville?"

Her head bobbed to a new angle of tilt and J decided that it was either ahead of him or behind, and that it was best that he acknowledge Madisonville.

"Of course, Madisonville, duh. And in the other direction?"

"A Motel Six, but that's a ways up along the 275."

"Thanks," J said, and took a bite of pie. He chewed and looked out the window. The waitress was still sitting there, doing everything anxious short of biting her nails. "Yes?" he asked.

"Is there someone I can call for you?" she asked. "Can I call you a cab?"

"No," J said. "There's no one to call. No need to call."

She paused, hovered. J sat.

"I don't know," she said.

"Yes?"

"I could probably just give you a ride if you want."

"Thanks, but I'm all set," J said.

He stood up. The pie hadn't tasted like anything anyway.

The waitress stood, too, assured him that he didn't need to leave. He reassured her that he was full, that it was time to get back on the road.

"You've got a Washington D.C. driver's license," she said.

J resumed walking. At the end of every left stride, a small bone in the bottom of his right foot ached where he'd broken his third metatarsal in his mid-twenties. It burned between each ache. To think, he thought, that a foolish misstep nearly twenty years ago still hurts. The night he'd broken it, he'd gone for a run in Inwood Hill Park, Manhattan's last vestige of uncut forest. It had snowed heavily that day and the trails had been a mess of mud and slush. But, the drenching muck, the filth, had rinsed him for the first time in weeks of his bi-polar obsessions about the love of his middle twenties, with whom he'd broken up twice in the preceding month, with whom he was destined to break again catastrophically in a borrowed Seattle room.

He felt rinsed so he called her.

She didn't answer and he called her again. Still no answer, and he began to drink, still full of energy, still running around his apartment, bouncing literally off the walls, his shoulder's impact on plastered brick satisfying and firm. His cats stared at him, howled, ran around as well. Two beers in, buzzed but hardly drunk, he called again and again and again.

Still no answer and he kicked at the air and lost his balance.

In falling, his foot slid back; he heard the bones snap. He had lain on the floor with his foot up on his futon, refusing to believe that he could have broken it in his apartment, afraid to think that this might be an alcohol-related injury—he'd only had a couple beers! He hadn't wanted to give up drinking.

J savored the ache and the burn. They made each stride count, though with each his foot hurt a little more. After an hour of this, he sat on a twisted guardrail overgrown with what might or might not be poison ivy, overhung with the junk trees that overtook untended forest clearings. He took off his shoe and massaged his foot, and he laughed. He laughed at himself, sitting on an overgrown guardrail in the middle of the night with his shoe off. He laughed and thought that he hadn't laughed since—since—well since the drugs he'd taken with Hayley, whenever ago that was. He hadn't really laughed since he'd been her.

A car crept along the road, its high beams making shadows of the woods. Its sloth, it couldn't have been traveling more than fifteen miles an hour, made J think that it sought him. His perch hid him in the shadow of a slightly older maple. Who would look for him? The waitress, he answered his own question. He could reveal himself, get a ride as far as the motel. No, he thought, if he was walking, he was walking. He pulled his head back into the shadows and let the car pass. He put his shoe back on, the hot spot in his foot somewhat relieved by the short airing, and resumed walking. What hubris, he thought, to think that it was the waitress and that she was looking for him. Likely it had been an over-cautious drunk, someone as likely to run over J as not. J picked up his stride. The diner food did not rest easy in his stomach and he finally began to feel exhausted. He'd begun to feel again, for fuck's sake: this was good.

The car came back in the other direction, its lights directly in J's eyes this time. He stepped off the road, his forearm over his face, wishing that he hadn't dumped the suit jacket in the dumpster on the far corner of the diner's parking lot. The car pulled alongside him. It was indeed the waitress. She reached over and popped open the passenger door. "Get in," she said. "I'll drive you to the Motel Six."

He thought to refuse, and then thought that refusal would constitute an ethics of walking. J did not want to establish an ethics for whatever it was that he refused to acknowledge he was doing. Plus, it would be rude to refuse the ride. He got in the car, thanked the waitress. It felt fantastic to sit. They tried to talk during the brief ride to the motel—barely five minutes, most of those just to get to the interstate, and then a dash at vertiginous speed on the interstate—and their attempted conversation sort of failed. The waitress might have lived nearby, J might have a job in Cincinnati doing something…They arrived, and the waitress offered to wait in the car to make sure J was able to get a room. He thanked her again, went in, easily procured a room-key from a half-asleep clerk behind Plexiglass, their exchange made through a concavity in the counter that passed beneath the bulletproof barrier.

J walked back to the car holding up his key.

"Where are you headed anyway?" the waitress asked.

"Would you like to come in for one of whatever's in the minibar?" J asked.

The waitress missed a beat, and then started her car; said, "No thank you."

"It's on me," J said.

"You have the best of luck with your walking," she said.

"I'm sorry, I just—"

"It's fine," she said, and drove off.

He slunk into the room, flung his clothes onto what passed for a desk, noted that there wasn't even a minibar anyway, of course there wasn't, and collapsed onto the bed, barely taking time to pull back the bedspread. Immediately, he fell asleep. In his sleep, he heard, "*Viya'as Elohim et-chayat ha'aretz leminah,*" and animals began to not so much emerge as fill in the empty space of the firmament. In fact, it was as if the grass plains had always harbored gazelle and ibis and lion and hyena, the trees apes and giraffes and elk, the mountains bear and leopards and sheep, the water leviathan and their myriad inferiors. The snake walked upon its hind legs and it spoke in Hebrew.

CHAPTER FORTY-THREE

J WOKE TO THE cleaning service knocking on the motel room door. He yelled at them to come back later. He was told that if he wasn't out of the room in fifteen minutes, they would charge him for an additional night. He looked longingly at the bathroom, more particularly, at its shower. Forty bucks for twenty-four hours of which he'd only use maybe thirty-five minutes; forty bucks just to shower. He'd siphoned money out of the always-level bank account the three kings provided; that paired with his monastic lifestyle these last years had allowed him to accrue sufficient savings to not need to think twice about spending the money. But the principle of the thing offended.

He pulled on his soiled suit, urinated, and scrubbed his teeth with his index finger over the sink.

As soon as he began walking again, it became apparent that he'd need to buy proper walking shoes. Hours later, wincing, he came to a small town center comprising a diner and several real estate offices, a movie theater, and a few shops. He went into the diner first. He limped to the counter before the hostess could intercept him, uncertain of his ability to summon his reassuring smile over his foot pain.

"What can I get you, boss?" the grill-clerk asked.

J ordered a menu's worth of food and topped it off with an inquiry as to a place he could buy sneakers.

"You looking for something that'll make you more comfortable getting to the office or something that lets you perform in an athletic capacity?"

"I'm walking," J admitted, "to New York City."

"Some kind of charity?" asked the grill-clerk, a tuna melt and fries magically already ready.

"Charity?" J asked.

"Which?"

"Why do you think I'm with a charity?"

"Must be for some kind of charity," the man said. "If you just wanted to get to New York, you could fly or take the train. You could drive. For the price of walking shoes, you'd be halfway to a bus ticket."

"What if I like to walk?"

"Then you would walk one of those trails they got for hikers, that Appalachian Trail, or that one out west what that all the ladies do, the PCT, and then there's got to be something up and down the Rocky Mountains. You'd get yourself a pack and a tent and some hiking boots. You'd do it in the woods."

"None of those go from here to New York City."

"There's the American Discovery Trail, that gets you most of the way there."

"I'm not doing it in the woods," J said. "That would take too long."

"Makes no sense," the cook said while J wolfed his sandwich. "Quickest way isn't on foot."

"Wait," J said in a synaptic flash, a bounce of recognition.

The grill clerk leaned on his elbows across the counter from J and waited, attentive. J hadn't noticed it at first because the man wore a white paper overseas cap with blue piping, a white apron with the same, and a white polyester uniform shirt, that and he had his hair back. Also, it had been a few years, and the last time J had seen the man J had been on a night of no sleep, a sleep-deprived morning compounded by the emotional tumult of seeing E, of seeing the little girl towards whom J now...

"Never mind," J said, thinking better of mentioning to the man that they'd last met in a diner in Torrey, though that other version of the man, the version that let his dreads hang and his beard grow, certainly explained this version's knowledge of hiking trails.

"Hey," the man said, "all I'm saying is there's more than one store I could point you towards."

"You know a lot about hiking," J said.

J's diner man squinted.

"Hike out west much?"

"How do you mean?"

"There's beautiful trails near Torrey."

"Everybody seems to have a crush on that town," the man said, standing up straight. "On Utah really. But, whatever."

Nonetheless, the man gave J directions to a sporting goods store. J left the restaurant, nauseous with the memory of his scramble in the desert to Joe's place. Still, what else was J going to do? This wasn't the desert. He walked to the sporting goods store.

There, J selected a pair of simple running shoes. They were incredibly white and shiny. He tried them on with his now haggard suit pants and dress shirt, observed the combination in the mirror. *I look like a secretary*, he thought, *in a zombie film called 'Night of the Endless Commute.'* He looked like the office workers on Water Street where he'd gotten his very first big deal job. He'd walk amongst them on the narrow Dutch streets, completely shadowed by towers up Park Row, where he'd dally at J&R Music World, fiddling with clearance CDs before continuing on to the East Village, then still a marginal neighborhood reeling from a decades-long heroin fixation in Alphabet City to its east.

How far J was from being the kid in a suit hanging out at happy hour at Coyote Ugly, back when that had simply been a dive bar with sawdust on its floor and a business model that meant hiring young women straight off the Greyhound, hanging there and waiting for Lena to get home from work, to join him, and then to go around the corner to her apartment.

To look less like that version of a commuter, he bought clothes more appropriate for hiking, nylon shorts, and nylon side-zip over-pants, and a synthetic t-shirt and a fleece sweater to put over that, and some accouterment: a camelback and a poncho. He changed in the dressing room, stuffing his suit into the camelback's main compartment, and filling its water bladder from the fountain in front of the men's room. He completed the look with a pair of cheap sunglasses. This was a mission now, no time for dwelling on his various infinite walks in New York City, years earlier.

(Some of those walks for adventure; others in order to flee, or not so much flee, as get home after the world stopped.)

Back on the sidewalk, he caught a glimpse of himself in a storefront window. His legs looked odd exposed beneath the hem of his jogging shorts, but it was too warm for his overpants. The following day, when the temperature dropped and rain stripped the dead leaves from the wintering trees, he wore all of his new clothes, his suit jacket layered between fleece and poncho.

J walked without incident across hills and hills and hills and hills, all of them short and steep, until he came to love the uphill better than the downhill, until his body shed weight faster than he could eat hamburgers, which he ate at least four times-a-day, always with fries, extra fries, and soda. He walked without incident into the heart of November, shelter, providential, every twenty-five to thirty miles. He washed his clothing in a sink every other night, dried it over the radiator.

Without incident until an early twilight, day-lengths cratering, overtook him at the outskirts of Pittsburg. There, he asked a gas station attendant for safe walking directions into and through the city. The man wrote out a small map for him and insisted that he take a free pint of orange juice, which J ultimately accepted out of a sense of politeness though he was certain he had money enough saved to purchase the gas station itself, outright, or if not money, then credit on the card from the Three Kings that he continued to use without hiccup. The map led him through streets that seemed neither kept-up nor dangerous.

J marveled that he had not logged onto a computer in two weeks, had not checked up on the two children he loved, the children he simply assumed he'd find in New York, that they'd be there. That notion hinted, a hint he suppressed by observing that he noticed the absence of internet access ahead of his lack of phone usage, which, he realized too late, reinforced the hint rather than suppressing it.

At the end of a quiet block of two-story brick houses, each with a small front yard bound by a low wire fence that cast checked shadows under the sodium streetlamps, J came to what looked like an armory, its roofline notched for archers. A line of men queued in front of its closed metal double door. The men all carried small bundles and had the appearance of wearing clothing that didn't quite match them. J noticed a burly man with an untrimmed beard and grease smudges on one cheek wearing a crisp, sparkling red t-shirt with the bubbly logo of a summer camp. Another man, despite his rags, sported a slicked back Roffler hair-do.

"I've been sent to a homeless shelter," J marveled. He considered staying in it, he really did. For one thing, he'd never been inside a shelter, had barely even ever had a conversation with a genuinely homeless person. Staying there would continue the sensibility of walking. J had so often felt himself a refugee, and there was the man in the van, who if he'd lived—he did live still—but if he survived, would have been/would be a refugee. Perhaps it was time for J to experience the institutional mercy of a shelter.

On the other hand, J worried for his personal security. He carried with him both real money and the means of accessing even

more money. His childhood had been filled with stories of the
homeless killing each other for shoes. He looked down at his own
feet. The white shoes gleamed even in the shadowed street corner
from which he watched.

The shelter's doors opened.

Two people came out and set up a card table at the entrance.
J watched the men in line sign some papers on the table and hand
over what looked like cash. It seemed that one of the workers then
stamped the back of their hands. Strange, J thought. He wondered
whether this was to allow the men reentry should they go outside
to smoke, or was simply a way of keeping track of them, or if it was
a measure to prevent them from staying multiple nights in a row.

J wondered where he might wander, if he didn't go into the
shelter. He imagined that the neighborhood did not improve on
the far side of the armory, and he further suspected that there might
be an awful lot of post-industrial despair before he made it to the
kind of interstate corridor beset by motels. The door opened as
one of the homeless men went in and J caught darkness broken by
flashing colored lights and a quick still of loud disco.

He heard the engine of a vehicle behind him and turned to see
a white van approach. The van stopped in front of him and a man
in a suit jumped out and ran up. J took a step backwards.

"Repent!" the man said.

"Excuse me?" J asked.

"Repent while there is yet time!"

J considered it, repenting. His life, after all, was full of sin,
if one believed in that kind of thing. Certainly, his dreams were
indicative of some imperative to do something.

"Repent!"

J allowed that perhaps the Lord had sent this screaming man.

"Repent! Repent! Do it now! Repent!"

Or, perhaps, finally, the man in the box truck dreaming had
somehow sent this screaming man.

"Repent unto the Lord!"

"Stop shouting already," J said. "I'll repent."

"Repent! Sorry, what?" the man said. "Really?"

"Sure. Why not?"

Really: why not? J had plenty to repent for; and, it wasn't as if anything he'd done up until now had made anything, any of it, better.

"Seriously?" the man said. "You're not just saying that?"

"For fuck's sake," J began.

"Lord be praised!" the man shouted. "So you won't go in there?" He pointed at the armory, whose line of men was now more than half absorbed. "Hallelujah!"

"That's the big deal?" J asked. "You don't want me to go to a homeless shelter?"

"Homeless shelter?" the man asked.

"That homeless shelter," J said, pointing at the armory. "That's your problem?"

The man began to laugh. "You're only out looking for supper," he said.

"Excuse me?" J asked.

"This is the problem!" the man yelled, apparently reinvigorated, to a woman who'd stepped out of the other side of the van. "This is what I've been talking about!"

"Sure it is, honey," the woman said.

"The innocent!"

"Of course, honey."

"Those in search of shelter! The meek!"

"Sure," she said.

"This poor man nearly went into there by accident! This man, this man pious enough to repent when penance he needed not, very nearly entered upon that temple of Gomorrah, unawares!"

J thought to argue that he wasn't homeless, had plenty of money, wasn't so necessarily not in need of penance.

Could he consider the man's edict to repent heavenly anyway? Should he? The question set up a binary between a world created and ordered and a world at random odds with itself. In the former, nothing was accidental, in which case meaning must be attached the man's edict. Indeed, meaning must be attached to each of his words, which had the effect of giving every word gravity both on its own and in its syntactic orientation. But, J thought, if each word has meaning independent of its syntax, independent of the words to its right and left, then the whole world comprises a series of ciphers of one. And, those ciphers have additional meaning by virtue of their organization.

Absolutely overwhelming.

Alternately, well alternately: no God. Still, J thought, isn't there a chance that there's a world with a loose God, one who's sloppy, an absentminded deity, a creator who creates, then moves on to other projects, then checks back in? If God was indeed unbounded by time, might He not instead look at His overall work, what humans supposed the history of the world, from bang to bang, as a kind of two-dimensional composition, and might not that composition require large dark areas, in which God's presence is not felt, to highlight the areas of bright color in which it is?

"Sir," the man said. "We can help you find a place to sleep for the night."

"Oh," J said.

"See?" the man said to the woman. "Poor guy's clearly out of it. Thought he needed to repent when he didn't even know what that place was."

"What is that place?" J asked.

"Evil."

"Evil?"

"Without pause or penance."

"Evil? Really? How? Who are those people?"

"Sodomites."

"Sodomites?"

"The inhabitants of Sodom, of Gomorrah, of Jericho. The damned."

The inhospitable, J thought, didn't seem likely.

"Should I invite him to stay with us?" the man asked the woman.

"You've basically just did," the woman said.

"Sure," J murmured, still marveling at the armory, it a worthwhile mystery now. "Sure, I'll stay with you."

He climbed into the van without waiting for an invitation to do so, and sat down in the second row of bench seats, halfway back, watching the line of men out the van's window.

He'd been outreached! J suppressed giddy laughter. He imagined the vehicle ordinarily shepherded parishioners to church picnics, or abortion protests, or to wherever it was pastors took their masses. J ought to know the answer to that; he was in the employ of the Christians, after all. Or was, he corrected himself, exhaling at this epiphany. He wondered if Chase worried about him, if his disappearance had been noted. Being outreached wasn't so bad, J thought.

Indeed, it all seemed to lead to a comfortable seat in a van with a driver.

Of course they noted his absence; just that he'd burned his relationships with Hayley and Chase too badly for either to care to worry. And Art? Art was governor. Art was governor and J didn't yet know what it meant to Art that J had punched a man at the museum they'd built.

It wouldn't have surprised J if the couple took him to a church basement and set him up with beans and hotdogs on a Styrofoam plate. There might be a whole new life in it, one in which he became the friendly janitor of an evangelical congregation, the smiling success story of the van's driver, rescued from effort, and struggle, and consciousness.

It might be the end at last.

Wouldn't it be something if years later Art stumbled upon him working in a church?

Nothing, J assured himself, can save you from the fate of the man in the van. And he pictured the bodies tangled and massed against the front wall of the van's box, warned away from the intake at the exit only by the slight sweet of un-burnt diesel, only that to indicate their drowsiness wasn't the lulling of a suspension swaying over dirt roads. He thought about E's two children, the little girl who'd smiled at him over the booth-back in the Torrey diner clutching her little sister's hand.

A night, he could spend a night with these people, whatever the intolerance they meant by Sodomites. Was their inhospitality towards God's ensigns so mistaken given God's enmity of them? Or that of the doomed of Gomorrah, the doomed inhabitants of Jericho, of Moab?

CHAPTER FORTY-FOUR

THEY TOOK HIM NOT to a church, but to a plain house in what seemed an okay neighborhood twenty minutes away from the armory. They supposed he'd want a shower; he did. When he emerged, clean, back in his athletic clothes, the woman, Lorraine, had prepared him a plate of food. She invited him to sit and eat. She had changed into frumpy pajamas swaddled in an oversized bathrobe, exchanged contacts for thick-framed glasses. She looked motherly, like she'd waited up for a late-working favorite son. Her husband had gone to bed already, she explained to J, he worked early, but she would stay up to keep J company, make sure he had everything he needed. Besides, she liked a cup of steamed milk before bed. J was careful to pull his chair all the way into the table and take small bites, chewing thoroughly, eating slowly.

Lorraine asked about his homelessness: its duration and causes. J explained, as best he could, the truth, that he was walking from Cincinnati to New York City of his own volition, that he wasn't homeless per se—though no less grateful for her hospitality and compassion. To his surprise, she wasn't perturbed by his confession nor fazed by that fact that he'd walked some three hundred miles to reach her. She did not evict him to a taxi and hotel. She sipped her steamed milk and longed aloud for the days in which she smoked cigarettes.

"Is this penance?" she asked J.

He cut a small bite of Salisbury steak, a homemade approximation of a food whose microwavable incarnation J had subsisted upon in his last years living in his New York apartment. So this, he thought, is the muse of all that, the real thing. He wondered if Art worried, if Jeremiah and Christian did: stacking new folders of findings on top of untouched ones on his desk. Since the period Christian liked to call "J's great dereliction," they'd checked up on him whenever he missed even a single day without calling in.

"Penance for what?"

"Does it matter?"

He ate more bites of food, overly aware of the sound his fork's tines made against the ceramic plate. It was as if he was only picking at his food even though he was eating.

"Can I show you something?" she asked.

He allowed that she could.

She walked across the kitchen and opened a sparkling clean, metal cabinet door and took down a shoebox. How cliché, he thought, but in a way that admired cliché for ordering the world. She sat back down and took a stack of old and uneven photographs from the box. She selected one, pushed it across the table to J.

"Look how happy he is," she said.

The man in the photo did look happy. He was chunky in the way that athletic men in their thirties confined to desks tend to thicken. He leaned against a shiny vehicle, black in the black and white picture, dressed in almost civilian wear, but that his jacket buttoned like a uniform jacket, and a medal of some sort hung over his breast. His hands were folded behind him, between the seat of his pants and the car, which gave the impression that he, while pleased to pose for the camera, wasn't quite used to it either, or, J supposed, that he was very concerned about keeping his jacket clean. Or even, the man might be standing at parade rest. In the background, a large horse pulled an open cart down the street.

"He was my grandfather's boss," she said.

"I see."

"The administrator of a ghetto for Jews."

"Which?" J asked.

"Which?"

"Yes. Which?"

"That's what you would want to know? The Jews are all dead. My grandfather's boss was executed in 1947 by the Polish."

"Seriously, which ghetto?"

"He's so happy in this photo. My grandfather was happy, too, I was told, when he wasn't griping about living in Poland and the danger of cholera and dysentery the ghetto posed. They didn't need any penance, so why shouldn't we need it for them? Why shouldn't we make a pilgrimage?"

"I don't follow at all," J said.

"Another," she said.

She pushed over a second photo. A small triangle of grass in the front left corner of the picture indicated to J that he was seeing the full breadth of a column of men that extended beyond the frame's short edges in both directions. The men sat on the ground, their hands behind their heads, facing towards the photo's front right corner. He counted: each row in the column was seven men wide. A picket fence in poor repair bound them on the far side of the photo. In the upper left-hand corner, the corner furthest from the photographer, a few forms, slightly unfocused, standing, might have been guards. Behind these, on the other side of the fence, a group of indistinct forms that seemed to rise up may have been onlookers. Many of the men on the ground had beards, none of them wore hats, all of them were in civilian clothing, drab civilian clothing. Most of them, J noticed, were old.

"These men are about to be killed," she said.

He looked at them again. Not all of them were old, just the ones in the foreground. They didn't all have their hands behind their heads, as J had first thought, either, though all of their hands were lifted. Some held their faces, as if in grief, or to hide from the photographer. Another looked more as if he was rubbing the back of his head, as if puzzled or confused, but the too-wide posture of his mouth, the upward disposition of his eyes, made it seem like his puzzlement was really a suppression of an outdone imagination, a space beyond thinking or knowing or doing. As if, J thought, this man's internal monologue was set to, 'you don't know, you don't know,' a monologue whose uncertainty held out some promise of everything being something other than what it seemed.

And what it seemed…what did it seem to the people near the guards in the back of the picture hanging over the fence looking in? They were onlookers, weren't they? They certainly didn't look like additional guards, though they were sufficiently out of focus that J had to judge this by the attitude of their silhouettes, the eagerness of their clustering, the way they rose in height, as if they were giving each other boosts, or had found the one rise that let them see over the fence.

"This one," she said, tapping a man in the photo with her nail. "He knows, he knows."

The man's cheeks were filled; it looked like he was blowing out air against their pressure; his elbows pointed straight forward, his hands on his neck below his black hair; he was shaven, his shirt clean, better nourished. He knew.

Whereas some of the old men's expressions reminded J of the slightly confused grimaces he'd seen when he'd visited his grandmother during her post-illness recuperation in a nursing home, this man's didn't. At the home, he'd seen the same look on patients asked to walk down hallways by younger, smilingly forceful attendants. It was a look at once suspicious of the attendants while masked by a fear of having their suspicion found out. It was a look that ebbed in and out of confusion of place and action and self. He'd interpreted it as the patients' vague anxiety that whatever posed as rehabilitation would likely be mildly unpleasant, certainly an indignity. But the man with his cheeks inflated: He was a man trying to figure out how and where and when the execution would take place, a man trying to decide how to face that execution and trying to psyche himself up to that decided manner of facing it. He was a man who'd despaired of escape, not remotely entertaining hope of pardon, but who considered standing and dashing that he might be shot now.

"From there the vans. Gassed," she said.

J looked again at the man she'd tapped. This too could be his dreamer...or maybe his dreamer was the old guy who squinted as if he was facing the sun, or the middle-aged gaunt man with the strong nose who covered his ears as if to block out the noise of explosions or keep the voices in his head from emerging, or this man with the white bandage tied around his brow like the bandana of a rebel leader, or...but before he could ask or ascertain, a new photo had covered the one of the murdered men in waiting.

The new photograph was of young people in a park. They wore suits but with their collars askew, like the suits were casual clothes. They had their arms around each other's shoulders. They mostly could have passed for any contemporary group of friends just out of adolescence jaunting in flaunted dress-up-wear.

"They look happy, but also them," and she made a small sharp click in the back of her mouth and a slash against her neck with her hand.

J gently stroked the photo with the tips of his right hand's middle three fingers.

"Are they so different from my grandfather's boss? They're happy and then they're killed."

"But they're so attractive," J said, and then processing what Lorraine had said: "How can you say that? They're not Nazis!"

"So?"

"So! So? So they're nothing like your murdering grandfather!"

"My grandfather's boss."

"What do you think he did for his boss?"

"You can't yell. My husband."

J took a deep breath and tried to look at the photo without thinking about Lorraine, but she pulled the picture of the man with the car out again and set it beside the picture of the young people in the park.

"He doesn't look it, like he believes he needs to do penance, does he?" she asked. "They don't either. They all end up dead. They're happy and then they're dead. Repent. Do penance. If you believe you should, then you should. We're not happy, and we'll also be dead one day. Why the penance...that's not so much what matters."

"Her," J said, pointing at a woman in the front right of the frame, further forward than her friends and on the edge of the picture, so that it almost seemed as if she was goofily leaning in. She was beautiful, J thought, they were all beautiful. Despite a crease in the picture and some discoloration, despite the fact that she was indeed leaning, and that her dress therefore obscured her body's contours, J could tell: she was what he had always sought.

It was her face, its breadth, her chin, her eyes, her thick hair cut short. Her he wanted to make smile, though the woman behind her was more model-perfect, and the man the model-perfect woman leaned upon was a handsome, incredibly handsome version of the girl J wanted. In fact, when he looked, that man was perhaps the most handsome man J had ever seen, more masculine and more refined than even Art.

Much as J wanted to, he didn't ask Lorraine how she'd come to have all of these photos. Not asking made a dark ominousness of their collection.

J didn't have good words or descriptions for any of the people really, just that they were strikingly attractive, certainly not the appropriate subjects of genocide, of Holocaust, of anti-Semitism.

Certainly not the appropriate subjects of Holocaust: the Salisbury steak he'd eaten came back up. He barely swallowed back his vomit, bile burning and gamy on his tonsils.

Who was the appropriate subject of Holocaust, of anti-Semitism, of genocide? How could anyone be the appropriate subject?

If he could ask the question then he must believe someone was.

No. No! He refused to believe that he believed that. He pulled the photo of the men by the fence out and began to cry.

Lorraine touched his shoulder.

"I didn't know," J said.

Lorraine shushed soothingly and rubbed his back with her hand.

"I know," she said. "It's very sad."

"I didn't know that I'd accepted that a certain type of person was meant to be the victim of the Holocaust. I didn't know. I didn't know. I didn't know that I had did that!"

She crouched beside his chair and put her arms around him and pulled his head into her chest and stroked his hair.

He wailed.

"They did that to me!" he said into her chest. "They made me think there was a kind of person who was suitable for anti-Semitism, for genocide, for Holocaust! They did that to me!"

She held him and he could feel her skin, wet against his face. He could smell the astringency of her cheap bath soap and the mild warmth of bedclothes not on their first wear. He hadn't cried since he held Jeremiah, but these weren't tears for a shitty month and lost love interests: these tears were for the recognition that he was the dream of man being slowly gassed to death, and that the beliefs of all those who'd come after that man had formed that man's dream into who J was.

He pulled himself away from Lorraine. She kept a hand on his back, comfortingly, and handed him a napkin from the table. He blew his nose and then pointed again at the young woman in the picture again.

"Her, too?" he asked. "She was also killed?"

"I can only think yes," Lorraine said. "All of them."

All of them, he thought, the purpose of the ghetto clear: to transform viable humans, these people, into the gaunt victims waiting for gassing in the other photo. First, J thought, you make them ugly. You make them people who deport each other to the camps. You make them weak and haggard and nebbish and disoriented. You make them joyless and then you can kill them. Then you can kill them.

What tender mercy, what empathetic care, the murderers afforded themselves, to first inflict the misery out of which it is only humane to put the immiserated, to make of their murder humaneness.

He felt through his chest the shaking pulse that comes before crying, before even more crying. He blew his nose and sighed and put another bite of the Salisbury steak into his mouth and began to chew before eating horrified him and he spat it out.

Once made appropriate for genocide could they be made back again? He dreaded seeing what the young woman and her group looked like by the end. He would do anything to be able to spend by her side her every living moment, whatever she was turned into. Once the flesh was stripped from beneath the skin and the will stripped from the human and the capacity for joy defenestrated, with it the capacity for horror, could that person, if that person was one of the few who didn't die, be reconstituted, unrived? Could those things flensed be shoved back between skeleton and skin? Would those things, replaced, place properly, assemble?

Wouldn't there be gaps and shards and fragments?

"The food has something wrong?" Lorraine asked.

"No," J said. "It's that…"

It was that he wondered if the same question didn't also apply to a people as a whole: once made nebbishe, ugly, shorn of their numbers, their young, halved, wrecked, could they be reintegrated? Reconstructed?

"I showed you only to make a point."

"What kind of a point could you have hoped to make?" J wailed.

"Hush, you'll wake my husband."

"Does he know?"

"I didn't mean to upset you so much," she said.

"Your husband? Does he know?"

"Does my husband know what?"

J didn't know what either. He asked whether she had more photos. She did, and J looked at them, but he was all used up.

He looked at the photos of skinny little children, all the same height, their heads shaven, escorted in long columns chaperoned by only a few armed adults towards Lodz's trains, onward to Chelmno. He looked and didn't feel anything. He had felt something. He had felt something about the Holocaust for the first time in so long. It didn't make him feel any better that he had now that he didn't. J tried to impose the faces of E's children on these faces. Nothing doing. There were other photos, but he didn't look at them.

"Cup of steamed milk, then bed?" Lorraine asked.

"Are you happy?"

He looked at her. She tousled his hair. He thought again that he was used up. And he'd have to sleep here. He would.

"Do you believe that you should do penance?" J asked.

She ran her fingers along his scalp and clenched her hand so that she pulled the hair on the top of his head just a bit, which, J had to admit, felt really good.

"You must be tired from so much walking," she said.

He almost thought that she would follow him into the neatly made guest bed. He slept unmolested, and in the morning, over thin bitter coffee and cold cereal, it occurred to him that Lorraine's husband was her penance, and taking J in was her penance, and living was her penance, knowing and yet living was her penance. And he would have, he knew, comforted her had she come unto him in the night.

CHAPTER FORTY-FIVE

J WALKED AND HE walked; he crossed the small communities and rural sprawl that ran the stretch of the Alleghany Plateau; he walked through Harrisburg's suburbs and through Allentown and back out through its northern suburbs. He walked and he walked and he crossed the Pocono Mountains and he crossed the Delaware River into New Jersey, and he walked through New Jersey. His body adapted to walking's rhythms. His feet contoured to his shoes, and his shoes contoured to the pavement. He slept in motels and he slept in culverts. He replaced his camelback with a slightly larger pack, one sufficient to accommodate a small sleeping bag, and a down coat, down mittens, and a sleeping pad and a tarp.

The walking offered little diversion, left his thoughts to entertain themselves, which they did with an increasingly ecstatic madness, a madness that showed him the landscapes of the wilderness trails he'd shirked, showed him waterfall-cut cliffs and lichen-speckled boulders and not-head-high trees stunted by exposure. The thoughts happened simultaneous and repetitive. In the ensuing noise, his thinking collided memories of childhood and yeshiva and anxieties about the world's end and the loneliness of a life without E or Chase or Allie or Hayley and the apparently innumerable specifics of the sex he never had with women he had never met, and these collisions formed sound and giggling and color and one foot before the other.

Then his mind left him, allowed him to become his walking so that there was only one foot in front of the other, a still and perfect reverie interrupted by the occasional need to ask directions or for food or to summon the wherewithal to pitch his wig in brush or dustings of snow or on concrete, the asking quiet and still, too.

His mind returned to him purged and empty, capable of infinite escape and cognition, capable of levitation, of withstanding coals beneath his feet or nails imbedded in his back, beyond needing such proof of its powers. In that space, he found his memory of his first job in New York City, near St. Marks place, and he ran through the names of all of his fellow employees, of the woman, even younger than him, who'd told J he would look cute in a tuxedo, and of her brother, a year older than J, who'd taken him out for Puerto Rican food, and introduced him to mofongo, and laughed with a kindness that J hadn't deserved that J needn't look so anxious: the man wasn't going to leap across the table to kiss J.

J began to observe, and the observations became a rhythm that followed the syntax of Celan's poems or of a psalm or of Genesis, a syntax of wonder punctuated by Lorraine's pictures of Lodz and of Chelmno. The sandstone landscape of Joe's redoubt came back to him, a paved earth speckled in green.

He contemplated the possibility that he'd been meant to pursue Allie and his mind elected emptiness.

Joe had shown him a spot where the stone seeped thousand-year-old water. Where the water seeped, the stone exfoliated in million-ton flakes. The whole thing was in a state of erosion. Passing through a suburban sprawl so massive it had forgotten the name of the small town, sacked by post-industrial collapse, from which it once bloomed, J conceded that the whole of the earth followed an entropic course: the sandstone exfoliated and collapsed, the mud hills of the southwest washed away. Here, sprawl grew like an immune response, like an allergic reaction to riddled urban centers, a response whose damages eclipsed those of the problem it permanently walled in. The whole world entropic: J's dreams of creation seemed themselves a lie, or at minimum destructive, a blighting of the nothingness that preceded comingled light and dark, dry and sea.

Then time was a decay, not just an axis against which decay was measured, and life was a decay, all of it was a decay, an erosion, a lossy emission of heat that sullied cold, which in turn, too, lost heat. Time was the off-gassing of the void, which was perfect and complete; time was the imperfection, the lack of completion, emitted, extruded, escaped, exiled from the void. Creation was the imperfection of the void, the void's entropy, endless.

The world was no more finished than it was flat; its completion no more desirable than the fact that walking long enough would lead one to one's point of origin. It was all so melodramatic; but it also was melodramatic. He newly empathized with Walter's collection of perfectly-worn things, things that began but didn't end, captures of time stalled, potential counterarguments to apocalypse, but even these were stalled not halted, even frozen things waited for thaw, for doom.

He was alone, and he wanted to reach the end of being alone.

All alone there isn't even conflict, isn't drama, isn't story.

A scratch on J's leg didn't heal. J bedded tired and woke tired. J thought the end must be close, that the life-force of the universe, the dream of the dreamer, was waning. He'd thought this before but this time he was nearly forty and his mind had the power to lift buildings, to ward marauders from his nightly city-park perches, to make his body walk despite its deterioration, despite the evolution of scratch into pussy gash. Certainly his clarity transcended the dream's confines. He walked faster, walked further, walked longer.

As he encroached on New York City, well into his fourth week on foot, and entered its surrounding patchwork of elegantly wooded suburbs, sprawl, and nightmarish small cities, the weather turned. It rained rains that froze, snowed snows that melted into super-chilled rivulets. He bought a rain shell and rain pants at an outdoor goods store and kept walking. It began to blow. The winds were so strong that the melt and the freeze, alike, found even the discreetest of slips in seams, sleeted in long horizontal streaks around the interior of his jacket, turned his skin putrid and purpled.

J walked anyway. The sky blackened. It hurled erratically. At first J dashed between awnings and overhangs, took shelter when the freeze fell from the sky, and then he determined that he had to walk anyway. He continued on, soaked and shivered. The darkness that plagued the Egyptians reigned for days, artificial light useless against the gloom, the sun obliterated. J would have wondered if there'd been volcanic eruptions or oil well fires, but the sky had turned against him when he left New York, and it made sense that it turn against him upon his return.

Random parts of his body worked less well. The end was simply near. He walked; he walked towards E's two girls.

And finally, one late morning, after a night spent in the lee of a Ft. Lee megastore's cinder brick, he set foot on the George Washington Bridge and the wind swept the sky clear of clouds then slowed. The sun rejoiced in the icicles it freed from the bridge's thick piping to the dense estuary below and the sun liberated moisture from the sodden ground in long patches of steam that rose from the riverbanks and from between the mess of six-story brick buildings that filled the steep rise of the Hudson's east shore. J stepped timidly onto the bridge, his sneakers malformed to his clumped feet from drying over the motel room's cranked heater. This was it. This was the day.

CHAPTER FORTY-SIX

HALFWAY ACROSS THE BRIDGE, J stopped and looked down towards New York harbor. The tide pushed floes, greyed, trapezoidal, upriver, steaming and disintegrating. To the south, the buildings, scoured by days of wet, glistened brand new, tall glints of blue and green metallic glass falsely claiming man's ability to build, to create, to forestall. He took off his pack. He no longer needed it. It tumbled from the bridge and disappeared into the swirling below. It would be a lie to say that J didn't consider following the pack over the railing.

He stepped off the bridge and into Washington Heights. Muck in sidewalk cracks passed for slush before dirtied six-story deco buildings whose battleship-grey-gloss lobbies were lit by bare compact-fluorescents screwed into incandescent fixtures. He walked uphill to Broadway. He became aware of how much everything hurt. He was tired, tired and achy.

J leaned against a building to catch his breath. He went into a bodega and bought some prepackaged desert that promptly turned his stomach. He couldn't walk any further. He stumbled to a bus stop.

From his old neighborhood, Inwood, there had been an express bus that for four dollars would have taken him, but it got on the highway well north of the George Washington Bridge. For lack of knowing better, he got on the first southbound bus that stopped. He found a seat midway back and collapsed into its hard plastic, orange perch.

The bus crept, moved perhaps even slower than walking. It stopped at the end of practically every block and made time enough for small old women, bundled against precipitation that had long ceased, to bring aboard their folding shopping carts freighted to the outside limit of these ladies' ability to wheel with plastic-bagged paper shopping bags. The bus knelt for these ladies and when it straightened and shut its doors, it clutched the outside air, acrid with snow's answer to mildew's musk. Blended conversations mixed with the bus' irregular pneumatic sighs and the engine and horn noise of the traffic around them, cars and cabs and gypsy cabs and delivery vans and police cars and bicycles swerving and keening on buckling streets already driven dry and patched with metal plates that clanged like explosions, this set against the nearly subsonic drone of other people's headphones. The combination soothed J, as did the smell of warm bus, which blanched the cold's acrid tang from J's upper palette after every stop, a consoling confection, musty with clothing too long exposed to any number of toxicities: tobacco, mothballs, drycleaners, luncheonette grills, Chinese kitchens.

Compared to the suburbs' uniformity and the benighted urban centers between Cincinnati and here, uptown Manhattan, the real uptown, seemed provincial and happy, north of the December decorative onslaught, especially in the sun, in the post-storm. Yellow awnings that dated back at least three generations advertised odd-goods stores, bodegas and small restaurants. J felt a bit like he might vomit blood, like the gash in his leg might be gangrenous, like he might slough a digit or two. He held it together, let the sounds and sights and smells insulate him from the people who cycled though the surrounding seats. No one took the bus as far. J had time though.

He intended to meet the girls at the ice-skating rink in Central Park. For lack of better methods, he'd adopted the scheme of TV kidnappers: he planned to pose as a family friend and pick the girls up after their skating lessons before their nanny got there. He would bring them to the dreamer, he thought, and somehow that made sense, sense of the kind Isaac made to Abraham on Mount Moriah.

When the bus eventually reached 125th street, J swayed to the bus-driver's booth and asked how he might get to ice-skating in Central.

"What? Wollman Rink? You?"

J averred. The bus driver sighed and told him to hold on. They pulled into a stop and new passengers pressed J back against the barrier behind the driver's seat in their crush to the seats and standing room behind him. The bus began again and J, standing still, meekly reminded the driver of his presence. The driver, who leaned back and forth to spin his big wheel and bring the bus back into the travel lane, ignored J for half a block before letting J know that he was in luck; this was the bus that connected the Cloisters with the Met, and then continued all the way on down 5th Avenue to 37th Street before cutting over to Penn Station. The bus driver would let J know when they got to 5th & 62nd. J didn't care that the bus continued onto Penn Station, but he took it as a divine sign, a nod from his dreamer, that the first bus he'd boarded at the top of Manhattan would take him all the way down to the bottom of Central Park. He swayed back down the bus aisle, clutching each of the poles along the way, until one of the old ladies repositioned her cart so that he tripped over her knees to reach the window seat beside her.

No one could tell that he'd just walked hundreds of miles carrying a pack.

The sun, risen to near its meridian, burnt off even the steam, and the streets were dry but for the occasional puddle where a wheelchair carve-out in the sidewalk had reservoired a gutter's flow. The neighborhood changed again. The Metro North tracks dipped into the ground, and with that dip ended the innocuous stores whose awnings' hooks and sidewalks' fronts overflowed with cheap suitcases and knock-off sunglasses and plastic wind-up frogs that awkwardly swam in small tubs of water and metal children's scooters and miniature folding bicycles whose seats rose high in mockery of a clown's ride.

In their place, tall, clean, pre-war apartment buildings lined daily-washed, broad sidewalks whose iron-hoop-fence-bound cutouts sprouted mature maple and locust, the denuded trees tangled in strings of lights whose plastic Caribbean palette echoed, in brighter hues, the uniforms of the doormen who paced rubber-ized burgundy welcome runners under wreathed canopies that reached all the way to the street. Where lobby windows were visible, so were white electric menorahs with yolk-orange bulbs for candle flames, and behind these menorahs, Christmas trees. J was close. He patted his hair down. He practiced smiling, showing his teeth to his translucent reflection in the bus window.

Eventually the bus pulled into the turnabout before the Metropolitan Museum of Art. Tourists teemed, everything did, life mushrooming after days battened by freezing rain. J had once met the love of his middle twenties on these very white marble steps, early in their dating in weather as beautiful as this, weather almost warm enough for the short sleeves of the coconut-buttoned, orange Hawaiian shirt he'd worn with a pair of white carpenter jeans, motorcycle boots, and a stiff brimmed cotton-checked hat meant for Floridian dog-track bettors twice his twenty-five years. She had laughed and laughed at him and he had loved her, then, before his feelings about his feelings swung, and swung back, and then back again, before all the phone calls and the broken foot.

Later, after they'd broken up with finality, J had begun the work by which he'd finally moved past the obsessive, ruminat-ing, second-guessing part of his thinking habits, to at last come to genuinely enjoy his own company, the work that allowed for his healthy relationship, the one with E. How long ago it was that his mind worked as it should.

How very long ago.

J again had the sense that something antithetical to déjà vu was upon him. This time, his remembering didn't seem to create the past event but eradicate it, and with it its attendant emotions. He couldn't imagine ever dressing to amuse again. He couldn't imagine loving someone like the love of his twenties anymore, a society girl a year out of a Pioneer Valley women's college earnestly endeavoring on behalf of a series of arcane non-profits. He was withered now, wrung out. His red athletic overpants and yellow poncho wouldn't be mistaken for colorful whimsy nor would his tanned skin be mistaken for vain fancy.

J had to use the hand railing to get off the bus, had to bring both feet to rest on every tread like the town-promoter in Baker had all those years ago going down the staircase before J's trailer. He moaned at the memory, grieved that in experiencing it he was likely to lose forever the feeling of being strong he'd felt roughnecking in Montana, once upon a time. Once upon a time! Fuck.

He walked into the park in a crush of Christmas tourists. He drifted through shopping chatter and out onto a stone bridge that crossed the park's loop road. He could see the scimitar of concrete terrace that sat upon the skate rental shop ahead through the crowns of the trees. Then he descended and the woods were dense enough to block his view. He still had too much time and thought about stopping at a pushcart and picking up hot pretzels for the girls, or roasted nuts maybe—then he thought that might perhaps be a better activity to do with them, something normal, a treat that would reassure them.

How was he to rescue them?

He felt a queasy at the thought he might need to reassure them: what the fuck was he doing here? He'd been walking for weeks, come this far.

How was he to keep them safe, spirit them from danger, once they were in his charge? Truthfully, he wasn't sure. He knew that they needed to leave the city. Dimly, he imagined getting back to Walter's, retrieving the Bedouin rifle and holing up on a mountain, living off the land. But what use could that be against the end of the world?

He would take them to the dreamer.

Walter's ranch. The land. The rifle.

A pulse of faster walkers passed leaving a pocket of cold in their wake. J shivered.

His hands trembled to think of the world unwoven, the firmament unraveled into pre-creation nothingness, watching that dissipation slowly overtake them, chase them uphill like the waters must have Noah's last neighbors, him keeping the girls a step uphill, his gun trained in their wake. What could he possibly shoot? Still, he felt compelled to try, to try to save those two girls, these two girls, the two girls that he loved.

His hands shook. He bought himself a water and also a pretzel, after all, because the words with which to request a pretzel were already formed in his head and thus accidentally came out of his mouth. He found that the pretzel in his hand, positioned to contain the mustard's drip, prevented him from opening the water in his other hand.

He forced himself to walk as slowly as he could.

Much too soon, beyond the perfume and manure-waft up from 57th Street's carriage cue, the path split to access the upper and lower levels of the rink-house. Barely mid-afternoon, and already the earlier sun had gone into retreat, dashed bands of office lights visible, dirty against the grey sky light, to the south. J didn't want to turn towards them, towards their implicit chill, but the path to the right led around to the front of the complex, and its teeny antiquated parking area. He chose left, the path leading him towards a little bridge over the runoff creek from beneath the rink. Clusters of children, coats color-coded by instructional institution, busied about on the ice, uneven wheels oscillating counterclockwise under the guidance of laughing teenagers. A group of girls in jade looked appropriately heighted for E's children's ages. He watched them as he walked as close as seemed nonchalant to the mid-torso-tall wooden wall. The girls played at holding hands and pin wheeling each other, hysterical at flourished kicks and bobs.

J pined for such extravagant fancies, the fancies of a moment that doesn't yet know it has already ended.

He and E had used to visit the Cloisters before brunch on weekend mornings and gaze upon the tapestries that depicted the hunt for the unicorn. In the first, the unicorn was like these girls, free amongst the forest animals, millions of different flowers and herbs embroidered, full color, in the hanging. The last tapestry in the series depicted the unicorn captive in a round corral barely as wide as the unicorn was long. That last image was every bit as floral as the first, except that it showed purity contained, didn't show any of the hunters or ladies in their elaborate trappings that played a part in the intermediate panels. The unicorn's ability to purify water with its horn, to make manifest chastity, was abandoned once it was possessed; chastity captured was jailed and abandoned, the sport ended. The unicorn began free of humans and ended bereft of them.

Or maybe the tapestries were part of more than one unicorn story, and only the viewer's need for order formed their sequence.

J mourned these memories while he watched the girls skate, grieved the remembered sense of loveliness of wandering the Cloister's gardens, of marveling at tapestries sewn in the fourteenth-century. He wondered once again whether this moment was the only moment and everything else simply a projection contained within it, memory this moment's entropic shiver.

He found a bench off to the side where he did not seem conspicuous watching the girls. He set the pretzel on his lap and opened his water. One of the teenagers blew a whistle and the little girls skated as fast as they could to the edge of the ice and then sashayed off to surround the whistler.

The teenager clapped and the girls giggled and cheered. The teenager and another her age distributed brown paper bags to their charges. J sat on the edge of his seat watching. If he walked over, all of this would end.

He wondered how close he might come before they would become aware of him and cease this day-dreamy innocence.

Now he recognized E's oldest daughter. She had on a flouncy white tutu over her puffy pink coveralls and fleecy earmuffs over her pompomed, knit hat as if her mother (or her nanny) had dressed her for a postcard photo shoot. Her younger sister sat next to her.

What strange covenant made the beauty of children a pleasure only voyeuristically available? Why couldn't he go closer? J loved them. And yet he knew that his love, expressed, would, like the instruments meant to measure an electron upon that electron, skew.

Both sisters retreated to the same bench facing the rink. They sat, legs dangling over the webbed rubber flooring. Heavy skates penduluming asynchronously, they fished small milk cartons out of their bags and opened them before reaching in again. Both retrieved sandwiches, cut diagonally, stacked and wrapped in cellophane. They sipped their milk and pulled at the cellophane. It took them a very long time to unwrap their food. J thought that someone ought to help them, but then all the girls seemed to take a very long time to unwrap their food. It disconcerted him that these little girls could be so inadequate to the task of feeding themselves.

They took such small bites.

The older of the two told some kind of story to some other girls who'd gathered around them while she ate. Her smaller sister seemed for all the world like she was singing a song to her food for only her food to hear. It surprised J that it seemed right to him that the girls he cared for would be the center of attention, queens of their peers. Even in all that he had been central, J had felt appropriately peripheral; in all that he was still, he felt so, tangential even to his own experience, his own existence.

The older girl set her sandwich down. Hardly consumed after a quarter hour of effort! And what had he ever done? She took an apple from the bag. She held it in both hands to bite into it. His life was filled with activity and yet the actual making of a thing was relegated to his dreams. She was six, would be seven soon. Surely she must be old enough to eat a full apple? A full sandwich?

J had made no marriage, no home, no child, built nothing with his hands. His inventions were at best the ephemeral impressions of false identities.

Here was this little girl. He couldn't articulate what she was. J's creations were of his dreams; in sleep he rendered the creatures of paradise and marveled at the names Adam assigned them. He knew that even if she were his daughter, even if he did rescue her, she would not tolerate his examination into the nature of her being. She would not consent to his constant handling of her, to his gawking at her fingers, cheeks, hair, behavior, marveling though his handling might be. Where was Adam to name this creature, this girl? Even if J was acknowledged as her parent, he could hope for little more than better proximity to her independent development. Neither E, nor judge, nor anyone would grant him any custody.

"Ever wonder if the oldest wasn't yours?"

J started, and Chase set a hand on his leg.

"How are you here?" J asked.

"This isn't a storyline we're going to want to see to its climax."

"How?"

"Best case scenario: you get arrested here, in the park, before you leave with them."

"But the end..."

Chase took J's hand between hers, the leather of her gloves cool and warm against his purpling skin, and asked, "Aren't you tired?"

The older of the two girls looked over at them and smiled her same over-the-back-of-a-diner-booth-in-Torrey smile. J turned his head away.

"Can't I?"

"Even if the oldest was yours."

"Mustn't I?"

They sat a moment like that: J's head turned away from Chase and the girls alike, Chase holding his hand in hers. He hated the wall of building walls he saw, ever taller away from him, the older, ornate skyscrapers on the park's southern border much like buttresses for the flat glass and metal tall behind them. Finally, Chase told J that he needn't be seen weeping here; they should walk. Walking would give his tears anonymity.

"Hold me," J said.

"Come on. Let's walk," she said.

They stood, both of Chase's arms awkwardly around his back as if she held a blanket over a victim of trauma, someone suffering from shock. J could swear he saw E's oldest daughter wave.

Then he felt a kind of solace, because there was no way that Chase could be there, unless there was a purpose, unless she too was a product of the dream.

Chase must be like him, ordinary and dreamt, and the dream simply put them in each other's paths to help each other. Or she was an angel after all. Or, perhaps, these were the same thing. Maybe they were all angels.

CHAPTER FORTY-SEVEN

J TOOK ILL AS soon as they got to Chase's hotel. He ran a fever that a century earlier would have been interpreted as brought on by nerves, a fever that made light of his laying-in at Joe and Allie's. Doctors visited the room. The grave J lay in this time in wait of whether God would smite him in the night was as posh as a grave might be: an elite hotel's elite bed. Barely, J avoided hospitalization, slipping in and out of delirium, infection in his leg, infection in his lungs, weathered misery throughout his being. When it was done, Adam had been cast from *Gan Eden* and a one-legged angel with a flaming sword guarded the gate of the garden. Either out of penance or anger or both, Adam no longer talked to his wife. So it was over then, paradise, J acceded, when his head cleared under a wrap of cold sweat; and he found his hand still between Chase's.

Winter had broken now.

She fed him simple broths spooned on heirloom-grade silver out of translucent china. He was too weak to leave the suite, but she insisted that he walk around it for five-minute intervals, walks on which he rested by clutching the doorframes that separated the three rooms. Chase kept closed the drapes, which ran the full twelve-foot height of the room and crumpled on the floor in pools of raw silk. If J was near them when one of her many phone calls pulled Chase into another room, he'd part the fabric slightly and stare across the tree-topped expanse of the park, even the moderate daylight forcing him to look from a shaded angle like a sniper hidden in the bridal trains of a mass matrimony.

A week into J's post-fever convalescence, Chase mistook a knock for room service, and resisted the male visitor's attempted entry, following him, instead, into the hallway. J struggled to overhear their conversation, but at best caught the occasional sharp vowel. He wondered if one or both of them were in hiding.

His strength returned and, despite his earlier premonitions, the gash in his leg healed. His walks extended to ten minutes, then fifteen, which was an awkwardly long span in which to wander the three rooms. He and Chase avoided conversation, mutually or individually he wasn't sure. In long stretches, though, seemingly at her whimsy, time of day independent, she read aloud from whatever book was in front of her. Like this, J followed the middle movement, the red herring pursuit, of an Agatha Christie novel; he heard about a knight who crossed a bridge made out of the blade of a sword to rescue an abducted queen; he learned how many cows must be returned for each stolen, and how many for each that died by negligence under the watch of a caretaker, and how many for each that died by accident; he fell asleep to a description of an elaborate nineteenth-century dining room designed to give the impression of a ship's cabin; he woke to two bungling Parisian clerks embarked on rural enterprise, one of whom had contracted the clap from their maidservant. He heard about a man recovering from the kind of illness that comes on in middle-age and drives one to a hungered despair in which the cabinets themselves, bare, empty, seem consumable, a week's worth of what to chew on, the wallpaper, the windows; heard how the man remembered this hunger only after his restlessness rose to such spasms that he set off to visit his mother in an isle south at sea. J drifted out of consciousness.

He asked Chase if she might read him poetry.

"Celan?"

"That would do," he said.

"Why did you sleep with Hayley?"

Margarete and Shulamith and which are you?

He thought to respond that he'd thought Chase hadn't loved him anymore. But, not only was that a lie, but recused to the hotel suite it seemed an absurd excuse. He didn't feel ready to admit that he'd simply grown tired of waiting; that he'd grown exhausted of trying to serve Art, stay faithful to her, and remain vigilant. He couldn't admit that Hayley had presented herself and because he was of interest to her, that kind of interest to her, he felt good, and that he'd wanted to indulge in that feeling good. He liked Hayley, he missed her, he was ashamed of his treatment of Hayley. It seemed empty to say how existentially lonely it was to be alone in the dream of a dying man.

He should have said, "Art," which would have been true and also a demand.

Instead, he turned to the wall and pretended to sleep. Chase climbed into the bed next to him. She spooned his back and dug a hand into his hair. He lay still, afraid to move, thought of Lorraine's hand in his hair. He felt Chase's body gently shake behind him, felt the warmth of her back against the chill brought on by the room's too-high ceilings. Then her body relaxed, quieted. Even after her breath turned deep and regular and slow, he continued to lay that way, eyes closed, awake. He had nothing, he thought, to offer his dreamer. Yet the dream, or his dreamer, would not let him forget, would not let him escape. And this realization, fostered in the shelter of Chase's sleeping body, brought him to the third stage of his relationship with his existential dilemma.

He was insignificant. More importantly, his will was insignificant. He plodded at the whim of a dream that did not depend on his active participation, on his elective choice, to derive whatever it was it derived from his life and servitude.

He was neither able to manipulate the dream, nor save the dreamer, nor serve as the dreamer's last hope.

The dream did not care about him.

Now he knew. His dreamer dreamt J for reasons that J could not hope to understand, through mechanisms equally unfathomable. Though his dreamer was dying, his dreamer did not depend on J for anything, or at least not for anything J could consciously offer of his own will.

Then what is left?

He was insignificant.

He could not act. He could not escape.

He opened his eyes and stared at the wall.

He understood what it meant to not have a story now.

Now he understood, at last, the horror of the van, of the gas, of the grave.

J was the man in the photo with his elbows up, sitting on the ground before the guards, his hands over his ears because he lacked the will to cover his eyes but dared not try to see what those around him saw.

He had become the appropriate subject.

He was in the van and the gentle bumpiness of the road and the sweet diesel smell were all asking him to sleep, but he dared not, dared not, close his eyes. J rolled into Chase. She shifted in her sleep, moved her head onto his chest. He longed to cry out, though to no one, to nothing, simply to cry out, to scream, to wail, to curse, to moan, to weep, to mourn, to exhaust himself with reverberations of his own breath forced from his chest. But he would not wake Chase, would not alarm her. He stroked her hair with his free hand, pushed it gently behind her ear.

He drifted off.

When he woke, the room was dark and the curtains glowed lightly with the moon and the city reflected. He ran his knuckles over Chase's cheek. She shifted and made what he imagined to be a happy noise, so he ran them over her cheek again. His own face felt taut, as if he'd cried in his sleep and the tears had since dried taut his skin.

Chase moved her hand on his chest and then lifted it up to his cheek. He ran his hand over her scalp, his fingers combing her hair. She pulled herself up to kiss him. Her breath was ever so slightly bad, warm and sleep-soured, familiar, grounding. He rolled to face her, his hand around her back to support her as she came off of him. They lay that way, side-by-side against each other, kissing in the dark atop the covers, each with one arm awkwardly tucked under the other, with one arm fondling the other.

At some point their clothes came off, though J could not tell when or how, as if the gentle motion of their bodies was the gradual push of the equinox against the stilled sap in the park's trees. Naked then, J's legs slipped between Chases'. Still they kissed, kissed as if with a dependency on a passion they'd exhausted earlier in an evening. Then, equally without decision, or even action, he was inside of her, as if his cock had simply formed within her, his erection within her: they made love for their second ever time, the shadows cast by the moon's night arc seemingly moving more than they, and he clutched at Chase with all his strength when he came.

Over the next three days, they gradually became fierce with each other, spoiled and energetic. They ordered from the dark allies of the food service menu to discover new flavors off of each other's bodies. They did things they didn't mean to do, and meant things they didn't do.

Between, Chase whispered the discoveries of her childhood, what it felt like to trudge barefoot across the sand bottoms of small washes in the desert past Walter's ranch; the sub-harmonic

throbbing of a fishing rod's handle when a trout or whitefish struggled for its life; her stubborn refusal to admit or leverage her father's
filmmaking fame.

J answered that when God showed Adam King David's life,
then said that David would die at birth, Adam gave sixty of his own
years to David, keeping only nine hundred and forty for himself.
David, who knew this, also knew that the *Melech HaMavet* would
not take a man while he was learning Torah, and so on David's
sixtieth birthday, he learned Torah all night. But in the middle of
the night, there was a thunderclap over his tent, and at that clap
he lost focus a moment and in that moment the angel took him.

"It isn't fair," Chase said.

"David was God's favorite and spoke to God all the time,
knew his place in heaven, and still, still he didn't want to die. And
Adam, Adam knew he had a thousand years and only would give
up sixty of them."

"It's not fair that God always wins," Chase said.

"I'm winning now," J said. "I'm with you."

Then he described all the places he'd seen as they were created,
and as they were after, when Adam roamed *Gan Eden*, and after
still, when Adam wandered the rest of the earth beyond Paradise,
avoiding his wife.

"Would you have avoided Eve?" Chase asked.

"Eve, maybe; but never you," J said.

And Chase traced J's ribs with her right finger, her elbow
upon his navel. She told him, in a stutteringly quiet voice, how
she'd first met Arthur, on the veranda of a small bar in a teeny
town above Santa Fe. She told of how over a drink beyond what
she should have drunk, Arthur had confessed to her his confusion
after a conversion experience, a conversion experience, a sudden
discovery of overwhelming love, love that ambushed Arthur when
a man, who found Art sitting on his skateboard, smoking a rollie
in the Saturday morning shade of an empty Barelas warehouse,
had approached Arthur and asked Arthur if he would step around

the corner to help him distribute sandwiches because the lady who usually helped was home sick. Sandwiches! That was all it took: Art believed in God after because he had loved divinely then. But even Art resisted the easiness of this irrational access to truth, to which Chase had consoled, a hand against his chest, between his breasts, her breast but barely against him: isn't it more beautiful to accept the belief and with it the love that belief entitles in you?

Chase had never met anyone like Arthur before, someone so physically beautiful, whose physical presence disappeared before his words, before the urgency of his feelings. And Arthur, Arthur claimed he'd never had a conversation like that one with anyone before, that he wanted to always have those conversations, and thus always Chase.

"What happened?" J asked.

"I went home with him," she said.

"Not that."

"Oh. Arthur joined the man's church," she said.

"I meant, what happened with you?"

"We married," Chase said, pulling her arm from beneath J's neck to prop herself up. "What is it you want to know? He had this passion. I helped him find an ambition for it. Gave him direction. Then the three kings came along with their honorary doctorates and schemes."

"Were they what happened?" J asked. "Was that why you left him? When we met, you guys were separated. Are they what happened?"

Chase made a fist full of J's chest hair and pulled, and J gutturalized involuntary pleasure.

"Tell me more," she said, "about us."

J explained how he and Chase would live in each part of the newly created world, the berries and fruits they'd pick and the animals they'd snare, the fish they'd tickle out of streams.

"A world to be destroyed by flood," Chase said and bit J's nipple ever so gently too hard.

"All that was destroyed grows back," J gasped.

"What dies is dead."

She laid her splayed right hand above his sternum, placed her weight somewhat upon it.

"Real freedom," J said, hard of breath, "freed from the confines of the garden to a world without a sole commandment," and dared to trace with his free hand the contour towards her femur.

"A cursed world, everything lost."

She rolled her weight further onto her palm, upon his diaphragm.

"Must everything stay lost forever?" his hand as far down her leg as it would go, barely able to breathe, his fingers moving back up from her knee.

"We are lost forever," she said.

"That's freedom," J said, her fingers contracting to grab in his chest hair again, his chest constricted beneath her weight, his right nipple hard beneath her breast. "If we are lost that's freedom. We can run. Let's run until we're found."

She rolled around to straddle him, heels tucked beneath her thighs astride his thighs, and ran both her hands down his chest, and scratched her nails down his chest, and scratched his chest harder, harder until he bled, but she would not let him inside her until he threw her from him, threw her onto her stomach, would not let him inside her until he threw her and twisted her arms behind her in the bed sheets, the sheets in his right fist, her hair in his other clutch, and fucked her until she screamed into the pillow clenched in her teeth, goose bumps on her thighs between his thighs, fucked her while she screamed into the pillow clenched in her teeth.

"Let's run," he said afterwards, sprawled, the sheets irreparable, in need of burning, watching the movement of her trapezius beneath her naked skin, of her dorsi and supraspinatus, where she stood, the way those muscles anticipated the movements of her spine beneath her skin, and her shoulder blades and pelvic bones, where she'd retreated to stand before the dressing table, the vanity. She turned away, broke her gaze from the mirror, turned to look across the room at him, her legs together, her breasts bare and unsupported.

"This is a dream," she said. "It can't last."

"This dream stretches on forever."

"This," she said, slamming her fist on the vanity top against which she leaned. "This won't last."

"Eight years," J said, "already."

"No," she said.

"Please."

"We need to get out of this room," Chase said, and began pulling on clothing.

There was a suit waiting for J, of course, and a shirt. He put them on over his sweat and blood and come. He put them on to trap her body's effluvia against his skin, safe from the volatile action of evaporative ethers.

They walked outside like a proper man and woman. J compensated with formal dress for what he lacked in beauty. Or maybe Chase was so beautiful that her weight against his arm lent him poise enough to be worthy of walking beside her. The afternoon was colorful with the first summer dresses and colognes that smelled of foreign cities and languages that summoned Alexandria's great library when the Caliph's army began burning papyrus for heat. The air and the light and the smells made J feel strong like he hadn't felt since Montana, and city-savvy like he hadn't felt since his early thirties. And yet, his heart rate burned, stomach acid pulsed against his esophagus, his mind stumbled over desperate utterances hardly contained.

Still alone, he thought despite himself.

Several blocks east of the hotel, they came to a bar with its walls opened to the street, and stopped to sip iced Lillet from wine glasses.

"You've already left Art," J complained, puckering with herbal aperitif.

"But I also haven't," she said.

"I want to have a child with you."

"Why?"

It wasn't a question but an expression of repugnance and despair.

"I want to make something."

"Not with me."

"Don't you want a child?"

"Let's walk," she said.

They left their glasses in the warm light of the late day sun, his a yellow third full, hers more, and turned north. Joggers passed them enveloped in small tornados of deodorant and detergent that flicked the spun surface of J's thoughts.

"I've never made anything," he said.

"Make a home somewhere," she said. "Make yourself free."

"So you can ignore me again?"

"This time I'm asking you to stay. I'm asking you to make a home I can visit."

"We'll be together when you visit."

"We'll always be together," she said.

"But not actually with each other except when you're in town."

"When I can be with you," she said, "I'll be with you."

"It's not enough."

"You love Art."

"Is this how you would love him?"

"Every minute I can, I'll be with you."

"No," he said.

"I'll come often."

"No. Still no."

"I'll always wish it was you I was with."

"Chase," he said. "No."

Their pace quickened as if one was running from the other, or as if both were running from the other at the same speed, in the same direction. Exertion felt good, J thought, though his pores prickled with sweat and he knew he'd smell like a cat buried in its own spoiled litter by the end of their stroll.

"Then what?" she asked. "What?"

"I'm going to build a school," J said, "with my hands. In New Mexico."

"That," Chase said, "is about the dumbest thing I've ever heard."

"Then a memorial, by hand, out of mud."

"A memorial to what?"

"Does it matter?"

"Usually."

But J was giddy with adrenalin and walking and with the breathing of air laced with too much oxygen so that it numbed the tissues above his septum.

"I can't do anything else!" he shouted, and they stopped where they were in the sidewalk.

"All right," she said. "But I can't leave Art."

"Why? Why can't you leave Art?"

"And you can't ask me why."

His heart rate…and he suppressed it.

"You can't, J. You can't ask me why. Please."

They spent another few days in the hotel, days during which J suffered excruciating desire for her body that went unsatisfied even when his cock was inside her, so that he tossed and turned, with wanting, with frustration. Then they took separate flights back to New Mexico. Chase returned to Art. J went to Walter's ranch to retrieve his truck that he might move to a place that he could stay for Chase to visit him.

CHAPTER FORTY-EIGHT

J DROVE OFF TOWARDS Utah, intending to get to Montana the long way round, or to maybe check out the far coast, where he hadn't spent time yet. A reboot, a restart, something. He couldn't go back to the museum project and he wanted space enough for Chase to long towards him. J entered Utah not so much wiser than when he'd arrived in it last as more resigned to what he did know. He took back roads, which allowed him to watch colored rock and sand rise into geometric shapes like the housing project towers that topped the angled rows of six-story brick complexes visible from his first Manhattan apartment, visible over the 207th Street subway yards, and then to watch the geologic up-thrusts relent into juniper-scrubbed low passes, fir-forested high ones, the snow almost down to the road on these. The land was mostly empty, the towns as small as those in the patch of Montana at the Dakotas where he was headed.

He dawdled.

He would turn forty in a couple of months, genuinely turn forty this time. Seven years since his discovery that he existed in the dream of the man being gassed in the van. What had he done, really done in that time? J figured he'd done nothing but search for solace, in that time. Solace! A principle more profound than pleasure. And where hadn't he sought it? Where ought he seek it? The old answers, lubricated with regular use, whirred till they settled where they always settled, settled with the woman from whom he travelled.

Solace in Chase's arms. But why should solace lie in anyone's arms? Be a thing found in arms? The statuesque desert was a place filled with angels and projections, an echo of the Holocaust in which everything knew the whole story except J, who must be led and guided and reprimanded. Just like his namesake, J thought, Jacob, who needed a conniving Rebecca and wrestling angels and duplicitous uncles to show him the way, who needed a certain ladder. J's own ladders had been steep staircases between streets, first as a ten-year-old in Jerusalem, then as a young adult in Inwood, where he'd climbed up from Broadway at 215th Street, and up from Marble Hill to Riverdale proper at 242nd.

What solace?

J made a detour into Blanding to pick up groceries. Tried to buy beer, but despite claiming to be the gateway to adventure, the town was dry. Then, on the far edge of municipal control, twelve blocks of beat-up conveniences behind, an endless stretch of juniper desert to every other vantage, he found a gas station that sold beer just fine. J decided to limit himself to two, and so sought out the largest cans on display that weren't independently equal to two beers—twenty-four-ouncers were clearly cheating, let alone forties—settled on eighteen-ounce, Budweiser Chelados.

He drove an hour past town, until the sun was low enough to tint the distant San Juans' snowcaps' orange, and until the land to either side was but barely bound by cow-fencing, two barbed strands strung along a mix of metal fence posts and desiccated lengths of juniper.

He parked off the side of the road, pulled a sleeping bag out of the bed of the truck along with his bag of groceries, put on his unlaced work boots, and crossed the fencing. He walked until he couldn't see his car, the San Juans to the north purple now, lit by the sunk sun's refraction so that they glowed with foreign adventure as once had Fordham heights with neon and streetlights when he'd

traversed the bridge into the Bronx alone in his twenties, unteth-
ered, searching for communion in communities not bilingual but
Spanish-speaking, him also not bilingual, but wracked with desire
for the smells and peoples and bodies, for the fleeting daydreams
of mysterious empire and enterprise that if an appropriate occupation of adolescence, only still persisted into early adulthood as the
suppression of loneliness during those solo weekend walks.

Behind the San Juans, the La Salle range, named such by Fran-
ciscan monks, who, constrained to the sere basin, had concluded
that the snowcaps above them must blister with heat, be salt, the salt
mountains, then, miniature behind the San Juans, blue tipped black.

Scrounging old brush wasn't hard, and J assembled a small fire
the way his friend in Baker had taught him.

This, too, he thought, that he'd learned how to do this, knew
how to cook steak over an open flame.

He ate his charred meat and sipped his canned beer, more
spice and tomato than lager, and watched what was left of the light
disappear from the distant mountains. The air, which when heated
by daytime sun smelled of dust, calmed to a heady sage scent that J
first mistook for lavender, for Ft. Tryon's monastic gardens at The
Cloisters, and then for rosemary. He wondered what one did alone
at a bush campsite. He didn't have a book, didn't have a light to
read the book he didn't have anyway. He thought to sing, but the
only songs he could bring to mind where the national anthem and
'Happy Birthday,' neither of which jived.

He shivered; with neither fire nor sun, it was cold.

He tried to make up a song; his voice offered the opening
stanzas to *Shir ha'Ma'alot*, the chant that precedes the blessings
after eating. The words sounded tinny and empty in the void,
not to mention wrong. He stopped, and a few moments later the
song echoed back at him, thinned further still by distance and the
uneven surface of a rock wall deep in the dark.

The sky was the color of the edge of the atmosphere, the
infinitely black blue bordering upon the light that astronauts

photograph. J had nothing to do. Stars became visible. He thought he should plan out his next steps. He scratched and considered scorpions and ticks.

He lay back on his sleeping bag, a thick quilted Walmart affair with a rubberized bottom that required neither tent nor pad. The dark deepened, bringing with it ever-increasing numbers of stars. Maybe, J thought, this would be a good time to mourn the victims of the Holocaust, the murdered. That seemed so abstract—as if mourning was a scheduled activity! In Judaism it sort of was: *Shiva, Yartzeit,* special *Kaddish* on special occasions—he couldn't summon anything anyway. He tried to just focus on the factories of the Lodz ghetto, nothing doing. He recalled Lorraine's photos but they bore no neural chemistry.

He tried to remember the names of the children of Belchatow, still nothing.

He realized that he was flipping through images of victims the way some men flip through images of women, him hoping that one of these would evoke a particular emotional state the way those men sought arousal. He wondered if this was why his father had stayed in the synagogue on Yom Kippur during the special services for mourners, though his father had not technically been a mourner, but offering prayers for his uncles, who, having married outside the faith, had no one to say their names to God.

I'm a victim of the Holocaust, J thought. All of this is a victim of the Holocaust. None of us outlive the man in the van. This brought him to the final image in his long list, the charred Torah scroll.

J pulled the sleeping bag around his shoulders. He wasn't ready to get into it, didn't want to build another fire. To think that he'd only first ever slept in a sleeping bag in the back of Chase's truck—excluding sleeping bags at sleepovers, indoors. That was different—J had made it halfway through his life without using a sleeping bag,

without sleeping under the stars. And now, these past few years...
he felt bad about dropping his last sleeping bag in the Hudson.

Noah, J thought, survived. What must it be like, he wondered,
to be the oldest man alive, all those who came before you killed at
once? It took Noah some hundred years to build his ark, a hundred
years during which his neighbors asked what he was doing and he
told them to repent. And years later, J thought, how had Noah
ever grappled with explaining to his new neighbors, his offspring's
offspring, that there had once been a different world, and that he,
Noah, had seen it destroyed?

For that matter, Lot also attempted to save his neighbors—well
not really, J corrected himself; Abraham argued with God to save
them. Lot just fled. Still, there's not a single story in the bible of a
harbinger undone, of warnings heeded. Prophets preached penance,
it seemed, simply to exonerate God of His wrath's wreaking.

The things that seemed profound while lying with a two-beer-
buzz under the stars of the heavens. How could J have ever have
thought that he could create babies? Build a school? Chase was
right: he was ridiculous.

Can a dream dream?

Had he missed some moment in his early twenties, when new
to New York, still struck with awe that the buildings all around
him had been built by men and women not any different than
himself? Had J missed a moment in which he might have turned
the whole thing right? Fulfilled some destiny? But he had turned it
right. He'd found Esther, moved in with her, built a life with her. J
had evolved from taking the D train to the Sears on Fordham Road
to pay his credit card bill with a check, in person, to someone who
ran a business, had friends. He'd never before been nostalgic for
that time in his life in which he'd tried to befriend the attractive
women on his subway commute, women who'd so completely
seen through his clumsy attempts that they didn't even bother to
acknowledge them. Why, J wondered, had he always so insisted
on seeking out people whose lifestyles and cultures had nothing in

common with his own? Why hadn't he been better able to accept his station, his caste, his selection?

That was it. J wasn't nostalgic for his twenties, and he had proved perfectly competent at establishing a boringly normal, relatively privileged, completely satisfying life: it was his selection, the revelation of the dream and the dreamer, that he wanted a way out of…as if some choice would have led to him not being dreamt! J was confusing destiny with revelation! He was mistaking recognition for a destination amongst destinations.

The Amoraim of the Babylonian Talmud argued about whether the fifteen-thousand that didn't die in their graves on the fortieth anniversary of Moses shattering the tablets were pardoned, or whether the last of the generation born into slavery had already died in their graves the year prior. The pardon made more sense to J. After all, the children of Israel in the desert understood who was meant to die and why. Surely, the next generation must have lain in their graves without real fear; surely they must have known whether in that fortieth year there were left among them any destined to die.

Speaking of graves, J thought to himself; he shed the sleeping bag and spread it out on the desert floor. His teeth began chattering before he even got a chance to get into the thing. Definitely time for him to turn it in, sleep.

That they lay in their graves, that they repeated the act six additional nights to ensure that God had indeed finished punishing them (or out of disbelief that he could've finished), surely indicated that there were those among them that should not have entered the Promised Land! Though the word punished, punished rather than purged. That all of them lay in their graves, not just the generation that had sinned, implied that any of them might have died, or believed that they might have died. This in turn implied that all the children of Israel, all Jews, participated in the Golden Calf, all Jews were born into slavery and all Jews were born in the desert in the presence of God, strong in their faith, entitled to enter into Israel, destined to bring the walls of Jericho down.

Or it was out of compassion that those clearly exempt also dug their own graves that they might not point out the sin and punishment of those condemned; or if not exactly compassion, then solidarity: the killing of any Jew equivalent to the killing of every Jew.

Forty years of food falling from the sky and, once a year, death in the ground. If they'd lain in graves out of solidarity that solidarity, too, would have been a rebellion against God, an announcement that He was wrong, that they were all the same. Or they whispered, those condemned Jews did, they whispered that God forgot us once, that God took us out of the desert with great signs and a mighty hand not to bring us into the promised land but to die in the desert. That God had done all this for the Glory of God. That God had forgotten us once for hundreds of years in slavery, and now again when there were no other nations before which to show off His might. Who is to say that He won't forget not to kill all of us, won't forget to take us across the Jordan?

Were solidarity and compassion different?

Did God always punish the solidarity of peoples?

Fifteen thousand times forty, J thought, is six hundred thousand. Six million.

Six extra nights.

And then Joshua to lead them to slay everything in their path.

And if the last fifteen thousand were pardoned? A commutation at the far end of a circuitous commute from Egypt to the Jordan? What an ancillary and irrelevant commutation. A fortieth saved. Surely that was closer to leaving a survivor of a massacre to report on the massacre than a genuine act of mercy.

And yet, and yet, and yet: forty years.

Those condemned were given as many as forty years to reproduce, to raise children, to birth their replacements, their legacy. But the pardoned, if they were pardoned, that fortieth: J couldn't help but think that the Holocaust's survivors were such, that the Jews left after 1945 were such, an afterthought afterthoughtedly spared. Yet each of those fifteen thousand must have rejoiced in the mercy of God, must have found His mercy infinite.

He should sleep; J knew this. Who could sleep when contemplating those who went to bed and didn't wake? Who could sleep so soon after learning that they had slept away nearly a quarter of a year?

Those additional six nights, a refusal, and a refusal based in what? Trauma? Failure to believe? Supposed miscalculation of the date? In what?

Did they think God merciful that He let them live?

Did they live in dread each of those forty years, not knowing which would be their last?

Where they spared solely to tell of God's wrath and God's mercy?

Were all of the generations of slavery indeed killed, but all of Israel, who had only known the desert, manna and annual death, certain that these things would be forever? Or were the generations born into slavery killed because they had questioned Joshua when he first brought them to Jericho, could not believe that they could ever conquer such a city?

Did God kill the oppressed that their children might be confident and conquering?

Did God traumatize the children that they might be ruthless and savage and without qualm?

And would not this entire world be destroyed when the man in the van succumbed to the gas? And if the gas spared him, did it not spare him simply for a bullet at the mass grave in the woods? Hadn't God made Noah a promise that He would never destroy the world again? And wasn't this the world? And wouldn't it be destroyed? And weren't those who lay in their graves for a week waiting to die destroyed even though they were spared? Didn't that violate the agreement? An agreement made by walking between the split-apart halves of sacrificial animals, consecrated with the rainbow after storms? Were J's inescapable perambulations an attempt to reconstruct the covenant wrought by walking between the split-apart halves of sacrificial animals? What sign was there to indicate an end to Holocausts? After what ominous groundswell could God's chosen look at what spot to see that all would be well?

What if that was God's promise to Noah, that when the Talmud claimed that every man contained the world entire, that was a literal statement, that each man held the capacity to dream an infinite future, that death for the dying lay on the far side of infinity, dying a stepping out of time not in the manner of lost consciousness, but of atemporal achieve, the space of chaos, of God?

J sipped a bit more of his Chelado and scratched at his butt some more. But then why dream J?

"Why dream me? Why me? And why let me know?" J yelled to the sky, agitated, twitching on his bedroll.

Why make him with the capacity for a purpose, with the desire for a purpose and then deny him knowledge of that purpose? But then why give all those carted off to gas chambers and marched off to pits in the wood and shot in their homes, worked to death and starved, why give all of them desires and purposes and a deep, deep attachment to the idea of continuing to be alive and an expectation of some legacy if they were simply to be killed? What of their great-great-grandparents who raised children in good faith that their lines would be continued? And of their great-great-grandparents' great-great-grandparents? And theirs, all the way back to David and back to Moses and back to Abraham, who was given to see the history of his children, children as numberless as the stars, numerous as the grains of sand, why did not he, Abraham, why did not all of them, cover their heads in ashes, their bodies in sack cloths, why did they not tear at their flesh and refuse to bring forth any children when they knew, once they knew, that all of them, all of them would be killed one gloomy half-decade some five-and-a-half thousand years after Adam pointed at a line of animals and named names?

Because Abraham would have sacrificed his only son, Isaac, the son that he loved, despite the angels telling him to stop, had not their tears melted his knife, had not God Himself come down to tell Abraham that it was enough.

How traumatized must Abraham have been by the thought of what he would do that he couldn't stop from doing it.

And what of Ishmael? Why did the verse say 'your only one' when there was Ishmael?

And if the angels melted the knife with their tears, then with what blade did Abraham and Isaac sacrifice the providential ram, hung up in the bushes, whose one horn they blew, and whose other horn would be the shofar that heralded the Messiah?

"Why dream me?" J asked again.

And that question seemed empty, and used up, and already asked, and solipsistic, and naïve. Juvenile. J hated that question. Why, he wondered, did parents kvell at their eight-year-old's formulation of that question, of that: why am I here? It was a question precisely appropriate for eight-year-olds and teeny-bopper pop-stars. Do we really all imagine that each of us is exemplary? Are we owed answers, owed meaning, any more than we're owed happiness? Perhaps, J wasn't exemplary. Perhaps he was created as an extra, a prop in someone else's grand drama. Perhaps, just as the dying man's dream included even these incredibly faint stars that seem to stretch almost to the borders of even fainter stars in a sky, that upon looking, seemed not so much white against black as a constant white differentiated by intensity, by varying levels of dim, so too the dreamer's dream must be filled with people, however inconsequential most or even all might be, and the dreamer's dream would be incomplete without a lonely man sipping a Chelado at the interstices of New Mexico, Utah and Colorado, driving away from a woman with both his eyes in the rearview, desperate for a glimpse of her following.

But would an extra have to pee as badly as he did? And as desperately not wish to leave the comfort of his sleeping bag?

But then, J resisted, resisting both the notion of being a prop and the necessity of getting out of his sleeping bag, why was he made aware that this was dream? And why didn't that clarity specify whether everyone else was part of the dream dreaming him, or the product of other dreams somehow comingled in this space, or not dreams at all? And what if he was wrong about the whole dream thing but somehow that too was a necessity of the dream?

If the dreamer succumbed before J, would J disappear? And how would that appear to those around him? Did he appear to those around him? He stopped himself, slunk out of his sleeping bag and walked ten paces downhill to pee, staring up at the stars.

God had belatedly answered the prayers of the Jewish slaves in Egypt, and then left them, let them languish in a desert to die in increments fifteen thousand strong. Why had none of them fought back? J thought bitterly, his pee loud on the hard-pack dirt and dust-dry juniper needles.

How did one fight back? Not by defraying the work caused by their own deaths; not by digging their own graves.

At Babi Yar, Einsatzengroup A shot to death 34,000 Jews from Kiev in two days, and those people stood quietly, naked, in family groups, at the edge of the pits, directed by men with bullwhips who never needed use their lashes, and stood, resigned, quiet, soothing their children while waiting execution, this depiction relayed by Einsatzengroup A's commandant at his Nuremberg trial and confirmed by several German tourists who witnessed the whole thing—tourists! What the fuck!—the commandant accounting for this quietude as a failure by the Jews he killed to value their lives the way Germans valued theirs, claiming that it was actually harder for the men shooting, who were overworked and enervated, than those they shot.

None of this is new, J thought. These are just the facts whose citations do all the work on their own.

He zipped his fly, and an unpeed last drip of urine wet his underwear. Its chill tickled a shiver out of him. He walked back to his little encampment, the dead fire, the couple of bags, the sleeping bag, and picked up his can of Chelado, shook it. It rattled. He sipped the last sip and crushed the can.

Are there even Jews anymore then? Could that radical nonviolence that created the space within which to comfort one's children, to pray to God the blessing for getting ready to die—always blessings!—could that have survived? Or was that it? Judaism destroyed; and if destroyed, and if God, then were the true Jews in the true Promised Land, elsewhere with God, the Moshiach come? The Messiah's shofar the horn of a death camp siren? Then what was this drifting planet without its creator's chosen people?

(A dream, J thought, detritus.)

Was the will to power, to survival, always at odds with dignity?

Was it actually easier for the calm, dignified martyr than for those who did evil? Irrelevant, the murdered hadn't been given a choice of participation (obviously).

Were those families protecting each other or acceding to the deity that decreed their deaths?

For whom does one dig one's own grave?

Tomorrow J would drive.

But what of desire? His desire? J's desire? And he thought back to Noah, who'd made sure God wouldn't do it again—or at least complied with God's mode of committing not to—and then gotten drunk. Noah must have been on at least speaking terms with his neighbors, they stopped by to ask what he was building, after all. He lived for hundreds of years, wasn't nomadic, had children who married the neighbors' children, had shared grandbabies with those neighbors. It was one thing for God to judge all those people evil. One thing for parishioners thousands of years out to accept their comeuppance, but for Noah! Everyone he'd ever known save his descendants and their spouses was killed. Noah must have seen them die: The waters came from the heavens and from the earth. His neighbors must have clung to the boat, clung until Noah beat their knuckles loose from the gunwales. When there was enough water for the ark to float, what then? Did he float past roofs to which his neighbors had climbed and ignore their pleas for rescue? Watch them stand on tiptoes, their noses barely above the surface? Drift over the bubbled last exhaust of his friends?

What of his in-laws, the parents of his three sons' wives? How did he deal with them? There's a bad joke in that, J thought.

The Midrashim say that the water that came out of the ground was boiling hot.

The Torah claims water is a metaphor for Torah. That deprived of either Torah or water for more than three days man perishes, whether physically or spiritually. And the water of Noah's flood, the water of Sodom and Gomorrah, and the water of the Red Sea when it folded over the Egyptians: then it was Torah that destroyed them. If God destroys by Torah just as God creates by Torah spoken, then what were cyanide gas and carbon monoxide and bullets? Was God's most recent annihilation of His people not even worthy of the divine? An offhand, guttural thing left to the nation of Amalek, left to the other? Or was that not God?

J wasn't even a believer, for fuck's sake, so why ponder it?

J laughed aloud at himself in the desert dark at the idea that his commitment to reason and enlightenment produced his atheism but did not preclude his existence in the dream of a man being gassed to death.

He could smell juniper giving fragrance to the cold of the night and the stars seemed bright enough to cast shadows; if he wasn't so redolent in the settled immobility of his resting body he might turn his head to see the starlight shadows on the ground around him.

The stars are bright, J thought, because it is dark.

He laughed at himself again. The laughter made him almost content.

When the water rose higher, and the ark began to float, Noah must have drifted past higher ground on which refugees must have climbed ever upwards until in some parody of drowning ants, a last stood atop a pile of his dead fellows, his dead fellows stacked at the tip of a mountain until water had boiled the flesh from the corpses' bones beneath him and the settling mass immersed him. Who was the last to die in the flood? What horrors Noah must have seen!

J wished he'd gone to see the Ark recreation on one of those three visits to the northern Kentucky.

Would Noah have sacrificed those three sons, one of whom was destined to geld him, to save the world? And what of the birds! Yes, he took two of each kind—except those that were kosher, of which he took eight that he might sacrifice six when he landed— but what of all the other birds that must've flown and flown, wings heavy with water, feathers soaked and battered, no place to land until they spied his ark's massive roof, a roof large enough to house two of every species of animal—except those that were kosher, of which he housed eight, that six might be sacrificed when he landed—and did they not try to land there? And how did Noah shoo them off? How did he bring himself to shoo them off? Or were his hands already strong from beating on the knuckles of those that had reached for the sides of his ark? Or did the giant Og really cling to the roof like a giant umbrella, making it his job to force death upon those last of the winged creatures unselected for the ark's sanctuary? Or were none of the birds explicitly saved, only those that managed to land—two of each alone, except those which were kosher of which eight were spared that six might be sacrificed, perched on Og's back like sparrows on a hippo's hide?

There's always an Og or a Lilith or a singing boy with a bullet in his head, crawling from the bodies of his peers to the chicken coop of a hostile peasant.

No, J thought, it was impossible that Noah did not feel himself complicit in the decimation of all he'd known.

Noah wanted numbness, anesthesia, amnesia.

J, too: he wanted for solace, for an end to the empty.

It was such a large and abstract and obviously unfulfillable desire, the kind of desire that Chase would argue couldn't be made into a story. Your character needs a concrete objective, she would explain were she beside J, an opportunity for conflict.

"I want to have a story," J sniveled in his sleeping bag, its aperture open enough only for his nose and mouth and eyes, the stars and the stars and the stars above him. "I so want to have a story. I want a resolution to my conflict."

He wanted to be in a romance.

On a quest.

This, though, J's journey, felt like tragedy, or satire, or a satire of tragedy.

The man in the van would want him to have a story, J thought. And if the man didn't, then the man wasn't anybody J needed to observe.

The man shouldn't be anybody J needed to observe, but the man kept forcing J back into a relationship that never did anything; or so it seemed.

"Chase," he said aloud to the stars, which were bright because it was dark.

"Chase," J said to the imagined echoing leaves of mountains-away quakies fluttering in the down draft of cooling pooling air, imagined because the leaves had fallen from the trees months ago.

For whom did one dig one's own grave?

CHAPTER FORTY-NINE

IN THE MORNING, HIS groceries were strewn across the desert, or at least their wrappers were, frost melting off their shiny edges; whether by coyotes or raccoons or particularly ferocious ground mice, he knew not. He made a feeble attempt to collect the detritus of the scavenged food, the multicolored wrappers whose silver bellies, exposed, caught the morning sunlight as finely as any of Delilah's elaborate table service. Then he abandoned the effort: why clean up a world destined for doom? Apocalyptic, he thought, eschatological. Lazy. How did faiths bound up in end-time fascination reconcile God's pact with Noah?

He dismissed that thought, too, eye bleary with the trace of thirty-six ounces of tomato and Tabasco tainted Budweiser. He trudged up to the truck and sighed.

They reconciled eschatology with the rainbow by assuming that the end was something other than the destruction of the world.

And if Noah was a rapture of one (family)?

J sighed again, wished, again, that he had the sort of brain that shut off, and pulled the truck around and onto the highway circling back towards New Mexico. It was time J accepted that he was headed back to the ranch; there to build whatever it was he was going to build.

PART FIVE

All letters give form to absence.
Hence, God is the child of His Name.
—*Reb Tal*

~~Edmond Jabes
The Book of Questions: Volume 1
(Translated by Rosemarie Waldrop)

CHAPTER FIFTY

WALTER LET HIM SLEEP in the house the first night back. Then, after they'd discussed J's elaborate plans over thin sips of whiskey drunk from mason jars on the porch, Walter forced J to live outdoors.

"What the hell," J complained. "If you don't want me building on your land, just say that."

"I want you building on the land," Walter replied. "I want you doing it right."

"Fine," J said. "I'll stay in town."

"No you won't," Walter said. "You'll begin your monument by constructing shelter. Till you build that, you'll live in the cold and the heat. You'll lay out under the stars."

"Jesus Christ, Walter, can I at least get a blanket?"

"A blanket," Walter agreed. "One."

"And a tarp?"

"No," Walter said. "Nothing synthetic. Nothing that could be used for war. No metal. Like Solomon's temple."

J looked past the border of the porch. Walter's land spread out arid with January drought, speckled with the juniper and sagebrush greying. Nothing, J supposed, was possible without doing. He'd lived outdoors most all the way to New York from DC. This couldn't be much worse. Still, he wondered at what other restrictions Walter might impose on him. J dared not ask how he was to prepare food for fear that this might suggest to Walter that he be made to grow, capture or kill his sustenance. He rinsed his teeth with the remainder of the whiskey, asked for a refill.

"But last one," Walter said.

J sipped his next whiskey as slowly as possible. He wanted to ask Walter about Chase, about what her connection to Art might be that she wouldn't leave him. He found that he lacked the chutzpah.

Instead, he tried to ask Walter about what happened between him and Delilah. Walter grunted, told J that he'd keep his things, the rifle, for example, safe for him in the house until he was done with building whatever it was he was building. J wondered whether Walter had designed his rules to discourage J, force him to retreat to civilization, to the creation of whatever was next for Art and Co., to his meandering path of non-discovery. But, that thought also seemed like a test or like Joe asking him to leave. To know which tests were the tests! J finished the last sip of whiskey, and Walter waived towards the land.

"What?" J asked.

"Well?"

"Now?"

"What would you wait on?" Walter asked.

"Is there a place you'd prefer I build it?"

"Dealer's choice," Walter said, standing.

With that, J stepped off the porch, banished into exile. Walter walked into the house and came back out with an army blanket and a mug of tea. He threw the blanket to J, and then sat down with the tea on the porch.

"I don't suppose you've got a tea for me?" J asked.

"Pretend I'm not here," Walter said.

"Are you just going to sit there?"

Walter just sat and sipped.

J stood holding the blanket awkwardly and blinking at the sun.

He supposed he ought to begin, but had no idea what to do first. He folded the blanket and set it down on the ground neatly.

For a few minutes, he stood next to the blanket, gradually turning around, looking to see what there was. He didn't like being directly in front of Walter's gaze. He walked in a slow circle around the house. The view changed from bluff-studded, sage desert to mountains and then back again. It occurred to him that he'd need water to make anything without access to modern construction materials, not that he had a clear sense of what he wanted to make.

He'd need to make bricks in any case.

J thought to research how the Israelites had made brick for Pharaoh, and rejoiced that Walter hadn't had the same thought.

There was the creek that Chase had fished in as a child. It lay an hour of trudging away from the house. J imagined he'd leave the property from time-to-time, really, whenever he wanted to eat, or clean up. He decided not to build next to the creek. He circled a second time, found himself between the house and the mountains. The shower's glass walls protruded from a porchless corner of the house here. A hundred yards on, the ground sunk in a small concavity. J walked over to it. A low rise of exposed sandstone formed its floor and overhung a dry arroyo.

Here, he'd build here.

Still, he didn't know what, or how. He walked back to the front of the house and got his blanket, carried it over to the concavity, set it down on the rock. The concavity was really the mouth of a very occasional, minor runoff, the rock exposed from some distant massive flash flood. He stood for a while, occasionally turning in a tight circle as if he was surveying though he wasn't. It was hot. He grew thirsty. He would have to fashion alternate drainage for the small runoff to keep the building site dry. He looked back at the house. Walter was in the shower showering. This, then, was his disposition: sage desert stretching towards low-rise swells, backdropped by mountain, and in the other direction, a naked old man playing peeping-tom from a show shower. J sat down.

Chase came by with sandwiches in a brown paper bag.

She sat beside him on the blanket. They ate, sitting cross-legged, not talking. J considered trying to make love to her. When they'd finished eating, she stood up, brushed off her jeans, and walked away with the sandwiches' paper refuse.

J expected her to return, but he presently heard the sound of her car starting, and then caught sight of the dust trailing her down the dirt road. He hoped she'd come back with dinner. For most of the rest of the day, he sat on the blanket, staring at the concavity's confines and contents. From time to time, he'd stand up and pace a bit, once going so far as to scoop some surface dust together with his hands. It was more like sand, and it rasped the outside of his palms, making only small mounds before pooling back down.

The day turned dusky and Chase didn't return.

J felt jailed by the concavity's dim rise, and so didn't leave it to seek out food. When it grew cold, he folded the blanket over himself as if it was a sleeping bag. Wrapped this way, he could choose to either cover his toes or his neck, not both. Didn't they know he'd just been ill? But even that thought passed presently, subsumed by the coxcomb's worth of empty effort he'd expended trying to determine how best to apply himself.

Eventually he fell asleep, and slept until the night air chilled him through the blanket. He awoke to a sky celestial white; the house disappeared by its own darkness; the bluffs and the mountains outlined by the blank absence of stars.

Shivering, J stood up and promptly stumbled over a sagebrush root. He tried to move around in his pit. Bright as the sky was, he couldn't make out what was where on the ground. He resigned himself to staying put. With the blanket wrapped around him, he sat, knees clutched to his chest as he'd been taught in high school health class. Like that, still cold, he waited the long hours before morning, sometimes nodding off, always reawoken by a sense of falling. When morning did come, and the air began to warm, he finally fell asleep. He slept until it was hot, and then woke sweating. Then it was too hot to live. He stumbled back to the house, but paused on the porch steps. The front door was locked closed. There were no sounds from inside. Walter's truck was there, though, which meant Walter was there, which meant that Walter was granting him a dignified moment in which to recant his retreat.

Walter couldn't expect him to live off manna from heaven. J's old F150 was still parked on the land, and the keys ought to be under the mat. He found them there, and drove into town to outfit himself for a prolonged campaign. He returned with a truck bed full of tools. As soon as J began unloading these, Walter ran out, demanded that no iron be used, "Solomon's temple rules."

"Solomon's temple didn't contain iron, but they had metal tools," J complained.

"Those tools were confined to the quarry so that the sound of no iron tool was heard on the mount," Walter said.

"The fuck?"

"No metal tools," Walter insisted.

"I'll limit them to the quarry," J said.

Walter agreed to this, but not to J's renewed plea to sleep indoors since he was allowed to use his truck and such, and J set out to find what other of Walter's prized views he might ruin by digging a pit for the making of mud bricks. He selected a spot for its simple proximity to both the project and the house. The creek, though, was a long ways away. This, then, would be his first project: an aqueduct to bring water closer.

CHAPTER FIFTY-ONE

HE SIMPLY BEGAN DIGGING at the stream.

Water immediately diverted into his beginning trough, and he realized that he needed to wait to connect his trench until after it was done. For the next six weeks, he dug all day, every day. If it wasn't an apprenticeship in building, it was at least a physical preparation for hard labor. The trench he built didn't nearly stretch all the way to his building site, or to his original mud quarry, but it did get him to a good place to dig dirt next to a graded double-track along which he figured he could wheel his bricks.

This time though, the water simply washed into his trench and then back out again. There wasn't enough pitch, he realized, and his duct left the flow at too hard an angle. Six week's labor wasted, and the day-lit air had declined from cool to chill, and he still had no house, though he'd brought more blankets to the site, and a proper bedroll, and lots of clothing, even a tarp. If Walter objected, he didn't say anything. J set out to make his aqueduct a third time. This time, he spent a week walking, observing the creek and how it flowed and where the land drained otherwise, one evening of which he spent with Chase, who came to share a bottle of fancy Scotch in celebration of his actual fortieth birthday. Eventually, he elected to make a trough out of boards that would join the creek above a section of steeper rapids and carry the water at a more moderate grade than the creek itself, the trough gradually and progressively elevated on trellises of crisscrossed two-by-fours, until he could lead the water beyond the rise of the creek's recess, and then across to a dry wash that flowed towards his brick-making foundry.

He snuck the wood in during the middle of the night so that Walter wouldn't accuse him of further cheating—though against what rules he cheated, J couldn't tell.

But, then, J also couldn't tell why he was building in the first place.

It was well after the solstice before a frigid trickle of mountain runoff coursed down three hundred yards of hand-sawn plywood strips nailed into a narrow box and caulked at the seams. J had had the insight to make the intake removable; and as soon as he ensured that he could get water to flow to his dry wash, he stopped it. He spent another month etching a trench in the wash so that the water wouldn't dissipate, and another month digging a receiving pit for the water, and still another month lining all of these with plastic drop cloth and then filling the trench with stones so that his thin trickle wouldn't simply seep into the ground or burn up in the sun.

Then it was summer, and he had lived three seasons outdoors, wrapped in blankets under a contraband tarp, his isolation mitigated only occasionally by resupply trips into town and a weekly cigar and whiskey with Walter, who seemed to tolerate the tradition mostly to reinforce J's sense of crude living by way of contrast, and Chase's occasional conjugal visits, these, because sexual, always timed to follow J's weeklies with Walter, for which J was allowed indoors to shower.

J accepted that it was better to make love properly clean and rinse off sex in the creek than the other way around. There was something of the mikvah to it.

By the time J figured out how to reliably make nice large adobe blocks, late fall, he had enough bungled misshapen ones to erect a simple shelter, roofed with branches foraged from the creek's banks and his tattered tarp. He'd also realized that his structure, his memorial to he knew not what, would be a circular tower. The tower would be solid, and slightly conical, ringed by a spiral staircase that slowly consumed its center mass.

When he had the first course of bricks on the ground, his structure a foot-high circle loosely mortared with mud, Art came to visit him. Art, like Chase, like everyone in the long narrative of J's quest, brought sandwiches, and they sat and ate these on the ground between J's shelter and the nascent structure, their backs to Walter's house.

They ate in silence at first, and J realized that, despite himself, he still felt the same fealty to the man. J believed in Art in a way that he'd only ever asked others to believe in the identities he'd created as a marketer and a lobbyist. Strangely, though J possessed a psyche custom-built for ruminating on paradox, he felt no angst at the contradiction between making love to Chase and loving Art. When they'd finished the sandwiches, Art took out a flask and from it filled two silver thimbles double the size of shot glasses.

They sipped their whiskey.

When the last dead leaves on the scrub oaks on the hills above rattled in warning, they braced themselves against the small breezes that started there and broke the warmth of the strong sun on their faces.

"Why this?" Art finally asked.

J didn't answer but clinked his silver cup against Art's.

"Isn't this bit of the earth beautiful enough already?"

J hugged his knees against the wind and squinted, happy, into the sun.

"Whatever it is you're building, it's only going to defile the beauty of what's already here," Art said.

"Like Yid World?"

"You didn't give it any time."

"Really?"

"You never even went inside!" But Art blushed and lifted his eyebrows plaintively even as he exclaimed.

J mildly suggested that Art lived in a house built on land once also wild and bare.

"You're not building a house."

"I need this."

"This is a disfigurement for disfigurement's sake."

"And if my tower was ancient, and in a third world country, if it was a cultural heritage site?" J asked.

"If you built a school or a hospital, maybe I could see that."

"How about a museum?"

"Seriously! Something that serves people!"

"What is this about? Walter's property? Is it still about the damn rifle?"

"Fuck Walter," Art said.

"Aren't there things that serve people that aren't houses or hospitals or schools?"

"You've decided to do this thing at the expense of serving your people. It's rather artless, tedious, don't you think?"

"What do you know of art?" J asked.

"I know that if you're an artist of anything, masonry ain't it."

"No, my medium is extravagant mockery, whole museum's worth of desecration, theme parks of humiliating frivolity…"

"Please!" Art said. "Just…please…ok?"

Art hugged his knees to his chest. J let his knees go under the pressure of mimicry, but Art wasn't paying attention. After a while, Art said, "I'm sorry. I'm sorry about the museum."

J shivered at a bigger gust that stripped much of what still clung to the scrub oak.

"I can't believe you didn't even make a joke about your name in all that talk of art, Art."

"Don't dismiss your work."

"You're dismissing my work, Art."

"Your real work."

"What even is that?"

Art gestured in frustration.

"You believe that man is created in God's image?" J asked.

"God!"

"Seriously," J said.

"What seriously? Come work for me in Santa Fe. Help me communicate my initiatives."

"If man is made in God's image then man has the power to create, too. Man has the power to create in his own image, and what he creates in his own image is also in God's image."

"Seriously?"

"Even if not His image per se, if building is an expression of humanity, a creation of humanity, then it's an expression of God."

"Do you even believe in God, J?"

"You do."

"Christ!" Art said, renewing his whiskey. "Anyway, that creation all refers to procreation, children."

"Not an option for me," J said, passing his cup over for a refill as well.

"You're depressed," Art said.

"And where are your children, Arthur?"

They sipped for a while in silence, the desert sun higher.

"You really think you're making in God's image?" Art finally muttered.

"I'm not a believer," J said.

"He's not a believer, he says! After all that talk of God's image."

"You're the one who told me, who showed me that damn eagle and that goose."

"And yet, Jacob, here you are belaboring me with talk of God and you don't even believe. Because if we're relying on my belief, then you belong either back in DC or at the state capitol with me."

"I just want a fucking pulpit to yell back at Him from, ok?" and when J said it, said it with a force and anger that startled a flush of newly grown quail into abortive grey and white flight from the arroyo below, J knew it was true.

CHAPTER FIFTY-TWO

It would be a mistake to say that J's progress was now rapid, but it was at least progress. With each new course of bricks, the spire added one further stair upwards. J spent his greatest energy on these stairs, carefully forming a new mold for each of them, each a single block, and, unlike the other bricks, which he simply air-dried, he fired these in his small hut in a homemade kiln over greasy, cottonwood punk.

Because they were large, and still fragile, these steps were difficult for J to move. He devised a set of rollers made of long wood strip runners and thin poles hand lashed to them. These he used first to get the stair-blocks onto his wheelbarrow, and then from wheelbarrow to their position on the spire, so that, his efforts looked, in miniature, like those of the Jewish slaves building Pitom and Ramses after all.

By the first blush of spring, the structure was taller than a man, a height it gained in seven tall steps. Its interior was still a solid mass, and J would pace the platform it made in the evenings. He thought to spend a night atop it with Chase, but she refused this, still viewing his construction as an obstinacy about her continued marriage.

Walter, who had always seemed old, began to be old. With his age came a new level of cantankerousness. He was increasingly proprietary about the tower. He now regularly invited Louis and a few other friends to sit on his porch and watch J build. But though word had begun to spread about the folk monstrosity, the post-modern land art structure rising on a desert ranch near the mountains, would-be visitors, art-tourists, curiosity-seekers, were chased off by Walter, who claimed he would brook no outside influence on his tower. J was glad of the privacy, and tolerant of Louis, who still threatened to drag him to brothels and steakhouses and society parties, such as they were, in Albuquerque.

CHAPTER FIFTY-THREE

AND SO THE TOWER rose, about ten feet a year, so that J spent his forty-third birthday twenty feet up, level with the roof of Walter's house, too blessedly tired to contemplate the ten-year-anniversary of his discovery that he existed in the dream of man slowly gassed during the Holocaust. The work energized him. He spent his forty-fourth birthday thirty feet in the air, and Walter asked him how forty-five felt. It took J a moment to remember that everyone but Chase had his age wrong by a year. He went back to work.

The dreams, if they continued, did so in secret, their action lost in the morass of sleep. His dreamer was quiet: not less relevant but less actively present. J's sense of the dream in which he existed receded as well. He no longer suffered the nauseous sensation, sometimes ecstatic, sometimes horrific, invariably debilitating, of existing at the whim of a creator with urgent and unknowable needs. For the first time since his early thirties, J felt a measure of calm. Now that he had a shelter, he took the time to set up a regular shower and a dishwashing station, though he continued to cook over the fire pit nee kiln that heated his hovel.

Chase no longer timed her visits to follow his porch sits with Walter. She didn't visit all that much at all. His porch sits with Walter were now more about J's caring for the old man.

J worried about Walter, alone but for J, on the ranch.

Forty-five; a birthday nearly forty feet up in the air.

CHAPTER FIFTY-FOUR

THIS, J THOUGHT, ADMIRING his structure, couldn't be taken away the way his work on the oil pipelines had. He was strong again. His tower was not fucking Yid World; he shuddered. He simply built what was in him to build. Even if he was forced from the structure, the structure would remain. He was making something at last.

The tower sat between Chase and J, stood in for whatever it was he thought she could offer but wouldn't: was for her his monolithic resentment at what he imagined himself denied.

Their sex lost some level of connectedness and left them angry and needy and alone. J did not indulge in empathizing with what it must have been for her, these many years of not having him, who Chase clearly loved, available for anything other than occasional outdoor liaisons on her father's ranch. Their conversation waltzed at fragmented ends, unknowingly trampling toes. She came to visit less; J welcomed her absence.

Anything to not think now; anything to not feel now.

Nothing except for the tower.

His devotion, his tower.

CHAPTER FIFTY-FIVE

Another year passed and the tower was almost fifty feet tall; another and it was well over fifty feet. The house no longer mattered and the structure could be seen at a distance. Local fussing about permits and zoning migrated from dinner talks to petty public offices. Art quietly suppressed these, or so Walter let on, either out of loyalty or guilt or familial obligation, one of these, J supposed. Another year, J forty-eight now—forty-eight!—and the spire sixty-something feet tall.

Walter, nearly eighty, asked to be brought up it. J took him in the late afternoon. Walter walked slowly up the great winding steps. He admired their burnished hard surfaces, slightly red from the clay in the sand.

Though the adobe mix was somewhat self-leveling, the steps' surfaces retained an imprimatur of J's hands where he'd packed the mud and straw into wooden molds. They carried something of the open flame over which they'd been kilned, a memory of cottonwood grease, soot and raw flame. Their smoothness seemed a virtue, earned and unique, a dark gloss spiral against the tower's rough body.

The tower's body was rough, crumbly even. Simple blocks formed it, air-dried bricks, each ten-inches-by-ten-by-twenty, that being the largest size J could easily work with. These bricks were laid edgewise, radial. The tower's circumference contracted as it went higher. With each new course, the bricks sat at sharper angles, leaving increasing gaps between them. J had filled these voids with the clay-rich mud he used for mortar. The mortar eroded where it was exposed to air, leaving grooves between courses, hollows between rows, chinks to which Walter clawed for lack of a handrail.

As they climbed higher, Walter grew progressively enamored of the thing so firmly wedded to his land and this made J ever more apprehensive. The steps were steep and winding and exposed. Walter tottered in towards the tower's wall each time he lifted his right foot up to the next tread, and then pressed with both hands on his right knee, jerking his body forward, to bring his left leg up. J stayed a pace behind, his right hand cupped beneath Walter's elbow. He wasn't at all certain that he could actually catch Walter should he falter. J hoped he might push Walter's balance back to where it belonged before stumble turned to tumble, to fall.

On top, not nearly far enough in from the edge, Walter paused and leaned back and clasped J's shoulder.

"This is right, J," Walter said. "This is exactly right."

Then, Walter wanted to drink whiskey at the top, kept walking too close to the edge, wanted to wait for the stars, see if they were closer from this vantage. J wouldn't allow the old man any of it: too dangerous.

CHAPTER FIFTY-SIX

THE COURSES WERE SMALLER now, the highest less than half the surface area of the first, and though the work of getting bricks up had become far more arduous, J made faster progress. He added more than twenty feet the year he turned forty-nine. Chase and Art were absent from his life. He added in excess of thirty feet the following year. Mary came by and Walter chased her off with a gun he couldn't hold steady while J watched silently from the shadow of his tower, surprised that he recognized her. Even E, apparently, wrote letters that J never saw. This J knew because Walter wasn't the least bit coy about having sequestered them.

J's fiftieth year, and the tower was better than a hundred-and-twenty feet tall, its top a mere stride-and-a-half across.

CHAPTER FIFTY-SEVEN

THEN CAME DELILAH.

She came, she claimed, because of Walter's age. When she came, she surveyed the great mess of things that had happened to the man to whom she'd once been married, and to the child she'd raised, and to that child's husband and to that child's lover. She came when the height of the tower was such that, despite J's former familiarity with the much greater altitudes of airplanes and mountains, J felt he could graze the heavens from it.

Delilah spent three weeks surveying, three weeks interrogating and keeping her own counsel. Then, several things happened all at once.

Delilah told Walter she would stay.

Delilah told Chase that at forty-five, she still had nearly half a life in which to choose happiness. Delilah did not tell J that she had told Chase this, and so he couldn't point out to her that all those many years ago Delilah had told him he wasn't her daughter's type.

J, having quickly added the remainder of a dozen more feet, cast and kilned his final step, a capstone for the tower, perfectly round and barely big enough to stand upon.

These happenings didn't immediately lead to anything.

J spent weeks raising his capstone, the final step, up onto the last course of his tower, a rough surface one-hundred-forty feet above the sandstone base of the concavity. J placed it but did not ascend onto it.

He decided to fast.

It was clear now.

J wanted to be pure when he reached the spire's top. J was afraid to stand atop it. His ankle would bear no High Priest's shackle and chain should he be smitten for impurity when in the Holy of Holies: best to fast and purge (and pray).

Chase, for her part, simply flew back to DC as her work itinerary dictated, ignoring her adoptive mother's admonitions.

Walter slid happily back into the care of a wife.

CHAPTER FIFTY-EIGHT

IT'S IMPORTANT TO POINT out that though there's almost nothing to say about those years building, that's not for lack of J doing.

J spent almost every hour of that decade at hard labor. The work soothed him. He lived almost entirely without creature comforts. The work became everything for him. And if he knew after he first yelled at Art that early day while they sat on the first course of bricks, eating and drinking and fighting, if J knew after he yelled it out that the tower was meant to reach to the heavens to confront the dreamer or God or whatever…well…it wasn't until he'd cast that perfect last round step, forming its slight concavity as elegantly as might the gentlest moki swirl away a pothole in rain's rush high upon a mesa, it wasn't until then that he understood that he'd been building a prayer, that his building was a prayer, that this prayer was all that was left unto him.

It wasn't until he gradually hoisted the capstone up those hundred-and-forty feet, until he tipped it onto its mortar, not ready yet to stand upon it, that he knew that it was a prayer and that he was grateful for this prayer, for this devotion of his forties. He was so grateful. Though it had cost the sacrifice of all he had left, he was grateful for it over everything else. If his dreamer had bequeathed J anything, it was this gift of a prayer.

J was still only, if barely, fifty. Fifty! Already fifty. But finally, at fifty, he had built something, found a peace of sorts, peace in his acceptance that instead of children or family or wealth or recognition, his would be to have this prayer, this spire, his chance to stand atop it.

It's important to point out that there isn't ever much to say about a decade of productive meditation: meditation is not a narrative, nor, for that matter, is prayer a story.

CHAPTER FIFTY-NINE

J SET OFF TO fast and purify himself.

He tucked a blanket under his arm and hiked up into the mountains. He followed thin game trails and overgrown corridors between trees, ever either pushing through tall weeds topped with yellow and white flowers, or monitoring brown needle beds for aberrant roots. The years of daily repetitive tasks had trained him to disassociate himself from his body's exertions. Walking became an easy rhythm despite his route's aggressive incline, which is not to say that he remained cool: he sweated profusely, smelt himself between the overheated pine, his shirt damp and abrasive against his chest, his head and ears overheating, salt stinging his eyes. He could do it though, could for hours without pause, as if the body that had once welded in the northern plains' oil fields and once walked across the Utah desert from Boulder to Joe's house and had once meandered madly north along the eastern seaboard from Washington to New York City had at last been kilned hard.

As high as he climbed, whenever he turned around to face downhill, flatten his feet, and rest his calves, he could see the spire behind him. The mountain he climbed was taller than it, but its height was different. The mountain was part of the earth. J was certain that his tower somehow punctured the earthly, as if the heavens were an even blanket, lower where the land lay lower, higher when above a peak. Or maybe he simply viewed his spire as other than of this world's physics. For after all, planes flew much higher right where the tower was and yet his tower, of the points upon the earth, reached highest towards the celestial. And if the spire did rupture the envelope between earthly and divine, then surely it must also penetrate the dream.

At last.

He reached a small meadow in the run-out of a wintertime avalanche path, its deposition zone bounded by groves of aspen, white bark and airy leaves shimmering in fall's die-off, multihued, white, yellow, red, green, orange, black.

He discovered that he was out of breath, that his eyes stung and his calves ached. This was it, he decided. This would be his purification spot. He laid his blanket on the ground and sat down.

All righty, he thought. *I sit, and then I go up that damn tower, and then we'll see, we'll see for sure.*

But what was it that he intended to see? It had to do with his dreamer, J knew that. It had to do with J's lack of consequence to that man whose unjust murder existed in some measure of time so radically different than J's own that J's entire existence could continue, inconsequentially, during the twilight dream of the dreamer's death by gas. The notion that he might feel entitled to demand something of a man in the midst of being murdered washed over J with some glimmer of the nauseous ecstatic state he remembered from the early years after his discovery of the dream.

Against this ecstatic unease, J's quietude, learned of a decade's labor, struggled to quell his ill-formed petulant demand: *dream me free, dream me different, dream me love I can hold on to, dream me with agency, dream me free,* demands made of a man who managed, *who bothered,* to dream J at all, demands of a man with far greater cause for complaint than J. Nonetheless, J's horror at his own audacity was only intellectual. That his relationship to his dreamer's death no longer evoked a visceral response contented J, as did the sense of ecstatic anxiety recaptured. He had neither choice nor agency in his creator's condition.

Was he so shallow as to need a dying man's acknowledgment? Approval? Was he that narcissistic? To seek validation from a progenitor in the unconscious throes of carbon monoxide poisoning?

Dare he pray?

It wasn't as if any dreamer exerted active control over the contents of a dream—and such an impossible dream! A dream of the future, a dream that extended indefinitely forward, a dream occupied by beings fully sentient. I'm trapped, J thought. And yet he must climb the tower, he must confront his maker.

By maker, J asked himself, *do I not actually mean God?* J wasn't a believer. But...but...if J could, for argument's sake, allow for God, then God, after all, was responsible for all of it: his dreamer's condition, his death, J's eventual death and J's confinement to a finite consciousness of elapsing duration.

This altered J's line of reasoning.

God, it should follow, could be held accountable. After rain there were rainbows. But shouldn't the symbol of the pact God made with Noah to never again destroy the world, a covenant God entered by walking alongside Noah through the cloven bodies of sacrificial animals, shouldn't the symbol of that *precede* rain? Or at least *coincide* with rain? That the rainbow followed rain implied that God's investment was not in reassuring those He had created in His image that this rain would not wipe them from the face of the earth. The rainbow demonstrated to God's creations that He had kept His word, that the rain could have continued; not reassurance, but threat, a reminder to those who rejoiced at the cessation of downpour that God might equally well have *not* chosen to cause to stop His torrents.

But if with each rain God needed to reconfirm that He had again kept His word, to remind Himself that He wasn't going to destroy all of His creations...didn't every rainbow reassert that God ought actually have destroyed His creations again, that they were sinners as unworthy of preservation as Noah's neighbors, preserved only on account of His mercy (or word)...or maybe the rainbow wasn't for humans at all! Maybe, the rainbow's audience was God, a reminder for Him that He had once used the essence of life to end life. But that wasn't any different, J realized, if it reminded God, then mustn't it remind humans that God needed that reminding? That their creator might forego or forget to preserve them, His creation?

Unless, the rainbow was a kind of heavenly mea culpa for collective human traumatic memory, and the rainbow was a covenant to not wreak again the world's end, because of the impact on the righteous of the destruction of the wicked. But, if the rainbow was an apology, even for that, then God had erred. If God could err...*Jacob*, J told himself, *you're not a believer.*

And yet, if J had seen and understood rainbows as such, then surely must his dreamer have too.

Then once again, yet again: how could his dreamer reconcile his understanding of the covenant with Noah with the fact of the Holocaust? And was God's understanding of the world so radically unknowable that the annihilation of His chosen did not violate His covenant with Noah?

Was the covenant only to not destroy by drowning? Or was the destruction of humans now bound by fractional rules? Killing two-thirds of all Jews not quite meeting the criteria for God's covenant with Noah? Was there an expiration date on the covenant? Or was it that in God's chronology, through some trick of His unknowability and atemporality, the Holocaust preceded the covenant with Noah, preceded the flood even. Was it that God's rainbow signified a covenant that there would be an after to all apocalypses? Was the rainbow not a promise not to destroy but a vow to remake after destruction?

This contoured chronology made a unique sense to J, for the Holocaust, because it created J's world, had the virtue of having always existed, and being therefore somehow both forefront and afterthought.

By this logic, how many more great exterminations lay ahead that, in divine logic, were a priori the covenant? When would it be safe for the Children of Israel to stop sleeping in their own graves each night and take their confident places amongst the living? Why bother to repopulate the world when apocalypse might apocalpyt again at anytime? When there was no way to tell when or how or to whom.

Who could presume to know God, to understand Him?

Why shouldn't one presume?

J wasn't a believer.

By being unknowable, J decided, God was unreliable. Was it any wonder then—and J marveled that he'd taken all these years to draw this parallel—that the offspring of the flood's survivors had wandered to a single place, a single Babylonian plain, taken refuge in coalescence despite divine decree to spread out, and built a tower of their own? And what were towers then but ziggurats upon which temples placed might have their prayers more readily heard in heaven? Did they not hope to make something more perma-nent than a world too-easily flooded? Were they not only seeking a foothold from which to negotiate with an erratic deity? Was it wrong to wish to beseech God? Were they not simply seeking a vantage from which to remind God of their existence? Was the problem of the ziggurat that of the golden calf, whose bare back was meant as a mount for an invisible God that He might be worshiped, a sin of anxiety, of a failure to believe in a covenant consecrated in rainbow or a God who might sustain his prophet Moses even forty days and nights, or was the city of Babel's tower indeed a means by which to breach the fortress of heaven? Did they not, haunted by images of the drowning slowly deprived of land, seek to create a stand higher than the heavens from which the rain fell?

Mightn't Israel itself be a kind of Babel then?

A tower?

Wasn't Israel a collaboration that warred against God's unreliability in which the offspring of survivors, what survivors there were, resurrected for themselves a common language to build a common thing that they might make a name for themselves? That at such time as the world sought to overcome them, they might stand above the earth's destructive might and withstand it? But to conspire to such might, what actions would be without their reach, their willingness: what wouldn't they do? And if they did all that such might allowed, at what point would God, witnessing them, say:

Behold, one nation and one language to all of them, and this they begin to do; and now...will not be secure from them, all that they will scheme to do.

Come, let Us go down...

And even if not God, at what point would someone else, as had once the Romans, witnessing what they began, say the same and scatter them unto the earth?

For that matter, was not America also founded by the traumatized refugees of another land come together, too, to make for themselves a name beneath a common language? And where had God been to deal with the ziggurat constructed by the outcasts of England and Ireland and Scotland and Germany and Italy and Poland and Russia and Greece and Armenia? Why had God not dispersed them, foreseen askance the schemes of those no longer denied any entry to whatever their power leads them to scheme? Survivors. Victims.

Oppressors.

Saviors.

What exactly had it been that would no longer have been able to be secured from the wicked scheming of those traumatized peoples assembled upon the plains of Shinar, building their ziggurat, their prayer?

And what was J? He was neither victim nor survivor. What was his tower? A refuge? A stand at equality? A pulpit? He'd built it alone, had not common language, nor effort, nor people. J was not Nimrod.

Did he build his tower to reach his dreamer or for his dreamer to reach God?

Was his tower so that his dreamer might reach unto God and negotiate?

Was that it? Was it so that his dreamer from the tower's peak might reach unto heaven and plead?

Plead what?

Plead thus:

Nu. Please.

Please. I am a father.

I have two beautiful girls. I am a dutiful father.

I have a wife that I love. I am a person. Please let me live.

I am sacred. My family depends upon me. I am not ready for death. Please.

Please. My people need me. Do not let me die tangled in my neighbors' death. Please do not let me die naked amongst strangers, in Gullus, in exile, alone.

Do not let me die in the back of a van. Do not let me die smeared in the excrement of those around me, smothered with the fear of those around me. Please do not let me die in my own feces, in my own fear. Please don't leave my body to the hands of my murderers, to a pit in the ground. Please, my Lord, don't do this to me. Please!

Do not deny me the sacred chance to return this sacred physical form to you in a pure state.

Do not deny me the sacred washing of my lifeless body and the vigilance of my beloved against those who would violate my lifeless body and the simple cotton shroud of my lifeless body's modesty and the simple pine box open to ground water that I might return to the dirt the dust that you have lent.

Do not deny me the Mishnaiot learned in my name by those who remember me.

Do not deny me the yahrtzeit prayers of my mourners, my loved ones, my survivors.

Do not deny me my survivors, Lord!

Do not deny me those who would remember me!

Do not forget me, my Lord!

Do not forsake me, my Lord!

My Lord! My Lord!

Do not forsake me, Lord!

Please, my Lord!

Hear me, Lord, please!

Please do not forsake me!

Lord, please!

Or:

The dreamer on top of the tower would present his toddler's pudgy clutch on his forefinger while he spooned her evening warm milk and rice, her hand turning from pink to mottled red and white with her exertion.

Yes, it could be the tower wasn't J's prayer at all but the dreamer's. But who was J to coin for his dreamer a prayer? To presume his dreamer's will? He didn't know his dreamer's will. J couldn't know.

Eighteen years: *Chai*, a lifetime, and still he didn't know.

J couldn't know.

To tell of the room in which the dreamer fed his child, of the way he felt her sense of safety while she held his finger, of the comfort of eating and of holding a father's finger, of the quiet of their home, lit at night, the infant asleep beside the dreamer's wife in another room…to tell of that could only dilute the fact of the image itself: Love was, love is. Love, a small child's clutch on her parent's too big finger. That is all.

And when had the fact one loved ever warranted one's salvation from death?

J remembered E's two children.

It grew dark. J remained seated, too accustomed to his ability to remain solitary and immobile to notice this ability of his, to note its difference from the frenetic state he'd occupied eighteen years earlier when first he'd come to realize he existed in a dream. God, J meditated, created language, Hebrew, with two letters, aleph and tet, Hebrew's A-to-Z, the alphabet, and with that language created the world. He fractured language at Babel with a sentence or two in an account that seemed like a footnote to creation.

Why, J wanted to know, was it so bad for people to possess potent capacity to accomplish their desires?

Could those desires, the people who longed them, really pose a genuine threat? Could their tower actually have reached God? The language says that God *came down, yaredet,* God *descended,* to see what the people were up to. Descended from where? Could they actually have reached Him? Did He continue to hover above, this high but not higher? Did God hover at a height between descent and departure? Between coming on down to walk amongst us and departing altogether to create new worlds?

It was unthinkable in the context of the biblical depiction of God that He would actually have been under duress and attack. Nonetheless, the passage does not say that God punished them for sin, nor that He separated them that they might be devout. It says that He split them apart because if they completed their city, nothing would be beyond their capacity. What could the people have chosen to do with that unlimited capacity that would so have threatened God? What strength would they have gained by finishing their city and its tower?

Babel, Babylon, Babel and one day, millennia after the tower, millennia later even than secular scholars of exegesis claim Moses' five books were composed, Babel conquered Israel, and led her people into exile there. And when Babel allowed Israel to return home, allowed Israel to rebuild her temple, much of Israel chose the lives they'd made in exile. The upset persisted. Ten tribes were lost. The remaining two would soon resume their wandering. Their wandering would culminate, just shy of two thousand years later, in the gas chambers and at the edge of mass graves and in the streets and squares of Europe and West Asia and North Africa.

Then, those remaining, who by all rights shouldn't even be called survivors, unless one was to call Noah a survivor, both really ought to be called remnants, tattered cuttings rived from their forming fabric, the traumatized genesis of something altogether new, these people, who lived though they shouldn't have lived, though the genocide of their people was a complete success, these leavings wandered to a place and they built a nation, said, let us make a name for ourselves, and they chose a single language, though none of them had spoken it as either first or second tongue before, the language of their disregarded prayers not the same as this new language that they forged from that one, and they dared the world to forbid them whatever they set out to do, whether it was moral or not, whether it was palatable or not, whether it was good or not. Not might be but is, J thought: Israel is the Tower of Babel.

Israel is the Tower of Babel.

That was his memorial.

CHAPTER SIXTY

J LOST CONTACT WITH his ethereal meditation's carpet ride with a rupture like waking, like falling back into his body. He could feel his legs' lack-of-feeling, and, through that tingling numbness, the pebbles and twigs that underlay his blanket. His arms were rough with chill, covered in goose bumps. His lower back ached. He felt hungry and unfocused and a bit angry. He wanted to be back in his space of pure contemplation, but each time he caught the edge of a thought about Babel and its tower and their relationship to Israel all those thousands of years later, he found insight just out of reach. He wanted to move, to stretch, and he worried that if he moved he'd permanently lose the rapturous state he'd been in. His desire to sleep was offset by the aches in his limbs, his stiffness. It occurred to him that he'd passed through middle age building a mud tower, was now nearly old. He felt that this should amuse him, make him laugh.

He didn't see any reason, any change in his thinking or station, that should mandate that he be older, but he was older. He felt the same as he had when he was young, but he was older. He was too old, probably, to settle down to family and children. He heard, or thought that he heard, a deer or something more sinister in the shadows past his sitting point. The moon began to rise and the far wall of his valley to glow, each tree crisp and lit and clear. The moon rose until it was upon him, its beam cold and exposing.

The tranquility of the tower felt distant. The notion that he'd stepped out of the messy action of living and into some grand parable plagued him, plagued him to think that his existence wasn't only limited to a dream, but to the narrower dimension of biblical telling, from which he barely touched down from time to time to engage with some female or other, that engagement, those women, his only real touch.

They formed a list too: Esther, Mary, Chase, Hayley, and all the ones before Esther. Each of them, even, now seemed like a mood or a sensation rather than a sentient entity with which to form a new separate consciousness that transcended them both. They were a *nostalgia*. Different nostalgias. Chase and he had tried to make a story, but thoughts of her felt like voluntary visits to melancholy and want and regret of something greater than himself that he'd never quite access.

CHAPTER SIXTY-ONE

With the beginning glow of the day, the air still cold, its atoms as yet unexcited, J regained awareness. His head rested on the intersection of his crossed calves; his arms slumped to either side.

Shit, he thought, this is going to hurt.

He tried to sit up, but his back, numb, didn't respond. He set a hand on either side of his knees and pushed gently, the ground's cool damp palpable against his palms even through the blanket. His back twinged, warned him off that approach. J sighed, and then toppled onto his side.

Blood began to return to his lower calves and ankles and feet. He seethed at the tingling. Gradually, he straightened his legs, extended his toes as much as his work boots would allow. His ear pinched, pressed into the thorned ground past the blanket's perimeter.

Through the tall flowers, hyssop and red paintbrush, he saw a marmot climb onto a granite boulder, its coat rich glinting brown. J wanted to straighten his back, his shoulder was pressed into what must have been the sharpest rock ever, but he willed himself to wait. Gradually, the tingling in his feet began to subside. Another marmot joined the first on the rock. The two of them stared out across the sloped meadow, oddly callisthenic in their inertness. A large black bird, either a crow or a vulture, J couldn't quite discern which from his angle, flew low towards him, circled once at twenty feet, and then continued.

"I'm still alive, asshole," J muttered loudly enough to alert the marmots, which turned their heads broadside, each observing him with one eye.

He flexed his legs again to confirm their renewed circulation, and then, very slowly, straightened his spine, easing off and pausing at each twinge. When his back finally came straight, he made the short flop to lie flat on it. He looked up at the unblemished sky of a day still less than an hour old. The stalk of something sawed at his right ear. At least the sharp rock no longer dug into his shoulder. He wondered whether it was better to move or to lie like this until the time came to go back down, with the smell of earth, or rotten mud, thick against his cheek. His stomach hurt from not eating. His mouth tasted of moths and algae. He decided that water, at least, was necessary. Surprisingly, sitting up wasn't bad, though his head swam a moment at the couple of extra feet of altitude. Next step, he thought, standing. That was all right as well; though he felt himself sway with each breeze, overcompensate at each still.

J opted to clear his head by moving, and set off for a band of aspen at the bottom of a scree field on the assumption that they hid a creek. At first, his feet clamored like string puppets under ungainly control. Eventually, he found that he was walking. Then, he was at the trees. Instead of water, he discovered a run of grey gravel, flanked by purple-fringed tamarisk and clumps of three-foot tall green stalks terminating in white flowers. The defeat made J's knees weak, made his eyes tear, made him want to rip something. He hung onto the trunk of an aspen while his sight wavered with lightheadedness, then bit down on his lower lip to clear his head.

"Well, this is it," he said aloud. "No water. That's ok. You can live without water."

He knew, of course, that this wasn't true. He knew that he could look further afield for water, that somewhere on the mountain there was likely a creek or a snowfield. But he decided that the sting of his defeat, the unrewarded effort it had cost him to ascend to the dry creek bed, was actually a conscious prod by whatever logic ruled the dreamer's dreaming to not abandon his blanket, to not drink. He could make it another day without water.

He plucked a stone from the creek bed and put it in his mouth.

Dust, neutral and warm, replaced the taste of mouse hide. Sucking on the stone soothed if not slaked his sense of thirst. He set off for his blanket, the downhill trip easier than the ascent, though each step had a kind of bright uncertainty, as if his extremities floated ever so slightly. And walking downhill, he realized how foolish he'd been to travel uphill in search of a stream when he could have walked laterally to intercept its path. The blanket's corners had folded over in the light gusts that punctuated the day's easy breeze. J carefully turned these back, and smoothed the blanket with his palms, before gradually lowering himself again.

As compensation for not drinking, he allowed himself to sit with his legs uncrossed. He stretched them downhill in front of him. In this position, he could see the plains below. They shimmered in the mid-morning heat, appeared a great wasteland from where he sat. He could see his spire, miniaturized, like something misplaced from a Bedouin desert, a minaret with no city to call to prayer, just the house beyond it, anomalous and low.

The view felt like an anchor; J wanted untethering. He wanted to be away from the spire, away from Chase's world. He turned around to face uphill, but now his legs were positioned awkwardly. Besides, he could still feel the spire behind him. Just turning his back on it too closely mirrored the ostrich's escape. With an unsighed sigh, resolute in his refusal to complain at the inconvenience of this ritual he himself had devised, J stood, and dragging his blanket behind him by a corner like a weary toddler off to his bed, J walked another mile to change his aspect on the mountain. He crossed a rounded ridge and came to a stand of fir that tapered into aspen after a hundred feet.

At the transition between aspen and fir, he found a stream.

Wide-eyed in front of the water, he debated whether or not to drink.

The water did seem like a reward. On the other hand, on his prior attempt to drink, he'd felt chastised. He sucked on his dried lips. I'm choosing to do this, J thought, so it should be up to me. But, if a ritual of one's choosing didn't extend past oneself, then it wasn't much of a ritual. Besides, if he believed that there was something to address at the top of the spire, then he must believe that his preparations were proscribed by that entity. Perhaps, he thought, he was supposed to question less: when there was no water, J was not meant to drink; when there was water, J was meant to drink.

No tests, only occurrences.

J stood thinking about how much he should be thinking, lightly swaying, blanket trailing behind.

By this logic, he need not even use the words "punishment" and "reward." The divine wasn't training him, it was creating as it felt fit, providing and withholding according to a logic beyond J's understanding. If, however, the logic of his existence was beyond his capacity, then it was foolish to think that he could communicate with it, beseech it, from his tower or from anywhere else. Then he had to think that the presence favored some actions or abandon the hope that the tower presented.

Even J couldn't follow where this train left him.

The creek might be a test: true. Truth: drinking stream water would give him the shits, but probably not for a few days. By then, he'd have ascended (and descended) his tower. J dropped to his knees and dunked his head to gulp great mouthfuls of water. He sat up, cold, clear, water gushing from hair and face and chest in long glistening runs.

For a moment, his sense of refreshment was ecstatic: the stomach cramp came hard and fast.

He battled the contraction a moment, then did his best to turn away from the stream before his torso bucked and the stream water came up.

He supported himself on his hands, panting between stinging heaves.

In a fermata between convulsions, he left his body and saw himself below, as if in a bad TV rendition of angelic death. He liked what he saw, and it saddened him. A man, muscular and wet down to his waist, his grey hair is blacked with drench around his face, on hands and knees on a tilted piece of meadow at the border of evergreens startlingly sunlit next to a shimmering line of white aspen, their leaves, in this light, more the blue of new growth than the season's browning green, a thinness of water winding down between their rows from a granite-banded mountaintop above. It was a pretty and perfect kind of sight, a natural version of the appointments Delilah would set on a breakfast table, except that the man was compulsively vomiting. Then J was back in his body again. The soft open tissue in his nostrils and at the back of his throat and at the margin of his gums and around his eyes stung with bile.

He vomited what felt like a last wave of empty nothing, a string of green spit, and collapsed to his side, weak, breathing deep gasping breaths.

He lay like this a few minutes until his heart rate settled and his breathing slowed to normal. Then, moaning lightly, he eased himself back to the creek and splashed water over his face. He tested a mouthful of water timidly sucked out of cupped hands, his nose still putrid with bile. He swished the water around his mouth, his mouth warming the water, his teeth tender with stomach acid. He spit it out and sucked in another, swallowed this one. There was a moment of queasiness; then his stomach accepted it. He willed himself to wait before sucking down a second handful. Like this, he gradually slaked, blissfully aware of nothing but his relationship with measures of stream.

A bit of breeze pooled down the valley and soothed his drying face and arms. He pulled his blanket to, and under, himself. The blanket's wool defined patterns on his fingertips as if it was a coarse scouring pad. He stared once again into the unblemished sky. Its surface rippled and warped. J realized he was seeing the world from beneath the surface of tears. He didn't know why he cried, but it seemed all right that he did.

He lay like this a while longer, his tears, like glacial snouts, running courses down his face that ended where the wind dried them. The sky shivered and J heard his skin rippling like a tarp over a pickup bed at highway speeds. Everything he'd ever known was everywhere and in him and him at once the way the light and dark had been one with earth and sea in J's early dreams of creation. There they were: Delilah and Esther and Chase and Walter and Rumkowski—not a rabbi now, but a heckled administrator—and the Chicago priest, but dressed as pontiff, and Hayley and another woman with two girls who looked like they were E's girls, but older, and there was a space of darkness filled with limbs—the dreamer, J thought, the dreamer—and J's grandfather was there, and his parents, and there was the aide, except that she was wearing nothing but brown Mary Janes, and the bodies and a tremendous desire to be awake that felt like an unrealized cough, and a tremendous desire to be asleep—the dreamer, the dreamer—there was J's growing-up yeshiva and huge tangles of tomatoes and hops and squash vines growing over the building—and there was a low teak ceiling with an elaborate gold etching of a mermaid battling a bull. Then his cock was inside of a woman straddling him, her legs wide and her pelvic bone like a palm between her legs against his pelvic bone, and then he wasn't—the dreamer! the dreamer…and there was a jolt and the limbs turned and there was a crack of light and through it fields near their wooded ends—back inside the woman again and the girls with their heads shaved and Chase and the Baltimore missionary's wife and the missionary and a pulpit and a park and an afternoon.

And the afternoon was a walk along a creek with tall green trees J couldn't identify and there was a woman at his side who he could feel, who leaned against him from time to time, but he never looked over at her because when she leaned J knew where her hip bone gave way to flesh and where her flesh gave way to ribs, because in the warmth of her body they, dreamer and he, J, could feel the edge of her aureole where it tensed at touch, because her chin sometimes lingered on his shoulder and he knows the way her cheeks slope, and they knew the way her hair draped, and J also knows the curvature of her eyes and her nose and her ass and he knew the flat spot at the base of her spine, a shelf, palm-sized between her ass cheeks; they, with her, walk along the path and there was a pigeon awkwardly hopping on one foot next to a bush and the woman whispers that this is the Moses of the birds and the bush is too hot for it to stand beside and J said behold the bush was not consumed and they know the way her stomach would shiver if he were to deny it the touch of his hand held just above it and they knew the way her thought would be naked if J asks for it, and then the path bends to follow the stream and there is a man fishing with a long cane pole and a string and no reel and no creel and the woman takes their hand, J's and the dreamer's, J's or the dream-er's, the dreamer's and J's both, their hand in her hand! In both her hands! And she holds it along her side between them so that he can feel his pants and the bottom hem of her skirt and at least J knows this much: that she will be the woman who leans forward in the picture and that the two girls who were Esther's are also the dreamer's and that maybe God was slowly allowing the world to continue despite his destroying the world.

Then Rumkowski, the light—the dreamer! the dreamer—the sun settled into a corner of a no longer aberrant sky. The dreamer dreamt again, his wakedness undone, and J couldn't tell whether he was relieved to be back on the solid surface of an intangible reality that would never be, his own world, or whether he wished the dreamer awake, the dreamer stumbling through carbon monoxide haze to find the back door of the van, some accident of rutted road jarring the door bolt back, the dreamer pitched out, mere hundreds of yards from the mass grave, stumbling, then running, into the woods, the dreamer saved and J ended.

The dreamer saved and J ended.

J's lack of agency was bliss for a second, and then, more than anything, he wanted the afternoon and the woman and the walk in the park along the stream, the woman whose features had already slipped away, whose warmth was just the chill of the breeze on his numbing arm.

There was an explosion and smoke rose into the sky; and J thought, this is it, a sign. He would go up the tower. He sat up slowly, his body like a desaturated photograph, a grey scale memory of a world in color.

He pulled his knees towards him, inhaled, exhaled: if the dreamer woke, J would cease to exist.

If the dreamer were to escape his grave, then J would be damned to his.

J would climb his tower.

He must speak.

He must ask why his people are condemned to sleep in their graves, night in, night out. Even if he lacked words for it, he knew what he wanted now, what he needed, and it was a burning plain.

J stood, scooping water into his hands to drink while he walked rather than stoop to drink from the stream, as if he was one of Joshua's long-ago troops. He left the blanket behind. He didn't bother to put his shirt back on. In pants and boots, he walked around the curvature of the mountain, his elevation constant, so that when he descended he might descend directly towards his spire.

CHAPTER SIXTY-TWO

J CAME AROUND THE corner of a ridge and the valley with the house and the spire lay below. The smoke, which had made a clean white column, had largely dissipated in the wind except for where it cloaked the tower. A second explosion swelled the valley, pushing a mirage of bent air towards J again.

When it cleared, J could see that a vertical sliver of his spire was gone. He paused, the perfect air and day alive in his hair.

Another explosion. J began to run. How could he have imagined the smoke was a sign from God? This was happening in the material world: an assault on his tower. Before the smoke could fully clear there was another explosion and another, the echoes of each meeting the outgoing waveforms of the next, creating an uneven series of spikes and troughs such that silence and deafening intermingled.

J ran towards it, towards the wafting cordite, into an air ruined with dust and fractured sparks that threatened pinon needles and dry tree branches and whatever of the meadows was already dead that it might conflagrate and consume the living. Here was his dream of an ecstatic apocalypse. He remembered his long-ago punch, his desire to burn down Yid World. Here was his itch for armed adventure. J ran, though he'd fasted two days, though he could hardly see the ground, which he knew was knotted with roots and rocks. J ran. J ran though the running was long. By the time the ground flattened and he knew he was only two miles from the site, the explosions had stopped, though J's ears still registered a series of concussions. When the wind shifted and the smoke cleared enough for J to see—the sky forever blemished by stripes of earth and brick and munitions and dreams and years-of-making— where the tower should have been, a column of dust milled with the lazy efficacy of a tornado warming.

He slowed to a walk.

The house, he saw when the dust bent away from it, had been battered by falling adobe chunks. Who and how and why? God come down, of course, or the dreamer, or both. But why and how and who? Who would take away his one last chance to look backwards towards his creator? Towards the man forever condemned to the gas and the van? The spire had been solid earth, impregnable.

Nothing should have been able to destroy it (except God, come down to deal with J lest nothing be denied J; the cruelty of that denial, when all J wished was to learn what it was he was meant to do, how it was he might serve his dreamer, reconcile the horror of the man being gassed to death and the nothingness of existing in that man's dream, without any access to that man).

J wondered whether it might not still be there, though he knew this was simple denial, a refusal to accept that after all his effort, still he would not be able to confront his dreamer.

He came to the house. The sweat on his chest turned first to mud, and then dust covered that mud again. White, grey and red dust coated his hair and face and pants. His lungs ached from breathing dust. His eyes stung with it. He thought to go into the house to get away from the dust, but pushed on to the spire. A hundred feet before the edge of the declivity that had been the tower's site, heaps of shattered adobe block set in shifting silt impeded his progress.

He tried to climb over these and slipped and slid. His eyes stung with caked dust. He tried to wipe them with his hands, but his hands were also caked in dust and only rubbed the irritants deeper. He put a finger in his mouth to suck the dirt off of it to fix his eyes, but his mouth was dust and dirt too. He reached the top of the choss, stood, ankle deep in silt. Where his tower had been, dust hovered like an unformed genie fully free of an oil lamp's spout. The sandstone slab that had once served as a foundation: obliterated; a crater, black and scarred, seeped water and oil in thin veins through unwieldy fissures.

Coughing, J turned to make his way away from the site. Coming down the debris mound, he tripped and tumbled to the bottom, scraping his shins and arms, banging his cheek. He made it to the front of the house, hobbled and bent over. He pulled the door open to discover that the air in there was no better, the windows having all shattered in the explosions.

He made his way to the shower that once faced the mountains and the buttes and then witnessed the tower, risen, before it. Glass everywhere, the suspended tank collapsed onto the granite slab, water spraying ineffectually into the dust from sundered supply lines. He turned around, still hunched, his wrist still in front of his mouth as if to double for a dust mask or as if to stifle.

He made his way to the bedroom with the iron bed. This room, though windowless, was nonetheless silted over, too, dust exhaled into the room beneath and around the door. At least the air was, mercifully, somewhat clearer. J closed the door behind him and then went into the bathroom, which was somewhat less choked. He turned on the elbowed faucet, but the pressure had been sapped by the burst supply lines in the ruined glass shower. Water collected over the spout and pattered in a thin trickle. He stooped beneath this, the drip hammering a small spot on his scalp like water torture, not nearly enough to wash the dust from him. He turned each eye, in turn, to the flow, cleared them nearly enough to see. Opened his mouth and filled it and spat and filled it and spat and filled it again and still spat, the dirt in his mouth endless. Then he coughed in long waves, expectorated hard chunks of phlegm and tower.

When the coughing slowed, he left the bathroom. In a bedroom drawer, he found an undershirt, which he tore into strips and tied around his mouth for a mask, and a western shirt, which he snapped loosely over his dust-caked chest. He went back into the living room and collected his rifle, the Bedouin rifle Walter had given him for his fortieth birthday, and a box of shells. He loaded the gun under his shirt hem, worried at the dust entering the mechanisms.

J was going to kill a man as soon as he knew which man to kill.

He left the house and went to his pickup, the hood and cab roof dented by falling brick, the bed half-a-foot deep in fallen rubble, the windshield spider-webbed. Miraculously, the truck started.

J drove out of the dust cloud. Past it, he kicked out the windshield altogether, rode towards town with the wind tearing his eyes, tears flushing them and streaking his cheeks, and the gun propped alongside him. He debated whether to go to Louis', where Walter might be holed up, or Delilah's house, or Chase and Art's home. Before he could choose any of these, he came to the gas station and general store that sat at the intersection of the road that went to Walter's and the two-lane that eventually crossed the interstate. There were cars and trucks massed here, and J realized he needed food and drink and a bathroom. He drove around back to where the bathrooms were, wishing to avoid the men he saw on the porch until he'd washed up some. He managed to get the dust off his face and hands, but his cheek was bruised and bloody, and his pants were torn around his shins, and his wet fingers left long dark streaks in the dust that permeated his hair.

Fuck it, he thought.

He walked around to the front of the building, everything in him sore and aching, the adrenaline sitting in his days-empty stomach a corrosive lubricant. The men on the porch were crowded around two young guys in National Guard uniforms. At first no one noticed him, and he overheard "bunker-buster" and "special project" and "crazy-ass tower." Then they became aware, and the two soldiers stopped, and their eyes drooped, and one of them exclaimed in what sounded like a question and an excuse that they'd been told no one was there, that no one lived in the house and that it was all right to do.

"Who told you?" J asked.

Everyone looked at him, everyone silent and shuffling and not answering.

"Did you blow up the tower?"

"Man, it was our training mission, to see what the charges could do."

"Who gave you those orders?"

"Who the fuck are you?" this from the other soldier.

"We checked, there wasn't anyone there, just like the governor said," this from the first soldier again.

"Shut up!" this from the second.

But J had stopped listening at governor, and his heart was broken and hardened. Art then, Art had destroyed his tower. Art, to whom he had been loyal; Art, who he loved; Art, who was perfect and claimed that he had faith; Art, who knew J was dreamt, and therefore thought J was closer to God; Art for whom J had debased the very idea of a Jew; Art had destroyed J's final chance to reach his dreamer. Art had destroyed the one thing that J had ever made.

Art.

Art had taken everything.

Dazed and sad, his wounds and the fasting and the running and the lack of sleep now present and debilitating, J collected snacks and an energy drink from the store's shelves, only to realize that his wallet wasn't with him. The girl at the counter told him to just take the stuff. He thought to refuse this charity, then instead limited himself to a white bread and egg salad sandwich and the energy drink. He knew her, after all, the cashier.

He asked her where Walter was.

She told him that Delilah had been by with Walter on their way to see their daughter a couple of days ago.

"Their daughter Chase?"

"If that's their."

But the girl didn't know where they might be seeing her, her information gained by forgotten eavesdropping.

J ate and drank while he drove, forced below forty on the interstate by the lack of a windshield, a steady stream of dust trailing him from the truck's bed. By the outskirts of Albuquerque, the traffic was consistent enough that passing drivers honked and swore as they went around him. Lost in his heartbreak, J didn't even hear them. His liege had destroyed his final project. And wasn't that project, at least in part, for Art as well? Hadn't Art's quests all been to remedy the world's flaws? Wasn't a monument that allowed conversation with God the ultimate means of salvation?

He reached the house in the suburbs and a Guardsman was posted at the door. J drove past and parked around the corner, stashed the rifle behind the bench seat.

Despite his attempt to approach casually, the soldier, M-16 across her chest, gawked at him.

"Are you all right, sir?" she asked.

"Is Art here?"

"Would you like me to call you help, sir?"

"I'm fine," J sputtered angrily. "I need to see Art or Chase. Let me pass."

"I can't let you in, sir," she said.

"Well could you tell him I'm here?"

"Sir, you can not go in there."

"Goddamn it, tell him Jacob Paul's outside," J said.

"Sorry, sir."

"Art!" J yelled. "Chase! Goddamn it, Art! Come out!"

"Sir!"

"Art!" J yelled again, refraining from following the name with threats in front of this armed woman.

"Is he even here?" he asked.

"You have to leave, sir."

"He isn't, is he? If he was, you'd tell him someone was here. If he was and he was shutting himself off this badly, you'd have radioed assistance."

"Sir, you need to go."

She had the weapon pointed at him. He raised his open palm to shoulder height and walked backwards and away. When he glanced back on the way to the truck he saw her speaking into the radio microphone clipped to her epaulet. At least, he thought, he'd parked around the corner and she wouldn't be able to radio his license plate. Then he realized that was silly. Art had access to the truck's plate number. Besides, if Art wanted him restrained, the Guardsman would have had orders to do so. He got back in the truck and set off for Santa Fe, drove without thinking, consumed by a hollow darkness that existed outside of time and language. The governor's mansion was swarming with Guardsmen. They'd extended a perimeter with roadblocks and jersey barriers. Art was preparing for war, and this realization woke J. The war could only be with him. And if with him, then Art had destroyed his tower as part of a larger declaration. J smiled. Art was clearly afraid of him if he'd done all this. J watched the maneuverings through his missing windshield from two blocks away. In the night, he thought, sniping, as would the Bedouin who once made the gun, as would Chase's grandfather.

He drove away. He would need money, amongst other things. He found a rare pay phone and dialed Delilah collect, marveling that the archaic form of charging a call still persisted. Some member of Delilah's staff accepted the charges. The staff member interrupted J's hysteria to ask if this was really the emergency.

"Yes," J said. "Yes, this is an emergency!"

"The emergency?"

"Sure! Yes! The emergency!"

"The one?"

"Yes, yes, the one!"

At which, the staffer gave directions to an Albuquerque hotel at which Delilah had left a package in case of the emergency for J. J drove back south, carefully husbanding the gas from the seven-gallon jerry can, thankful for the downward bent of the road between New Mexico's two cities. He coasted into the parking lot of the small hotel Delilah's staffer had named, the truck hiccupping on vapors mostly imaginary. The lobby, while not opulent, dated back to a period in which even middling hotels had striven for the grandiose, and the high, tiled ceiling, made the place dark and cool, which amplified the sense of mildewed carpet.

The clerk wore a uniform suited best to a pre-war bellhop, and the clerk, too, seemed preserved from some lost epoch, preserved but poorly. Remarkably, the clerk seemed completely oblivious to J's decrepit condition. Instead, the clerk simply handed J a room key, an actual key attached to an old plastic, diamond-shaped fob, and said J would find everything in the room. Before bothering with the room, J went back to the truck, wrapped the gun in a horse blanket excavated from beneath the dust of the truck's bed, and took it with him into the hotel.

The room was small, high ceilinged and wainscoted. The sink was in the main room, rendered from heavy porcelain and wedged like a pie slice into a corner, the spigots' silver mermaids splayed around marble spindles. There was a leather briefcase with a wooden handle on an overwrought bureau. There was a suit in the closet, alongside a few fresh shirts. It struck J: this was the seventh and last of the suits. Well, it was all coming together, the end, the resolution, some finality. He smiled. He didn't need to look in the bureau to know he'd find undergarments and ties in it. He elected to bathe before opening the suitcase. He threw the deadbolt and the security latch on the door. The bathroom was so small that J had to pull down his pants before he went in, this action taking skin from his shins with the pants' fabric, reminiscent of his arrival at Joe and Allie's.

Despite the bathroom's small size, a tall-sided claw-foot tub with silver faucets was crammed into all of the space that wasn't the toilet or the door's swing. J marveled that Delilah, even when prioritizing discretion, found a hotel that belonged to her world's aesthetics. It took inordinate effort to scale the tub's side, and only after he was in it did he realize it didn't have a shower.

He sat on the tub's rear edge, leaning back against the bathroom plaster wall while the water ran, wondering what was in the brief-case, depressed that others continued to anticipate all his moves and guide whatever it was he did. And yet those moves were coming to an end. The last suit. The tower's destruction. Eighteen years. A lifetime. The water rose around his ankles and he mused that this was the kind of room old ladies nostalgic for lost empires lived in on the pensions of dwindled ancient fortunes, and that it was also the kind of room in which men not quite yet of middle-age, but convinced that they were, quietly killed themselves.

CHAPTER SIXTY-THREE

Naked, abraded, wet, with a delicious dread, with the sense that he was finally unsealing the secret orders for which he'd prepared all these years, under the delighted suspicion that in lieu of a tower and its divinity, his communion was with some underworldly cabal, J set the briefcase on the room's small writing table, which was wedged between the bed and the tall window. He sat in a high back chair and pulled it in to the table, sighed, paused to glance at the peeling green paint on the window's center mullion, undid the briefcase's two latches, took another deep breath, and opened it.

The top cover was divided into expandable compartments, each banded with a stitched strip of maroon-pinstriped brown elastic. These contained a cell phone, chargers suited to the voltages and outlet styles of multiple nationalities, two sets of car keys, two passports, multiple identifications, and several sets of currency as well as a thin bar of gold. J touched each of these with his forefinger, stroked them, without removing them. A manila folder sat on top of the briefcase's main contents. J extracted this. Beneath it were several sets of documents, an Iridium satellite phone, an automatic pistol, the pistol's magazine, and a box of bullets. J touched each of these as well, and then, using the thumb and forefinger of each hand, pushed the briefcase back with measured precision.

Then, when there was exactly enough space to open the folder in front of the briefcase, he did so.

A sheet of letterhead, embossed with what he imagined must be the coat of arms of some branch of the Hapsburgs, titled Ark 2.0, read:

Welcome to the Levi family emergency contingency plan. In the event of catastrophe, on either a grand scale or of a scope more limited, this plan will provide for your safe escape and extraction. Please begin by plugging in both the cellular and satellite phones; though they have been packed with a provisional charge, secure communications are the key to any plan's efficacy, and these depend on your communication devices' prolonged operation. If the emergency includes a localized radiological, biological or chemical event, please immediately deploy the anti-contamination suit located in the wardrobe.

J plugged in both phones to a set of outlets conveniently located on the base of the lamp at the far side of the writing table. He then returned to the letter.

The other family members have been equipped elsewhere with similar rooms and comparable packages. Both communication devices contain the numbers of the other family members' new communications devices. They also contain their former contact numbers. To the extent possible, refrain from contacting pre-event devices, as the security of those lines cannot be guaranteed. Upon establishing communication, select a rendezvous point a-f, domestic, or 1-8, international. Directions to these rendezvous points are pre-programmed into the GPS devices installed in the vehicles with which you have been provided. Keys for these vehicles may be found in the briefcase.

J skimmed through the directions for locating the vehicles and powered on the cell phone and punched through to the phone book. Sure enough, Art, Chase, Walter, Delilah and several others were all listed, as were numbers for things ominously titled: coyotes, medical-surgical, security, medical-nonsurgical, armament, targeted security, medical-aesthetic, money exchange, counsel, identity, treasure exchange. He debated whom to call first, and on what version of their phone. He hovered over Chase's number, and then decided that if Delilah had set this plan in motion, then it was her he should call.

He tried Delilah's emergency cell and sat numbers. They went unanswered. He dialed her regular cell number, and she answered immediately, demanding to know who it was.

"It's J, Delilah."

"What number are you calling from?"

"From the contingency plan cell phone."

"What?"

J began to repeat himself, but Delilah said to never mind. "Where are you?" she demanded.

"At the contingency plan hotel room," J said.

"What?" Delilah asked, clearly confused and irritated.

"Where are you?" J asked.

"We're at the hospital in Albuquerque. We've been leaving you messages for two days. Where the hell have you been?"

"At the hospital? I'm going to fucking kill Art."

"What? Why are you going to kill...never mind," Delilah said. "Did you get my messages?"

"No, my cell phone was destroyed."

"Destroyed?"

"In the explosions. Isn't that how..."

"Explosions?" Delilah cut him off.

"At the..."

"Enough. The point is that Walter had a collapse. A heart attack and then a series of small strokes, or the other way around, or both. No one can tell us anything for sure, or at least I don't understand any of it. He's asking for you. Where are you?"

"I'm coming," J said. "What hospital?"

Delilah began giving him directions, and he discovered, with some great irritation, that *Ark 2.0* had overlooked the inclusion of pen, pencil or pad. He scrambled to get the ones provided by the hotel that were on the bureau at the foot of the bed, and then the pen didn't write till he'd scribbled, flicked and licked it, so that he had to have Delilah repeat everything, which she did in a frantic high-pitch, insisting that he hurry, and then he had to have her repeat things a third time because he'd distracted himself by considering that the pen didn't work because no one had used the room in a very long time because the room had been reserved all of that time for him (or another Levi).

J took the suit out of the closet. Dressed, the set of ID that reflected his usual legal identity selected and assembled in the provided billfold along with domestic currency, J closed the brief-case unceremoniously and set off to find the vehicle labeled 'sedan,' though the 'tactical utility' option did project a certain allure, the gun back in the horse blanket and back under his arm, anomalous against the suit jacket's clean, refined fabric. The sedan proved to be an armored five series BMW, at the German provenance of which J ordinarily would have balked. It was parked in a back corner of an underground parking lot across the street from the hotel. He tried to override the GPS' welcome screen, which demanded that he select domestic or international, and upon the selection, gave him options a-f or 1-8, but was unsuccessful. J decided to wing it, despite his at best nominal familiarity with Albuquerque's cartography.

On the way to the hospital, he attempted to call Chase no less than three times, but each time, midway through what passed for a dialing process on a cell phone with a contact list, he had to pay attention to confusing directions and ambiguous street signage. When he arrived at the hospital, pistol locked in the glove compart-ment, rifle in the backseat foot well, disguised there by the horse blanket and further disguised by the windows' dark tint, he again put off calling her in the interest of sooner reaching Walter's room.

Walter's room was on the top floor of the hospital where he'd been moved from the ICU only hours earlier. His bed was tilted up to bring a hospital tray closer to his mouth. An IV fed into his forearm above a paper bracelet whose enormousness called attention to Walter's reduced frame. Another tube ran under his nostrils. Delilah sat on a chair beside his bed, perhaps the plainest, most industrial chair she'd ever sat in, a simple chrome frame with a seat upholstered in purplish carpet. Her bearing was as ever it had been, but she'd cut her hair into a kind of bob, and let the grey show at its roots.

She attempted to feed Walter something once-canned from the tray, and Walter seemed perturbed by, and resistant to, the approaching spoon. Walter! Walter, who as long as J had known him had carefully constructed a patina of worn ordinariness, who'd spent fortunes to look like a ranch hand, Walter, finally, was without disguise and genuinely vulnerable. He was old and frail and in a bed, somewhat confused, waited upon. J leaned into the room to knock on the open door and Delilah frowned and waived him in.

"Good," she said, "You're here." And in a louder voice: "Walter, Jacob's here to see you."

"Jacob," Walter said, and J's heart broke for how much strain there was in a voice that achieved so little volume.

"Hey, Walter," J said, his own voice booming and annunciative. "How are you?"

Walter motioned J to come closer. J came closer until Walter, Delilah, and he were bunched together. Walter grabbed J's wrist, and J had the uncomfortable sense of being stronger than the man who held him, of feigning being restrained out of a sense of obligation.

"Did you talk to him?" Walter asked, suddenly very present, very focused.

"Talk to who, Walter?"

"To him! To him! Did he answer you?"

J looked over at Delilah, his arm still in Walter's grip.

"Don't look at her!" Walter strained, and J turned back. "On the tower, did God speak, did He answer you!"

"I'm sorry," J said.

"He didn't answer," Walter said, letting go and falling back into his inclined bed. "He didn't answer."

"I didn't get to ask."

"So maybe He's not there, and maybe He doesn't care."

"No, I didn't get to ask, the tower was destroyed."

"What?" Delilah asked.

"This is what I was trying to tell you," J began explaining to Delilah.

"God destroyed the tower!" Walter began sitting up again.

"Art destroyed the tower," J said.

"God destroyed the tower!"

"It was Art!" J said again, loudly. Louder, "Arthur blew up the tower!"

"The tower's gone and there are no answers," Walter said, falling back again, clutching J's arm again. "There are to be no answers after all."

"I'm sorry," J said.

"Art blew up your tower?" Delilah asked.

"What do the doctors say about Walter?" J asked.

"I'm right here," Walter said.

"Well?" J asked.

"We don't really know anything, then, do we?" Walter said.

"Do the doctors have any ideas?" J asked.

"Doctors?" Walter asked.

"They've got him on thinning agents and they'll put in a pacemaker tomorrow," Delilah said.

"Fuck the doctors," Walter said. "I'm talking about God!"

"I'm sorry," J said. "My tower's blown up."

"I'm talking about fucking God! Fuck doctors!"

"I'm sorry," Delilah said.

"I'm so sorry," J said to Delilah, nodding at Walter.

"I'm right here, man!"

"All those years of work," she said.

"You didn't do it."

"All these years," Walter said. "To find you, to provide you with a course, to let you develop as you were wont to develop, so that you would build the tower, and then you build the tower. You build the tower! You fucking made the thing! And barely in time before I'm gone! And after all that!"

"After all what?" J asked.

"Can I talk to you in the hallway, Jacob?" Delilah asked.

"After all what, Walter? What have you known that you haven't told me?"

"Maybe that's its own answer," Walter said. "An answer in the refusal, the decimation of the means of asking."

"Come," Delilah said.

"What can't you say in front of me?" Walter demanded.

"It's not about you," Delilah said.

"Don't lie to me."

"You waited for me all these years?" J asked.

"I told Art about Chase and J," Delilah said.

"What about Chase and J?" Walter asked.

"Oh come on," Delilah said.

"Is this true?" Walter asked.

"Ignore him," Delilah said. "Art's kicked Chase out, that's good. But I didn't think he would..."

"Kicked Chase out?" J said, still in shock that Delilah knew, and that Delilah had told, and that Art knew, and that this must clearly be why Art was at war.

It was war then. It really was.

"Yes, but Walter collapsed and..."

"Who the hell is he to kick Chase out?" J asked.

"He should keep a whore in his bed!" Walter said.

"She's your daughter!" J said.

"She knew," Walter said. "I was very clear with her about your status."

"I meant for Art to kick her out," Delilah said. "I thought that would finish it."

"Finish it?"

"Surely Art knew."

"But you had to force him to confront it."

"I couldn't imagine anyone could destroy your tower," she said, "let alone want to."

"Or destroy the house?" J asked.

"The house?" Walter said.

"He wouldn't destroy Walter's house," Delilah said, making frantic gestures to J about Walter.

"Oh, who gives a shit," Walter said. "You don't need to protect me, Delilah. Fuck the house. The house doesn't matter. It's that we can't talk to God."

"Of course you can't talk to God!" Delilah said. "It's ridiculous!"

"It was as it was foretold!"

"You can't blow up a 120-foot tower and not damage the house next to it," J said.

"You were dreamt," Walter said. "You alone, and we took you in, cared for you; you an orphan, wayward, in need of patrimony. And this! This is what you do!"

"I didn't blow up the tower."

"You do this! You, you...sully, you sully my daughter, betray your friend, Arthur, your boss! You betray me! Yes, certainly, sir: you betray me!"

"I'm a man," J said. "Chase is a woman. We're adults."

"You were either the underling uplifted or the adoptive son, those were your available roles," Walter said. "Hell! You were dreamt, that's your role. What use have dreams with doomed love? What use have they with adultery and betrayal? And now, now there are no answers. There is no tower."

"And how have you known all this about me? And why have you never told me any of it? While I've struggled to find a way? While I've wandered lost? Alone?"

"He makes Chase happy!" Delilah said.

"Makes Chase happy!" Walter said throwing up his hands.

"Why am I dreamt?" J asked. "What do you know? What can you tell me?"

"Jacob!" Delilah said. "Walter would do better without worrying about all this!"

"Fuck Walter!" J said. "It was my tower, and my being dreamt, and I didn't blow up the damn house. Art did."

"I said, fuck the house!" Walter said.

"I'm going to find, Chase," J said. "And then I'm going to fucking kill Art."

"You'll kill no one!" Walter said.

"Walter's heart can't take this stress!" Delilah said.

"Tell me what you've kept from me!"

"Fuck my heart!"

"Fuck his heart!" J said. "I'm going to kill Art."

"Don't you dare! Chastity…" But here Walter fell into a fit of hacking that bent him up from his rest and brought his chest over his legs. Delilah hunched over him, lifting her head only long enough to mouth to J to get out.

CHAPTER SIXTY-FOUR

J STORMED DOWN THE hallway to the elevator bank, too absorbed in the great drama surrounding him to notice the charged energy and excited chatter of the staff waiting with him. Walter had known! In the elevator car, J failed to overhear the loud speculations of the doctors and nurses, nor did he observe the clusters around every screen, computer or television, in the hospital. He treated these groupings and their carnival atmosphere as simple obstacles, impediments to his haste, best dodged as quickly as possible. Who cared about any of it—the dream, the dreamer, how these people had guided or misguided him, who and what they were: Chase, he wanted Chase; and he wanted Art dead.

He made it into the car and onto the street, driving fast, before he even bothered to think about where he might be going. Even while punching up Chase's number, still theoretically aimless, he didn't slow down, making the car, heavy with armor, careen as if indeed evacuating an endangered dignitary.

Chase didn't answer any of his three calls. J didn't leave messages for her because he couldn't figure out how to put his current state of arms into a voicemail. He tried her emergency plan numbers, but, needless to say, she didn't answer those either. Meanwhile, J continued to whip around street corners at the tail end of yellow lights, haphazardly weaving through the city's early evening traffic, the sun in partial decline, half the cars with headlights on already. J idly wondered who maintained the emergency contingency plan, who kept the vehicles fueled, lubed and running, who updated the phone numbers in all of the communication devices. Then he called Art because why the hell not, and that act carried a measure of elation and breathlessness.

Art did answer his phone.

J announced himself as the caller.

"All right," Art said.

"What the fuck?" J said.

"You're what-the-fuck-ing me?" Art said.

"She was loyal to you," J said.

"She was fucking you!" Art exclaimed.

"She refused to leave you. I refused to leave you," J said. "I still refuse to leave you."

"You're out," Art said. "In exile. Her too. I expect never to see either of you again."

"Easy for you to say when you've got both your house and the governor's mansion surrounded with militia."

"I'm not afraid of you."

"I'm not afraid of you!"

"Fine. Just leave. Don't come back. Disappear. Find the earth's ends and jump. Don't write. Don't call."

"If you're not afraid of me, then why do you have the whole fucking National Guard out?" J asked.

"They're not out for you," Art said.

"Then for what?"

"You've been away for years, asshole. This is the world," Art said and hung up.

J tossed the phone on the passenger seat, mimed shooting it with his right hand. He punched the radio's power button. The news reports were garbled and hard to decipher. J began to delineate place names: DC, Salem, Somalia, Manchester, Iran, Mexico

City, Louisville, Fayetteville, Monrovia, Nagadoches, Wichita, St. Louis, Zinder, Batkun, Meridian, Abuja.

J had never heard such a convolution of geographies. He began to understand that the government had forestalled an elaborate terrorist plot, but elected to retaliate against the nations through which the would-be attackers passed and operated. A homegrown radical group, long opposed to American international intervention, claiming that the government had contrived the attack in order to extend American hegemony—or perhaps they believed the American hegemony had engendered the attacks, and therefore deserved them, J couldn't quite tell which.

J pulled the BMW over in front of a sports bar and went in.

Inside, the bar's umpteen screens displayed every concurrent game of every in-season sport. Where was the war? J expected to see a mélange of news stations, each broadcasting its own version and coverage. He thought he would witness warplanes, and troop transports, and smoldering Small Business Administration trailers, and FBI agents in body armor carrying assault rifles raiding suburban houses in neighborhoods that could have been in any of the fifty states. Nothing. Just sports. It was supposed to be a war, a real war, here in the dream, a war that transcended whatever was between J and Art and Chase!

J drank a beer and ate a plate of chicken wings, sucked the spare sauce from his fingers, drank another beer, waited for the TVs to catch up, to show pictures of explosions, portrayals of destruction, the appropriate accompanying images of the bereaved, the maimed, the dead, waited for pundits in newsrooms usually reserved for nascent national election returns to explain graphs projecting hypothetical death counts. He expected to see faraway nations subjected to high-altitude bombing raids, bombs, whose intelligence bordered on artificial thought, carefully destroying concrete abstractions, the physical manifestations of institutions, government buildings, factories, storerooms, armories. Where were the arrests of domestic radicals?

Finally that special hour came in which J imagined that powerful men remained active while their domains recreated and retired, worried and hid. J asked his server about the war, and why they weren't showing it.

"War?"

"Don't you know?"

"Seriously? War?"

The man was visibly frightened and J felt magnanimous catching this poor gentleman up, though J still couldn't believe the sports channels hadn't interrupted play to broadcast the news. J couldn't believe it, that was, until the man, hearing the details of J's clarification, began to laugh.

"Where you been, old man? Those attacks happened over years."

"But I just heard on the radio..."

"Nothing new happened, my friend. These TVs would've shown it. Must've been some kind of news analysis retrospective some kind of thing you was listening to."

"But,"

"No new war, my man, just the old one. Shit's normal."

"But all the security and the news and..."

"You need to get out more."

The server slapped J on his shoulder and handed him his check. No new wars, J thought. So there were old ones. Persistent ones. One new one: a war between Art and J.

J returned to his car, sated, calmed, and methodically drove back to Santa Fe.

He parked the car several blocks away from the mansion, well away from the National Guard barricades. He took off his jacket and tie, folded them, and placed them on the passenger seat. The Bedouin rifle was oiled and cleaned. Regardless, he unloaded it, ran a brush down the barrel, blew out the chamber, and then reloaded it. He withdrew the pistol from the glove compartment and checked its action before tucking it into his waistband. Finally, he resigned himself to leaving the vehicle. Despite the obvious logic of concealing the rifle, J carried it slung over his shoulder. He was a soldier now. He'd hide himself in order to reach his objective; he wouldn't hide his gun. As it turned out, a system of alleys and backyards through unlit blocks made it quite easy to reach the small park across the street from the mansion. Several Guardsmen kept a sloppy patrol of the park's walking path. J easily eluded them. He climbed a cinder privacy wall in front of a small public bathroom to reach its roof, kicking off his shoes first so that he could jam his toes into the small open circles in the blocks. The roof was shaded by a massive eucalyptus tree. J lay prone under its willowing tendrils, a shadow amongst shadows, mere feet above eye-level, at best a block away from the governor's living room. The night was thankfully still, forgiving J the need to adjust the gun's sights for windage.

The sights, of course, were manual. No scope. But something about his position and ambition was itself telescopic. J could make out not only Art's form, taller, better proportioned than the others assembled in the room, but his facial expressions, the creases in his sleeves where they'd been rolled up and now draped open around his wrists, the stray hairs that had come uncoiffed from his swept do, and the new small lines around his mouth that, unlike his other signs of age, pointed at a hardening, at loss, at flaws. J adjusted the sights for the distance, laid a second bullet next to the chamber so that he could rapidly reload if the window's shatter deflected his first shot. The perfect kill shot would aim for the head, but J felt that it was Arthur's heart that had betrayed him. He would aim for Arthur's heart.

J paused to consider that a shot now would kill Art in front of his innocent advisors, and decided that was acceptable. He considered that he would likely not escape. He decided that was all right, too. Seventh suit: the end. The tower was gone.

Having come to peace with his eventual capture, he removed the pistol from his waistband, unloaded it, and set it on the roof.

There was no need to kill his pursuers. Better to undo the ability to do so.

J aimed. This would be it, then. He would finally shoot. He would finally kill. He would kill Art. To think that finally the someone who J would shoot and kill was Art. Art was the man who had shown him the eagle and the goose and dream of the crusade. Art was the man he loved. Art was the man who had given him work, who had thrown his fortieth birthday party, who was married to Chase all those years, who stood up for J, who believed in J. Art was Christian strength. Art was a Zionist. Art was a man who'd wanted to build a better Holocaust museum, wanted to make a memorial to the Jews of Eastern Europe.

Art was the man Chase had refused to leave.

Art was the man J had refused to leave.

None of that mattered.

Art had cast out Chastity. Art had destroyed the tower. Art had started the war. From the very beginning, J had always been going to kill Art. J flicked off the safety, began slowing and lengthening his breath so that it might make a deep and inevitable rhythm from which the bullet would of its own accord emerge, fired from a perfect, placid weapon.

J watched Art talking to the others. He watched Art push his hand up into his hair and then let his hair drop, then let himself drop into the chair behind his desk, and then stand up again. Art was, above all else, the one man to whom J had sworn fealty.

J watched Art gesture with his hands frantically. Art was J's liege. J thought about killing someone else in the room. Karl was there; J could kill Karl. Killing Karl would make a point. Undoubtedly Karl had participated in the decisions to exile Chase and to destroy the tower. J still didn't know whether Karl had rescued him from Art or destroyed him for Chase those ten years ago. J's fortieth birthday didn't matter anymore anyway. J wasn't going to kill someone else to make a point to Art. J was going to kill Art, the man he loved.

Art was around the desk now, his hand on an assistant's shoulder looking at a chart, his back to the window. It was a good shot.

If J was to retreat, if he was to show mercy…well…of what meaning is mercy unbeknownst to the spared? J needed a rainbow to let Art know J had spared him. J could fire upon an inanimate object as a sign of his power and mercy and fealty. The pen stand he'd given Art as a birthday gift would be aptly symbolic. J could shoot it and it would shatter and everything in that room would stop. J watched Art laugh. One of the others walked over to the buffet and poured from a decanter into several rocks glasses, and then used tongs to add only one ice cube to Art's glass, bringing it to Art before preparing the other drinks. J watched Art take the drink and briefly set his hand on the man's bicep; J longed for the feel of Art's hand. J couldn't even imagine, couldn't dream, of how that hand would feel were it on his bicep, not anymore.

Art had destroyed the tower.

Art had saved J's old gift for more than a decade.

Arthur had exiled Chastity.

J reengaged the rifle's safety, reloaded the pistol and put it back in his waistband, and climbed down from the roof, petrified that he'd slip, or drop something loudly, or crunch dead branches beneath his feet.

He reached his car the way he came, drained, as if he'd survived on coffee and now his stomach had rebelled, or as if someone had turned off loud music, or as if he'd come to the far crest of a cocaine bender. He sat in the armored BMW, his weapons all stowed, and thought that he might cry a bit. Nothing came. Instead, he sat dry-eyed and abstractly bitter. He started the ignition and drove slowly, aimlessly away; dialed Chase again, told her voicemail that he didn't know what was next or how to express that lack of a next and the fear of an end. He began to express his realization that any salvation of his dreamer would be at the expense of the dream, and of he and she in it, but the voicemail cut him off mid-sentence, gave him the option of satisfaction or re-recording. He elected to rerecord:

The tower was gone; Walter was hospitalized; they were both in exile.

That seemed too despairing and melodramatic. He rerecorded again, told her to call him, left it at that.

CHAPTER SIXTY-FIVE

HE IDLY DROVE THE back streets of Santa Fe, slipping between adobe duplicates and suburban neighborhoods exempt from the homogenizing building codes. Late in the night, he stopped for gas. An unevenly idling Bronco II on the far side of the filling island played Emmylou Harris into the station's floodlit moment in an otherwise still and dark night. Music, J thought, and felt a wave of nostalgia for the twang he'd first associated with Chase all those years ago leaving the Bronx and for fiddled Klezmer and for the swells of a proper adagio. He engaged the BMW's stereo, and what he got was the Pixies playing music that made sense to a version of himself that was twenty years younger, ten years younger, a day younger. He changed stations until he found something both unpresuming and inoffensive. This lasted long enough for him to get past the city's aureole, linking back roads south towards Albuquerque. Then, he switched back to the station that had been playing Pixies, it now onto something synthesized but organic and needy that made him feel the way he'd felt in the hotel room overlooking Central Park making love to Chase after she told him that she wouldn't have his kid and she wouldn't leave Art and that he couldn't ask why.

J arrived back at Walter's ranch under all of the moon. The dust had drifted off or settled, though strands of wind lifted small eddies off the choss heap like holographic helixes. He sat in the car observing the wreckage through the windshield, first in the beam of his headlights, and then more completely with those off and the moon broadly illuminating all that had been. He'd felt that tears might come to him in the last minutes of his drive, or when the actual destruction confronted him, but he couldn't summon any response at all. He got out of the car, the rifle still with him, still loaded, the pistol tucked into his waistband, and went into the house.

He reached for the light switch inside the front door, and then remembered how bright lights indoors made the outside impenetrably dark, how this is what had divided him from Art when he looked in through the window at that man desperately working in the afterhours of public government. J didn't want to be cast out of the night, out of the outdoors yet. He left the light off, stood in place until his eyes adjusted enough to make out shapes in the dim glow the moon shed through a few shattered skylights.

It smelled, and J wondered whether the gas lines weren't severed and whether his reluctance to employ electricity might not have saved him. It seemed so arbitrary: a fixed and consistent physics inside of a dream. But then, if there was a creator, why need there be a physics at all? What great effort would it be for Him to suspend gravity, or mute the weather, or do away with the behavior of particles and atoms? Why not fail to let electricity spark gas? Why not leave a tower standing despite the explosive power of National Guard-deployed munitions?

Why not say it: why not allow a gas chamber full of innocents to breathe cyanide as easily as ordinary air and live?

This of course was the real question, had always been the real question, because fuck the tower, and fuck the house, and fuck J even: not why couldn't, but why didn't God save the Jews in 1938 and 1939 and 1940 and 1941 and 1942 and 1943 and 1944 and 1945? And if it was that those Jews were called home to heaven, then why hadn't God saved those Jews remaining from the trauma of surviving?

J wandered the house, absently touching surfaces, tracing long lines in the new dust. This touching wasn't so very different from what he'd done with the contents of the briefcase, and if the biblically proscribed method of land acquisition was a pacing of the perimeter of a plot, then stroking objects might be a divine mode of relinquishment. He relinquished the pistol to the dust of the dining room table.

He continued on through the house. In his new state of exhaustion—remarkable to think that this day had begun by slowly toppling over to unbend his cramped spine, that this same day he'd vomited stream water, had been his dreamer, his hand inside the hands of the woman in the park—it proved easier to continue walking than to stop and determine what must be done next. Motion required no decisions. His slow shuffle, the gun heavy on its sling over his shoulder, gradually returned him to his path into the mountains. He walked back up through the strata of growth and meadow and rock, no tower behind him now, no attempt at access to dreamer or to God waiting below.

The moon gradually fell. In its wake, stars renewed the sky. Their blank white the infinite *neshamot* shunted from their bodies by German death camps and mass shootings. Dimmer behind these newly bright were those liberated of worldly life by Cossacks and pits of fire and Spanish pyres; further out still, dim and distant, were the beneficiaries of Roman aggression and Greek aggression; beyond, those set free of their earthly pursuits by Babylonian conquest sputtered on the last of their tallow. At the very limits of his extra-dilated pupils, the last whispered blink of the generations before the flood, drowned and boiled, slipped the edge of this universe for some statistical probability of extra-dimensionality. These or the moon, J thought, and it was a choice.

The foliage changed around him, the air thinned. He was nearly to where he'd stopped before to fast and purge and purify. What then? Nothing then, he guessed. The stars faded and J imagined he could hear the trumpeters announcing Apollo's chariot and it was almost the light of *viyihee boker.* J reached his spot, and the world glowed with the rays the sun sent bending around orange lime-stone ridges to announce its imminent form. The grass was still flattened where J had laid out his blanket to meditate two days earlier. He stood in the center of the spot and turned. Three-quar-ters of the way through his rotation, he saw it.

The animal was hung-up on silvering deadwood, white against the grey scree that ran down the cliff from the relaxed wide granite bowl above to the meadow in which J stood, a big horn tangled in deadfall caught in the avalanche chute's chokepoint, a ram strug-gling to free itself.

J leveled the rifle and fired and the ram fell.

The ram fell downhill over the log, an ass first, uneven, awkward tumble that J immediately repented. Yet there was nothing for it but to go to the dead animal. The rifle for a staff he heavily leaned upon, J made his way up the chute, the loose scree sliding out from beneath his feet, sections steep enough that he could touch the ground in front of him even as he stood. Halfway to the ram, the sun came over the top of the chute, blinding him. He stood blinking, unbalanced, his vision spotty. He leaned forward to not fall backwards. On the ground before him, he saw a big knife in a rotted leather sheath. Carefully stooping he hefted it. The twine hilt was warm to his palm and the leather around the blade crumbled to his touch. He pulled the knife free, and by the time the edge was clear it had already found blood along his palm.

He held the knife up like a visor, its blade haloed and large where it eclipsed the sun. J debated whether his find was new or old, whether its edge had first been dulled separating scalps from sculls, or whether a hunter had lost it mere seasons ago, its leather turned to crumbling by the sliding snow's violent abrasion and the alti-tude's exaggerated ultraviolet radiation. He did not doubt the blade's intent. Nor, did he doubt the knife's providence, a clear signal that the ram had been provided a proviso Art. Was this then Mt. Moriah?

Was Art, Isaac? J, Abraham? He searched himself for some resistance of his role of priest offering sacrifice and found no resistance.

For now, at least, rebellion, rebelliousness, was denied J.

Thus, dually armed, the rifle in one hand, still his crutch on the ever-steepening scree, the knife in his other hand, he kept upwards until he reached the animal. The ram lay at an angle with its hooves uphill and its head lower than its hind. The bullet had caught it upper mid-torso, but missed the heart.

It was alive. Blood in its nostrils inflated into glistening bubbles.

The bubbles burst every second or third breath.

Its side heaved and it stank of shit and it made a depleted, involuble whinnying scream when on irregular intervals it tried to move its rear legs, which only straightened and shuddered as if in epileptic seizure. J seized up. He lifted his hand to his nose and in the process lost his balance. To save himself from falling, he reached forward and clutched the ram's horn with his left hand, giving up his grip on the rifle. The gun tumbled a ways down the chute behind him. J swayed uneasily, holding onto the horn.

The ram shat again, and frothed more blood, and tried to twitch and whinnied its scream.

"This is it then?" J screamed upwards. Why not upwards? God might be there as well as anywhere. J screamed upwards, swaying and light-headed with the sunlight and the altitude and the precariousness of his stance. "You want that I should be the shochet? The gun from the distance isn't enough. You would have me sever the animal's neck with a knife? And all this so that I should know that it is Your will that I let Art live? And all this so that I should know that it was not Your will that I ascend my tower and speak to You?"

J swayed, the animal ever more desperate, ever more putrid. J began to cry. The animal shuddered its rear legs and screamed.

"Am I Zipporah? Am I saving Your Moses by sacrificing this ram for You? Is that what You want? The covenant with *Avraham Avinu?* A foreskin? *Brit Milah*, a pound of flesh, a life, circumcised? That it?"

The animal thrashed its head, beating its eye bloody on the rock, trying to get up but unable to move its legs. The animal made its noise again, the noise filtered through blood in its thorax.

"Fine! Fine!" J yelled. "Why not? Sure!"

What a thing, J thought, to kill out of mercy. As if this mercy now absolved him of having shot the creature.

He leaned over the animal and put the knife against its neck. It reacted to the blade with shuddered and frantic whinnying. J pulled the blade across its throat and it bled but it did not die. He drew it across again, this time severing trachea and jugular both. The animal shuddered and bled more, froth forming around the neck wound, blood draining into the grey rock, into the scree.

"Enough?" J called, still to the sky, still clinging to the horn, covered in blood. "Is it ever enough? Is there ever blood sacrifice enough?"

He could make the animal die faster by cutting further, by severing the nerves that connected head to body. To do so, he would have to sever the spine. If he severed the spine, the head might come free.

"Enough?" J wailed.

If it came free, J would lose the anchor that kept him upright in the chute. He let the animal bleed. J was afraid and he let the animal bleed.

What was J's cruelty compared to God's? God, who created a world that it might worship Him, and then demanded that worship take the form of blood sacrifice, God, who made men such that these sacrifices cost, that their cost traumatized, that the acts that let loose blood were all either of martyrdom or of those things immoral in any other name but God's.

The horn became heavy with the full weight of the head and the heaving sides stopped heaving and the rear legs collapsed out of their shuddering and the animal only excreted a final loose stool. Blood and grime covered J so completely that he couldn't find a free surface with which to wipe his face. J wondered whether it would ever be enough, but it was a feeble thought.

He understood now.

J would choose himself, for however little longer, if that meant an animal suffering, if that meant the man in the back of the box truck forever damned to his twilight extermination.

J needed him dying, after all. He needed the Holocaust in order to exist, and he needed it to never end, to never quite finish its work, to never elapse, lest he cease.

And God? What covenant? Humans have free will! If some thought to kill all those around them, and if some chose to make blood sacrifice…

All right then, J conceded. *All right then*. He would submit. He would step out of his grave. Seven nights, seven suits, whatever, it was time to leave the desert and cross the Jordan. J would accept that he had been spared.

He sawed at the horn he held onto, though doing so once again threatened his perch, a danger against which he compensated by falling to his knees in the loose rock. He sawed at horn. It broke free of the animal with a bloody stump of skull and hide. Leaning against the animal's torso with his elbow—elbow deep in gore, so to speak, and now that the sheep was dead, lice jumped and fled its wool, buzzed around J, clung to him—J sawed off this stump as well. He then reversed the horn, and using the animal as a work surface, carefully etched his way around the plug of bone that formed its tip, broke it free with a quick rap of the knife's hilt. He held before him three feet of twisting horn, translucent and yellow as old ivory when up to the light, as elegant and visceral and bloody a *shofar* as ever there'd been, though it was still filled with marrow. This he tapped out, and picked out with the knife and the other horn and with sticks from the deadfall.

When it was mostly clear, he lifted the horn, fist around its tip, the other firmly grasping the middle of a bend, and put it to his lips. The horn tasted of the ram's death and the salt and sweet and stink sung vital through J's famished senses. He blew and it made an empty gasping sound and spittle and gore misted out the open end and rose with the meadow's sun-heated air rising and rained back upon him.

The horn tasted of rust and excrement and dust and hair.

He tried again, his cheeks swollen and red with clenched exhalation, his eyes teary with exertion. Nothing still. A third time and a fourth. He experimented. Pursed his lips. Changed positions. At last, in a great sputtering expulsion of breath and spit and vibrato, he forced a long loud trumpet from the horn.

He blew again, *Tikeeyah*,

again, *Truah*,

long blast and staccato blasts, the organic and pealing and surreal trumpeting that swore God's repugnance with human sacrifice and swore that one day a messiah would come, or at least swore that humans would take comfort and blood in believing these promises true. The sound echoed back from the other wall of the canyon and then back again. J blew again, a series of short blasts and then a blast that exhumed the last of the tower's dust from his bronchial deeps. He set the horn down, rested on his fists, dizzy, vision spotted.

Echo after echo after J stopped, each echo progressively distant like the layers of the prior night's stars, the shofar symphonic, its call the sound of the Messiah at last summoned from every corner of the earth, heralded in every corner of the earth.

From below, on the belly of the last echo, returned a hallo, long and mimicking.

J looked down the chute, carefully turning to not throw himself off balance. Down, down below, a thousand feet below, in the spotlight of the sun channeled through the chute, stood Chase.

J looked at himself, covered in blood, in dust, in gore, in shit. He looked at the savaged ram, mutilated, ruined, dead, providential. J could shove the knife into his own heart. He could. He could sacrifice his life. He could reject the conditions of his existence. For Chase, he could display for Chase right now his commitment to some standard that stood despite the divine. He could resist. He could.

Or he could accept.

He had already accepted, long ago.

J set down the knife and the horn. He plunge-stepped his way down the scree, more sliding than walking, skiing almost, glissading.

He scurried down from the mountain.

He slid towards the woman who waited.

He slid towards the spot where the chute's angle lessened and where the woman waited.

He raced when he could race. When the sun warmed him, he smiled, and when Chase could make him out she tilted her head and turned up her lips and was ever as beautiful as she'd been all those years ago in Andy's Bar's doorway.

He said, "I love you," and she held his face in her hands.

He said, "I have a story for you."

Acknowledgements

It took seven years to write this book, I am fortunate and grateful to not have had to spend them alone. I owe a tremendous debt to Jacob White, who, while at *Green Mountains Review*, published an early version of the prelude and first chapter, and a greater debt still to Joshua Mohr, without whose excellent editorial services there would have been no Yid World. I also want to thank the many generous folks who read drafts of this over the last seven years, Scott Black, Matt Batt, Charmaine Cadeau, Matthew Kirkpatrick, Rich Wistisen, and Jacqueline Osherow, amongst others, and the far greater number who've supported, or at least tolerated, me in the very long process of writing and revising and revising and revising this book.

A huge shout out to my people over at C&R, who accepted the least coherent cover letter I've ever conceived: to you, John and Andrew.

C&R PRESS TITLES

NONFICTION

Women in the Literary Landscape by Doris Weatherford, et al
Credo: An Anthology of Manifestos & Sourcebook for Creative
Writing by Rita Banerjee and Diana Norma Szokolyai

FICTION

Last Tower to Heaven by Jacob Paul
History of the Cat in Nine Chapters or Less by Anis Shivani
No Good, Very Bad Asian by Lelund Cheuk
Surrendering Appomattox by Jacob M. Appel
Made by Mary by Laura Catherine Brown
Ivy vs. Dogg by Brian Leung
While You Were Gone by Sybil Baker
Cloud Diary by Steve Mitchell
Spectrum by Martin Ott
That Man in Our Lives by Xu Xi

SHORT FICTION

Notes From the Mother Tongue by An Tran
The Protester Has Been Released by Janet Sarbanes

ESSAY AND CREATIVE NONFICTION

In the Room of Persistent Sorry by Kristina Marie Darling
the internet is for real by Chris Campanioni
Immigration Essays by Sybil Baker
Je suis l'autre: Essays and Interrogations
by Kristina Marie Darling
Death of Art by Chris Campanioni

POETRY

A Family Is a House by Dustin Pearson
The Miracles by Amy Lemmon
Banjo's Inside Coyote by Kelli Allen
Objects in Motion by Jonathan Katz
My Stunt Double by Travis Denton
Lessons in Camoflauge by Martin Ott
Millennial Roost by Dustin Pearson
Dark Horse by Kristina Marie Darling
All My Heroes are Broke by Ariel Francisco
Holdfast by Christian Anton Gerard
Ex Domestica by E.G. Cunningham
Like Lesser Gods by Bruce McEver
Notes from the Negro Side of the Moon by Earl Braggs
Imagine Not Drowning by Kelli Allen
Notes to the Beloved by Michelle Bitting
Free Boat: Collected Lies and Love Poems by John Reed
Les Fauves by Barbara Crooker
Tall as You are Tall Between Them by Annie Christain
The Couple Who Fell to Earth by Michelle Bitting
Notes to the Beloved by Michelle Bitting

CPSIA information can be obtained
at www.ICGtesting.com
Printed in the USA
FSHW012056240819
61339FS